Castle Rouge

Castle Rouge

An Irene Adler Novel

Carole Nelson Douglas

FORGE®

A Tom Doherty Associates Book
New York

CASTLE ROUGE: AN IRENE ADLER NOVEL

Copyright © 2002 by Carole Nelson Douglas

Edited by Claire Eddy

Maps by Darla Tagrin

A Forge Book
Published by Tom Doherty Associates, LLC
175 Fifth Avenue
New York, NY 10010

www.tor.com

Forge® is a registered trademark of Tom Doherty Associates, LLC.

Library of Congress Cataloging-in-Publication Data

Douglas, Carole Nelson.
    Castle Rouge : an Irene Adler novel / Carole Nelson Douglas.—1st ed.
        p. cm.
    "A Tom Doherty Associates Book."
    ISBN 0-312-86941-X (acid-free paper)
 1. Adler, Irene (Fictitious character)—Fiction.   2. Holmes, Sherlock (Fictitious character)—
Fiction.   3. Women detectives—France—Paris—Fiction.   4. Transylvania (Romania)—
Fiction.   5. Jack, the Ripper—Fiction.   6. London (England)—Fiction.   7. Paris
(France)—Fiction.   I. Title.

PS3554.O8237 C215 2002
813'.54—dc21

                                                                              2002026057

First Edition: September 2002

0 9 8 7 6 5 4 3 2 1

For Jennifer Waddell,
first a fan, then a student assistant,
always a writer herself, and always fabulous in every role,
with many thanks for coming along on all the journeys
with Irene, Louie, and me

Contents

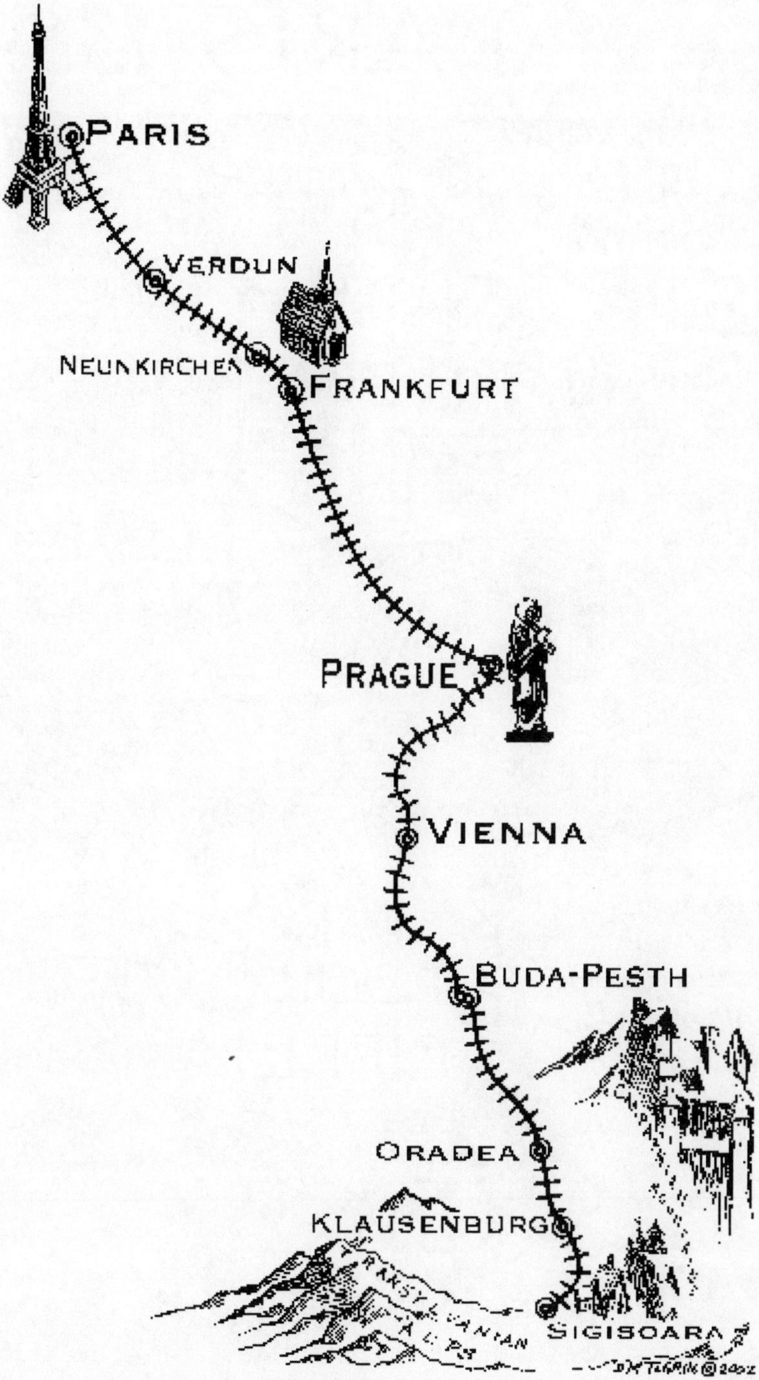

PARIS
VERDUN
NEUNKIRCHEN
FRANKFURT
PRAGUE
VIENNA
BUDA-PESTH
CARPATHIAN MTS
ORADEA
KLAUSENBURG
TRANSYLVANIAN ALPS
SIGISOARA

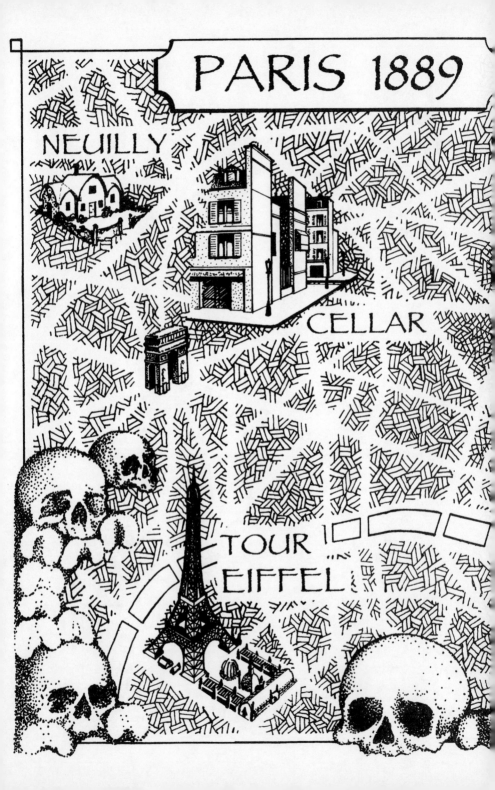

Castle Rouge

...she has a soul of steel. The face of the most beautiful of women and the mind of the most resolute of men.
—Sir Arthur Conan Doyle, *A SCANDAL IN BOHEMIA*

Editor's Note

With the release of this volume I finally sail past a rough patch in my ongoing effort to collate various and obscure nineteenth-century historical documents into a coherent whole.

If the reading public and the scholastic establishment have been impatient at the time this task has consumed, they must bear in mind how many threads go into weaving this series of tapestries.

Not only am I integrating the newly found and exhaustive Penelope Huxleigh diaries recording her life and adventures with Irene Adler, the only woman to have earned Sherlock Holmes's respect, but also "lost" episodes from the supposed Dr. Watson accounts of the Sherlockian Canon as well as additional and mysterious entries from a yellow-bound narrative that have been inserted into this portion of the Huxleigh diaries, but are admittedly foreign materials I found with them.

That the subject matter of all these separate documents is the most notorious serial killer of all time, the still *publicly* unidentified slayer of women prostitutes known as Jack the Ripper, only makes the task more delicate.

In the previous account that I titled *Chapel Noir*, shocking revelations fixed on one suspect among many for the role of Whitechapel killer at the time. James Kelly was an upholsterer by trade and a convicted wife murderer who slipped away from an asylum early in his incarceration and was at large in Whitechapel before the Ripper slaughters began. Even more damning, Kelly left London immediately after the appalling mutilation of Mary Jane Kelly, generally considered to be the Ripper's last act of destruction. He walked to the coast, whence he embarked for Brussels and from there walked to Paris. He remained at large for an unbelievable thirty-nine years, until, aged and confused, he surrendered himself to British authorities and ended his days in the asylum for which he had been destined far earlier in his career.

In *Chapel Noir*, Irene Adler and her cohorts not only encountered Kelly but also came across a truly fiendish cult with which Kelly appeared to be affiliated. Their own investigations into the notion of a *group* of maniacal individuals is buttressed by excerpts I used from the "yellow book" (kept by an unknown individual who seemed to be investigating the cult) that had somehow come into Nell Huxleigh's possession at some point.

Irene Adler herself, through her deductive abilities—admittedly more instinctive than Sherlock Holmes's scientifically based investigations—had concluded that a subtle and sacrilegious pattern underlay the latest Paris depredations against women, particularly women of loose moral character. She determined that the attacks occurred on certain saints' days and in the geographic pattern of a Chi-Rho, an ancient Christian symbol for the Christ figure on the cross. It is represented by an "X" crossing through the letter "P." Another disturbing religious element in the Paris crimes was discovering a cavern where the cult met, in which the graffito immediately erased in Whitechapel—*The Juwes are the men That Will not be Blamed for nothing*—had been inscribed on the wall, in French and in human blood.

Although Nell Huxleigh prides herself on her Christian devotion, it was Irene Adler who first detected the pattern that referenced elements of Judaism, Catholicism, and Satanism. My documentation doesn't yet give me any insight on Adler's religious upbringing or philosophy, other than that, like many artistically inclined persons, she is most suspicious of overtly religious expressions. And, of course, compared to her biographer, Nell Huxleigh, she is markedly lacking in the usual outward demonstrations of religious belief and piety.

The religious question is extremely intriguing, given that a Whitechapel murder site also had been decorated with a line of graffito about the Jews, either an apologia or an attempt to implicate them in the Ripper murders.

We must bear in mind the rampant anti-Semitic feeling during this period in western Europe, extending as far east as Russia, which was conducting brutal pogroms that forced the mass emigration of Jews to western Europe, including Whitechapel, and America, where they were less welcome than even the Irish. Hitler did not arise in a historical-sociological vacuum.

With all these new factors thrown into the speculative stewpot that is the Ripper question, I confess that I approached the next volume of the Huxleigh diaries with confusion and trepidation. Yet even I could not have predicted what I found. I have endeavored only to present it and the supporting materials as reasonably and calmly as possible, in honest chronological sequence, so that history may judge.

I have done all that I can. It is up to posterity to decide if it wishes to believe the stunning revelations implicit in these conjoined narratives. Certainly the conclusion that all three narratives reach, each in their own separate and harrowing way, is so shocking as to be unbelievable, save that it makes perfect sense, even as the modern mind may shudder at its implications for the historical participants' future, and for, in hindsight, our own brutal and bloody past.

Fiona Witherspoon, Ph.D., A.I.A.*
April 2002

*Advocates of Irene Adler

Cast of Continuing Characters

Irene Adler Norton: an American abroad who outwitted the King of Bohemia and Sherlock Holmes in the Conan Doyle story, "A Scandal in Bohemia," reintroduced as the diva-turned-detective protagonist of her own adventures in the novel, *Good Night, Mr. Holmes*

Sherlock Holmes: the London consulting detective building a global reputation for feats of deduction

Godfrey Norton: the British barrister who married Irene just before they escaped to Paris to elude Holmes and the King

Penelope "Nell" Huxleigh: the orphaned British parson's daughter Irene rescued from poverty in London in 1881; a former governess and "typewriter girl" who lived with Irene and worked for Godfrey before they met and married, and who now resides with them in Paris

Quentin Stanhope: the uncle of Nell's former charges when she worked as a London governess; now a British agent in eastern Europe and the Mideast, he reappeared in *A Soul of Steel* (formerly *Irene at Large*)

John H. Watson, M.D.: British medical man and Sherlock Holmes's sometimes roommate and frequent companion in crime solving

Pink: another American, although no innocent abroad; met in

Chapel Noir at a Paris brothel where a double murder occurred; a young woman with a taste for the sensational and her own agenda

Bram Stoker: acquaintance of Irene and Nell; the theatrical manager for Britain's foremost actor, Henry Irving; an aspiring writer of sensational stories. He figured in *The Adventuress* (formerly *Good Morning, Irene*) and, more suspiciously, in *Chapel Noir*.

William F. (Buffalo Bill) Cody and **Red Tomahawk:** appearing with the Wild West show in Paris. Both assisted Irene in tracking the Ripper suspect in *Chapel Noir*.

Wilhelm Gottsreich Sigismond von Ormstein, King of Bohemia: the Crown Prince who courted Irene years before, then feared she might disrupt his forthcoming royal marriage. He hired Sherlock Holmes to recover a photograph of Irene and the Prince together, but she escaped, promising never to use the photo against the King. They met again in *Another Scandal in Bohemia* (formerly *Irene's Last Waltz*).

Queen Clotilde of Bohemia: former Danish princess who married the King after his pursuit of Irene and found herself a pawn in a political intrigue in *Another Scandal in Bohemia*.

James Kelly: a demented Liverpool upholsterer who stabbed his wife to death and escaped a madhouse, residing in Whitechapel during the Jack the Ripper murders of autumn, 1888. Immediately after the last Ripper slaying, he fled to France, where Ripperlike murders soon occurred, as related in *Chapel Noir*.

Inspector François le Villard: a Paris detective and admirer of Holmes who has translated the English detective's monographs into French. He worked with Irene Adler Norton on the Montpensier case in *The Adventuress* (formerly *Good Morning, Irene*).

Baron Alphonse de Rothschild: head of the international banking family's most powerful branch and of the finest intelligence network in Europe, frequent employer of Irene, Godfrey, and Nell in various capacities, especially in *Another Scandal in Bohemia*

Albert Edward: familiarly known as Bertie, the Prince of Wales, royal rake and bon vivant and heir to *Queen Victoria*

Sarah Bernhardt: the leading actress of the age, a self-made success, extravagant impresaria, and friend of Irene Adler

Prelude

I often have this strange and moving dream
Of an unknown woman....
—PAUL VERLAINE, *MON RÊVE FAMILIER*, 1866

❧ FROM A YELLOW BOOK ❧

She cleaves the night like a sailing ship. The ruffled wake of her trailing skirts leaves a silvered moon path on the greasy black cobblestones. Water and dirt have crept up her ragged hems for a foot or more, swelling her skirts into anchors instead of sails. They momentarily sweep up the damp and slime before it flows shut like sludge behind her.

She has long since lost the will to lift them from the muck.

She does not so much walk as stagger deliberately, like a noble-woman in a state procession. She is unaccompanied, alone, but each step she takes is emphatic. Each pauses. No marcher to some stately processional, she. The only music the night makes are bursts of raucous song from the public-house doors she passes by.

Each feverishly lit portal exhales a hot, bright breath of ale, laughter, and sour sweat.

The spring night is chill. Mist steams off the cobblestones in the scrofulous patches of gaslight that fail to illuminate the poorer quarter.

Drinking songs—robust, merry, deluded—barely penetrate her deadened mind.

She has no coppers to buy even a tankard of ale, much less lodging for the night. She can sell herself, but not if she is too worn to exchange coy words with the lone men who prowl beyond the frail, flickering halos crowning the gaslights.

She knows they are there. Should one find her, and pay her instead of running away after, she will have the choice of food or drink or some crowded corner out of the night fog.

He will have to lift the street-soaked skirts for her, though.

She has a history, but she does not remember it. She had family once, but they do not remember her. Once she had employment, but her fingers and eyes gave out, and the younger girls from the country could do the work better, at first, as she had.

Her fingers grow numb along with her feet, her face. If a carriage came clattering down the street, she wouldn't have the heart to dodge it. In fact, the thought of an onrushing carriage, black as a funeral coach, is a welcome dream. It would stop her feet in their monotonous march. She would like to stop all movement now, finally. All. Her bodice expands with a breath, just a little. This duel with whalebone stays for space is too difficult. Who can outblow Leviathan? She remembers the big, black-bound book in a place she had once called home.

What country is this, what city?

Who can say? It could be London, Paris, Prague, Helsinki. It is a city not her own. Yet she claims no country but her own mind.

What child is this?

She does not know. Country, city, self. Not anymore.

If only Leviathan would come and carry her away, as it did Job. Or was that Jonah? Away into the dark inside of the sea, where nothing moves.

Something does move. It careens into her. Somebody.

Drugged with hopelessness, paralyzed by hunger, drained of all thought and will, she sinks. The dark of a byway swallows her. She doesn't feel her cheek scrape rough brick, her back slam into ungiving wall.

He is muttering at her, Leviathan, but she can't understand the words and doesn't care to anyway. He is lifting her heavy, sopping, filthy skirts, and she feels the absence of their constant weight as a dim animal relief, not quite understood.

He is poking at her buckram bodice, that well-built wall to keep her from breathing. He is poking with a stick, a sharp stick, but what has her life become but a poking with a sharp stick. . . .

A hot tongue cuts across her throat. Something warm and wonderful floods down her chest. Honey, warm honey. She sinks, hearing the irritating clop of nearing horses. She is too far away to throw herself under their iron feet. She is too far away to do anything, even when the force that had caught her ebbs away like mist.

Perhaps this time she, too, will ebb away like mist.

Now the carriage has stopped and the horses, but the trickle of hot liquid at her throat has not.

She is, as far as she can tell, still alive.

What a pity.

1.

Evening in Paris

༺ᘒᘓ༻

⟨ F R O M   A   J O U R N A L ⟩

 I was born Elizabeth, but they call me Pink.

I have had to steel myself often in life.

First against my stepfather, Jack Ford, a drunken brute. Then against the men who said I had no right to exist as I was, who would patronize me.

Now against a woman who would appeal to my conscience.

I am an exposer and righter of wrongs. An undercover investigator. My mission is above conscience. My mission *is* my conscience.

She would divert me.

I do not like it, not even when she assembles Bertie, Prince of Wales; Baron de Rothschild; Bram Stoker; and Sarah Bernhardt into one room in Paris.

Hers.

Beyond this convocation of capitol B's the only person of interest who is missing is Sherlock Holmes, the renowned English consulting detective. Even this cold-blooded Brit hesitated—a few moments—in forsaking her and Paris for London and fresh insight into the most appalling murderer of the age, Jack the Ripper.

I should perhaps figure her into this scene: Irene Adler Norton, ex-diva, ex-American, ex-Pinkerton agent.

She is now also a woman deprived of the two personal props in her life: her husband, Godfrey Norton, and her friend and supporter, Nell Huxleigh, both English, both taken in mysterious ways by mysterious enemies.

I think of women in Greek tragedies: Hecuba in *The Trojan Women*, Medea mourning her faithless man and sacrificing her children, Electra murdering her mother. Women who like Samson shake the pillars they are bound to and make the known world tremble.

She is very dangerous right now, Irene Adler Norton, and I don't care to be here for the catastrophe.

She has blackmailed me, this woman, this implacable Fury. She has reached into me like the stage artist she was and captured my attention. She has sunk her tiny, precise teeth into my soul, found my aching vulnerabilities and bound me with silken fibers of steel.

She has offered me a story to end all stories. She has promised me Jack the Ripper.

I am proud of her and I do not trust her and I will serve my own purpose, not hers. Meanwhile, here I sit among some of the Great of our Age, and listen to them flounder in the face of one irrational killer.

"My dear Irene," says Bram Stoker, the first to arrive. "I am . . . speechless. Godfrey. Nell. Gone. I think of Irving. It would be as if God had died."

Bram Stoker. Manager of the finest actor in England (the world to hear him tell it), Henry Irving. An auld acquaintance of Irene Adler Norton. He is not so much of an old friend that she has not ruled him out as a new suspect in the recent Ripperlike murders of Paris. In the London Ripper crimes of last autumn as well? Possibly. My special system of notes that only I can read records it all.

Nell had used to "take notes" for Irene when she solved cases the Pinkertons sent her way. Now I take notes. These are my property, for publication later, when I, Elizabeth Jane Cochrane, am released from my vow of silence and fully free to be the daredevil girl reporter who has made my reputation: Nellie Bly, who will go anywhere to expose any wrong. That suits her.

"Bram. Thank you for coming." Irene takes his big hands in hers. They gaze at each other, people in a common profession feeling loss as it happens in the real world, not on a stage.

He is still a suspect in her cast of characters, a theatrical man married to an icy beauty, devoted to a domineering actor who both employs and uses him. Sweet-tempered Bram Stoker, free after midnight in any capital of the world, loving women or loathing them? Jack the Ripper? After what we have learned, she and I, it could be.

"It slays me," he says now, "to think of dear, sweet Miss Huxleigh in villainous hands." He delivers the line with conviction.

Such a big, bluff, hearty soul. Even I who detest the Englishman's sense of superiority adore Bram. He is Irish, after all, and they are battering my own country into submission with their energy and optimism despite the most shattering prejudice. Big redhaired bear, genial, social, interested in such dark topics as bubble up in his short stories . . . Iron Maidens and vengeance and blood, always blood.

His huge hands tighten on Irene's delicate ones. His are bone and muscle, masculine force. Hers are steel in velvet, feminine survival.

If Bram Stoker is Jack the Ripper, he is lost.

Baron de Rothschild arrives next. An older man, refined, powerful, quiet in that power. He, too, takes her hands. I am struck by the image of courtiers coming to pay respects to a bereaved queen. She has won hearts as well as minds.

Not mine.

He kisses the back of each hand. "Any agent, any amount of money, they are yours to command."

"Thank you," she murmurs, and shows him to a chair.

It is a seat no better or worse than any other in the room. This is a war council of equals, and she is Madam Chairman.

Sarah Bernhardt wafts in on a perfumed zephyr of ostrich boa and red hair as frothy, all fabric-swathed whipcord figure with a leopard on a leash.

"Irene! My darling! My adorable Nell and Godfrey missing! I have traveled all over the world. If you need the aid of any person of power anywhere, just let me know."

The leopard paces back and forth between the two women's skirts, purring.

The Divine Sarah bows to the Baron, nods at Bram Stoker, and arranges herself on a sofa between them.

The leopard watches Irene Adler Norton with bright predatory eyes, its vertical pupils black stab wounds in the glory of jungle-green iris.

Next comes the first of all of them: portly, blustering Bertie.

I cannot stand the man, though he is Prince of Wales now and will become King of England . . . if his black-bombazine-clad pincushion of a Mama ever dies. She has made mourning into an industry for thirty years. Bertie, christened Edward Albert, is fat, self-indulgent, and British.

But then, aren't all the English fat and blustering? Well, except for Sherlock Holmes, who is not fat, and Godfrey Norton, who is apparently not only not fat, but also not self-indulgent, a rare quality in an Englishman and in any man for that matter. At least in my limited experience. Actually, more than one man has been my mentor, but they are exceptions.

So is she, Irene Adler Norton, and that is why she is so dangerous, even to me, who am used to being dangerous to others.

Inspector François le Villard comes last, hat in hand, waxed mustaches gleaming like very pointed India ink calligraphy. He accepts a solitary chair.

I wonder if Sherlock Holmes has assembled a similar company of high and low and in-between in London to serve his purposes as he returns to put Whitechapel upside down in a search for a new motive that will unmask the Ripper at last.

But I think that Mr. Holmes is a mostly solitary creature, like the web-weaving spider, and works and waits alone. Certainly he was appalled by the idea that I wanted to return to London. He claimed I had a duty to accompany the bereaved Madam Norton. I have no duty but to my higher purpose.

Still, I find it most agreeable to sit here in this Paris hotel room, among the Mostly Great and Merely Interesting, taking notes as is my wont, and as was requested specifically by our hostess.

It is the actress who makes the opening speech.

"My dear Irene, I speak for all of us, I believe, when I beg to know what we may do to assist you? This sudden disappearance of Miss Penelope, not to mention your dearly beloved spouse, is what you call in English heart-rendering, I think. You play a scene more tragic than any written for me on the stage. Ask anything of us you will. Your wish is our necessity."

A grand sentiment, but the Prince stirs uneasily, no matter how slightly. "Anything" is not a word the high and mighty toss around like a head of cabbage. Not in America and not here.

"I thank you for your good will," Irene says quietly.

I had not looked closely at her, being busy memorizing the appearance and address of the famous folk in the room. And, I did not like to stare Loss in the face, either.

She is bearing up remarkably well to scrutiny, this woman who had learned scant hours ago that her husband and her long-time companion had both vanished from the earth as if plucked up by eagles, the husband in forgotten reaches of eastern Europe, the companion vanished in the vast wilderness of the gigantic *Exposition universelle* at the heart of Parisian civility in the Champ de Mars under the Eiffel Tower.

She wears a steel-gray taffeta gown as resolute as autumn rain, though it is summer.

Nothing could dampen the drive of her spirit, but her demeanor is still and serious this afternoon. Her calculated calm, however, makes everyone else restive. In their edgy rustle I detect the odor of unwilling overcommitment. She makes them nervous and had intended to.

"My dear friends," she says finally in a low tone that trembles like the finest cello strings, "if I may call so many who are mighty in the world that."

They stutter, murmur, shout that she indeed may.

"You have already put your worldwide spy network at my service, Baron de Rothschild. I can ask no more. Your Royal Highness," she nods at the Prince, "has already offered that 'anything' I might wish for."

So Bertie was not forthcoming with any solid support. What a hypocritical prig! The talk is that he is always hard up for money. Mama keeps her knuckles on the purse strings.

"Sarah, you have your network of not so much spies as devoted admirers, and I may indeed need to call upon some of them in time.

"Inspector le Villard. I know the Paris police are doing all they can and more than many metropolitan forces ever would, including welcoming the activities of our advance American scouting party, Buffalo Bill Cody and Red Tomahawk."

She turns last to the husky Irishman. "And Bram, I have high hopes for you and your wandering soul. I am hoping you will serve as European scout for Pink and myself, for I fear this trial will lead us far from Paris."

The Baron and the Prince and the inspector look relieved. The actress smug. Bram Stoker looks both pleased and shocked.

I realized that Madam Irene has divided and conquered once again, as she had finessed me not hours ago. The two richest men in the room will be eager to offer whatever small requests she makes, having seen the specter of truly draining ambition. The actress will leave feeling useful, an emotion not common to the profession, and will consider that a contribution of great worth in itself.

The inspector will be grateful if, and when, Irene removes herself from his jurisdiction, and I am convinced that she soon will.

And Bram Stoker, luckless Bram Stoker, the poorest and least famous personality, has just been named Knight Errant, the only one present she intends to lean upon in any major way whatsoever.

I wonder if it is because, next to the inspector, he is the least important of the persons gathered together. Excepting me, of course, who is a nobody and happy to live in a land where nobodies can become somebodies. The thought makes me homesick for New York, but I suppose it will be a while before I snag a big enough story to telegraph home and follow fast on its heels for the resulting sensation and acclaim.

Then Irene seizes the moment and turns the joint call of condolence into something quite different. It is enough to make me sit up and take notes even faster.

"You realize, my friends," she says, eyeing each person in turn, "that we have gathered together in this room the world's most eminent collection of experts on the murderer known as Jack the Ripper."

Protesting waves of demurs in English and French wash against her stone-gray figure to no avail. They had come here to say what they could do for her. Now she is telling them what they can do for the world.

"It is true," she goes on. "What we knew of Jack the Ripper before these recent murders in Paris is now virtually useless. Even Sherlock Holmes has scurried back to London to reinvestigate the events there from the new perspective these Paris atrocities demand."

I doubt that the man I have met "scurries," but I know the description pleases Irene, who had perhaps hoped for his more direct assistance.

"I do not think," she adds, turning her attention to Inspector le Villard, "that our esteemed colleagues are aware of James Kelly's history and actions here in Paris."

"James Kelly!" The Prince of Wales grows immediately interested. "A very English name. I know at least one. Who is this particular man?"

"He may well be the Ripper, Your Highness," Le Villard admits with a bob to the Prince. "I regret to say that he was in the custody of the Paris police after being found and confronted by Sherlock Holmes—"

"And by," Irene interjects, "Miss Pink, myself, and, of course, our dear Nell."

A pause holds while all present acknowledge Nell's alarming absence with respectful silence.

"Indeed," Inspector le Villard says, nervously tweaking his waxed mustaches into sharper points. "I am told that the presence of all you ladies had a very disturbing effect upon him."

(*Not to mention upon Sherlock Holmes*, I jot down in my notes.)

"We were gowned," Irene explains to the room at large, "as ladies of ill repute."

"How I wish I had been there to see that!" the Prince exclaims.

"I as well," says Sarah.

"And I." Bram Stoker.

The Baron de Rothschild expresses no such desire, which makes him the only true gentleman in the group in my estimation.

"The point is," Irene says, "James Kelly had a history of both despising and consorting with fallen women. His behavior when confronted by Sherlock Holmes in the guise of a French priest, and by we three dressed as women of the street, was odd. He alternated between cowering in fear from our very presence . . . and leaping up to put a knife blade to hapless Nell's throat."

"Ah!" Sarah clutches for her own scrawny neck with an actress's instant empathy. "Poor Nell! Of all the ones least bold, the one most . . . mild."

Theatrics do not impress an ex-diva like Irene Adler. "Nell was bold enough to unsheath her hatpin and stab what might be Jack the Ripper in the wrist."

"Might be?" the Baron asks.

Irene turns to the inspector, politely waiting for his opinion.

He preens his mustaches again. "This James Kelly indeed has a sinister history. An upholsterer by trade, he came into some money from a man he had never known to be his father. Instead of enjoying his good fortune, he denounced his long-suffering mother as a whore and moved to London. There he had killed his own wife several years ago, very near the debased district called Whitechapel, by screwing a clasp knife into her ear during an angry fit. He accused her of being a whore merely for marrying him. Convicted of murder, he obtained release from a madhouse a few years later. I cannot imagine that English madhouses release such fellows, but there it is. He certainly was at large in Whitechapel during the Ripper crimes and, what is most damning, just after the unthinkable slaughter of Marie Jeanne Kelly, he walked eighty miles to Dover and then sailed to Dieppe. From Belgium he came to France, thence making his way to Paris."

"Where," Irene notes, "he managed to forge a link between himself and a member of the British royal family."

"Oh, I say now!" Bertie assumes full royal pout, pulling his embroidered waistcoat down over a substantial belly. "I have heard enough of these foul rumors trying to connect the Royal family to this Ripper fellow. That is the sort of outrageous gossip the sensational papers revel in. I can assure you that no member of my family would consort with the sort of persons to be found in Whitechapel."

"But Paris is not Whitechapel," Irene says, "and the connection is not a rumor, as unsuspected as it might be to Your Highness. The inspector mentioned that Kelly was an upholsterer. He was apparently a good enough one to find finishing work with a reputable firm here in Paris, one that was creating a unique and exquisite piece of furniture for Your Highness, that was in fact, the structure upon which the two murdered residents of the *maison de rendezvous* were discovered."

The Prince is almost moved enough to bound up from his sofa seat. Almost, but not quite. It is too soon after lunch, which no doubt had been twelve courses.

"No! The scoundrel! You are saying he had a hand in my, er, custom-appointed couch? This is revolting."

"Your Highness must have known the events that occurred upon the object in question during your absence."

"I was told that the piece was ruined and, of course, I would never reclaim anything that had played a part in a scene so opposite to the refined and joyous purpose for which it was intended."

Here I nearly snort my disbelief and contempt. This *siége d'amour* was a spoiled nobleman's toy for cavorting with two bought women at once. To consider this a "refined" use was more than an upright and plainspoken American could stand.

Fortunately, Irene has lived in Europe long enough to avoid plainspeaking when irony will do.

Instead of launching the lecture I would have at this prince of lechery, she merely remarks, "Your Highness has put your finger on the most interesting feature of some of these latter-day Paris slayings: the choice of a refined scene of the crime, and of refined victims. Yes, one could simply say that James Kelly strayed onto the scene in the course of installing the furniture. Certainly, judging from the encounter we three women had with him later, he was unable to restrain himself from violence when in the presence of women of a certain type."

"Whores," Sarah announces in her most ringing, stagy tones, and in English. "Oh, don't frown at me, Bertie. You know you adore the female in every incarnation, from maid to mistress."

"So I was within moments of encountering this monster?" Bertie notes with a shiver.

"So was Bram," Irene adds.

The heavy-set Irishman, who'd been content to cede his usual role as raconteur to Irene during this macabre discussion, finds himself the sudden center of attention. His cheeks pink above his bushy red beard. For all his hearty manner, he is a sensitive soul.

"I had accompanied Irving to the *maison* on previous visits to Paris," he says quickly. "Now that I am in Paris alone, I went only to pay my respects to the, er, madame."

He always refers to Irving as a demigod, presumably recognizable to all by his last name alone. Perhaps that is the role of a manager.

This all-consuming position includes accompanying the Great Man to Paris scenes as scandalous as the cancan clubs and various *maisons de rendezvous*. When Englishmen visit Paris, there is only one thing they want to do, apparently. Except for Sherlock Holmes, which raises other, equally interesting speculations in my reportorial mind. Also raising speculation are the more macabre outings of Irving and Stoker along with hundreds of daily gawkers: the public display case of unidentified corpses at the infamous Paris Morgue.

I realize how cleverly Irene has turned a condolence call into an interrogation, for two of the four men in this room had been present at the scene of the first two Paris murders and a third, the Baron de Rothschild, spirited both the Prince and later Irene and Nell from that same *maison.*

I can see by the drooping of the inspector's very disciplined mustaches that he had not known of the Prince's presence in the house of sin and death, nor the fact that the . . . device upon which two women died had been commissioned especially for His Royal Highness. Being French and worldly, the inspector would not condemn the perverse intention, only the murderous turn its use had taken.

"Kelly possessed a certain religious mania," Irene muses for the benefit of her friends and suspects.

I began to wonder if even the inspector and I are excepted from the suspect category, for of course I, too, had been present that night and had found the butchered bodies. Probably we are not. I am beginning to see that, like Sherlock Holmes, Irene is relentless in the pursuit of truth, though her approach is far less direct than his.

I also begin to see that she arranges scenes like a playwright. First she assembles the dramatis personae, then she lets them speak among each other and thus speak the truth to her, all unknowing.

It's a theatrical approach that requires much patience and rehearsal before any denouement can be expected.

"Nothing in Jack the Ripper's London murders indicated a religious mania," the Prince says finally, after long mulling over Irene's comment.

The inspector answers for her. "Allow me, Your Highness. I have studied the case most avidly. In all such murders of fallen women a religious mania is suspected. As the purported *billet-doux* from the Ripper said, 'I am down on whores.' Usually such reactions are moral. I believe that it is the frustration of the natural instincts that creates such madmen. In Paris, in France, we have made houses of prostitution legal for decades and inspect the women to ensure good health. It has eliminated much unnecessary disease and is the only reasonable approach to the situation. England and London are not so enlightened. Men who have contracted foul diseases from whores become murderously infuriated. It is no wonder that these Ripper slayings, and others that frequently occur in this Whitechapel district, are more common to England than to France."

"Until now," Irene notes.

The inspector flashes her an impatient look. "What? Two women at a reputable house?"

I shudder to think what Nell would have to say about the very French notion of a "reputable" whorehouse were she here to ride scout on the discussion.

The inspector natters on. "The third woman was either an unlucky laundress or one of the lone unfortunates, *femmes isloée*, who plies the streets on her own."

"You have not addressed," Irene says, "the strange subterranean aspect of these Paris killings. That is another aspect purely Parisian: cellars, sewers, catacombs. Even the morgue and the wax museum were used to display the bodies in some bizarre manner."

The inspector shrugs, a classic French response to the mystery of life.

"The *Musée Grévin*," he says grandly, "is far more than a wax museum, especially during *l'Exposition universelle* and the inauguration of *La Tour Eiffel*. It is a landmark of Paris. Might not even a madman wish to pay tribute to the attractions of the City of Light in planning his crimes?"

"The Ripper managed to keep to obscure and hidden ways in London," Irene points out.

"London!" The inspector barely restrains himself from spitting. "Whitechapel. Paris has no such sinkhole as this. It is no mystery that the Paris murders involve a finer sort of victim."

"Then the Ripper has moved to Paris and grown nice."

Bram Stoker speaks up at long last. "The bloody rites I heard of in the cavern beneath the fairgrounds don't sound very refined. Were I to write such a scene, I'd be accused of sensation-mongering. I agree with what the man in the street said during the Ripper attacks last autumn. No Englishman would do it."

"Nor any Frenchman!" the inspector shouts, his mustaches twitching like cockroach feelers.

Amazing how no nationality on earth would spawn a Ripper so long as any man of that race is present.

"The Jews," the Baron says quietly, "are often accused, and falsely, of atrocities toward Christians. Oddly enough, the facts prove the atrocities are inevitably committed against them. Us," he adds.

"That is the trouble!" When the Prince of Wales finally speaks again, he does so passionately. "There are all sorts of political scapegoats abounding that one faction or the other would like to accuse of the Ripper's crimes, including members of England's royal family! I have been repeatedly criticized for consorting with Jews and merchants and jockeys and, er, women."

"And does Your Highness deny any of it?" Irene asks, a trifle archly.

The Prince, like any pampered aristocrat, responds to the coy like a cat to a whisker tickle. That is one thing I grant Sherlock Holmes. He is not pampered and he is not an aristocrat.

"Well, no," Bertie says, demonstrating the disarming honesty that makes him tolerated if not beloved. "Drat the fellow! He has caused endless trouble, and I wish they would lock him away."

" 'They' is always us, Your Highness," Irene says. "And that is why 'we' must do something about Jack the Ripper. I take it I have your permission to try."

The inspector snorts delicately, being French.

Irene needs no one's permission, but she wishes some of the people in this room to see that she has a royal mandate.

"I would be delighted," the Prince says, smiling a bow in her direction. Bertie has always enjoyed deferring to women, except his mother. Irene has never underestimated official approval.

She smiles back. Like a privateer of old, she has won the royal letter of mark.

She is free to hoist the Jolly Roger and to board and commandeer any ships she chooses.

Lord help us, she already has the U.S.S. Nellie Bly in her fleet and I shudder to think what freebooters she will add to her armada.

2.

Plainsmen in France

*The red man does not wear his heart upon his sleeve for
government claws to peck at. One knows what he proposes
to do after he has done it. The red man is conspicuously
among the things that are not always what they seem.*
—HELEN CODY WELMORE, *THE LAST OF THE GREAT SCOUTS*, 1899

⊰FROM A JOURNAL⊱

 There are many things for which I will never forgive Irene Adler Norton, but I guess the one that is least her fault is the thorn that rankles most. The fact is that the Paris Ripper could only be the London Ripper on the move and that the real story had its roots back in London where it all began the previous autumn of 1888.

So Sherlock Holmes telling me that I owed it to Irene to nursemaid her in Paris didn't sit well at the time he declared this to be the case, and it especially didn't go down like butter now that I was tied to a secondary investigation while he was back in Blighty chasing the Real Ripper.

Irene and I strolled through the now-familiar grounds of

l'Exposition universelle, brushing skirt hems with shopgirls and ladies of leisure sharing a holiday spirit and utter ignorance of the horrific and hidden events that had transpired here but two days before.

Our expedition with that pack of Rothschild agents and Buffalo Bill to hunt down the Paris Ripper had reached such a shocking and savage climax that every man in sight thought I should be spared further discussion of the particulars. I had heard only such snippets from Inspector François le Villard as he regarded necessary for my nursemaiding of Irene or as fit for my foreign and female ears.

I could hardly prod Irene to dissect the matter in every lurid detail yet, since her long-time companion Nell had vanished at the height of the horrors. The only concrete result of our pursuit of the Paris Ripper was one missing English spinster and a sinister sign later in our hotel room that Irene's English husband, Godfrey, journeying from Prague to Transylvania on business for the enormously influential Rothschild banking family, was also in unknown but likely hostile hands.

It had not been a good night for the British.

If Sherlock Holmes had not as good as threatened me with arrest to keep me at Irene's side, I would be off on investigations of my own. I so resented being pent up on the sidelines with the women while the men made history.

"I suppose," Irene said, apparently unaware of my irritation, pausing to gaze at the fountains exploding like Old Faithful beneath the pierced iron silhouette of the Eiffel Tower, "that you would like to analyze the crimes that occurred here as they fit into a larger picture."

"You bet I would! But I daren't ask the natural questions any reporter would want to know because of Nell vanishing so abruptly at the height of the atrocities. The last I saw of her was you yelling at her to leave the cavern when that madman James Kelly came rushing at her. Do you suppose he caught up with her? And, if so, why so far away from where we all were? And why did Kelly go for her particularly?"

Irene's gaze lowered to meet my eyes. I saw then that they focused on something far different from spectacular fountains or my humble opinions.

"You almost sound envious of Nell being the Ripper's target, and indeed it could have as easily been *you* and not Nell missing now. Perhaps." Did her soft monotone almost hint that this would be the far, far better thing for all concerned?

I would not be shamed, not by her. Not again. "Certainly I am better qualified to fend for myself in desperate circumstances than Nell is. I have survived a madhouse, after all, a sweatshop, and brothels on two continents."

"If fending for oneself is still an issue." She turned her gaze again at the plumes of tumbling water.

"Nell must be alive!"

"Why?"

"Why not leave her body at the panorama building where she was apparently abducted, then?"

"Perhaps he needed her for future . . . rites."

"From what I understand, which is too little, the participants were willing sacrifices. I do not see Nell ever becoming a willing sacrifice."

"The people controlling events wished to leave no trail, that much is true," she said absently. "In that they failed. Nell was able to unclasp her lapel watch, so that it dropped to the floor to mark the spot where she was taken. That clue allowed Red Tomahawk to note the signs they'd left and begin tracking the party immediately."

"They left in the gypsy wagon, isn't that right?"

"In *a* gypsy wagon. There may have been more about than the one we observed by the campfire earlier."

" 'The one we observed!' I was allowed to observe very little that night in that mob of people. Observation is my work, my gift, my livelihood. You should have brought me to the forefront. I might have noticed something vital."

"Nell would have been incensed if I'd given you preference. It was bad enough you went to the morgue along with me."

"Oh, for heaven's sake! This petty rivalry has cost us all a pretty penny. You would be only half so distracted if only one of your . . . associates were missing."

"You are saying that I would not take your abduction as seriously as Nell's?"

"You know that I can take care of myself."

"Nell may do better than you think."

"If she is alive." I had not meant to be brutal, but Irene had pointed out the reality first, after all. Apparently reality was harder to face when it was turned back on one.

"You're right. We can't know that," she said through tight lips. "Yet I cannot help but suspect that Nell was apprehended in much the same manner and for the same purpose that Godfrey was abducted at about the same time on the opposite side of Europe. What that purpose is, I don't know, but I intend to find out. And since it is a purpose, I am hopeful that their lives, rather than their deaths, are the key to it."

After that, talk seemed as dangerous as dueling. Mutually silent, we made our way to the huge arena prepared for the Wild West Show.

En route I found myself thinking of Sherlock Holmes again. He already had some repute as a wonder of deduction. Now I wondered where he wandered. In Whitechapel, obviously, returning to the scene of the Ripper crimes with fresh insight into which of dozens of suspects might be the actual killer. Did he track a rogue Red Indian from Buffalo Bill's Wild West Show? The great scout and showman had admitted that some of his native warriors had parted company with the cast to remain in London. Long Wolf was the most famous instance, but another man had also jumped ship, so to speak, there.

Irene, to give her credit, had first brought up the possibility that a Red Man, encountering European society and the thousands of women and girls who plied the prostitute's trade in such great capitals as London and Paris, might succumb to a barbaric slaughtering. It was not so long ago that those of their tribe, or neighboring ones, had raped, burned, and mutilated settlers of the West. What would such a savage soul make of the poor white women who solicited pennies on the streets of Whitechapel in such numbers?

Sherlock Holmes was the quintessential Englishman in my view: superior, opinionated, and desperately in need of showing up. It was rather amusing to watch his vaunted logic dither in the presence of the beauteous and bright Irene. He had even admitted within my hearing that she was the only woman ever to have outwitted him.

I truly did not see what he saw in her, for she seemed sadly disorganized and dependent now, relying upon the kindness of friends, trusting to Indian scouts instead of her own pluck. And the men all kowtowed to her great losses like courtiers to a widowed Queen Victoria!

This was not where the mystery would unwind. At least Sherlock Holmes had hied to London to reinvestigate the Ripper's Reign of Terror there. Oh, to be in England now!

I would so dearly love to beat him to the identity of the Ripper. AMERICAN GIRL BESTS EUROPE'S GREATEST SLEUTH. What headlines that would make on my side of the Atlantic!

A plain lantern sat on the huge table in Buffalo Bill Cody's tent, its vivid light painting his long wavy yellow locks into tongues of flame.

He stood hunched over a map of England, not of the Wild West.

Hunched beside him was the thrillingly authentic figure of Red Tomahawk, whose nose was as aquiline as any Spanish aristocrat's, whose earth-colored skin shone like tanned leather, whose figure radiated the sheen of bone and feather and deerskin.

The scene resembled a lithograph of the Indian Wars, save that we were plunked in the middle of a great fairgrounds in the world's most civilized city. Once I was done with Paris, France, and London, England, and other points east of the great U.S. of A., I determined to go West some day soon to record the doings there, though the exciting conflicts of yesteryear were over and done with in this advanced year of 1889.

So I envisioned again the savage scene that we four violently different people gathered here had witnessed on these very holiday grounds: the gathered madmen—and women—leaping and screaming and slinging weapons as if partaking in an Indian war dance, though they were surely the debased product of a half dozen European countries. No doubt the Europeans prided themselves at having evolved beyond savagery, but these demented Gypsies and lowlifes gave such snobbery the lie.

And the three other witnesses to this murderous scene were an odd blend of New World and Old: the courtly Wild West scout better known by the colorful name of Buffalo Bill instead of William F. Cody. The colorfully garbed Red Man, a sharp shadow of the fierce plains warriors his dead brothers had been, his name and tracking abilities testifying to his proud and violent heritage, Red Tomahawk. The American-born dethroned European diva turned very private detective, Irene Adler.

They consulted like old warriors, despite their disparity, despite my presence, which they ignored. I began to see that "taking notes," as Nell had so often done, effectively rendered one invisible.

I didn't mind. I was most effective when invisible. Until I chose to be very visible indeed.

"So you found the horse with the misshapen shoe?" Irene asked Red Tomahawk.

Her tone was no different than if she had addressed the Baron de Rothschild. Indeed, it was perhaps more respectful, for Red

Tomahawk's native abilities bordered on the magical in the eyes of whites and Europeans, much as did Sherlock Holmes's vaunted reading of the smallest signs of evidence.

He grunted, displaying the admirable taciturn nature of his race. His finger stabbed the map. "From here. To here. To here. The horse with the damaged shoe only took them to the edge of the settlement. Then the wagon went on."

"The Gypsy wagon you followed through the exposition grounds earlier?" Buffalo Bill asked.

Red Tomahawk nodded, setting his feathers atremble. "I followed the trail, east where the sun awakens, to a city they call Verdun."

"Verdun! On foot all that way?"

Red Tomahawk eyed Irene. "All our horses were shot out from under the Red Man. So we walk."

She understood that he spoke of not-so-ancient wrongs. "Did no one comment on your appearance?"

"I wore hat and coat, like Long Wolf in London. Most strange garb. When tracking bear it is well to wear bear hide."

"Why only as far as Verdun?" Buffalo Bill asked. He not only had no trouble believing in Red Tomahawk's startlingly long foot journey; he wondered why it was not wholly epic! Why not Frankfurt or Prague or Vienna or any of the great cities beyond Verdun?

Red Tomahawk tapped the point on the map again. "No more wagon. Iron Horse."

I loved that expression. So apt. The railway engine had indeed been a Trojan horse, an Iron Horse snorting and steaming its way across Indian lands like a giant plow, domesticating the land, making the flesh-and-blood horse obsolete. And the buffalo. And the Red Man.

"They drove the wagon to a railway station?" Irene asked.

"Hoofprints lost in boot tracks, in Iron Horse tracks."

"Have you no idea where they went from there, Red Tomahawk?" she asked, her voice throbbing with naked hope as only a performer's can.

"East, where White Man come from. Everywhere I go east, there are more and more White Men. No Red Men."

"Ah, but go far enough east," Buffalo Bill put in, "and there are Yellow Men, millions of them."

"I have gone far enough east to know that I will not like the end of it." Red Tomahawk's forefinger stabbed the map again. "That is where wagon went, and all who were on it. The horse came back the same way Red Tomahawk did. I crossed its path more than once, but when I found the wagon it pulled, there were only these dark tribes you call Gypsies aboard. They may know something of these war dances in the caves, but I was not one they would answer to."

"They answered to you in the cavern, when you threw your war tomahawk," Irene pointed out.

The Indian said nothing.

"It was bravely done," Buffalo Bill noted. "Only a war whoop would stop those Devil's imps from their obscene business. Pistol shots were like snapping lapdogs in that hellish scene."

"It's true," Irene said, "that the Rothschild agents were horrified into inaction. It took us Americans to stop the butchery."

Buffalo Bill nodded, grinning. "No fiercer warriors, on horseback or on foot, than the American Indian. That's why I delight in bringing their cavalry prowess to the attention of the crowned heads of Europe. Those princes and kings are pretty proud of their mounted forces in their fancy helmets and uniforms on their warm-blooded patrician horseflesh, but a bareback Cheyenne on a rangy paint pony can ride rings around them. Rode rings around me."

"White Brother ride all right," Red Tomahawk conceded. "Ride our buffalo to death."

Buffalo Bill cleared his throat. "We had settlers to feed."

"Iron Horse to feed."

Buffalo Bill nodded. "But now we can afford to celebrate the Indian and the pony of the plains, and the horsemen who ride them.

Now we can corral the buffalo like cows, those that remain, and build up the herds."

"Corral the Indians, too?"

I had expected Red Tomahawk to answer his boss and fellow American, but it was Irene who had spoken.

"Listen," said Buffalo Bill. "If these Indians weren't on the reservations, they'd be dead. Many of the Indians in my show would be imprisoned at home. I maintain their freedom."

"Freedom of movement," she said, running her finger along the red veins of roads upon the map. "Where could our mysterious party go from Verdun? And does not their hasty escape imply that they are heading somewhere specific, and possibly conveying a prisoner with them?"

"Could be," Buffalo Bill admitted. "And where to go? I don't know. South to Italy. North to Germany, perhaps Berlin. Or east as Red Tomahawk thinks. There's the most land that way, if distance is what they crave."

"We know they crave blood," Irene said. "Why they want Nell . . . oh, it is a mystery meant to madden! We cannot afford to dally with insanity when we are chasing it."

"You think this is related to those women murdered here in Paris?" the scout asked. As he respected Red Tomahawk in matters of tracking, he bowed to Irene Adler in matters of murder.

"And London," she answered.

Buffalo Bill whistled his surprise. "Those are mad acts, all. Do you really believe a madman—madmen, as we have seen here in Paris—is so methodical as that? What do you opine, Red Tomahawk?"

The Indian thought first, as was his wont, before delivering himself of a diagnosis. "These are crazy men. They are not at war. They do not fight for their tribe. There is firewater in their blood. They kill their own squaws? No sense in that. Squaws too valuable workers. They wound, they kill for no good reason. Not for land. Not to turn back White Man, who is like the waves of grass and springs up ten-thousands full under the very hooves of our horses and our buffalo. They are crazy-drunk."

"It's true," Irene observed, "that liquor plays a part in their debauchery."

I could tell that the word "debauchery" meant nothing to Red Tomahawk.

"What do you think, Pink?" she asked, turning to me at last.

Nell had been right: she had a most annoying habit of rhyming a person's name with the word before it.

I was struck by how swiftly I, Nellie Bly, had been subsumed into the role of Irene's quiet companion and amanuensis, Nell Huxleigh. As long as it suited my purpose, I would serve. When it didn't, I would prove myself a very different sort of Nell indeed!

"I think," said I, "that we need to better understand exactly what happened in the cavern on these grounds the other night."

I won support from an unexpected quarter.

"No one can track," said Red Tomahawk, "without knowing the ways of the prey." He looked at Irene, a regard as steady as his ax hand. "She will scout for you when you go east." It was a question presented as a certainty.

"With me," Irene corrected. "And the red-bearded man as well."

The Indian nodded. "He walks the lone ways, like a scout. He is a man of the city, but there is prairie in his soul."

"There is room for more in my party," Irene said.

Red Tomahawk looked at his employer. "I have a contract to stay. I am a performer now. Like Sitting Bull."

I doubt that anyone in that tent had the slightest impression that Red Tomahawk or Sitting Bull, the legendary Sioux chief who also appeared in the Wild West Show, were mere contract players on the world stage.

When we returned to our hotel room, Irene doffed her bonnet as if it were a crown of thorns. She ran her fingertips into the hair at her temples, perhaps seeking to push the migraine away.

"Verdun! Would you believe that our modest party has driven this band of maniacs out of Paris! Is there any sherry in the decanter?"

She threw herself into the lounge chair, crossed her feet on the ottoman, and picked up her cigarette case and lucifers from the small round table beside it.

I poured two generous glasses of sherry. A *sommelier* would object, but we were two American women alone at last, and I had never seen anyone as able to become completely herself, or the opposite of it, as Irene Adler.

"Thank you." She regarded me with weary amusement. "Nell would never abet my vices so readily."

"No doubt that is why you acquired a husband." It was a bold observation. I was speaking of her Lost as if they were Perfectly Fine.

"Having done so, I intend to keep him. And Nell. So." She exhaled an exceedingly thin stream of smoke. "You wish to analyze every gory detail of our recent encounter in the cavern."

I sat in a matching lounge chair and sipped sherry, dislodging my feet from their ladylike slippers.

"Yes! I saw the woman at the morgue, her clothes on pegs above her naked body as if displayed on a line. I saw the mutilations to the breast and . . . generative organs. The cavern showed me where such an atrocity had likely occurred."

"Not the organs. That is the point."

"It is?"

"Jack the Ripper was an . . . organ man, not the begging organ-grinder on the corner you pass by without noticing but a new and nasty variety. He reveled in bowels and intestines. He cut off breasts and ears and noses and slit faces, to be sure, but his real work was excavating the body, cutting out the womb, draping entrails like Roman shades and rearranging guts like furniture."

"Is that why the upholsterer James Kelly is the leading candidate for the villain?" I refused to let her blunt speech scare me off the subject, as she had no doubt hoped it would.

"James Kelly is what we theater folk call 'typecast' for the role of Jack the Ripper. He is mad. He hates women. He hates particularly women who will couple with him, especially his wife, whom he killed for her trouble in marrying him, calling her a whore as he did it. He had just escaped the lunatic asylum and was in London, in Whitechapel, at the time of the Ripper killings last autumn. He fled to Paris after the last and most loathsome death, Mary Jane Kelly's. Here he has helped create erotic furniture for the high-class brothels of Paris, where more murders and mutilations of prostitutes have occurred."

Irene had not truly regarded me during this brutal recital, but now she turned the full power of her gaze upon me.

"You have never explained to me, Elizabeth Jane Cochrane, how it is that you have been able to pass yourself off as a woman of easy virtue in brothels in both London and Paris. I do not take you for a victim of anything but your own ambition. Is there no length to which you will not go to pursue a lurid subject matter?"

"Now you are sounding like Nell, Keeper of the Proprieties. It is none of your business how I do my job, or . . . what I am, maiden or harlot."

"Surely there is some middle ground," she said, smiling persuasively. "And if there is, I am assured that you have found it. Women have been forced to trick men into believing they are virgins when they are not for centuries. I have not yet heard, however, how it was possible to trick men into thinking a woman is no longer a virgin, when she is."

"You are accusing me of being a virgin?"

"If you wish to put it that way."

"That is indeed a serious charge."

"How you love to turn convention on its head. So did I. Once."

"It was easy in London. Even in the uppity East End, prostitution is illegal, however much it is winked at by Brits with monocles in their upper-class eyes."

"Yes, but you must have encountered a hitch here in Paris. Prostitution is legal and strictly regulated against disease. How were you able to pass the inspections? A speculum does not lie, at least to the existence of a hymen." She eyed me with a combination of dubiousness and respect. "The examinations are rough and humiliating."

"So was my life at home with Jack Ford. I would do anything to escape that. A wife is far more the humiliated creature than a Paris prostitute."

"I am a wife and do not consider myself humiliated in the least."

"Oh, the sainted Godfrey, to hear Nell talk! I cannot wait to see this mythical beast."

"I sincerely hope that you soon do."

Her tone's intensity made my cheeks flare with heat, but I spoke past that humiliating habit of mine, from which my nickname derived.

"Here you are, so eager to keep Miss Nell from learning the rough edges of life. Let me tell you of a few rough edges she would never stomach. An intact hymen is the bride's badge of innocence, the harlot's one-time prize. I didn't reckon that Paris would require such piggish examinations, but . . . I made certain to . . . disable mine before they could investigate me."

"You deflowered yourself. It must have been painful. You are as formidable in your way as Red Tomahawk."

"Thanks. Now that your curiosity is satisfied—"

"Not mere curiosity, Pink. That is so crass. You know that certain information is crucial."

"And the means of my masquerade is that crucial?"

"I needed to know to what lengths you'd go."

"Happy?"

"No. I wonder if you have escaped Jack Ford as thoroughly as you think."

"He was no King of Bohemia, that is true, but a petty tyrant in his own mad way. James Kelly puts me in mind of him."

"James Kelly. Gone, too. With the Gypsies-O."

"You really think he's gone off with that lot? And Nell? He did show a fancy for her when we three and Sherlock Holmes cornered him in his rooms."

"If a knife at the throat betokens a fancy. . . ." But she frowned, and I knew I had hit home.

If she had to twist the means of my masquerade from me—and she was right, though I'd never admit it to her or any other soul—it had been humiliating. My best, most meaningful stories came from subjecting myself to humiliations ordinary people endure every day. And then there were the more spectacular stunts I did to keep my pen name in the public eye.

"He went after Nell," she went on in a memory-driven singsong. "In the cavern. Right for her. I urged her to run away. For her safety. In that flight she found . . . what? Who? Capture, that much is clear. I don't know if he found her. I hope not."

"Somehow I did not envision Jack the Ripper in league with Gypsies. It smacks of an operetta."

"No one envisioned the London killings as part of a . . . grand design. Or a common infection, at least. The Ripper has become an umbrella for all the ills that murderers do. Under the funereal ribs of his name shelter an entire nation of suspects, from lowest to highest, like the figures portrayed in a Parisian panorama display.

"If he is a single man, he may hide in a multitude. If he is many, he may trickle away like single poisonous raindrops into a muddy puddle of mankind. Yet we tracked down Kelly, as did Sherlock Holmes. Surely two such different hunting parties meeting at the same source means something."

"It means that Sherlock Holmes is as subject to misconjecture as the rest of humankind."

Irene smiled palely at my response. "Poor man."

"I would not call that self-sufficient and arrogant creature 'poor.' "

"The ultraintelligent are often mistaken for arrogant when they are merely right." She sipped her sherry. "I meant 'poor man' because he eats and drinks reason and now he has put himself in the

position of pursuing unreason. He should never have agreed to med-
dle in the flurry to find Jack the Ripper." She leaned her cheek on
her hand. "I wonder what he will make of *Psychopathia Sexualis*."

"More than 'poor Nell' ever would! And she is the one of us all
most likely to encounter the Ripper."

"*Hmmm*," Irene said, and said no more.

"I can't see how you stand it! Nell was last seen pursued from
the site of a murderous orgy by a suspect for Jack the Ripper and
a candidate for these four latest Paris slaughters of women. Your
husband has gone missing in the wilds of Wherever. And you sit
in a Paris hotel room and speculate on the reading material of Sherlock Holmes!"

"Our enemies have stolen a march on us, Pink. If we jump up
leaping in every direction, they will gain even more distance and
time. We must settle the business in Paris before we move on, and
move on we will. I have already put inquiries in motion."

"Not through the Rothschilds."

"Not yet."

"Not through the Prince of Wales."

"He is of use in areas I do not yet need."

"Not through the Paris police."

"I have, as a matter of fact, asked for some small information
there."

"Not through Madame Sarah."

"No woman in Europe has more ex-lovers. We shall see if we
need the aid of any as we continue the hunt."

"And Buffalo Bill's trusty scout Red Tomahawk came to a dead
end at Verdun."

"An end may be a beginning," she said enigmatically.

"So with all these offers of aid, you accept only the company of
a suspect for the Ripper almost as far-fetched as a member of the
royal family itself, Bram Stoker."

"Apparently," Irene said with another Mona Lisa smile. "I am
not trying to annoy you, Pink, but patience is the one virtue that
Jack the Ripper does not have."

"Nor do I! That does not make me the Ripper."

Irene tilted her head even more, regarding me like a weary bird. "The Ripper could be a she. Now that is an interesting theory that I doubt has occurred to Sherlock Holmes."

3.

Somewhere in London

✧

I have never loved.

—HOLMES TO WATSON, ARTHUR CONAN DOYLE,
THE DEVIL'S FOOT

◁ FROM THE NOTES OF JOHN H. WATSON, M. D. ▷

 A telegram from my friend Sherlock Holmes was always to the point:

"Watson, if you can manage it, come to Baker Street at once. If you cannot manage it, come anyway, the sooner the better. I am working on the gravest case of my career."

My dear wife, Mary, was well used to Holmes's clarion calls to the hunt. She merely nodded when I told her my errand and glanced to the pocket of my Norfolk jacket, where my service revolver reposed, as she had suspected. Holmes had not requested its presence, but old Army instincts told me that it might not be amiss. Grave cases require strong medicine, as any doctor knows.

Unlike many wives, Mary never demurred when my former rooming partner demanded my attendance. As a doctor's wife she was used to my being called out unexpectedly. Also, she knew that we owed our very marriage to my friend's storied deductive abilities, and, even more, to his stout heart in the face of danger.

So she merely smoothed lapels that needed no straightening, tucked in the muffler she had knitted for me, and, smiling, kissed my cheek as she saw me out the door.

The spring evening radiated the abiding damp that comes between rains. Through the fog and smoke the streets shone like a black cat's well-licked coat.

I hailed a two-wheeler and soon the horse's brisk hooves were beating a rat-a-tat on the cobblestones of Baker Street.

Mrs. Hudson answered my knock, the gaslight behind her in the hall making a halo of her tendrils of snow-white hair.

"He's not here," she informed me, then turned to lead the way up stairs so familiar that my feet could trace their height and length in the pitch dark.

"Wasn't here for a fortnight," she grumbled. "Off to foreign shores, as he will, I think. When he came back, he was in and out again like a messenger boy." She paused in midflight, turning back to address me. "Won't eat. Oh, I'll bring his meals up, but if so much as a canary bird is pecking away at the food, I'd be surprised."

"On the trail, I suppose," I put in, knowing my comment wasn't needed as either a goad or a period to further conversation.

"That man lives on nerve and shag tobacco." Mrs. Hudson's snowy head shook as if to dislodge an avalanche of disapproval.

I could have added another bad habit to her list, but forebear to mention the seven-percent solution of cocaine that, along with playing the violin, rather well in my opinion, was my friend's only recreation.

"He works too hard," she said, mirroring my thoughts as she opened the door. "No doubt, *you*'ll have some refreshment, Doctor."

I required none but didn't care to join Holmes in rejecting her culinary attentions.

"I've a bit of cold kidney pie left over from dinner. He was out for it, of course. You know how to make yourself at home."

"Indeed I do." I turned from my quick perusal of the room to usher the kindhearted soul back down to her kitchen.

I sighed relief as the door closed, understanding for a moment Holmes's fondness for solitude. Everything here was just as it had been. Oh, not precisely, but close enough.

I wandered to the mantel and the Persian slipper. The same fragrant wad of shag plugged its up-curling toe. Where on earth was its mate? Now there was a mystery.

On the table in the corner, the clutter of chemical experiments winked glassily at me in the lamplight. I could smell sulphur . . . *hmmm*, kerosene, of course, and . . . ginger?

I felt like an actor visiting the beloved stage set for a play in which I was no longer employed. Each homely item in the chamber had the dear familiarity of an old friend, yet I felt somehow removed from these things, this place, perhaps even from the role I was here to reprise.

And yet, despite my distance, I still felt a flutter of stage fright. "The gravest case of my career." Did Holmes choose that word "grave" not merely in the sense of seriousness, but because of its additional freight of meaning? For its proximity to death and decay? I feared so. He was nothing if not exact.

The heel of my hand touched the crosshatched wooden butt of the pistol in my pocket, my forefinger caressing the cold silky steel of the trigger guard. Would I need this weapon before the night was out?

A scrabbling sound in the stairwell sent me to the door. For once I would not allow Holmes to burst onstage and put me in the role of mere audience to my own drama.

I pulled the door wide . . .

. . . and found an ancient rabbi in long, rusty black coat and hat fumbling to lift his cane high enough to knock on the door, only my face had replaced the sturdy wood.

"Now, Holmes," I chided, perhaps inspired by the earlier liberties of Mrs. Hudson. "You can't expect to fool me in that getup."

"Fool you, young man? I have no need to fool you. You look a fellow fully capable of doing it to yourself, as most of these young idiots are these days. This is 221B Baker Street?"

"Yes."

"Then invite me in, Mr. Holmes, since I am here at your invitation. Nay, command."

"I am Dr. Watson."

"I could use a doctor, I admit, for my rheumatism, but did not need to be called out on such a damp night with no Mr. Holmes present."

"He will be." I caught myself entering into the charade, so much in stooped character was Holmes. "I mean, *you* will be."

"I will be present if you step aside and allow me to enter the chamber."

At this pointed remark, I did as requested. In this way I was able to take an unobserved survey of Holmes's "visitor."

What an ideal disguise this one was! The high-crowned black hat, from which side curls hung before each ear, the stooped back and shoulders held so stiffly, elbows jacked out, the shuffling gait accentuated by the rhythmic thump of the cane, all were perfection.

I expected Holmes to straighten and turn with twinkling eyes as soon as he had fully entered the room, but he did not.

"A long journey for nothing," the slightly accented voice noted, no quaver about it.

A small mistake, that, which I would be only too happy to point out to Holmes when he had finally doffed the guise that had never deceived me from the first. Quaver was definitely required for this impersonation.

The old fellow stamped his cane on the carpet so hard I worried for Mrs. Hudson's peace of mind.

It was echoed, however, by a furious thumping from beyond our door: feet taking the steps two at a time.

I whirled to see what visitor was so impatient to arrive.

"Holmes!"

He paused in the doorway, the same tall, lean figure I had often seen stepping through just that frame like a painting come to life, wearing city top hat and a suit of modest but gentlemanly cut.

"Ah, Watson. You have introduced yourself to Rabbi Barshevich," he said. "Excellent. Pray be seated," he suggested to the old man with a bow. "Watson, you as well. But first shut the door, if you please. We will not wish to be disturbed."

"Er, Mrs. Hudson—"

"Yes, yes, I know the lady."

"She's returning with kidney pie."

"Kidney pie?"

His tone made it sound like raw entrails. "Very well, we will let it stay. A pity I don't keep some creature around the place that could eat it for us. Now, Rabbi, I require a summary of the International Working Men's Educational Club at number forty, Berner Street. I am assured that Baron Rothschild's emissaries have acquainted you with my needs and mission."

"Quite above themselves they were, and eager to smack the dust of Whitechapel from their smart city shoes. I received only your name and address and the instructions to visit you."

"I must apologize. I have just returned from abroad and am most eager to lay these Whitechapel matters to rest."

"If you can find and lay Jack the Ripper to rest, that will be all that is needed," the old man said robustly, thumping his cane on the carpet again.

"Surely you do not expect further depredations?"

"The monster seems to have vanished with the fog that hid his vile ways, but the suspicion his foul acts cast on my people still lingers."

"Tell me," Holmes said, suddenly drawing his feet up on the cushion of the basket chair like some swami. "That phrase, 'The Juwes are the men That Will not be Blamed for nothing.' What does that mean to you?"

"Nonsense. They are always scrawling vile phrases about Jews in Whitechapel. Children!"

"You think children wrote that chalked phrase?"

"Not real children." The old man tapped his temple with one horny forefinger. "Grown children who love to jeer and call names, and throw refuse when I pass. Then the young ones, too. They see and repeat, like monkeys. We Jews have always been blamed for much."

"No one is exempt from suspicion in this case," Holmes said. "Not even myself."

That last qualification forestalled the old man's forthcoming speech of protest.

"Besides several Jewish individuals," Holmes went on, "a number of Russians and Poles are suspected."

"Even gentiles, and even the high and mighty," the rabbi put in tartly, with some personal relish at the idea.

"Even those considered high and mighty," Holmes agreed, expressing his customary disdain for the twin social advantages of wealth and station.

"Then you rule no one out?"

"No one, no nationality, no race, no religion, no sex, fair or not."

"Do I take it, young man, that you wish to reassure me that you will be just?"

"I will be better than just. I will be logical."

"Logic." The old man chuckled. "That is one remedy that has not yet been applied to the Whitechapel Horrors."

When Mrs. Hudson had delivered her offering and left, when the rabbi had given Holmes the particulars he required and left, my friend turned his attentions to me.

"What, Dr. Watson, still waxing plump with prosperity and the married life in Paddington?"

He surprised me by sitting at the round table and tucking into the kidney pie like a sailor.

"Apparently you intend to put me on a fast immediately, Dr. Holmes."

He gave that sharp bark of laughter that seemed a social convention rather than real mirth, and pushed the platter toward my side of the table.

"Dig in, Watson. It is chill and damp out despite the season."

I sat, if I did not import any kidney pie to my plate. "Then this is an expedition of sorts."

"Or a sortie." Holmes grinned as he dashed some Tokay into the empty wine glasses.

"You have made progress since you sent me the telegram. Was it something the rabbi said?"

"I have made progress indeed, if crawling to the end of the most noxious sewer in England is to be considered an achievement."

"Surely not in that garb."

"No. I had to report to my betters just previously."

As always, Holmes gave a twist to the word "betters" that could only come from a man who considered himself on a higher plane entirely.

I had to agree with his cheerful self-esteem. I had never known a man who could so accurately pierce to the core truth of a situation or a character. From the smallest motes of physical evidence he could extrapolate to the largest conclusions about the good and evil rubbing shoulders in the human soul. This facility made him remote to the myopic concerns of ordinary mortals, but it did indeed lay open the way certain of us live our lives and die our deaths. He was very like a master surgeon, cutting through the skin and gristle and muscle and bone of the carapace of ordinary life to what lay beneath: to the extraordinary and complex systems of motive and passion and seven deadly sins that race like rampaging corpuscles through every vein of our beings and often erupt in paroxysms of crime and evildoing.

"Your betters," I repeated after my reverie had faded. "Not the police surely."

"Especially not in this case!" he snorted, his restless gray eyes

pouncing on the Persian slipper on the mantel. A cat spotting a
mouse in its hole across the room could not have looked more
intent.

He leaped upon his prey in the next moment, and shortly after
the familiar perfume of tobacco masked the chemical odors that
filled the chambers like noxious potpourri.

Scheherazade had her veils and her thousand-and-one tales to
beguile. Holmes had his veils of smoke to add dazzle to his chron-
icles of crime.

"The police have been thicker than usual," he rumbled over the
pipe. "The real crime is the vast numbers of footprints they have
left all over the area."

"Then this is a case of paramount importance, if so many police
are employed."

"Oh, indeed," he said airily. "Of such paramount importance
that they did not bother to call me in on it. No matter. Their
'betters' have beat them to it."

He had resumed his seat over the crumbles of pie crust on his
plate and now placed his elbows on the table. "I confess that the
police outflank me in only one respect."

"You confess?"

He shrugged. "I am, as you know, able to slip into the foulest
pits of London. Opium or thieves' den, I can don a suitably low
disguise and pass among them as their own."

"Nothing to envy," I said with a shudder, for well I knew the
diseases physical as well as spiritual that thrive in such ratholes of
human commerce and depravity.

"There is, however, one sinkhole of sin into which I am less
easy about inserting myself."

"Really."

"No doubt you have already discerned it, Watson, given your
superior experience in certain hidden corners of life."

"Well, I—" I had certainly not discerned where Holmes was
leading me and was not eager to claim residence in his "hidden
corners of life" without knowing to what he referred.

"Tut. Modesty does not become you, Watson, a stout-hearted, hale, and handsome fellow like you. In one area your expertise far exceeds my own, and no doubt that of most men. And I do not refer to the practice of medicine."

"I know my field, certainly, and something of human nature, as any good physician must."

Holmes held up a quelling hand. "I will hear no demurs from you on this topic, Watson. When it comes to women you are a Daniel come to judgment."

"Women! This case is about women?"

"Indeed. And what men do with them. As you know, I have always been somewhat mystified on that subject. Oh, I know the ways of the world, I simply do not understand why they are that way. Nor do I really care to."

"A man with no use for his fellow man is called a misanthrope. A man with no use for women is called—"

"A misogynist. I know the term, Watson. And I am not sure that having no 'use' for women makes me a misogynist when I see evidence of the 'use' most men put women to."

I sipped the excellent Tokay while I floundered for words. Though I had often twitted Holmes about his indifference to what certain coy writers call the fair sex, we had never really plumbed the vast chasm between myself as a married man and Holmes as the quintessential bachelor. Moreover, Holmes was a bachelor who did not use his freedom to 'play the field' with the ladies, but instead indulged his solitary, almost monkish, celibate bent.

There. I had used the word, even if only to myself, about the one condition in my friend I had never approached or explored. Celibate. Had he been religious, that would have explained much. But Holmes was a logician, and as indifferent to organized religion as he was to women. He was an ascetic esthete, an undebauched Bohemian, if such a contradiction in condition exists. Holmes was unique, and exulted in that fact. So did I, when I was not being irritated by it.

"Can you not guess," Holmes asked quietly, "what case I pursue?"

"No, I cannot!"

"It is the Ripper."

"The Ripper! You mentioned the case to the rabbi, but I thought those were comments in passing. You swore to me in this very room that you were not involved. 'Mere butchery, Watson,' you said. I have made notes. Besides, there has not been a Ripper slaying in several months. Surely the matter is dead."

"Apparently," he said cryptically through an immense huff of smoke. I could see that my indignant charges had hit home.

"It was necessary to mislead you, Watson. I was called into the case last autumn, although late, by a Personage of such eminence that even to hint at the name and position would be a betrayal any true Englishman would face an execution squad rather than reveal."

"Oh," I said, understanding immediately that he referred to Her Majesty, the Queen, herself. Sometimes Holmes ran the danger of being most transparent when he most wished to bemuse.

"I deeply regretted the necessity. You have been a most loyal old fellow and deserved more. But you do have a tendency to write down the particulars of my cases and are even eager to publish them. However, now—"

"Yes, I suppose old Toby and I do deserve a small treat now and again."

Holmes flashed me a look of impatience over the bowl of his favorite black clay pipe at my reference to the scent-hound he occasionally used on his cases. "No need to be testy about it. The matter was of national secrecy, and now it has grown into a matter of international discretion."

He had me there, hooked like a salmon in an icy Scottish stream. "International?"

"Indeed," he murmured to his oil-stained pipe bowl, his favorite accessory for cogitating. "See here, Watson. I defer to your superior experience in this one area and cast myself upon your mercy. Come

with me to Whitechapel, and show me how a gentleman might see
the place and might see opportunity there."

"A gentleman?"

"A man of good character, at least apparently. You cannot deny
that when you served in foreign climes you did not fail to sample
the . . . recreational aspects of the locality."

"I was in the Army, Holmes! And I am not a saint."

"Exactly why I value your knowledge now. I was never in the
Army, and while I do not aspire to sanctity, neither do I to sin. I
had long considered this an advantage in my calling, but am discovering this to be a handicap in this particular case."

"It is unlike you to admit a failing."

Holmes laughed into the smoke welling up from the pipe. "It
is humbling indeed when the lack of what is commonly considered
a moral failing proves a stumbling block to my investigation."

He leapt up as he was wont to, without warning, and made for
the bookshelf. He returned with a slim volume I had not seen
before, an odd stutter in his usually confident stride as he came
abreast of the mantel and glanced at something on it.

I consulted it myself, for its terrain was as unvarying as the
cursed wilds of Afghanistan. I saw nothing amiss: the jackknife pinning correspondence to the wood, the Persian slipper, the clutter,
the cabinet portrait of the dead adventuress, Irene Adler, the wad
of saved tobacco ends at the mantel's opposite end.

"Do you read German, Watson?"

"I can stumble through it. Medical texts, you know. 'Richard
von Krafft-Ebing.' I have heard of this doctor, although in a scandalous context."

"Excellent." Holmes cast himself into the basket chair and
huffed away on the pipe like a steam locomotive. "Tell me what is
so scandalous."

"He claims to have discovered a class of killers that he calls 'lust-
murderers.' "

"And he means by that?"

"That the lust to kill is also a carnal urge."

"And how does that make these killers different from those who slaughter in the name of greed or vengeance or pure madness?"

I perused the thick pages. "I am not sure. I have heard of but not read his work."

"And how is it that I have escaped knowledge of this most useful volume?" Holmes asked a bit querulously. His voice was a trifle high-pitched to begin with. When he felt overlooked, or worse, offended, it would rise to a strident tone.

"Holmes, these matters are discreetly discussed among men of the world, in clubs, at gentleman's bars. Such knowledge is not deemed fit for the public at large."

"Nor for women."

"Certainly not! I would shoot the man who would lay such filth before my Mary."

"Yet women, and occasionally children, seem to most often be the victims of such lust-murders, if one is to believe Krafft-Ebing."

Holmes may have eschewed certain knowledge. He was never not astute.

"First one needs to believe his theories, and they have been roundly abused."

"So were Galileo's."

"I cannot recall that you ever cared one iota about whether the sun revolves around the earth or vice versa. We have had words on this very issue."

"And I do not care one whit more about these tiresome empyrean arrangements," he said with a dismissive wave of a long, lean hand. It struck me for the first time that he had a conductor's hands, incredibly communicative when his face so often was not.

"I merely point out what is of more interest to me than the subject matter of the Baron's speculations: that new ideas are often roundly rejected. I suspect that the theories of Baron von Krafft-Ebing are of more immediate use to me and my work than any roundabout made by heavenly bodies for untold millennia."

I could not restrain a "*tsk*" of exasperation. That a man of scientific bent in the minutiae of evidence to be discerned by a microscope could ignore the magnificent yet grossly visible and daily dance of the planets and stars struck me as beyond belief.

Holmes shrugged and offered one of his rare, charming smiles, which were usually exerted with nervous clients and not myself.

"I am a reprobate, Watson, when it comes to matters which have no bearing on the intimate course of my investigations. However, I am willing to learn. And it appears that this Krafft-Ebing has, in his much-loathed and yet eagerly devoured book, described a legion of Jack the Rippers."

I began to page through it looking for an assemblage of words that would translate most readily to my stumbling eye. "How did you come across this book?"

"It was a gift."

I looked up amazed. Holmes received payment, sometimes in the form of costly trinkets from rich and titled persons, never anything as personal as mere "gifts."

His lips remained firmly shut, an expression that a stick of dynamite could not blast open, but I detected a dampened smile. A smug dampened smile.

"So you believe that this bizarre book will aid you in finding the Ripper, who appears to have finished his work with the ending of last year and has vanished into the foul mists from which he came."

Holmes's eyes narrowed, perhaps from the rank smoke the old clay bowl heaved up like Vesuvius.

"This is as foul a trail as I have ever followed, Watson, and already I know of decent women who have been devastated by it. I find that makes my blood boil. I am even finding the brutal despoilation of indecent women making my blood boil. No honest Englishman should tolerate what has been made of Whitechapel, both before and after Jack the Ripper. I mean to have him. That may require me to delve into deeper, darker matters than I ever have before, and you know my appetite for human horror, for the axe murderers and acid poisoners and all manner of human depravity. This Ripper has reached a new level of atrocity. I will understand it. I will understand him. And I will catch him. Are you game to go with me?"

"Of course, Holmes. I brought my old service revolver."

Holmes smiled, tightly. "Bullets may be our least line of defense against what will come. But it is heartening to know you stand with me on this."

4.

Pitiless Whitechapel

~~~

Here I am noble; I am boyar. The common people know me, and I am master. But a stranger in a strange land, he is no one; men know him not——and to know not is to care not for.

—THE COUNT TO JONATHAN HARKER, BRAM STOKER'S *DRACULA*

⊰FROM THE NOTES OF JOHN H. WATSON, M. D.⊱

Before we left on our unwholesome errand, Holmes had changed into one of the lounge suits that were becoming popular on the streets of London, an American habit, I believe, that no Harley Street physician would dare adapt, nor even a lowly Paddington doctor. The jacket lacked the flourishes of city attire: coat skirts or tails. In that respect it resembled the more casual dress worn at sporting events, save it was constructed in decent, sober black wool rather than loose-woven linen or sackcloth.

"I am told, Watson, that supposed gentlemen amble among the greasy lanes of Whitechapel, though all I have thus far seen there are would-be gentlemen tricked out in bits and pieces of their betters' attire, rather like the unfortunates themselves in their velvet-trimmed bonnets."

The hansom had left us off where Holmes had directed, at Fairclough and Berner Streets. The jointure of those two names brought a shudder to my sturdy frame, for they often figured in newspaper stories of various evils.

"You suspect a gentleman of the Ripper slayings?" I asked, keeping my tone low against eavesdroppers and my hands in my pockets against thieves.

"I? No. But that is the current fashionable theory among the Fleet Street speculators who pass themselves off as journalists. It is not bad enough that a homicidal monster stalks the alleyways; he must be a man of privilege and position. If I had a farthing, Watson, for all the far-fetched tales constructed around the acts of Jack the Ripper, I could . . . well, I could afford a finer blend of shag."

I coughed a bit at inhaling the foul stew that passed for air among these twisted byways. "What do you need of me?"

"You have no acquaintanceship of Whitechapel?"

"I am a married man, Holmes!"

"It was not always thus, Watson."

"No, but even then I should never find my way to Whitechapel. The disease potential alone would dissuade any man of sensibility."

"We are not looking for a man of sensibility." Holmes paused beneath one of the too-few gaslights to study the street. "We are hunting a man who revels in the opposite. That does not mean he cannot sleep on silken sheets elsewhere."

"And the Ripper letters?"

"Are they indeed from the monster? Possibly. But why then the Americanisms and the mock Cockney phonetics?" He gazed around the ill-lit scene, people lurching beyond the honest circle of gaslight like supernumeraries in some contemporary vision of urban hell. "I understand the opium addict, Watson. The drug brings phantoms, illusions. It makes pain seem like pleasure, for a while. I do not understand the men who come here looking for *that* particular delusion as any kind of surcease, or illusion of pleasure."

I followed his gaze to a staggering woman across the way.

She was a creature of the ignored and much-abused homeless classes: thick of frame with poor nutrance, thick of mind thanks to too many tankards, about as feminine as that quality is experienced in a drawing room as an andiron. To a physician, a walking cesspool of disease and decay. No wonder they were known as "unfortunates."

"Why bother slaying such a sad creature?" he went on. "Yet men willingly consort with such. Can you explain it?"

"The men are drunk as well."

"I am devoutly grateful that the occasional fine port does not bring me to such a condition."

I nodded to some tattered-looking men linking arms with lampposts along the lane. "Most of these men are brute laborers. Their work is low and vile and distasteful, and so are their scant and guilty pleasures, but I tell you, Holmes, the same game is played in more attractive guise in the West End nightly."

"Ah. So I understand. Or know for a fact. It is the same game you say, Watson. Then a man from a pristine playing surface might wish to . . . try his skill in a more . . . dangerous neighborhood."

"True, Holmes. The confirmed hedonist seeks sensation at its rawest. A demented aristocrat may wish to wallow in the city's worst sinkhole."

"There. That innocuously run-down building is an opium den of my . . . knowledge. I guarantee that all within are dead to the world, Watson. The life that goes on in these streets is another matter. When death strikes here it is usually not worth noting. Where does the Ripper begin and end? I begin to think he is eternal. Not a man, but a . . . mania."

"How can you find and accuse a mania, Holmes?"

"I don't know. I suspect it hasn't been done before." He paused under another lamp to light his pipe, nodding at the bobby who strolled past.

"You've been here before," I accused.

"Frequently. In many guises, including my own."

"Your own personage is not a disguise, Holmes."

"Is it not? One night I stood perhaps ten feet from the Ripper."

"You saw him?"

"I glimpsed his shadow. And chased another shadow, believing it more likely." He inhaled so deeply on the clay pipe the bowl glowed as cherry-red as fresh-spilt blood. "I went the wrong way. I pursued a witness, not a perpetrator. I left the Ripper behind to do his bloody work."

"You, Holmes?"

"I, Watson. The man I observed was berating a woman. He knocked her down but from my recent observations of the environs, knocking down women is more the commonplace than the exception. I took it for the usual street scene. By the time I returned, she was warm but no more. It was all I could do to remove myself from the vicinity without being hailed as the Ripper myself."

"Good God, Holmes! You were that close?"

"I was that far, and for that I shall never forgive myself. If I ever do somehow stand before St. Peter and he is inclined to admit me to the pearly gates, I shall take myself off directly in the opposite direction, merely for the evil I did that one night with one wrong decision. I did not understand the customs of the country, Watson. I am a stranger in a strange land."

"You are indeed, when you quote Holy Writ."

"How is it holy?"

" 'A stranger in a strange land.' It is what Ruth became for her mother-in-law Naomi's sake."

"These are persons I should know?"

"Well, yes. If one were well-read."

"I am perfectly well-read, Watson, merely not in those tiresome tomes that pass for essential in our day. In fact, I am so well-read that I now number Krafft-Ebing among my acquaintance." It was as close as Holmes ever came to a jocularity. He eyed me, head tilted like a robin expecting some unwise worm to rise to the surface.

"Do you think that this author would have useful insight on this place?"

"Vaguely. Promotes a bunch of lurid poppycock, if you ask me."

"How well you put it, Watson. Then you do not think his lurid poppycock is even worth the denouncing."

"We can discuss it, Holmes, once we are out of this dreadful place. I can certainly see how the Ripper was able to slink among these ill-lit byways and pounce upon his victims, then disappear, if that is what you brought me here to see."

"I brought you here to see what I could not see."

"There is nothing you cannot see."

"Exactly. I would be obliged if you would wander 'mongst the lost and the damned for a while longer. We can have a warming toddy back in Baker Street and compare notes."

"It will take more than a toddy to erase this stink from our nostrils."

"At least we can leave the vicinity and its foulnesses far behind. That is more than its residents can achieve. Ah." He stopped to stare at an unprepossessing brick building of four stories before us. "The International Working Men's Educational Club. It was near here that I so deserted sense and chased the wrong quarry. Now we are getting somewhere."

"Holmes, I am sure that any man would have made the same mistake."

"Ah, but I am not any man. Stand with me here by the road and let us dissect that abominable evening. It was nearly one of the clock. The club's front door, which you see there, was locked, but that gateway at the side was open, and led through a small yard to a rear entrance, so residents could come and go as they needed."

"Is this a legitimate club, Holmes?"

I saw a sickle-moon of smile in the dim lamplight. "It is not secretly a house of ill repute, Watson, unless you count Socialism as a social ill and they would say they are only here to reform social ills. Yes, it is what is said, and I have the rabbi's word on that, for what little credit he gives the young revolutionaries that assemble here, as you heard from his own lips."

"A wise man."

"That is what the title means, I believe, although arcane religious matters of any stripe are far beyond my ken. At any rate, I had taken a post opposite the club, in disguise of course."

"Why?"

"Why? Because a number of the early suspects were Jews. This is a central point where men of that race come and go. And after two murders that had particularly captured the public imagination, not to mention the usual string of women murdered in the district months and years before, I noted that the murders of Mary Ann Nicholls and Annie Chapman had occurred in a certain progression of dates. It seemed some pattern underlay the attacks."

"You were following a wild guess, admit it, Holmes!"

"I was following my own logic." He drew deeply on his pipe before speaking again. "I will admit that there are some few areas in which I am personally deficient and that they probably intersected here, to my chagrin and to the death of that woman, Elizabeth Stride. Chagrin, I am convinced, falls far lower on St. Peter's list of failings than unnecessary death. It is lucky that I do not believe in such postmortem fairy tales."

I did not know what to say. I had seen Holmes perplexed, Holmes afire with the hunt, Holmes triumphant. I had never seen Holmes humble, and I suspected that this was as close as I would ever come in my lifetime.

He gazed at the street opposite. "No woman killed in Whitechapel, Watson, during or before or after the Ripper's reign, was seen with so many men of varying appearance as Elizabeth Stride, this forty-four-year-old unfortunate who was missing two front teeth. I saw her with one myself, though I don't believe I can afford to discount the earlier men who crossed her path, some quite intimately, according to witnesses. From the testimony, there was a cordiality to the encounters that quite surprises me. Perhaps you can explain."

"It is a game, Holmes. The woman pretends interest in the man, she flatters and flirts. What she wants is the coins that will ease her life for a few hours, whether spent on beer or a bed indoors at a doss house. Usually she is so drunk she scarce knows what she is doing. So is he."

"A fine advertisement for such transactions, Watson. I have seen more personal interchanges in an opium den."

"Both parties in such exchanges are benighted, miserable souls, Holmes. All the world knows that. Still, the great cities of that world support ten thousands of prostitutes and many times more men to patronize them. It is a ritual as old as earth."

"No doubt why those stars and moons and planets keep such a wide berth of our own globe. Take yourself back to that night of twenty-nine September last year, Watson. By sometime between 7:00 and 8:00 P.M. Elizabeth Stride had earned sixpence through some cleaning work. She planned further and more profitable expeditions, for she borrowed a clothes brush from Charles Preston, a barber, and left a piece of velvet with Catharine Lane, a charwoman, two friends she encountered at Flower and Dean Street.

"By 11:00 P.M., two laborers saw her lingering with a man outside the Bricklayer's Arms pub in Settle Street as they entered. They were surprised that the couple were hugging and kissing in the open. The man was too respectably dressed for such behavior: smart black morning suit and coat, billycock hat, black mustache, about five-foot-five."

I nodded, seeing the picture painted like a scene in a play.

"The workmen couldn't resist taunting the woman. The man with her, they teased, resembled Leather Apron."

"Leather Apron! Good God, Holmes, quite a chilling fellow. He was one of the earliest suspects in the Ripper murders."

"One of the earliest and the least likely, save that he had all the earmarks of a suspect made to order for the press to convict in print, which they are even better at than Scotland Yard detectives are at letting the guilty go. Although, in this instance, I behaved remarkably like Scotland Yard's finest," he finished bitterly.

Holmes would indeed be chagrined with himself for committing the same blunders for which he so often berailed officialdom.

"This man did appear in the streets in a Leather Apron and when arrested was found to keep several nasty knives at home, was he not?" I asked.

"Indeed. He was a bootmaker, hence the apron and possibly the long knives at home. He bullied the ladies of the night, no doubt, and was Jewish. Worst of all, his name was Jack. Jack Pizer. He was the sort of neighborhood bogeyman that the police and press could wish for, a 'crazy Jew' to throw to the mob and the police courts, with a nickname created to terrify women and children in their beds," Holmes finished almost contemptuously.

"I can't deny that I would seize upon such a name for a story of mine."

"Of yours, or of mine?" Holmes asked acidly.

"Of . . . yours, of course. All stories of mine are . . . yours."

"*Hmmm*. Not as flattering as you might think, Watson. I distinctly forbid you to concoct any 'story' of this case. It is too awful to perpetuate in all its gory glory. At any rate, too much time has already been wasted on Leather Apron. But back to twenty-nine September, 1888. Sometime before midnight, Matthew Packer sold fruit to a man and a woman from his front room at forty-four Berner Street."

"Next-door to the murder site we now stand near!"

"Indeed so, Watson. No one is more quickly attuned to the nuances of street addresses than a doctor who is called out frequently in the night. In this instance I detect a clear superiority to the mere olfactory skills of Toby the bloodhound."

I knew that if I could view Holmes by a paraffin lamp I would see the twinkle in his eye as he so gently paid me back for my peevish complaint of a while previous in Baker Street.

"Poor old Packer!" he went on. "His testimony wavered like his aged hand. Although he identified the woman as Long Liz and described a man of thirty to five-and-thirty years as her companion, a dark-favored man of medium height, it remains a questionable sighting."

Holmes drew deeply on the pipe, expelling enough smoke for a miniature steam engine before he continued. He turned and looked down the street.

"The next witness is the only one to have heard a soon-to-be-dead woman speak. He was William Marshall, another laborer, and he was standing outside of his lodgings at sixty-four Berner Street when he noticed a couple standing outside next door. He remarked that neither appeared to be drunk but that the couple kissed. This appears to have been common behavior in the neighborhood. He reports that the man—middle-aged, stout, and clean-shaven, about five-foot-six—commented "You would say anything except your prayers," then walked the woman down the street toward Dutfield's yard." Holmes nodded to the gate across the way from us.

"It sounds as if he knew her, Holmes! That is an accusation, and people seldom accuse strangers."

"Apparently, however, there are no strangers in Whitechapel, with all the willy-nilly kissing."

"Was there anything unusual about this last man, other than his age? The other suspects have been decidedly below five-and-thirty, and I assume middle age refers to five-and-forty, or fifty or so."

"Yes, I find this fellow of particular interest and not only for the cryptic quality of his remark. He was quietly, clerkishly dressed: cutaway coat, dark trousers, peaked cap; nothing that would attract attention, although the nautical touch of the peaked cap is out of character and strangely sinister."

"Do you think so, Holmes?"

He shrugged and sucked upon the pipe stem again. I had the sense that I had just proven my only human intuitions again but could not see how or where.

"There was, however, a disappointing lack of facial description because William Marshall did not see it, no doubt because of an excess of kissing."

"Holmes, a kiss in Whitechapel is like a handshake elsewhere in London. It begins a bargain instead of seals it."

"I can only rejoice that I have been spared making that bargain. The clock is moving toward my appearance on the scene. It is now half-past twelve and Long Liz Stride, all five-foot-two of her, is still making herself puzzlingly public on the street. PC William Smith notes on his rounds that about where we keep watch now, Watson, opposite where her body would be discovered an hour later, a man and woman stood. He identified the woman as Stride, but was the first to notice a red flower on her jacket."

"And I suppose it is some damned different fellow with her."

"Ha!" Had we been at home in Baker Street, Holmes would have leaped up and begun pacing with excitement. "Five-foot-seven, Watson. Eight-and-twenty years old—note the precision of the professional observer—dark complexion, dark mustache; wearing a black diagonal cutaway coat, hard felt hat, white collar and tie."

"More than smart, a dandy."

"And carrying a parcel wrapped in newsprint six-to-eight-inches wide and eighteen-inches long."

"Well. Holmes, that was not fish and chips."

"No, Watson, that was not fish and chips. It was, in fact, the exact size and shape of a collection of knives useful for some impromptu street surgery, would you not say?"

"I'd say so more surely could I see the contents. It might have contained only . . . kitchen utensils."

"Ah yes, a man might feel an urgent need to purchase such items to carry through all the kissing corridors of Whitechapel in the dark of night. What is interesting is that a resident who passed this location at virtually the same hour saw nothing."

I mused upon this. "There is the gate beside the International Working Men's Educational Club. The couple could have ducked in there to transact business the moment PC Smith vanished."

Holmes nodded approval. "Just the sort of quick-witted insight on such matters I expected of you, Watson. However within five or ten minutes at 12:35 or 12:40, an innocent young man named Morris Eagle returned from seeing his lady friend home. I cannot tell you how encouraged I am, Watson, that such customs as seeing lady friends home do still occur in Whitechapel. He found the club's front door locked because of the lateness of the hour and went through the side gate. He strolled the length of the passage and saw no one. There vanishes the possible escape route of the couple seen earlier, Watson."

I gazed up and down the street, seeking another byway they could have nipped into.

"However," Holmes said, "Mr. Eagle admitted it was very dark, and he could have missed seeing someone in the passage. At any rate," he added casually, "I took up my post immediately after Mr. Eagle had passed, for I never saw him. And almost immediately, the street became a carnival again. I had arranged myself almost invisibly in this very spot when I looked up to see she who would shortly be identified as the dead body of Elizabeth Stride standing by Dutfield gateway. I have no idea how she came there. None! Even as I watched, a man came along the street and paused to talk to her. He was not *any* of the men witnesses would describe as having dallied with her previously."

"This is indeed a conundrum, Holmes."

"And this man was not the only stroller. Immediately another came by. The woman was wearing the red flower pinned to her black jacket that other witnesses mentioned. I saw it. The light is strong enough here for such details to leap into relief. Then events exploded into action."

I was now rapt in Holmes's story. Standing here in the dark and the damp, under the thin rays of the mist-shrouded street lamp made me feel the presence of the many people who had passed by here that night eight months ago. I could smell the dusky scent of mildew and the greasy miasma of pub food. Was it cooking grease that spotted the newsprint wrapping the last man's odd-shaped bundle . . . or blood? For a physician, I have an active imagination I try to disguise, but as a fictioneer my blood roars at the hint of a ripping good story!

I know that Holmes most distrusts this tendency in me, so I keep it sternly leashed. He continued his tale.

"This latest man with Stride was five-foot-five, thirty, dark hair, fair skin, small brown mustache. He was full in the face as a moon yet broad in the shoulders, like a laborer. He wore dark coat and trousers and peaked hat. He tried to pull the woman down into the street but managed only to spin her and cast her down on the footpath.

"She . . . bleated, Watson. Like a sacrificial lamb. Three times, none of them loud. I didn't know what to make of it. In any other place I would have rushed to the lady's rescue, but in Whitechapel I didn't know the customs of the country and felt obliged to observe without judgment until I had made a conclusion. Obviously where kissing between strangers is such common coin of the realm, so violence is also. The cries of "Murder!" to be heard in a Whitechapel night are as common as cries of 'Giddy up' in Rotten Row."

I doubt the upper-class riders of the Row would descend to a common "giddy up," but I ignored Holmes's sardonic humor and did as he said. I listened. The night was still, not in contradiction of Holmes's words, but almost in honor of his tale-telling. I knew the story's end, but the process of hearing it was agonizing.

"The second man who had been coming along the path bolted across the street to avoid the altercation. In doing so, he nearly threw himself into my arms. I was lighting my pipe but had to pocket it at his impetuous arrival. He was later identified as one Israel Schwartz and this is the tale he told police later: I was five-feet-eleven and thirty-five years old with light brown hair and mustache and a fair complexion. I wore an old black hard felt hat with a wide brim and a dark overcoat."

"Is that true, Holmes?"

He chuckled. "Israel Schwartz was an excellent and accurate witness. I am five-and-thirty. I am taller than that, but had, of course, disguised my height by my own personal method of shrink-

ing, or affecting to shrink. The clothing was from my supply of
odds and ends to which I added the lighter hair and mustache. The
wide-brimmed hat helped shade my features, which you notice
Schwartz could not describe.

"At any rate, the man who had downed the woman startled us
both by shouting the word "Lipski" in our direction. Now you must
know the history of Whitechapel and the great resentment toward
the influx of immigrant Jews who have come here because of the
fierce pogroms against their kind in Russia in recent years. A pogrom is an odd word to describe an ancient human tendency to
persecute, kill, and cast out some of its kind on very parochial
pretexts. A Jew named Israel Lipski was convicted of killing a Christian woman named Miriam Angel a few years ago. Was there ever
a victim's name that so called out for vengeance? Naturally, this
fanned the flames of religious and racial hatred, so any Jew seen on
the streets of Whitechapel may now be taunted by the name of the
deranged killer, Lipski.

"Israel Schwartz testified that he was convinced that the man
opposite had called him 'Lipski' by way of alerting his accomplice
across the street—myself—to his presence as a witness. I suppose
Schwartz's sharing the first name of the hated figure did not serve
to calm his fears.

"Schwartz's sudden flight caused me to take the epithet literally.
I immediately wondered if Lipski had escaped custody and could
he not be the perfect candidate for Jack the Ripper? This was not
an idle speculation. So, as Schwartz ran, I sprinted after him."

I leaped to the only conclusion for this tale, given recent history,
a horrifying fact. "You ran *away* from Berner Street." I watched
Holmes's heavy lidded eyes shut at my words, as if blotting out the
facts of that night.

"Not for long, Watson. But long enough. Schwartz fled to the
railway arch before he noticed that I was no longer behind him.

"Meanwhile, during the time I was absent from the scene, a
woman named Fanny Mortimer stood outside her lodging at thirty-

six Berner Street, two doors down from the murder site, and said she saw no one enter Dutfield's Yard at that time."

"That is impossible, Holmes!"

"This case is impossible. And if you think it unlikely that Israel Lipski could have been out and about the night of twenty-nine September, I will refer you to the particulars of another convicted murderer named James Kelly, an escaped lunatic who was a Ripper suspect and only two weeks ago figured as chief villain in a new series of vicious prostitute murders in France. I will recount his story at another, more amenable time. For now I am concerned with what appeared to happen on Berner Street the night of Long Liz Stride's murder.

"We are still at the hour of a quarter to one on Berner Street. I am returning from my foot race after Israel Schwartz, having decided that the busy events in Berner Street will be more fruitful. And I am worried about the woman.

"At that very moment, James Brown, a dock laborer, was returning home with a late supper. He spied a man and woman standing at the corner of Fairclough and Berner Streets outside the Board School. She was backed against the wall facing the man, who at five-feet-seven loomed over her. He was reportedly stout and clad in a long dark coat. Brown heard the woman say, 'No. Not tonight. Some other night.' He identified Stride in the mortuary later as that woman."

I frowned. "There was a man earlier who was reputedly five-foot-seven."

"Yes."

"Would Elizabeth Stride have been knocked to the ground outside Dutfield gate in one minute and be backed against a wall in Fairclough Street around the corner the next?"

"You tell me, Watson. How fast are these streetside transactions in Whitechapel?"

"They can take mere minutes, even moments. What happened next?"

"That is a puzzle. Fifteen minutes later, Brown, at home in Fairclough Street heard cries of 'Police!' and 'Murder!' This tallies with events reported by other witnesses. At 1:00 A.M. Louis Diemschutz—"

"Another Jew, Holmes."

"You see why suspicion falls upon such, besides the ancient distrust of the foreigner. Remember, though, that the International Working Men's Educational Club is just across the way. Diemschutz, a Russian Jew and street jewelry seller, is steward of the club. He drove his pony and cart into the Dutfield yard. The hardworking pony balked and shied away. Diemschutz noticed a small heap on the ground. He prodded with the whip handle, then got down and struck a match. It was, of course, Liz Stride.

"Diemschutz fled into the club, ran upstairs and sought his wife. Was she safe, or the woman who he told others lay drunk or dead in the yard? Obviously he had been too frightened to examine the body and may have sensed lurking danger. He later told the police he feared that the Ripper might have stood unseen only feet away from him in the dark, and escaped when he ran into the club.

"I am afraid that he was quite right, Watson. That is exactly what I did."

I opened my mouth, and could not close it, could not speak. Had this expedition and recital all been an elaborate confession not to a friend or a physician, but to a loyal biographer?

Was Sherlock Holmes telling me that he was Jack the Ripper?

5.

Inhospitable

※

A complete account of the case [of hypnotic suggestion] will be found, with authority and evidence, in a pamphlet entitled "EINE EXPERIMENTAL STUDIE AUF DEM GEBIETE DES HYPNOTISMUS," *by Dr. R. von Krafft-Ebing, Professor of Psychiatry and for nervous diseases, in the University of Gratz, 1889.*

—F. MARION CRAWFORD, FOOTNOTE TO

THE WITCH OF PRAGUE, 1891

⊰ F R O M   A   J O U R N A L ⊱

There are always many attractions in Paris worth visiting by the dedicated sight-seer. This was only June, yet the year of 1889 had already welcomed the inauguration of the Eiffel Tower, a sort of inverted thumbtack of embroidered iron, as well as a massive world exhibition.

Parisian sights of particular interest to the visiting girl reporter desperate for fodder for stories sensational enough to cable back to America are more rare. I myself had already explored the bowels of the Paris Morgue, various cellars, and a catacomb or two, and witnessed the results of violent death as well as glimpsed the mob violence that once made Paris cobblestones gleam redder than rubies with aristocratic blood.

One might think a visit to a Paris hospital too boring for words, but I was intrigued to see how this French institution compared to ones on my native soil. And, of course, I was mad to see the woman whose breast had been cut off.

Now, at last, I would glimpse an actual survivor of the unspeakable events that had transpired in the secret cavern beneath the electric lights and spouting fountains and thousands of strolling visitors of *l'Exposition universelle.*

"You think that this woman will remember enough of events to testify to us?" I asked Irene as we prepared to leave our hotel room while dusk darkened into evening. "And what language does she speak? Have the Paris police interrogated her? Why are they letting us see her?"

She answered my last question first. "They are not letting 'us' see her. They are permitting me access."

She could be as coldly precise as Sherlock Holmes when it suited her, and she wasn't even English!

Irene went on installing her hat atop her piled hair with a trio of formidable steel pins ornamented with finials of jet beads. The shafts disappeared into her coiffure like swords into sheaths, their hilts alone showing and providing surface glitter. In many ways, they reminded me of their owner.

Irene went on answering my questions. "She is Polish, the police say, saying also that they can get nothing sensible out of her."

"Perhaps they have asked nothing sensible of her."

"Quite right, Pink. They have either asked too much, too fast, or not enough. I believe," she added, still replying to my flurry of questions, "that her memory of that outrage will be erased. I do speak a smattering of Polish. I was prima donna of the Warsaw Imperial Opera once."

She regarded her hatted image in the mirror with utter inexpression. "I learned a few words, though it was long ago and far away."

"That won't do much good."

Irene turned and thus turned the same flat expression she had bestowed on the mirror upon me. It was like regarding the eyes of the walking dead.

"There are other skills," she said, "that I have acquired in my travels that may do more good. Are you ready?"

Well, I had been ready first, after all.

I don't know if it was by accident or design, but my—mentor, shall I say?—had undergone a strange shift in her mode of dress and her very demeanor since the horrific events in the Seine-side cavern, which events all who know about them are all sworn to conceal, more's the pity.

Somewhere among the wardrobe of an operatic diva prone to peacock display she had unearthed the simple, earth-colored garments of a sparrow. Today, in a gown of large-scale camel-and-charcoal plaid with a solid-gray jacket with matching revers, she suddenly could pass for a Quaker.

In fact, she seemed to mark the absence of Nell by assuming some of the coloration of Nell. On the other hand, she was a born chameleon and might be simply dressing in an unassuming fashion that wouldn't intimidate a frightened foreign woman of peasant class. It was always hard to tell what was clever effect or deep conviction with Irene. No doubt that was why she was so successful as a private inquiry agent.

"I am ready and rarin' to go," I said, stabbing pins willy-nilly into my own hat and hair. "Is there anything I should know before we arrive?"

"With reporters, I understand, speculation is always more alluring than mere fact."

"First comes speculation. Fact proves it. To find out facts, I must see for myself," I finished pointedly.

"So you shall. At St. Sulpice."

I certainly was glad of the time I'd spent in a madhouse, which resulted not only in a ripping good newspaper story, but my first book: *Ten Days in a Madhouse* by Nellie Bly.

Hospitals were but one step up from that in my opinion.

Perhaps it is the sight of those rows of iron beds, the rough-grained cotton cloths more resembling winding sheets than gentle bed linens.

The floors are hard and cold, the walls unadorned, the place reeks of carbolic acid, with the windows fastened tight as if to hold in pain and suffering.

The Paris hospital had no magic French touch to lighten its deprivations. Lit by too few lamps, the ward where our quarry lay looked like a dank underground mine populated with emaciated wailing women or fat moaning ones.

The matron in a striped apron who conducted us to our quarry's bedside was utterly disinterested in our identities or our mission. This was good news for us, but rather awful for the residents.

I must admit, with all that I have seen that is unpleasant, I felt a slight shiver as we approached that spare bed and the sparer figure that barely raised the profile of the sheets.

I tried to keep my eyes from her chest in the dim light but couldn't. The flatness seemed symmetrical. It was only one breast taken. Wasn't it? How would Irene's "smattering" of Polish include as extraordinary a word as "breast," that is not heard in public unless it belongs to a chicken or a duck, and even then is deemed crude by some?

Our guide left the light on a small bare table so it could cast our shadows large and distorted on the rough plain walls. Irene rustled straight to the bedside and took the woman's limp hand between hers, as if to warm that chill flesh.

She began crooning some thick, Slavic syllables. I am not at all certain that they were Polish. They may have been a combination of Slavic words, or some lullaby that she had made up, but I had reckoned without her remarkable voice. The words she uttered were so melodic, so tremulous with sympathy and sorrow, that it would take a heart of stone to resist them.

The pale lashes that lay upon the woman's bloodless cheeks like shadows lifted open. She was a study in ashen tones, this girl: her hair the color of blond lace, her skin a strange jaundiced match to her hair. She reminded me of a doll cut out of buff-colored paper: flat, monotone, almost lifeless.

Irene murmured more and stroked the hair at her temple. A faint flush of life-giving color appeared at her cheeks.

She muttered a word.

Irene leaned closer to hear it.

When the patient repeated it, I heard it. "*Merci.*"

The girl spoke some French!

Now Irene's chatter mixed French with the Slavic sounds. She was casting a braided twine of language like a line into the sea, drawing the girl up from her lifeless state.

I begin to hope that we might indeed learn something here.

Irene leaned over the pathetic creature, whispering, weaving her multilingual spell into a singsong like poetry. I noticed that the gold locket she wore on a long chain swung out when she bent forward, that it swung back and forth like the weight on a clock pendulum, a small gold sun that shone like a glimpse of high summer in the dreary hospital ward.

Irene glanced at me. "A chair?"

I looked around the huge barren chamber, seeing but one item of that sort. A wooden chair by the door, meant for the attending nurse, no doubt, who was not in attendance. My note-taking fingers itched. I saw an article on the neglect in French hospitals, which mirrored the neglect in hospitals the world over. . . .

"*Hurry!*" Irene's whisper tossed the English word into her European stew like a raw onion into well-simmered bouillabaisse.

I rushed to the chair, lifted it though it was awfully heavy, and lugged it back to the bedside.

No ailing heads on miserably flat pillows stirred at my revolutionary act. The only sound was the drag of my shoes on stone. I set the chair by Irene, who sank onto it as if it were a cushioned divan.

Only one of her hands now held the woman's in custody. The other had moved to the gold chain at her neck and was idly swinging the locket to and fro even as her voice had settled into a lulling singsong.

Now the poor girl's face looked positively feverish, hot spots of cerise blooming on her thin cheeks, her eyes blue and very black in the center, as if the pupil had exploded like a blossom.

Irene began to speak, still using an up-and-down rhythm. The girl answered her in a blaze of unintelligible syllables.

Irene eyed me, not surprised when she saw that I had withdrawn the notebook and pencil from my skirt pocket.

"Her name is Leska. Her family are Moravian sheepherders."

I made notes, amazed that Irene had delved as deep as family already.

"The Austrian grip upon their land drove them west," Irene murmured to me after another interminable exchange. "West beyond Austria. Cities proved harsher than the land. The family lost each other. A brother in Fribourg, married. A father buried in Bregenz. A mother in Dijon. Alone, this one came finally to Paris. She worked as a laundress."

These facts were spit out to me as whispered asides between long mutual exchanges in the hybrid language that Irene had drawn out of Leska. I noticed that she spoke slowly in answer to Irene, her gaze blank and directed to some spot beyond us both.

It was like an interview with the dead, or the near dead, and I had never seen the like of it. For a moment I didn't know if I blessed or cursed Sherlock Holmes for so arrogantly insisting I remain tethered to Irene.

Still, I was too busy noting down any tidbits Irene threw my way to give in to girlish shudders.

Irene was nodding as the young woman droned on. Her head moved up and down like a puppet's, but the gold locket below her throat still swung from side to side. I found the motion oddly soothing and had to blink myself alert to catch and record the rare English phrases Irene tossed over her shoulder to me from time to time. The girl seemed not to notice these abrupt asides.

"The next step," Irene hissed at me. "She became a *fille isolée*. She plied the streets alone, at her own risk."

The girl's hand withdrew from Irene's and folded as for prayer, some childish gesture she remembered in her distress. Her monotone grew higher-pitched, the singsong even more pronounced. She called for someone named Maria, perhaps her dead mother.

From what I had seen of the unfortunates forced to solicit on the streets themselves, no mother would wish to know of such a fate for her daughter. It was the lot of the women of Whitechapel; still mired in it a number of them had gone down to their gruesome deaths.

"A savior," Irene told me. "A holy man who speaks in tongues. Sin can be salvation."

I noted that all down, for it was coming fast now, Irene speaking half to me and half to the girl. Sin can be salvation? I suppose it could be regarded as the last straw before seeing the light.

"Ah! The act . . . the holy coupling . . . is salvation."

My pencil paused. This was a tenet of no religion I had ever heard of. They were all very sure about unmarried copulation being one of the quickest and surest highways to Hell.

"And then," Irene said, "the . . . end . . . the climax of coupling is salvation, says the Master."

I wrote it all down, though I had never heard such gibberish.

"God is . . . love." Irene leaned near and began to ask questions, as if to pin down the exact meaning of each word in their confusing dialogue. To me: "*Lust. Remember Krafft-Ebing, Pink. Lust-murders.*" She leaned so close she seemed about to snatch the syllables from the poor girl's lips as she uttered them. "Ah, bawdiness . . . no, lechery."

God is love. Lust? Lechery? Those last words I could not write down, though I have never been very religious.

This unfortunate must have been drugged with laudanum or some such. I was transcribing the ravings of a drug fiend and Irene was passing them on to me as if they were gold ore. I wondered which of the two was the more insane.

Irene put one hand to her forehead, as if it too could not contain such opposing concepts. "There must be . . . reparation." She nodded, then looked at me, pointing a finger so I should write. "*Pain. Denial.*"

The girl droned on, and suddenly Irene went silent. She slumped in the chair, exhausted.

Leska lay on the ashen linens, her eyes feverishly bright, her lips moving but no sound coming out, as if she were reciting the Catholic rosary. Her voice faded and she seemed to sleep, though her eyes remained eerily open.

Irene stirred, straightened. Looked at me one last time. "Sacrifice," she intoned.

She shook herself, then leaned over the barely conscious girl. Her voice sunk low again. Foreign words flowed like undiscovered rivers in forgotten lands. Again the lullaby, again a soft and soothing refrain. At the end she whispered one word over and over and finally it evolved into English: "Sleep. Sleep. Sleep."

I felt in need of that restorative myself, for my fingers were stiff with cold and my mind numb with something other than that, some spiritual chill perhaps, at all I had heard, though I am not religious, or even superstitious, as I will tell anyone.

"Sleep," Irene repeated with a sigh, leaning her head on her hand.

I saw that her eyes were dark wells of sadness, that she instructed herself as well as the injured woman, as if she doubted that her wish or command to sleep would do any good for either of them.

6.

Ripper Redux

～○○○～

In the East End we are used to shocking sights, but the sight I saw made the blood in my veins turn to ice... huddled against the wall, there was the body of a woman and a pool of blood was streaming along the gutter from her body... I remembered the man I had seen, and I started after him as fast as I could run, but he was lost to sight in the dark labyrinth of the East End mean streets.

—SGT. STEPHEN WHITE OF THE METROPOLITAN POLICE, 1888

❧FROM THE NOTES OF JOHN H. WATSON, M.D.❧

"I don't know what you're saying, Holmes." I was in fact very much afraid that I did, but dare not admit it either to him or myself.

"You mean that you were lurking in the dark yard beside the lifeless body of Elizabeth Stride when Louis Diemschutz found her? Good God, why?"

He stared across the street toward the gate of the very yard in question.

"Because *I* was the one who really found the body, Watson. I returned here from my fruitless chase of Israel Schwartz to discover the street deserted. After all the activity I had witnessed here in the past half an hour that was decidedly odd.

"Immediately I was struck by the tragic misdirection of my actions. The woman who was the object of all the night's attention was gone. Vanished. Of course I went first to the gate where I had last seen her and one of her many . . . swains."

"As I recall, Elizabeth Stride was the third victim attributed to Jack the Ripper, and had escaped the rather more thorough later mutilations."

Holmes did not answer me directly, resuming his narrative instead.

"I had little light and not much longer to examine her. She lay on her side, her legs drawn up and her right arm passed over her body as if she were sleeping. Her clothes were not disarranged, but the hands and wrists were sopping with blood and her throat was cut. Her left hand clutched a packet of cachous, the pills smokers use to freshen their breaths. The red flower pinned to her jacket looked like a stray gobbet of gore, but other than the slashed throat she had not been injured."

"So you had time to assess the condition?"

"Barely. The body was warm and the blood still flowing when I heard the gate opening and withdrew into a dark niche near a rear door. All was as Diemschutz reported to the police later, save that I too left as soon as he fled. I regained the still-empty street and was away before he brought others to the site and they cried bloody murder."

"I must say, Holmes, I am shocked and angry. I understand your need for secrecy about who commissioned your services in the Ripper case, and I would have respected that, of course. There is no reason, however, not to allow me to accompany you, as I have on so many other dangerous missions. Had I been present I could have examined the body from the viewpoint of a physician, and of a physician who has learned your methods of precise examination. I might have been of help!"

"You could not have saved her, Watson."

"I might have stayed as you pursued Schwartz, seen something, prevented the brute from acting this time."

"Ah, Watson, I can tell you from experience that imagining what one might have done is just that, an exercise in fancy and the very opposite to the stern logic I live by. And the reason for your absence that night was also just that: you are a doctor."

"But," I began, recognizing I was in danger of resorting to an indignant sputter, always a disastrous position in a debate.

I then grew silent as the true import of his words weighed on me like stones. *I was a doctor.* Jack the Ripper's dissections had been accorded almost medical skills. Any doctor loitering in Whitechapel that terrible autumn stood in danger of being accused of the Ripper's crimes.

My friend Sherlock Holmes sought to shield me even as he walked the streets with Jack the Ripper and his victims.

"I would have come anyway, Holmes," I muttered testily to hide my confusion.

"I know you would have, Watson, but the woman was beyond any human help."

Now I gazed in my own turn at the closed gate, picturing a woman's life blood coagulating on the pavement as she lay dying alone.

"She would not have felt much after the throat slash," I observed, more to comfort myself than to contribute to the knowledge of the death. As one trained to ease and save life, it opens abysses of speculation to contemplate the mind that can end life with one or two savage saws across the throat. It is not easy to accomplish with one clean cut, as I recalled had been the case with Elizabeth Stride, but great rage would do it. Or great skill.

"You wish to enter that building, don't you, Holmes?" I said, returning to the present and our reason for being here on this street, at last, together, pursuing a belated investigation.

"No, Watson, I wish to enter that building's cellar. Unless you care to dig, I suggest that the direct approach will be more convenient."

The building in question did not need a sign to announce its purpose as the International Working Men's Educational Club. Even as we had kept watch I had observed individuals of a working-class and Jewish appearance disappearing into its unimpressive portals.

Although I have traveled the globe far too widely to hold a man's race or religion against him, I feared that the opposite might be true. The Jews of Whitechapel were often made scapegoats for gentile debaucheries in the poorer quarter. We might not be welcome.

"We wear no suitable disguise," I pointed out.

"I hold the passkey of the rabbi's name. Besides, I could enter here at any time in appropriate guise. I wish you also to observe the place and its denizens."

So we climbed the few steps to the ground floor of that sectarian club. As I suspected of a working man's association, the men within were earnest if not highly educated.

No well-read Englishman could be unaware of the social unrest among the less-prosperous classes. None could argue that the crowded and corrupt conditions found in Whitechapel were not only intolerable but had made Jack the Ripper's attacks impossible to stop.

Whitechapel had become a cesspool, the stopped drain into which poured the dregs of the British Isles and Eastern Europe. The times had created a vast, shiftless population of former peasants clogging the great cities, flowing inward in a never-ending stream. The pogroms in Russia forced the Jews to choose death or flight. The Poles fled a variation brought by the same Eastern invaders who had bedeviled their land for centuries, along with many from many lands to the east. Ironically, these refugees came to the East End of London. Such people were poor, seldom spoke English, had few skills to sell.

All sank like stones into the lowest sections of our great city to mingle uneasily with our own unfortunates. These last were the legions of displaced farm workers forced from the wholesome country into the city-bred flotsam of humanity that had always blighted Mother London, including the homeless women who had no trade to ply but themselves.

"Why, Holmes," I had jibed him as we began our proposed jaunt across the street, "I knew you were a Bohemian, but I did not know you are a socialist."

"I am no 'ist' nor 'ian,' Watson. Merely an observer by inclination and trade. I take no political position except to note how these upheavals in nations may effect the commission of crime."

"Many believe a foreigner is Jack the Ripper, that no Englishman would slaughter women so fiendishly."

"And so they believed of Frenchmen in Paris," he murmured.

"Paris? Is that where you were? You say that they suspect the Ripper of having relocated to Paris?"

"Series of brutal murders occur everywhere, Watson. They are seldom recorded in sufficient detail and tallied in any sensible way that shows whether one man or a dozen may have done the deeds. It is always assumed that the lunatic's violence is so severe and mystifying that the deed stands alone . . . until the next lunatic attack occurs. There is never an attempt to follow or show a pattern."

"And did the Ripper show a pattern in Paris?"

"Several," Holmes said tightly.

Using the rabbi's name after knocking on the door, Holmes was shortly able to persuade a rather surly bearded fellow to speak to us, although we were obviously not 'working men' of any stripe.

"I'm searching for a man," Holmes began.

"We are all men here," was the short answer, accented but understandable.

"This man would have been a visitor, like ourselves."

"Then he would be an exception."

"That is what I hope," Holmes went on. "I hope he was exceptional enough for you to remember him. You come from the Ukraine, I perceive. I see the journey has cost a great deal, including the loss of your sister, no, brother, pardon me. No doubt it has been hard to obtain work as an ostler in a city in which so many Irish are naturally suited for the job and also as hungry for work. I cannot blame you for seeking betterment through uniting with other men in your situation. Certainly the English lessons you study here are a great help, for your mastery of such a difficult language is commendable, and at least your mother will soon arrive."

"What are you? Some Gypsy fortune-teller?"

"Alas, no. I could certainly use prescience in my profession but must rely on evidence instead. I am a consulting detective."

The man's shrewd eyes darkened with speculation. "And how did you discover about me?"

Holmes smiled slightly at the awkward construction that betrayed the fellow's serviceable yet imperfect command of English. "I am a student like yourself, only I deconstruct the articles of appearance instead of those of sentences. An instant's glance allowed me to notice the resemblance between your face and that of the tiny photographic likeness you wear on your watch fob. The fob was swinging during that instant or I would have never done your brother the disservice of taking him for your sister, however briefly. As for your origin, I am also a student of accented English. By the secure lodging of your tongue in your lower jaw, yours certainly springs from east of the Volga. Beyond that is the handkerchief that peeks out of your left inner breast pocket. The embroidery is of Russian style. I admit I hesitated for a moment there. Such handiwork is usually done by young women preparing for hope chests, or quite old women occupying time as best they may. However, your watch fob already paid tribute to your late brother and the handkerchief lay near your heart. I detected a mother, one whose arrival you expect soon in view of the loss of your brother. As for your history in working with horses, such men acquire calluses on certain areas of their fingers—on the second joints between the first and second fingers, for instance—that betray the constant rub of the reins through their hands."

The fellow tucked the visible portion of the handkerchief away and ran his fingertips over the visage of his brother. He may not have liked Holmes's insight into his family matters, but he couldn't deny it.

"What sort of man do you look for?" he asked.

"Of middle years, perhaps fifty. Not terribly tall but powerfully built. Dressed quietly, as a clerk, but affecting a peaked cap, to hide a lack of hair, I suspect. He would have been seeking quarters some months ago, say last summer."

Holmes's litany had been casual to the extreme. I admired the way he slipped past the fall's Ripper atrocities to a time when Whitechapel had been calm and mired only in the usual thefts, riots, and odd crimes of passion. I also recognized his method of disarming me when we first met on New Year's day of 1881 by reciting my personal history to me as if he had read the family Bible just before we met.

"I am a steward here," the man admitted. "I do in fact recall another fellow coming in about then, but he didn't want to rent a room, which of course we wouldn't have done now, would we, being we are devoted to working Jewish men?"

"No, this man would not have been Jewish."

"How is it Rabbi Barshevich allows you to noise his name about?"

"He trusts me," Holmes said simply.

Our interrogator nodded slowly, then continued. "It was June, I think. And he was interested in an assembly room, he said. Cellar, he wanted. Said they were a religious group and grew loud in their praises of the lord." He shrugged. "Who am I to judge ways of worship? At Passover we celebrate with the sacrifice of the lamb. Christians do not understand that, yet they worship a sacrificed man."

"Religion is indeed a complex matter," Holmes said. "I assume then that you did not rent the Englishman your cellar for his rites?"

"No." He frowned for a moment. "I don't trust those who descend beneath the earth to worship anything."

"So where did you send him?"

The man's eyes whipped to Holmes, as if both startled and hoping to startle in return. "Why to the nearest pub. They will take money for anything there."

"And that is—?"

"The Briar and Thistle, one street over."

"This Englishman you describe sounds oddly familiar," I mention as we trudged to the next address.

"As do most of the Ripper suspects. That is the devilish bit about this business, Watson. All these various suspects are types to be seen about Whitechapel day and night."

"So you are convinced an Englishman is the Ripper, after all?"

"I am convinced of nothing, because I have not seen all the evidence there is to gather. But Whitechapel is a global stew, and I absolve no race or religion from suspicion. Not even," he added with a rare glint of amusement, "Irish bartenders."

And that is exactly what we found at the Briar and Thistle, a pub crowded with the very cast of characters that make up the Ripper suspects and his victims, with an Irish bartender indeed presiding over the chaos.

"Finn's the name," he said. "Thanks be my friend Saul a street over recommended me. Clannish these Jews, but then I come from a clannish sort meself. How can I help you gennelmen?"

"We seek," said Holmes, "a private meeting place. I understand that you have a cellar that might accommodate."

"Accommodate what, is it?"

"We are a scientific brotherhood," Holmes said. "We wish to conduct experiments in the art of electricity as it passes from one body to another. A rather esoteric pursuit, requiring privacy and sequestering."

"Sequestering, is it? 'Tis a bit noisy up here, gents."

"All the better. We are a bit noisy below."

The man shook his head, which was covered in tightly curled red hair like a mop. "Then we should suit each other well."

"It is my ardent hope. I understand you have rented this space before, perhaps to an acquaintance of ours. Stout-set chap about fifty. Very sharp eyes."

"Aye, blue as the bay off Donegal and just as icy. Quite the businessman."

"And what was his business?" Holmes inquired.

"His business, Sor, as yours . . . is yours."

Holmes asked no more, but offered a pound for the privilege of inspecting the "premises."

I could not imagine his aim. All the Ripper's victims had been slain on the street, down wretched byways and alleys, it is true, but on the public cobblestones, in the open air of night.

The barman pointed us to the back of the building and a narrow circuitous passage where, even there, the usual commerce of the district was being contracted between drunken men and women.

A shambles of a door led down into greater darkness and odor. From the capacious pocket of his coat, Holmes pulled a small lantern. We paused halfway down the rough stone steps to light it.

Illumination, no matter how feeble, seemed to intensify our other senses. I inhaled the fetid, dank air, fearing for the wholeness of our lungs. A skittering sound punctuated by the rare drip or squeal below did little to encourage me. I would have brought a club instead of my revolver had I known we would be confronting sewer rats.

"What do you expect to find down here, Holmes?"

"A cellar. No doubt the hovels that pass as dwellings in this quarter have no such convenience, but this building is large enough and old enough to support an underground domain."

"You almost make it sound like an annex of Hell."

"Another concept, like the endlessly agitating heavens, that does not interest the true scientist, Watson. Had you not the rather lurid instincts of a teller of tales blended with your admirable medical precision, you would be more aware of the practical assets of a cellar, rather than their appeal to the gullible souls of the superstitious."

"One of the Ripper letters was signed, 'from Hell.' "

"Are they called 'Ripper letters' because they are proven to be from the uncaught killer of Whitechapel unfortunates, or because they captured the public imagination?"

"Who else would have sent them?"

"Cranks, Watson. They sent hundreds and thousands of other missives much less credible and much less . . . seductive. And perhaps the worst cranks of all, the journalists themselves, sought to stir up news."

"That would be utterly irresponsible."

"My point exactly. When have you seen any report of my modest efforts in the press that has not been riddled with error?"

"Well, the press tend to credit the police, above all."

"Then it should not be surprising that the police should credit the manipulations of the press. The so-called 'Ripper' letters read like a ransom note from one of your fictionalized accounts of my cases, Watson. They not only employ a number of crude 'Americanisms,' such as salutations like 'Dear Boss,' but the diction and spelling mimic Cockney expressions. Why stoop to the patois of two such different and geographically separated classes?"

"No reason at all. Unless . . . the writer was the very opposite of those qualities."

"This is my stout friend Watson. On the trail! So this would indicate that the Ripper is—?"

"An educated Englishman."

"Bravo!" Holmes clapped me on the shoulder. "Perhaps now you understand the net of silence that has fallen over the case since the fiendish evisceration and flaying of Mary Jane Kelly in her Miller's Court chamber on the ninth of November last. All London hopes and holds its breath that the world will hear no more of the Ripper."

✦ ✦ ✦

I had seen my friend Sherlock Holmes throw himself down on study floors to examine the weave of an Oriental rug, fiber by fiber.

Indeed, I was used to regarding him as a sort of human blood-hound who needed to put his eyes and magnifying glass to the ground. Then I would marvel at the conclusions of great moment he could glean from the smallest mote of evidence, be it a speck of a particular kind of clay or a drop of hitherto unseen blood.

But I had never expected to see him perform this investigative ritual upon a filthy cellar floor beneath a raucous public house in Whitechapel.

"A good thing you are not married, Holmes," I noted. "A spouse of any sensibility would swoon dead away at the sight of your garments after such an exercise as this."

"I am not married, Watson, for other reasons than to prevent the female sex from swooning. Lean a little closer with the lantern . . . a bit lower and to the right. There, there's the spot, old fellow! Now for a delicate extraction worthy of any dentist—"

"I am a fair hand at extractions myself."

"I doubt you have ever plumbed such a prize as this."

Holmes raised a tweezer into the lantern light. I could just glimpse a translucent curl caught between the tiny steel tongs.

"Candle wax, Holmes? I imagine a hole the age of this contains pieces of wax going back to the time of Charles II."

"I will admit that candle wax is a common remnant on the scene of several crimes possibly attributed to Jack the Ripper in Paris, but this is wax of another sort, Watson, from another country, I believe. I need a container for it," he announced peevishly, going face down on the packed stone and dirt again, still holding the miserable wisp of "prize" aloft.

"A container? All I have is a lantern and my pockets, which you would hardly find sanitary enough for a piece of precious evidence."

His head came up, turned over his shoulder. He frowned. "Of

course you have nothing useful about you, Watson. I quite forgot. Can you be good enough to go up those rickety stairs and ask . . . er, bribe, the proprietor for . . . the smallest glasses he might have, Watson. Cordial glasses would do. Two or three. And being clean would help."

"I shall have to leave you in the dark for I cannot navigate those stairs without light."

"Then be quick about it! I cannot move for fear of crushing these rare flakes of evidence."

I mounted the perilous stairs, grumbling to myself. I suppose I should go out and about with empty vials in my pockets, all in case Holmes discovered a flake of tobacco or a dab of beeswax worth preserving.

This Mr. Finn proved to be a businessman born who found even bribery too much trouble. I was forced to buy a double pint. My request for cordial glasses earned a hearty round of laughter. This was hardly the place to serve the finer liquors meant for such vessels. I explained my need for pocket-size glass containers and threw myself on his mercy. My abject need gave him such a sense of superiority that he ducked down behind the counter and solemnly lined up three tiny open-mouth glass objects on the bar.

I suppose my gaped-mouth reception of these items was worth his trouble. He explained that he had obtained these from an American who couldn't pay his bar bill and apparently traveled with his own bizarre set of measuring cups for whiskey. I had to pay him six pence before he handed over the three glasses after first swiping their interiors on his grimy apron on my request. Rather, I had requested that they be clean: the swipe was his interpretation of that condition.

I apportioned a glass to each of three pockets so they should not rattle and hastened to the pub's rear, where the scents of ale and elimination combined into a heady brew. Down the dark and shifty stairs again I went, to find my friend still stretched supine, like a corpse, just where I had left him.

"Excellent, Watson," he crowed as I handed over the first glass. "Strange things. What are they?"

"American shot glasses," I explained with pardonable smugness. "It appears that Americans seek to control their intake of spirits by using such Lilliputian glasses."

"Strange breed, the Americans," Holmes muttered, utterly disinterested in odd customs as long as they provided what he needed.

The small steel tongs Holmes had produced from his pocket—a tool I had never known him to carry before, a most suggestive fact—released the pale wax into the first receptacle.

Holmes's elbows worked like cricket legs, pulling himself forward.

"More light," he ordered.

I delivered, and in a moment he triumphantly lifted another crumb in the tongs. "Cork this time, Watson. Lovely brown cork. From Portugal, of course."

"Wine corks seem rather expected in the cellar of a pub, I should think."

"But not French wine in a Spanish bottle sealed with Portuguese cork."

"I agree that it does not seem quite English."

Holmes was ignoring me, his nose to the ground and literally sniffing. "Red Tomahawk's foreign firewater," he muttered to himself, not pausing to explain anything to me. "Scent and yet no scent. Ha! The savage is a connoisseur. But what is this stuff?"

"Red Tomahawk, Holmes?"

He waggled dismissive (and filthy) fingers at me from the floor. "Foreign cases make for strange allies, Watson. I have one more sample to find here and . . . aha! Another vial, noble physician."

I produced a second shot glass, feeling rather like the barman at the Officer's Club in Kandahar. My wounds from Maiwand ached in the damp underground. I unaccountably became wary of cobras in the dark corners beyond the circle of light the lantern threw.

Holmes sprang up with the combination of energy and utter limberness a youth of seventeen but half his age would have envied.

His dirty palms dusted off his filthy clothes before he reached for the last of the shot glasses in my hand. Another bit of candle wax drifted to its empty bottom.

"The way to transport our loot is thus."

He bent to retrieve the other shot glasses from the floor and nested them one atop the other. Over the top one he thrust his thumb, and then pushed the whole tower into his coat pocket.

"It's back to Baker Street and my laboratory, Watson. I believe the cellar floor here is sufficiently clean."

"I'm afraid that all you have accomplished is the transfer of dirt from one surface to another."

"Let the microscope be the judge of that, Watson. The microscope is often the judge of us all and will be even more so in the times to come."

I left that miserable cellar with Sherlock Holmes as confused as the police. I had no idea why a few cork crumbles and flakes of wax and glass and pottery shards, all things one would expect to find in a cellar that sheltered a modest supply of wine bottles, should excite my friend's attention.

We stood on the paving stones outside, breathing less-confined air, although no sweeter.

"I failed that night, Watson," Holmes said suddenly, pausing in relighting the old clay pipe. He drew so deeply on the pipe that the end of the bowl burned bloodred. "I need to explore the building's rear, then our expedition will be over."

"I see that my service revolver was unnecessary."

"We are not out of Whitechapel yet, Watson." Holmes marched around the side of the building to where the streetlight cast more shadow than light.

We had not even turned the second corner to the building's rear when he stopped. "I cannot credit it! Watson, the lantern!"

I had taken custody of the light and struggled to pull the shutters fully open to reveal what Holmes had discovered.

It was most like the crumpled pile of discarded clothes that had announced every Ripper victim last year.

"Right here, near the very spot. I cannot believe the audacity of the creature! Your diagnosis, Doctor. I will hold the light. And the revolver, though I believe our man is gone."

I knelt on the damp cobblestones, felt the neck. It was warm, as was the blood, which was still liquid.

"Quick, Holmes! Summon a bobby. She's still alive."

He flung back a few words of encouragement as he raced away. "By God, Watson, if you can keep her that way you may be the one man in all England who will be able to bring Jack the Ripper to justice and salve my conscience."

After he had vanished, I pressed the neck wound shut, unwinding Mary's knitted scarf to make a bloody bandage of it.

"It's all right, my dear," I murmured to ears that might soon be deaf for all time. "Help is coming and you are among friends."

7.

Taking the Air

PLAYING MAD WOMAN
NELLIE BLY TOO SHARP FOR THE
ISLAND DOCTORS
THE SUN FINISHES UP ITS STORY OF
THE "PRETTY CRAZY GIRL."

She is intelligent, capable and self-reliant, and...has gone about the business of maintaining herself in journalism in a practical, business-like way.
—*THE NEW YORK SUN, 1887*

⊰FROM A JOURNAL⊱

Irene surprised me the next day by proposing that we visit *Notre Dame de Paris.*

"Why?" I demanded.

"Because it is Paris in the spring?" She paused in pinning on her hat to add with brittle emphasis, "Because it is the first time, the first place, where Our Enemy showed itself."

"You mean the pistol shots."

"Rifle shots, Buffalo Bill believes, which makes them much more interesting."

"Then they were not merely some usual afterdark danger of Paris?"

"Knives and fists and the cancan are the usual afterdark dangers of Paris. Not rifles. I wish to reconsider the site, and the incident, by daylight."

"Should we be dallying to speculate with Nell and Godfrey gone missing?"

"No, of course not! We should be charging to the rescue. But where? Where first? Verdun, an innocuous city on the fringe of France? If there is an Enemy, where does it hide? Come from? Go to? We must have some notion of the who, what, and whyfore before we rush off anywhere."

"And visiting Notre Dame will provide us with this greatly needed 'notion?'"

"I hope so." Irene smiled tightly.

"Is not Bram Stoker to act as our escort?"

"Bram? No. Why?"

"Why not?"

"I have sent him east on a walking tour."

"On a walking tour?"

"Well, he will take the train first. And then he will walk."

"You had other plans for him."

"And you disapproved of my typically feminine weakness in relying on male escort. I decided you were right."

"I was merely pointing out an inconsistency in your character."

"Quite rightfully so. I have remedied it."

"But . . . I didn't really mean it."

"How unfortunate," she murmured. "Bram left Paris this morning by rail. It shall be some time before we see him again, I suspect."

"So he is forging eastward to all the adventure, as Sherlock Holmes ranges westward to London and Whitechapel, and we are merely going to visit Notre Dame Cathedral?"

"Which is an adventure in architecture," Irene said almost as piously as Nell might, drawing on her gloves. "Do be patient, Pink.

There is more going on in the world at large than even Nellie Bly can fathom."

The day was sublime. Paris sparkled under one of those skies marbleized by pale veins of cloud. The scents of burgeoning buds and leaves overpowered even the eternal odor of horse that is every major city's most dominant perfume.

Irene looked a fit subject for an *Academie* portrait painter in her pale yellow satin-faille gown worked with borders of blond lace at the hem and very fashionable three-quarter-length sleeve. This subtle gown was topped by a black fichu-wrap, an exquisite sleeveless overbodice of ribbon and lace that was caught at the narrow waist by a satin sash and ruffled into a peplum both front and back. She wore a broad-brimmed hat rather than the rapidly becoming passé bonnet.

I admit that I sighed for her sense of style even as it puzzled me. One would never guess she had faced deep personal losses only forty hours before. That is a testimony, I believe, to the stage arts she had mastered as an opera singer. The numb, stricken creature I had glimpsed for a few desperate hours had been banished to some hidden cell of her mind.

She paused where the carriage had left us, spinning a black-lace-edged parasol on her shaded shoulder like the most fragile of social butterflies as we stood in the crowded square before the great medieval cathedral.

Smiling, she seemed to sense my disapproval and said, "We were watched here before, Pink, in the dark of night. We may be watched here again, even and especially in daylight."

"You suspect the conspirators of remaining in Paris?"

"I suspect that some of them have never left it. Why should they? It is their conspiracy, and their city."

I was frankly puzzled and had no parasol to twirl so fetchingly, but only my stout walking stick to rely upon.

Irene strolled on, managing to drop her crocheted reticule while pausing to inspect the side of an unremarkable building in the square before the cathedral.

I gazed at the fallen object, suddenly realizing that if it were crocheted, Nell must have done it. The woman was a bear for constant make-work and thus very annoying, yet I felt an intolerable poignancy in this mute, fallen reminder of both her presence and her absence.

A gentleman, or a man at least, immediately retrieved the article, presenting it to Irene with a bow.

"*Madame.*"

Hence came rapid French, which freed me to observe, as I couldn't translate the words.

He was of the type known only in Paris as a *boulevardier*: a man of leisure, almost a dandy, dedicated to the arts, amusement, gossip, and flirtation. Like many French aristocrats who summered in the country or by the sea, his naturally olive skin had taken an even swarthier tint. Despite his agreeably regular features, the sun-beaten skin gave his pale eyes and teeth a piratical glint.

This man could be up to no good, I thought.

But his Parisian *bonhomie* appeared to have found a perfect partner in Irene. After briefly doffing his straw boater, he settled his striped jacket on his frame and inserted himself between us as a well-met escort, bowing and chattering with an aplomb that was lost upon me, as my command of French was about as good as Nell's. In other words, dreadful.

Irene accepted his company like a woman of the world accepting tribute. She gestured with her parasol at the passing parade, smiled, bowed, laughed, and nearly drove me mad with her utterly uncalled-for frivolity.

Truly, the woman had lost her mind, only now it showed itself as a complete disregard for reality.

I soon had enough. It was off to London and dogging Sherlock Holmes's footsteps for me. Condescension was better than lunacy any day!

I was about to excuse myself to return to the hotel and pack when Irene suddenly turned to me and spoke in English.

"Wasn't it near here, Pink, that the first shot stung the stone?"

"Here? Shot? When? Oh, the night we visited the Morgue." I turned around to place the church in my memory. "About here, I suppose."

Our escort chattered something and pointed upward, at the sky.

While we gawked, my glance passed over the featureless gray stones of the building beside us. Just above our heads, I spied a long white gash in the stone.

"*Exactement!*" our escort chortled with a small dance-step of exuberance.

In a moment he had seized both of us by the elbows and piloted us through a narrow door that had materialized before us like a magician's cabinet.

The plunge from a Paris of sunshine and sparrows to the cool dark inside a stone building was shocking. While I blinked to adjust my eyes to the lack of light, I smelled and heard the strike of a lucifer.

Irene's face was hellishly lit from below by the match she held to a candle stump she had extracted from the formerly elusive reticule.

Our escort was peering out through the sliver of door still open to the daylit square beyond the door.

"A bevy of French schoolchildren was just herded past like ducklings. We won't have been seen," he whispered in perfect English. So perfect that I knew at once this was Another Damned Englishman in our midst.

He turned to me. "I thought at first you were Nell." His tone was almost accusing.

"I am—" I began, meaning to drop my pen name, Nellie, but Irene interrupted.

"We'll explain later," she promised. "First, you saw where the bullet marked the stone?"

"Yes," he said. "A powerful one. Had that shot hit bone instead of stone—" He shuddered mockingly. "I agree with whoever diagnosed a rifle. Perhaps a heavy game rifle, or even an air rifle."

"Our diagnostician," Irene said, "was much perturbed by how a man would stalk the streets of Paris with a rifle in plain sight, even at night. The gaslights and the new electric lights do illuminate much."

The Englishman considered for barely a moment. "Nothing simpler. It must have been an air rifle then."

"I have never heard of such a weapon."

"And well you should not have. It is an obscure one, known only to a few, and mostly those of us in the spy trade. Not the sort of thing an honest man would have anything to do with."

"It shoots air?" Irene asked.

The man had quite a chuckle at her expense. "Lethal air, now that would be armament mighty nations would kill to possess, and someday perhaps they might. No, the air rifle is driven by air that expels the projectiles. It is a fiendish weapon, really, and can easily be disguised as a harmless walking stick."

"Ah," Irene nodded, "like a sword stick."

"Exactly."

"How can it be so slim, and how does it fire?"

"It can be a simple straight stick with a right-angle handle. The upper half can be curved, and I believe this was such a model." He nodded at the scarred stone above our heads. "The straight model requires the shooter to hold it against his cheek and site down the length of the stick. The curved design allows the bearer to shoot from the shoulder, which is less obvious. Using such a model indicates a seasoned shot, or a shooter who doesn't need the pinpoint accuracy of a lethal strike but something more in the way of a warning shot. Certainly he would not attract much attention with such a weapon after dark in Paris."

"Why is this wonder not better known?" Irene asked next.

"It has its limitations. Really, assassination is what it's best for."

"Lovely," said I.

He flashed me an assessing look. Apparently he was used to

women who swooned instead of waxed sarcastic at the thought of personal danger.

"A lovely weapon indeed," he responded. "The trick is that you must use an air pump to prime it. After that you have twenty shots before it fizzles. For those twenty shots you have one of the most murderous weapons on the planet. It is light, noiseless, easily disguised in public use and capable of pushing any type of bullet through an inch of wood planking at fifty yards at a pressure of four-to-five-hundred pounds. But the things have a range of three hundred and fifty yards, so are chillingly versatile. I have long wanted one, for they are of English invention and date to midcentury or before. I understand that the individually constructed ones are far superior to those manufactured, but have not been able to put my hands on one of those. As you can imagine, collectors and assassins snap them up like turtles do dragonflies. It is interesting."

"What could be more interesting than the history and mayhem of the air rifle?" Irene wondered a trifle sarcastically.

"That the bullet hit just above your heads. I can't believe that anyone who knew about and went to the trouble to acquire an air rifle would fail to use it accurately. This was definitely a warning shot."

"A warning shot, or a herding shot?"

He smiled at Irene's question, showing his teeth like a sauve shark. "All warning shots are herding shots. So where were you two herded that night?"

Irene pressed forward against the dark, the small candle flicker illuminating only narrow stone walls.

"After this passage, there is a cavern," she said, "and then a catacomb."

But in a few steps she stopped.

Rough piles of rock obstructed the way. As she lifted the candle, the light revealed that the low tide of rock had swelled into a barrier wall.

"We passed this way only a few nights ago, unobstructed, Pink and I."

"Pink?" the Englishman eyed me with incredulity.

"Pink," I repeated firmly.

His attention had returned to the dark narrow walls. "Here. The candle."

Irene obliged.

"Another bullet mark. And likely the last. The way is too narrow to miss from here on."

"Thank you," Irene said sardonically. "But there was a lot more way before us the last time we were here. Someone has loosened the stones to block any entry now."

He nodded, his silly hat casting a silly shadow on his serious face. "It took more than a few men to loosen that torrent of stone. These work buildings are apparently deserted."

"I don't believe the authorities, civil or religious, know of the underground catacombs yet," Irene said. "Or perhaps they do and simply don't care, as the bones may be Pagan."

"This area of Paris is not noted for catacombs," he agreed, turning a dazzling smile on me, "They run south of the river Seine. I believe we have mystified the charming Miss Pink for long enough. I will scout a discreet exit, then perhaps we can go somewhere more civil to discuss our business."

"Indeed. We will expect you at the hotel for tea. I shall give you the address."

"Indeed," he mocked her. "I am most anxious to learn what is worth calling me forth from the ruby mines of Afghanistan. Madam. Miss."

With a bow he tunneled into the darkness behind us and was gone.

"A rifle," Irene said. "The second such diagnosis. It confirms Buffalo Bill's, though with a perspective from an opposite corner of the world. Most interesting."

"Who *is* that rude Englishman?" I demanded. "This is Paris. I prefer the French."

"I am sorry. I have found Englishmen to be not only ubiquitous, but uniquely useful. You must admit that I play no favorites."

I shrugged. Her various alliances with the French Rothschilds, the English, and now the American plainsman clearly showed her to be a woman of international acquaintance. Perhaps she was merely an unemployed opera singer. They are used to multilingual performances.

I eyed my trunk longingly after we returned to our hotel room.

Sherlock Holmes was an arrogant, opinionated, aggravating Englishman, but I sensed that he was truly on the scent of the Ripper, while Irene's heart and mind had been subdivided and sent in every direction at once.

This one time, my money was on the Brit.

Meanwhile, Irene had ordered tea sent up to our room!

The cart and waiter arrived first. The Franco-English dandy came along on the waiter's departure, almost as if he had been waiting for that exit.

"My dear Irene!" He kissed both her hands after he knocked and entered our rooms, and threw his boater atop my trunk. "My God, this form of dress is annoying."

"Robes do not do in Paris unless you are playing Othello in Verdi's amazing opera," Irene said.

He threw himself into a chair, his long, loose limbs lying athwart it. "Your message arrived via the Rothschilds, though I was supposed to be unfindable. What can be so urgent?"

She sat before answering, behind the tea table, in the role, I realized, always taken by Nell.

She lifted the teapot cover, as if to ascertain that the water was steaming. When she drew back, small beads of moisture dewed her forehead like tears.

She set the cups on their saucers. Three.

I did not drink tea, but I don't think that mattered then, to her or to me.

She gazed into the small silver ewer of steamed milk, enumerated the flat dishes holding slices of lemon, the bowl swollen with lumps of sugar.

"Nell is missing," she said, pouring tea into cups and then milk.

He sprang up like a Jack in the box.

"My God, no!"

"Godfrey is missing."

He fell back as if shot, silent.

Irene moved the tea service like chess pieces on a board of sterling silver. Her eyes never left the tabletop. "It has something to do with Jack the Ripper."

"He is a monster, but an individual one."

"I am not so sure."

"He is many monsters?"

"We have two people missing. More than one person has accomplished this."

"Or . . . the incidents are unrelated."

She nodded. "Sugar?"

"I take salt in my tea."

She met his eyes for the first time. "So also do I . . . now. It is an eastern habit, is it not?"

"Afghani."

She waved a languid hand. "What am I to Afghan or Haemon to Hecuba? I need you in Bohemia."

"Nothing easier."

"And beyond Bohemia."

"Nothing easier. Will it lead to Nell?"

"Last suspected to be in Verdun."

"Paris, then Verdun?"

She nodded.

"Eastward then. I know it. Know it well."

"I know you do."

He suddenly glanced at me, and I saw the *boulevardier* was a fool's masque slipping from the face of a warrior.

"And Miss Pink?"

"My comrade in arms."

He measured me. I measured him. We were both not what we appeared to be. That we understood, if we did not understand each other, or remotely wish to.

"He should be rowing a boat on the Serpentine!" I exclaimed the moment the man was gone.

"That would indeed be a waste of his talents." Irene sipped cold tea as if it were ambrosia.

I suspected that all her senses were dulled, so intent was her mind on restoring her losses.

In truth, I had sensed some mettle beneath the fellow's manner, though I hated to admit it in an Englishman.

"You are accustomed to acting alone," Irene mused. "It is both admirable and a certain handicap. Perhaps it is my theatrical history but I am used to large casts acting in concert. You disparage my instinct to cast gentlemen of my acquaintance in leading roles. You consider it womanly weakness. On the contrary, no war was ever won by lone soldiers.

"This is a war, Pink. Undeclared perhaps, but nonetheless serious. I will use who I can where I can, and not apologize for it. Including you."

"There is something heartless in you."

"I hope so." She leaned forward and spoke to me, fiercely. "Sentiment or horror will not aid us in this battle. Only persistence. Consistency. Implacable pursuit. This is what has been directed at us. Me and mine."

She sat back to deliver herself of a speech for my benefit.

"As Buffalo Bill can rely upon the peerless tracking skills of Red Tomahawk, Indian of the Wild West, I can equally depend upon the insight and courage of *my* emissary from the Wild East.

"Quentin Stanhope is a valuable spy for the British Foreign Office," she went on. "More than that, he is a man who has absorbed the very nature of the foreign into his bones and blood. He is an explorer of what polite society wishes hidden. He has seen, drunk, slept, eaten, lived—and no doubt almost died—elements of uncivilized life that we can scarcely imagine.

"I do not accept his escort. I welcome his collaboration."

"Quentin. That name is familiar. . . ."

"He is a friend of Nell's, and thus my truest and best ally."

"A friend? Of Nell's? That seems hard to believe."

"Then let me modify my description. He is an admirer of Nell's."

"Really?"

There was no mistaking her meaning. The duplicitous rogue Englishman Quentin Stanhope was seriously taken by our little Nell.

Really! I was almost intrigued enough by this ridiculous notion to consider abandoning Sherlock Holmes to his Johnny-come-lately investigations in Whitechapel. Perhaps Jack the Ripper did not lurk in our future, but the savagely civilized Quentin Stanhope might prove to be of equal interest.

8.

Uneasy Allies

Case 21. Lustmurder
It satisfied me to seize the women by the neck and suck
their blood. Since I was twelve I experienced a peculiar
feeling of pleasure while wringing the necks of chickens. I
often killed great numbers of them and claimed that a
weasel had been in the hen-coop.

—RICHARD VON KRAFFT-EBING, *PSYCHOPATHIA SEXUALIS*

◄ F R O M   A   J O U R N A L ►

 "No more than one bag apiece," Irene decreed.

I raised my eyebrow.

This from the mistress of the well-rounded wardrobe?
Yet she was serious, and just how much soon came home
to me.

She vanished into Nell's bedroom and returned with a garment
draping her arm. "Nell's 'surprise' dress. It lifts the overskirt and
revers to reveal a more formal aspect. For Nell it was a matter of
economy," she added, stroking the pink-satin lining as if it were a
pet. "For me it shall be a matter of practicality, which Nell would

most approve. The skirts shall be a trifle short for me, but will permit more freedom of movement."

Irene's relentless will may have driven her to seek a more practical wardrobe among her lost friend's possessions. I also believe that dressing in Nell's clothes was an actress's way of donning her persona. She would move forward in the outward guise of her friend, absorbing her mental habits as well as her habiliments, beginning to think and feel as she did, setting herself on the trail in the very mind of the one lost.

I did not have such a theatrical approach. I went out to one of the fabled Parisian department stores, *Le Bon Marché* in this instance, and satisfied my own imitations of Nell by purchasing a checked coatdress of fine, light wool, much like that she had worn on our last outing to *l'Exposition universelle*. I topped it off with a hoydenish billed cap that quite made me feel like a newsboy hawking sensational late editions on the curb. Read all about it! NELLIE BLY TRACKS RIPPER TO VERDUN.

Oddly enough, clothed as Nell, I felt some of her stern island spirit dampening my natural American exuberance.

At such instants it occurred to me I might be invoking a dead woman's semblance and spirit. Yet somehow, that thought did not deter my resolve. I would give Irene's wild flight eastward a week of my time. Then I must return west to England and America. My absence would not go unnoticed that much longer.

I must admit that my heart beat a cancan of anxiety beneath my sober, checked coatfront as we made our way through the *Gare du Nord*, that monstrosity of a railway station, all echoing stone and the seagull-like cries of children and conductors.

When we reached our railway car and slung our single carpetbags into the brass racks above the seat, Irene smiled.

"That is all Nell and I had when fleeing Bohemia: a carpetbag each."

"You and Nell did this before? Traveled by train across Europe?"

"Yes. Only then nine of the King of Bohemia's best agents were on our track. This time, we are on the trail."

"To where? Pursuing whom?"

She ignored my questions and gazed out the window at the crowds milling back and forth on the platform like people at a carnival gawking at freaks behind glass.

"Ah, there he is! Do not look! We must not appear to recognize him. He will join us when the train is underway."

Our tickets were marked for Verdun. Irene seemed nervous now, withdrawing one of her slim dark cigars, then returning it to the exquisite case that held them. That blue enamel lid boasted a single, slanted capital "I" picked out in diamonds on the cover, one precious item she had not left behind, but it weighed little. She glanced at the passage, where late passengers were thronging past to find their compartments.

Apparently ours was private, for no one darkened our glass-inset door.

Irene consulted the small enameled watch she wore on a long chain around her neck. I had never seen her wear a watch before. She had left such practicalities to Nell until now.

"We leave in moments," she fretted. "I can't imagine what is keeping him."

"Mr. Stanhope, you mean?"

"Well, I wasn't expecting Red Tomahawk."

"I don't see that we need him."

"Red Tomahawk?"

"Mr. Stanhope. Or Mr. Stoker."

She shrugged and pushed the heavy velvet window curtains back even farther to gaze at the people milling on the platform amid clouds of steam.

The train throbbed, then jerked forward. Wheels creaked as they slowly groaned into motion, like a slugabed awaking in the morning.

I felt the unbidden thrill of beginning a journey to a strange place, despite my misgivings. And I was rather glad Mr. Stanhope had missed our train.

The car jerked and ground forward, barely in motion at first, but gaining speed and smoothness with every passing second.

Yes! The odious Englishman was indeed too late to accompany us.

Footsteps pounded the narrow passage beyond our compartment door.

Oh, no! I had been relieved too soon.

A flushed face under a peaked cap pressed against our etched glass until its nose was flattened like a piglet's.

Irene leaped up despite the unevenly lurching train and opened the door.

"Madame Norton?" the urchin asked, grinning.

At Irene's nod he thrust a misfolded newssheet at her. "For you."

"And for you," Irene answered in French equally as simple to understand, pressing a few sous into his palm to replace the paper.

He nodded and raced out of sight again.

She quickly went to the window, looking back to the station.

"Ah, he landed on all fours, but safely. Brave lad!" Before she finished speaking the train's rapid acceleration pushed her back against the plush green upholstery.

I couldn't help thinking of the man who had done that work, and of James Kelly, who had found other, more murderous uses for his upholsterer's chisels. . . .

But Irene rested against the padded velvet seemingly untroubled by macabre thoughts. She was reading the newspaper so suddenly delivered to her.

I tried to skim the text from the opposite seat, but the train's progress through the rail yards was too rough to permit easy reading, especially the surreptitious sort that I excelled at. And besides, the text was in some foreign language, not even French, I think, but German or some such.

We do not much study foreign languages in the U.S. Unlike the Europeans, we don't have neighboring states that use other tongues jammed up against our borders, and our foreign immigrants keep to themselves in sections of the city, or else learn English.

Irene read raptly, with the absorption of the linguist born. I could see how learning to sing in a handful of languages had taught her the major European tongues. It occurred to me then that the profession of opera singer was a demanding one requiring years of study to produce the impression that one could then waltz onto a stage in improbable costumes glittering with paste and foil and sing one's heart out like the Emperor's dying nightingale in five different foreign languages for three or four hours a night.

Irene sighed loudly enough for it to carry to the first balcony and set the paper down in her lap as if it were suddenly heavy.

"Well, we have lost our escort for the first stage of the journey."

At my mute questioning face, she added. "Quentin has gone ahead by horseback and coach. He says it is faster. But the Rothschild agents have been ahead of even him. Here is the Mannheim newspaper from two days ago. A village called Neunkirchen just over the French border near Worms—in Germany," she added, sensing my mystification.

I took the folded pages she handed me, remembering our lessons in Richard von Krafft-Ebing's *Psychopathia Sexualis*. German is the language said to underlie much of English, but I can claim no easy understanding of those twisted Gothic letters.

Of course the name "Neunkirchen" caught my eye.

Some of the words beneath the headline struck me with familiarity, but before I could interpret them, Irene did the task for me.

"The body of a young woman was found. 'As if torn apart by wolves.' Near the train station."

"At Neunkirchen."

" 'Newchurch,' I believe it means in English. It seems that the Ripper precedes us."

I sat up. "And Mr. Stanhope believes he can make better time than the train?"

"I believe he can," Irene said with a smile. "Civilization is a great retardant. I wish he could make as good time as Jack the Ripper, but that gentleman knows where he is going, and we do not."

"Are madmen that . . . competent?"

"When they are not so much mad, as evil. And I fear that this is the case."

I said nothing in answer, but my heart was beating with fear and anticipation, a state it often reached when I was launched on one of my famous 'stunts.'

I wanted to be on horseback flying along the hilltops with Quentin Stanhope instead of chuffing along the switchbacks in an iron box on wheels. I began to understand how a plains warrior like Red Tomahawk might feel touring with the Wild West Show.

"We will have to stop in Neunkirchen," Irene added with a frown.

I saw that she resented any pause in her haste to follow a possible route to Nell. "I will wire ahead from Verdun, so that we don't waste any time."

But we would waste time. Like Red Tomahawk we followed a trail, we did not break it. We were forced to keep our eyes and ears and mind to the ground just ahead, to slow down to observe traces, even if they were as obvious as dead bodies. To pause and think and worry and wonder.

No mystery why Jack the Ripper had eluded so many bobbies and gendarmes. He had the advantage of forging a trail, not following it.

We were all doomed to be a little too late, perhaps even Mr. Sherlock Holmes.

9.

The Devil His Own Way

"I incline to Cain's heresy," he used to say. *"I let my
brother go to the devil in his quaintly 'own way.'"*
—UTTERSON, THE LAWYER IN *THE STRANGE CASE OF DR. JEKYLL
AND MR. HYDE*, ROBERT LOUIS STEVENSON, 1886

⊰ F R O M   A   Y E L L O W   B O O K ⊱

Trains make him uneasy.

He finds their motion sickening. The way the tracks eat
up miles also upsets his usually steel stomach.

He is a prodigious walker, my large burly charge. It
offends him to see means other than time-tested foot or
hoof accomplishing such marvels of time and motion. What the
modern world worships—speed, ease, luxury—he despises as weak
and corrupt.

Therefore almost all in city life offends him. His is a soul born
to expand in the mighty cathedral and natural Gothic arch of forest,
in the empty chancel of deserted climes, under the heaven-thrusting
spires of mountains.

As we move slowly into landscape that swells to encompass his needs and enthusiasms, he feels more sharply the strictures of his recent life, no matter how much he has smashed through them.

It is all I can do to confine him to the compartment.

At times I think he would leap out the window like a goat and go clambering with his kind over the huge boulders that strew the mountain meadows like the severed heads of stone giants.

According to the tales of his previous travels, he has trudged across most of the continent in the most forbidding of weather, from searing heat to ice-bitter cold.

I myself have tasted the extremes of heat and cold in the past, and prefer temperance in this one area. In all other arenas, I am with my beast: life is best lived to excess, in the lofty halls of those who abide by no rules, among the gods of Olympus or Asgard . . . or Heaven before our friend Lucifer left it to its Bearded Old Man landlord.

My lad is quite religious, in his way.

Given his unwholesome pagan appetites, I find this contradiction most amusing.

He knows I study him and is flattered by that attention in his crude, boyish way.

He thinks he will be a person of importance someday.

He is already unaware that he has earned a sobriquet that puts half the known world in a panic.

Jack the Ripper.

Or . . . Attila the Hun. Vlad the Impaler, Ivan the Terrible. They all spring from the same deliciously tainted fountain of humanity that I so adore.

It is what has made them famous. Immortal. Or simply notorious on the grand scale.

I crave notoriety, but I also desire anonymity.

What a quandary. No wonder I am forced to work through lesser tools.

He will crouch sometimes on the floor of the compartment, at my feet, like a great shaggy mountain dog. Even sitting on a chair is a civilizing burden he cannot long endure.

It would be amusing to try to make a gentleman of him. Yet that would take more time than I have. And, actually, I prefer the easier task of making a monster of a gentleman. There I have what is called a "head start."

I smile to think of the chaos we have left behind in Paris.

The four dead women are the least of it.

It is like allowing a few drops of blood to drip into a pond. At first the large body of water appears to absorb the gaudy addition. Yet unseen the atoms of blood diffuse and spread out until, invisible, they tinge every wavelet that laps the shore. All waters, of baptism or birth or Mother Ocean, are tainted by the shed blood of the lambs and the lions. I see the thin crimson crust edging even the most holy spring. That has been my curse. And his as well.

It would be amusing to import this virile infection over water, to the States perhaps.

But there my boy would be too obviously a fish out of his bloody water. The East is in his veins, as is savagery. For a moment I toy with the notion of him encountering a Red Indian, surely one of the last savage races left on the planet.

The one upon our trail in Paris, for all his Wild West Show drollery, might actually be the match for him.

A pity I could not dally to make him part of my experiment. It is interesting that the Red Man shares with my beast a weakness for strong drink, a taste that first enhances strength and then, inevitably, saps it to the last pathetic drop.

Yet I have high hopes of my beast even on this score. Thus far the drink has only aided and abetted him. I am reminded of Mr. Stevenson's intriguing Mr. Hyde, or a misshapen dwarf like Quasimodo, that pagan sprite of Notre Dame. One of world literature's many monster-heroes, yet with the rotten soft-center of a Viennese sweet.

None of that for my beast. He murmurs as I stroke his unkempt head while he crouches beside me on the floor. I bleed in secret ways and that both calms and excites him.

I open my palm, where a brass fitting from a piece of luggage has carved away a small, burning tongue of flesh. He smells the blood, turns, licks it like a dog.

It is our Sacrament. His strange pale eyes meet mine. He wants what I will give him . . . when I am ready.

He will kill for me, but mainly for himself.

That is why I love him as no other.

Save one.

10.

A Stray Chicken

One of the most dangerous classes in the world is the drifting and friendless woman. She is the most harmless and often the most useful of mortals, but she is the inevitable inciter of crime in others. She is helpless...a stray chicken in a world of foxes. When she is gobbled up she is hardly missed.

—ARTHUR CONAN DOYLE, SHERLOCK HOLMES IN *THE DISAPPEARANCE OF LADY FRANCES CARFAX*

〉FROM A JOURNAL〈

This crude shed has neither the formal stone bier, the refrigeration that quells scent, nor the neat wooden clothing pegs of the Paris Morgue.

The girl's body lies atop a crude wooden board on sawhorses.

Wind whistles through the fir slats of the shed and plays among her locks of hair. She smells both sour and sweet, like some German cooking. My stomach lurches.

I can understand how the people of these remote villages believe the dead could walk. Her skirts tremble in the torchlight, touched by the wind but not breath.

Quentin Stanhope has gone before us like John the Baptist, announcing our advent. I only hope we do not catch up to him as a head upon a tray.

The stern German police official is stoic about showing two women the savaged body of a third woman.

"Her name was Liesl," he says in English stilted enough that I must translate it for my journal. "She sold flowers at the train station. An orphan, perhaps seventeen. Her flowers were scattered around her and her money was gone. There is not a copper left to pay for her burial. She had flowers but no funeral."

"But she wasn't found near the train station," Irene says, staring at the dead face as if she might recognize the features could they only speak, move.

"*Nein.* In a cave a short walk from the rail yard. A cave fit for dogs. Or wolves and bears."

"Wolves and bears," Irene repeats, in her deepest, darkest stage voice.

The man nods. He has a fleshy face that shadows work ruin in. He likes his schnapps and his sauerkraut and dumplings. He believes that caves fit for dogs and wolves and bears are best avoided. I can read all that by the smell of beets and peppermint on his breath.

"You have not removed her clothing," Irene notes.

"The wounds are obvious. The torn throat, the slashed bosom."

"We would like to be alone with her."

His face curdles with puzzlement and distaste. What would women want with a dead woman?

"Prayers," Irene explains, for a moment looking as modest and implacable as a nun.

It is enough.

He bows out of the shed, leaving us to the flickering torch and the features that flicker with deceptive life.

"I pray," she says, looking at me, "we do not find what we expect."

I can't do it. I know what she wants to know. I am as eager as she to know it. But for the life of me I can't do it: lift the dead creature's oddly sentient skirt, look like any lewd man on her privates, violate her in death as well as in life.

Irene draws up the cloth like a curtain, her face stone.

It is only two superficial slashes, in an "X." I turn away, cover my mouth, choke back my rising gorge. Is Sherlock Holmes pursuing such grisly examinations in London now? Or only cold, cerebral trails?

"Wolves," Irene spits out. "Caves."

"Is it the Ripper?"

"He has no time now. No . . . leisure. No time for pseudo-surgery. It is rip and tear and move on. Perhaps because we chase him."

"Us? We're responsible?"

"No." She brushes her brow as if to remove cobwebs only she can see. "He would do what he does without us. *To* us, if he could. He does not discriminate. But somebody does."

"What do you mean?"

"Somebody wants us on this trail. On his trail."

"To catch him?"

"Or for him to catch us."

"Us? Me? They know about me?"

"You are the internationally famous Nellie Bly."

"Not that international. Yet. Why don't they want Sherlock Holmes?"

"I'm not saying they don't, but Dr. John H. Watson is not missing, that I know of."

"Who is Dr. John H. Watson?"

"Sherlock Holmes's Nell."

"He has a friend, that man?"

"You're surprised?"

"He struck me as utterly self-sufficient, but . . . when he left our rooms, after—"

"After?"

"After he'd tried to convince you that you were up to facing Nell's loss."

"Did he try to do that?" Her tone was dreamy, distant.

"Try to convince you? Yes! You wouldn't listen."

"I couldn't hear then, not even Sherlock Holmes. That was . . . clever of him. A pity I . . . missed it."

"You missed much in those hours. You were as lost as Nell."

She shook her head. Threw off that despairing self of hers, even the memory, as a snake would shuck a dead skin.

"We will all be lost if we do not track and stop this criminal. He is rushed now. He has become used to being ignored, forgotten, overlooked. No more. He kills like a wolf on the run . . . to where? To somewhere that he can revert to his usual practices."

"You make it sound like a . . . an art form."

"It is a form, I'm convinced of that. Not so mindless as it seems."

"But it must be. No mind could conceive these attacks and remain sane."

"Didn't you absorb your Krafft-Ebing? These killers are perfectly sane until they kill. They are Dr. Jekylls and Mr. Hydes. On one hand the rational, organizing mind. On the other, the rampaging, tearing emotions."

She turned me to face the torchlight, to watch it flicker in her living features as it had danced on the face of the dead girl moments before.

"Don't you see it? The great rationality of Sherlock Holmes, for instance? Don't you sense the insanity that lingers beneath? The more that Reason rules, the more Insanity runs rampant beneath the surface. We are all like that. We are all just this far from being like that. Look at your rage toward your violent stepfather Jack Ford! You testified against him in a court of law as a child. Why do you subject yourself to madhouses and brothels except to expose other Jack Fords? Look at the rage of Jack Ford. You lived with a madman, Elizabeth Jane Cochrane. You made Nellie Bly to hunt him down. You are with me now to find another incarnation of him. Don't tell me I am an unnatural woman to protect mine, to fight the darkness that gouges at my kind. You are me, and I am you. And we both can become Jack Ford or Jack the Ripper if we let ourselves."

"No. I will never admit that."

"Then you will never catch Jack the Ripper, however many headlines you covet."

"I am more than headlines!"

"Prove it. Come with me even though you believe the hunt pointless."

"I . . . don't."

She looked at me. I did not look at her.

"Come with me," she said as softly as a siren, mocking my reluctance and my hunger at the same time. For a moment, I wondered if this was how Jack the Ripper felt, reluctant and hungry. And why. "You will be sorry, but you will get Jack Ford at last."

"He's dead," I said, meaning to object.

She only shook her head.

11.

Cold Comfort

❧

*He has always been of unstable mind and a person whom
one would expect to become actively insane from a
comparatively minor cause.*

—DR. W. ORANGE, SUPERINTENDENT, THE BROADMOOR
CRIMINAL LUNATIC ASYLUM, 1883

⊰ F R O M   A   J O U R N A L ⊱

At the train station, Irene consulted the schedules.

Or she appeared to.

She approached the ticketseller, a broad man of sixty with old-fashioned muttonchop whiskers as broad. Fortunately, he spoke some English, so I was able to follow the conversation, which quickly became one of Irene's casual interrogations.

"We need tickets to Frankfurt," she began, "but—"

He paused in shuffling through his papers.

"We were supposed to meet my brother here and travel on together. I wondered if he had bought a ticket yet. In the past day or two. He may have arrived here before me."

"Many men who could be your brother or another's have bought tickets in the past two days, men enough to be brother to half the Prussian army."

Irene smiled apologetically, with a helpless tilt of her head.

"My brother is rather headstrong. He may have grown annoyed because I am a trifle late. He is a man of middling height, dark-haired . . . but, Hortense!" She turned to me. "You have the portrait of Henry, don't you?"

At this cue I drew a cabinet photograph from my capacious handbag. When the small book opened, one side of the glass showed a photograph of Irene, the other a pastel portrait of a man.

"Henry." Irene beamed proudly.

"This is not a photograph." The ticketmaster leaned through his archway to squint at the likeness.

"Henry is afraid of cameras. So silly, but true. He could be persuaded to sit for a sketch, however."

I had to swallow a grin. Irene's first act on recovering her wits after Nell's abduction had been to drag me to a café in Montmartre, where a rather seedy artist nursing absinthe had listened to our long, joint, and sometimes conflicting descriptions of James Kelly, also known as Jack the Ripper to the Paris police, and had finally drawn this likeness to our mutual satisfaction.

Despite the portrait being handdrawn, the eyes had the wide, staring look found in some photographs. Otherwise, that was the only sign that the subject was quite mad.

The ticketmaster's callused finger poked at the celluloid protecting Kelly's face. "I saw a fellow like that. Your brother, you say? He had no money for a ticket, but insisted he must reach Frankfurt as soon as possible."

"Oh, Hortense!" Irene sighed heavily. "Henry has been gambling again! And after he promised our mother. . . . Sir, I apologize for my brother's behavior. If you can guess where he might have gone, we will find him and pay his way."

"Gone?" He regarded us as if we were the mad killers. "He's gone all right. To Frankfurt. Yesterday evening. He may have won the price of a ticket gambling, for he paid the entire fare with a fistful of coppers."

Irene nodded slowly while I shut the cabinet on James Kelly's loathsome face, but only temporarily.

No doubt that was what had become of the dead flower girl's hard-earned coppers: a ticket for James Kelly to another city he could terrorize.

While I reflected bitterly on this fact, Irene purchased two tickets for Frankfurt leaving within the half hour.

"Looks like that brother of yours keeps one step ahead of you," the ticketmaster noted, "and of his promises to his mother, too."

We stepped away from the window to one of the hard wooden benches strung along the platform, and sat.

The wind was chill. I heard a faint cry of "Flowers" on it. The smell of spiced nuts trailed from the chestnut vendor's stand some fifty feet away.

"Do you need a comfort station before we continue?" Irene asked. For a former prima donna she was unusually practical at times.

I sat beside her. "There is no comfort station on this journey."

She did not argue.

12.

Cork and Candle

Halifax is built of stone,
Heptonstall o' stone,
I' Halifax ther's bonny lassis,
I' Heptonstall ther's none.
—OLD CHILDREN'S RHYME

⊰FROM THE NOTES OF JOHN H. WATSON, M. D.⊱

A veteran of foreign wars like myself should not have been rattled by the swift arrival of the police and the even swifter removal of the pitiful yet breathing body under my care into the custody of the ambulance men.

Yet I was shocked beyond anything the chaos of combat had ever accomplished. Certainly I was loath to give up my patient, but the authorities were as rough with me as with any of the gawkers who soon gathered to murmur and bruit about the name of Jack the Ripper.

It was even more shocking when a pair of bobbies said I had to wait for the inspector and made clear that my medical title was only a liability at this time on this scene.

I couldn't even resort to the sometimes magical name of Sherlock Holmes, although with the police it was less of an "open sesame" than with other authorities in London. These were not even the London police, for Whitechapel had its own (and I might add, remarkably thickheaded) force.

So I fretted in that dark yard now lit by a constellation of lanterns, watching the cobblestones suffer under the boots of enough policemen to have Holmes crying to heaven at the stupidity of it all.

Holmes. Where was he? The police had come, presumably because he had found and warned a bobby on patrol. I had heard their shrill whistles calling to each other like hysterical birds, but nothing more of Holmes.

"And you say your name is Dr. Watson, sir?"

"I don't say it. That is my name. Dr. Watson of Paddington."

"A long way from Paddington, sir, at such a late hour. Does your wife know you're about?"

"Of course she does! A doctor is often called out at night on cases."

"Convenient, 'tisn't it, sir? What case brought you out tonight, all the way to Whitechapel?"

"Not a case of mine, exactly."

"No?"

"A case of a friend of mine's."

"Who is?"

"Not here at the moment."

"But he was here before?"

"Yes, of course. We found the poor woman together."

"Did you now? And where is he, did you say?"

"I didn't say. I sent him to alert you lot, while I attended to the . . . patient."

"But you said it was his case."

"Yes, well . . . but he isn't a doctor."

"Then how can he have 'cases'?"

"Ah, really, you are wasting your time, and these men are completely trampling the ground, destroying any evidence that might remain!"

At that moment I heard the report of a pistol in the distance.

My interrogation paused as every helmet in the vicinity lifted to gauge the distance and the caliber of the shot.

I desperately feared it was my old Army Adams, a sturdy, accurate and noisy firearm.

"Holmes!" I burst out, fearing for his life.

"Holmes? That is the name of your accomplice?"

"Blast it, man! Of course not. I am speaking of no accomplice, but of Sherlock Holmes, the consulting detective. Surely you have heard of him."

"Can't say that I have," rejoined the stolid, cockney voice of PC Whoever.

I groaned. "I must speak with Inspector Lestrade."

"Is this someone else you expect us to know?"

"Of Scotland Yard," I finished with the ringing conviction of a desperate man.

"Lestrade is coming," a familiar yet authoritatively strident voice announced. "And so is this sorry fellow I trapped six streets over in a yard as dark and hidden as this one."

Holmes, his face smudged with grime and the occasional darkening bruise, hauled a scowling, blinking, cringing figure into the lantern light.

I had never been so glad of seeing such a likely looking villain in my life. I meant the man in Holmes's custody, of course.

Our return to Baker Street was, thankfully, in such a wee hour that it was not observed by Mrs. Hudson. I shudder to think what that worthy Scots lady would think of Holmes's profligate ways with the condition of his clothing.

My vigil by the wounded young woman while waiting for the

police and ambulance to come and take her away and Holmes's pursuit of his quarry had done nothing for either of our appearances.

Holmes insisted that Inspector Lestrade, who had finally arrived on the scene and grandly dismissed us as both suspects and witnesses, would send for us when the poor girl was able to speak and would interview us then. Until that time, we could only find our weary way home. I stopped to wire Mary not to worry, for I could see no sense in making for Paddington when I'd so soon be needed in town again.

I must say that we both trudged up the stairs to 221B silent and solemn.

Holmes left me in the parlor setting out the foreign forms of the shot glasses on his chemistry table while he retired to his bedchamber to remove the blighted articles. To me these glassy artifacts seemed like remnants of another time now that a woman and her assailant had been found, but not to my ever-curious friend Sherlock Holmes.

In moments Holmes returned in his favorite mouse-colored dressing gown, humming happily off-key while putting his pipe-smoking kit together beside the Persian slipper on the mantel.

"It appears that I will have that most rare opportunity granted to few mortals, Watson," he noted.

"What is that, Holmes?"

"A chance to interview a victim of the Ripper . . . or a purported victim of some lust-murderer, at least. Not to mention a suspect for the Ripper himself. I am glad you were along last night, old fellow, not the least for your medical skills. This time I have a witness to my innocent appearance on the scene! What did you think of Whitechapel?"

"A hole, a filthy hole. I knew as much, but to see it in person reminds me of the Black Hole of Calcutta of legendary repute."

"Unfortunately all of Whitechapel could answer to that epithet, Watson. As long as civilized nations allow such sinkholes of poverty, despair, and neglect to exist, crime will have a field day. Crime, not

mere puzzles, Watson, not the intricate interplay of greed and vengeance and jealousy that have brought me some of my most per-
plexing cases, but crude, raw, brutal crime. Murder most
inexplicable and savage."

"Yet you seem to think that these case studies of Krafft-Ebing
shed some light on such senseless murders as Jack the Ripper's."

My comment plunged my friend into one of his gloomy reveries.

His thin cheeks bellowed in and out as he inhaled on the black
briarwood pipe until the tobacco truly took, and the pipe began to
exhale smoke like a fire-breathing dragon.

" 'Case studies,' " he quoted back at me finally. "A doctor's expression, and quite rightly so, yet such an appalling admission. It
turns Jack the Ripper—and James Kelly and Sweeney Todd and
Bluebeard, if you will—from a singular demon into a simple if
noxious mania common to more than one man. Does one really
fancy one solves anything by seeing Rippers produced in endless
links like strings of sausage?"

"I know about the legends of Bluebeard and Sweeney Todd, the
demon barber of Fleet Street, but who is James Kelly? You promised
earlier to tell me his story."

Holmes cast himself into the velvet-lined chair as if craving its
cradling softness. His eyes lit up with the joy of contemplating an
enigma.

"A demon upholsterer, if you will, Watson. A miserable man
from the miserable manufacturing and port city of Liverpool. A
bastard, quite literally. Yet a happy boy bound to the upholstery
trade with no greater ambitions than that.

"Then one day he discovers he has great expectations. It seems
his father is not dead but a successful merchant who has left young
James a tidy sum in his will. Of course, that only makes him a well-
provided-for bastard. His lifelong love for his mother turns to hate.
Then he is severed from his beloved trade and given the golden
opportunity of being sent to school, for him a prison not a boon.
One revelation, and not only his entire life changes but also his
feeling toward his fellow man . . . and woman, especially, as a certain

person of my acquaintance would remind me rather sharply, were she here."

"Are you referring rather coyly to my wife, Mary, Holmes?"

Holmes must have inhaled rather too deeply of his pipe; he coughed violently for at least a minute. I was forced to rush to him and apply a few sharp slaps to the back before he recovered.

"You do see what I mean, Watson? That Krafft-Ebing and his book make mice of monsters?"

"I suppose so. It must go back to our days of childhood tales, when we believed bogeymen actually hid in the wardrobe or beneath the bed. An uncaught killer like Jack the Ripper begins to take on the power of a legend. To realize that he might be only a pathetic maniac, ill-educated as well as ignorant, religiously deluded, and not so much clever as lucky . . . well, what would the papers have to write about?"

"The papers have made the Ripper, as have our imaginations. So, Watson, take your ignorant, deluded maniac and multiply him by many. That is what Krafft-Ebbing would have us all believe. Such men prowl every city, usually acting separately but joined by a common impulse and a common method of following it: bloody murder."

Holmes set down his pipe and rose. "Such men are often dipsomaniacs, according to Kraft-Ebbing, acting during some drunken nightmare. Certainly James Kelly drank. Hence my interest in bottle corks."

I followed Holmes to the table, where he was separating the three shot glasses into a single line, rather like the shells in those street games involving hidden nuts.

"A piece of cork and two pieces of wax. Not much to lead us to Jack the Ripper. Yet this trail may lead us to the source of all his evil. Imagine. Jack the Ripper hung on a bit of cork and sealing wax."

"Sealing wax? But you described the wax from the cellar floor as coming from candles."

"Some of it did. But this, this pale bit. . . ."

Holmes's tongs elevated a slender curl the size and texture of the half-moon tip on an infant's fingernail.

"This is not candle wax but sealing wax, and if it doesn't lead me to Jack the Ripper here in London, it will certainly lead me to the unholy coven that turned *le tout Paris* into an abattoir in the supposedly merry month of May."

I don't know which shocked me the most: to hear Sherlock Holmes declaim a French phrase like a Parisian born, or to learn that he suspected Jack the Ripper of moving on, and of collecting followers.

13.

'Twixt Heaven and Hell

~~⚬~~

At length the slight quivering of an eyelid, and immediately thereupon, an electric shock of a terror, deadly and indefinite, which sends the blood in torrents from the temples to the heart. And now the first positive effort to think. And the first endeavor to remember.

—EDGAR ALLAN POE, *THE PREMATURE BURIAL*

Darkness and motion.

That is all I remember, all I sense.

And now . . . darkness but no motion.

The stillness makes my stomach rebel, or it would, were there not a black hollow curled tauter than an empty fist where my stomach should be.

In fact, I can sense none of the ordinary limits to my being, only the ear-ringing shriek of silence when intense sound has suddenly stopped assailing one's ears, only a kind of throbbing that seems to indicate where I leave off and something . . . Other . . . begins.

Vaguely, the memory of a shrunken room, of a box, assembles around the entity I suspect of being "Me."

I try to move what would be my fingers, were they still there. To stretch the nerves and muscles I imagine until the flesh I assume touches . . . something.

No wall. No wood. Nothing.

I feel as if I am floating.

I must be dead, or halfway there. My "self" seems both swollen and weightless. Perhaps I have expanded and burst out of my box.

That I remember. The ungiving limits that I met both up and down and from side to side, as close as a shroud but as hard as Sherwood Forest yew.

If I am on my way to Heaven, why no light and no angelic chorus? If I am sinking into Hell, why no fire and demonic jeers? I know that I do not believe in the Papist limbo, though this state feels most like it. I would most dislike being forced to reconsider my denomination on the brink of paradise. Or of perdition.

The box may be gone, but I feel a barrier around my form nonetheless: it is as close as an insect's carapace and is hot as an iron poker and aches like a fever. This would confirm my worst surmise: Hell, it is then. I do not think that I have been so very bad but such determinations are up to the Deity, and I was always told He was a harsh Judge.

In fact, I hear amid the high-pitched whine of silence a distant voice. It comes from above me. It calls my name. "Nell."

Well. Would the Deity, or even the Devil, use the abbreviated form of my name rather than the full and formal "Penelope?" I think not. One does not judge with diminutives.

So. I may be . . . not quite dead.

"Nell."

Must I try to open my eyes? The lids are as heavy as a rosewood piano cover. As a copper coffin lid. I doubt that such luxurious substances are fit for the funereal accessories of someone as insignificant as I.

The box and the motion seem to be gone. It might be to my benefit to try to open what in another place and time were my eyes.

I seem to have forgotten the series of movements that achieve such a thing in an everyday world.

"Nell, for God's sake!"

The voice is beginning to sound irritated, or urgent. It is beginning to sound familiar. It invokes the Deity, so it is not the Devil. Perhaps. After what I have glimpsed of Hell, it is not safe to regard the Devil as anything but a near neighbor.

I hear a bellows fan the flames that lick at the edges of my mind. The bellows is myself. I had . . . sighed.

I feel my extremities stir, feel the first soft tingle of sensation growing into a buzzing, itching, screaming torment like a rectangle of fire.

I must open what passes for my eyes in this state. The act is so alien. I realize that I have embraced the darkness for the sights it impedes. I see flames and gibbering forms and sharp blades and blood. . . .

Suddenly the darkness behind my eyes has become more awful than any sight they might open upon. I blink them ajar, again and again, fighting the daylight that sears like a red-hot iron.

"Nell, you are all right?!"

I rather doubt it!

My bleary focus shows a face hanging above mine. Something familiar . . .

"Irene?" I ask.

There is no answer.

"Irene? You have found me!"

Then I must have been "lost."

Lost or not, I am suddenly buoyed by a swell of confidence and security. Of course Irene has found me. That is what she does. She finds things. And people. And sometimes evildoers. Am I an evildoer? Is that why I suffer so? It must be.

"Nell." The voice sounds despairing, and I suspect Hell again. We are fellow inmates of Gehenna, that is why it burns so.

"It's only I. Godfrey."

Godfrey!

Godfrey.

I have never heard of an archangel named Godfrey, but I am convinced that there is one, and that he has found me.

I am saved!

14.

Unknown in Whitechapel

※⋙⋘※

I am not retained by the police to supply their deficiencies.
—ARTHUR CONAN DOYLE, SHERLOCK HOLMES IN
THE BLUE CARBUNCLE

⊰ F R O M   T H E   N O T E S   O F   J O H N   H .   W A T S O N ,   M . D . ⊱

 "So I am saved," the girl said, sighing in her hospital bed.
She did not so much speak, as rasp.

Yet she was very lucky. The slash across her throat had
run like a placid river, broad but not deep. The wound
would heal into a thin pale scar, nature's very narrow
mother-of-pearl necklace, and her voice would recover completely
in time.

My friend Sherlock Holmes was not a man for the sick room.
He possessed too much wiry energy. The subdued hush required of
the hospital aggravated rather than soothed him.

Still, he knew when a client required cautious handling, and this
pathetic girl was indeed his client now and more deserving of cod-
dling than any titled aristocrat in distress.

"My dear young woman," Holmes said in that deliberately
kindly tone he adopted only for the deeply distressed, "you have

truly faced a terrible ordeal. Can you testify at all to the appearance of your attacker? It would be a great service."

Although this was very true and quite logical, it had no effect whatsoever upon a girl who had stumbled through a vale of despair into horrors Holmes and I could only guess at.

Nevertheless, she seemed to recognize in his controlled address a fellow sufferer of the human condition. Her eyes had a clarity her voice was incapable of at the moment, and she turned their pale blue sorrow upon him.

"Mr. Holmes," she said, having marked our introductions with touching precision. "I must admit to not much noticing anything around me last night. The man was a shadow who came from the shadows. He was taller than me, and he didn't stop to say sweet words but pushed me against a wall and had at it."

"Taller? As tall as I?"

That made her smile. "No."

"Dr. Watson?"

She glanced my way, and I fancy that her gaze warmed, as if she knew that I had tended her.

"Dr. Watson would have to stand up, as you do."

I complied, apologizing. Doctors are used to long hours in hospital wards and sit when they can.

"About as tall as Dr. Watson. The nurse said . . . was it really your wife's muffler I bled all over?"

"No, no, my dear. You are not to worry about that. It was *my* muffler, knitted by my wife. Mary would be pleased that it was at hand to help save your life."

"Would she?" A look of inexpressible pain crossed her face. "Kind, is she?"

"A veritable angel on earth."

"I thought I saw an angel. On the street that night."

"Were you . . . ?" Holmes began.

"Drinking? No. I had no money for it. Never did. It was from the shirt shop to the streets. I'd no time nor pence to do much of anything but walk. Most of the men stopped me, then ran away. It is all like a dream."

"And in this dream," Holmes insisted, "there was one last man and he cut you."

She put a pale hand to her pale throat and the paler bandage that swathed it.

"All I could think of was that my spilled blood would at least make a warm blanket."

Even Holmes was struck silent. Then he began again. "How tall?"

"I am five-foot-one. Perhaps five-foot-five."

"His complexion?"

"The night was dark, but there was a bar of streetlight just moving across his face. Fresh-faced. Was that the angel?"

"Eyes?"

"Not dark. Light. You could see through them to someplace else. I almost . . . got there."

"Facial hair?"

"I saw no mouth. Just a brush across."

"A mustache?"

"A mustache. My father had a mustache, but he is dead."

"Light or dark?"

Her eyes fixed on something above our heads, like an ascending saint. "Dark," came her dreamy voice. "His face was as round and pale as a moon, but his hair was dark. His mustache was small and brown, like a mouse."

"Mouse-colored mustache," Holmes repeated with a sharp glance at me. "Age?"

She shook her head. "Neither young nor old. Thirty?"

Holmes flashed me a triumphant glance, although puzzled. Her description, pried out feature by feature, matched exactly the man Holmes had captured and also one man who had accosted Elizabeth Stride, the man who had escaped while Holmes pursued the phantom of Israel Lipski.

While we silently consulted, our witness had fallen into a deep sleep. I gazed on her with the bittersweet surety of a physician. She would survive, but for what?

"Remarkable," Holmes murmured, whether referring to her testimony or her survival I could not tell. "Now we have a more unpleasant task ahead."

"More unpleasant?" I demanded, aghast.

"The man must be interviewed as well."

We walked out of the long lonely wards, our footsteps echoing.

"She is well-spoken," I noted. "And something of a seamstress apparently. Perhaps Mary could use—"

Holmes's glance was both impatient and sympathetic, but he said nothing.

"There are only two interesting features, as you would call 'em, Mr. Holmes, in this arrest," Inspector Lestrade said while we waited in a mean room at the Yard for the prisoner to be brought in.

Holmes could not contrive to look very interested in what our acquaintance from Scotland Yard found interesting, but I assumed that expression of rapt attention to symptoms so necessary to physicians.

The lean-faced inspector grimaced in my direction to acknowledge my effort.

"First," he said with slow importance, "it is a matter of interest to more at the Yard than me that Mr. Sherlock Holmes should bestir himself so far from Baker Street as Berner Street and just happen upon the first woman-murder attempt after Jack the Ripper was persuaded to retire."

If Lestrade had hoped to intimidate Holmes, he had got the wrong man in more instances than one.

"Second," the inspector said, leaning nearer the better to put his case, "it was most interesting that the only weapon to be found upon the fellow, in a deep pocket of his jacket, was no knife or blade at all, but this."

Lestrade reached to the table behind him and thumped to the top of his battered oak desk an ungainly crockery jar perhaps ten inches high.

Holmes immediately seized upon it for closer inspection, drawing his magnifying glass from his own jacket pocket. He applied it and his eye closely to the jar's thick lip.

"Some crude liquor container," Lestrade said, "but the contents are all gone, down the fellow's throat, no doubt. What say you, Mr. Holmes? I did not even find a razor thrust down that empty pottery throat. He could have clubbed the woman with this, but where's the knife?"

"I assume you have had the area searched between Dutfield Yard and Westworth Street where I cornered the fellow."

"Yes, and no trace of a knife."

"Perhaps, but there are a hundred places along such a route to conceal or discard such a weapon that even the police would not notice."

Holmes passed the jar's open mouth under his nostril and inhaled so delicately that I suspect I was the only one present to notice it.

His thumbnail flicked a bit of pale wax adhering to the lip almost fondly. Then he set it down again. "What do you know of our man, or, rather, what is he letting you know of himself?"

Lestrade frowned on the word "our," but his countenance smoothed immediately. He did not often have the chance to inform Holmes, rather than the other way around.

"We've done a pretty fast job of getting his facts and figgers together, if I do say so myself."

"And who else would say so?" Holmes asked with a smile so swift and small that Lestrade blinked to wonder if he had seen it at all. He also apparently missed the insult implicit in the remark. Sometimes Holmes couldn't resist baiting the more plodding emissaries of the law, though in private he accorded Lestrade more respect than he gave most of Scotland Yard.

Invited to perform, the inspector reeled off a list of details. "He is an immigrant. We had to send away for someone who could speak his language."

"That must not have been difficult," Holmes said. "Russians have poured into Whitechapel in recent years."

"Oh, so you think he's Russian?" He did not wait for Holmes to indicate what he thought, which was wise as Holmes did no such thing, and went on. "Not so much Russian as"—he glanced at his notes—"Georgian. It's a part of Russia, I suppose, but they take much pride in which exact part they call home, perhaps because it's such a big country."

I knew from my time in the Near East that there was a lot more to geographical pride and prejudice than that, but kept silent. It was always best to let Holmes lead the conversation, for I could never guess the many streams of suspicion that were always flowing in his busy mind.

"How have you interrogated him?"

"We have our methods, Mr. Holmes. They may not be as mysterious as yours but are no less important. As it happened, the Foreign Office was most happy to provide an interpreter, one who even spoke the particular dialect of this . . . Yuri Chernyshev chap."

At the mention of the Foreign Office, Holmes seized the jar again and subjected it to scrutiny. I believe he meant the gesture to hide his expression of satisfaction, for of course his brother Mycroft must have had something to do with it. I recalled again that the most eminent personages in England were interested in both the Ripper case and Holmes's progress with it.

"What has he allowed you to learn of him?" Holmes asked again, finally.

"He was a brushmaker in Vilna, wherever that may be. Russia is a very large land mass."

"Indeed," said Holmes, never glancing up from the mouth of the pottery jug. "From its far western islands to its eastern wastes, it girdles the globe over an expanse that would go from Cairo to Fiji, should Russia lie on a more temperate southerly longitude instead of the icy upper half of the map. Were it not for the frozen expanses of upper North America and Greenland—and a few modest European countries on the western fringe of Europe—Russia would girdle the globe. As it is, the nation extends from Nunyamo near the furthest extreme of Alaska to Gdynia above Warsaw. A mighty land indeed."

Lestrade's jaw dropped at this apparently idle excursion into geography, but less so than mine. If there was any subject my brilliant but erratically educated friend found less interesting than the clockwork operation of the heavens, it was the specific arrangement of the earth and sea below those heavens.

"At any rate," Lestrade finally went on, studiously consulting his notes, "this Chernyshev said the Czar's police came to his village of Vilna, wherever it was between, ah, Nunyami and Gardinia, and so taxed and beat the Jews that they fled like sheep to Europe and eventually he found his way to London and Whitechapel, where he resumed his work as a brushmaker."

"And his reason for being out that night?"

"He admits to being a member of the International Working Men's Educational Club, which we know as an organization of Jewish anarchists."

"But he denies attacking the young woman just outside of it?"

"Of course. There's not a Ripper suspect we've had in hand that did not deny everything."

"And does he admit to a state of drunkenness?"

"Admit? He is proud of it."

Holmes peered deep into the jar. "He claims to have emptied this jug by himself?"

"Absolutely. It is rarely attained here in England, being a popular village brew all over Russia. He claims to have wandered the streets all night, intending to drink until he could not stand."

"And these chips along the bottle's lip, could he explain them?"

"I happened to have noticed that very thing, Mr. Holmes," Lestrade said with a ferrety grin at me. "Looks as though the bottle might have been used as a bludgeon, although that poor woman was not struck with anything but a blade. So I asked him about that, through the interpreter, who said that men in his village used to gather in the forest and beat these jars against a tree trunk until the sealing fell off and they could drink. And that is how the chips came to be."

Holmes set the jar away from himself at the center of the desk, with the air of a cat tiring of a dead mouse. "Russia is a brutally large land, filled with peasants who follow peasant pursuits. I understand their miserable lots make them prodigious drinkers, especially of a potent distillation of rye. No doubt the spirit in this jar was that brew so common in Russia and yet so rare here."

"Given the fellow's condition when you ran him down, I can only hope it will continue to be rare here."

Holmes nodded, and stood.

"I say, Mr. Holmes, do you not wish to see this man for yourself? He is sober now, and we have retained the translator."

Holmes didn't hesitate. "That is most kind and prescient of you, Inspector Lestrade, but I have no need to interview the man. There is no doubt he attacked the woman we found, as you could have proved had not your fellow policemen trampled the ground about her body until all traces of a bootprint missing a large nail were erased. I suggest you examine the bottom of Chernyshev's boots, but it will only show the futility of prosecuting him. For want of a nail. . . . Still, I would keep an eye on him."

"But Mr. Holmes! This man may be the Ripper! Have you no interest in pursuing the matter?"

"No. He is all yours, I am happy to say. I'll bid you good day."

It was not often that I was as shocked as Inspector Lestrade by Holmes's unpredictable approaches to crime solving.

I finally scrambled out of my chair, nodded farewell to the stunned inspector, and hastened after Holmes.

15.

The Wild East Show

*Wild Magyar horsemen tumbled down the Carpathian
passes in the late ninth century....*
—THOMAS REIMER, A GERMAN HUNGARIAN HISTORIAN

⊰ FROM A JOURNAL ⊱

 Our train had pushed beyond Frankfurt toward Vienna
when I first spied the riders.

They came at a distant angle at first, then soon galloped
alongside us. The horses' ribbon-caparisoned halters, reins,
and saddles fluttered with rainbow motion, but the riders'
full-sleeved and trousered garb was no less colorful.

"I see why Colonel Cody hails the horsemen of the world in
his show," I noted, standing on the shuddering train to look out
the window with my nose pressed against the glass. "Who or what
are these wild men?"

"Magyars," Irene says, leaning forward to regard them. "Cousins
and mortal enemies of Turks and Huns. Hundreds of years of
mounted battle beat beneath the hooves of their steeds."

Her voice took on the thrilling tone of a melodrama, or an
endless Sarah Bernhardt death scene. She is like Bram Stoker: if it

is a cast of hundreds and cost thousands, it is Theater, even if it is real. Perhaps especially if it is real.

"Bandits do this," I said, breathless myself as I sat to pull out my journal and began scribbling penciled notes. "In the American West. They run down trains and stop them dead, then rob the passengers."

"Bandits operate worldwide." Irene reached into the side pocket of the "surprise" dress that carried something Nell never would have when she wore it: a small black pistol. "We move into mountainous country. That is where civilization loosens its grip and the Old Ways win out again."

"Do those men really mean to stop our train and rob us?"

Irene shook her head. "I don't think so. They are showing off. They are a mere distraction."

"A distraction for what?"

"Watch and see," she said with an irritating smile. It was not that the smile was irritating; it was the fact that she smiled at such an uneasy time that was irritating.

I saw that despite the drawn pistol, she was not afraid, not even were Billy the Kid to board our train.

Then neither should I be!

Our train did not stop, but the engine did jerk and spit up a long grade like a balky mount.

Not long after that I heard bootheels pounding down the passage.

At our door they stopped.

A fierce, mustachioed face peered in at us through the frosted glass.

The door sprung wide. A man in high-heeled boots of mad design and a military uniform trellised in gold braid invaded our compartment.

He strode at once to the window, tapping upon it with a long-barreled pistol that was as gilded as his uniform.

The riders came galloping alongside, men whose foot-long mustaches whipped back like their mounts' long black tails. They lifted sleeves as ruffled as a seventeenth-century English cavalier's and flourished rifles before they careened away at the same diagonal with which they had intercepted us. I watched the black manes of their pale gray mounts grow small and become as wispy as storm clouds on the horizon.

"What magnificent beasts!" I exclaimed.

"The horses, or the men?" Irene asked, turning from me to our guest—our invader—before I could, in all honesty, choose. "Well met, Bassanio."

"This is no Rialto." The officer sat without invitation, doffing his savage bearskin helmet.

I eyed his slanted black mustaches and eyebrows, his flushed, swarthy face. Surely a distant descendant of Genghis Khan or . . .

"Thanks for the cabled warning, Quentin," Irene said. "Kelly was seen in Neunkirchen. We are on the right trail."

He nodded, still catching his breath.

"Will you not lose your horse?" I interjected.

"It was borrowed." He tossed me a glance as a soldier might unleash a grenade.

I flushed. The horses were stage props, no more. As perhaps I was.

He glanced back, observed my high color, and made a brisk bow. "I am sorry my unannounced appearance startled you, Miss Pink."

"No more so than the Ripper," I replied as tartly as Nell might have.

At the same instant the expression in his eyes recognized, welcomed, and then blanched at my evocation.

I was surprised at myself as well. It was as if Nell accompanied us in some unseen way. Like Irene, I was unexpectedly taking on her coloration. Had this meek nonentity really had such an effect on us, on all of us?

From the sudden silence on the dashing Quentin Stanhope's part, apparently so.

"What have you learned?" Irene asked.

"Gypsies, of course, travel east. And west."

"You have learned nothing more of them?"

He lounged back in the velvet upholstery, the spurs on his bright leatherwork boots chiming. "I have found the horse with the misshapen shoe."

"Are you sure?"

"The American Indian's description was Johnny-on-the-spot: a mark like a mare's-tail cloud in the sky. Almost like a tilde to my eye."

"And—?" Irene was breathless with impatience.

"The caravan it pulled is heading east, accompanied by the usual packs of dogs and children walking alongside."

"And?"

"Nothing else. No passengers but Gypsies. No fleeing English upholsterer, no hooded devil worshipers. Just Gypsies: close-mouthed, grimy, proud."

"Then our party has all transferred to trains."

"Perhaps not."

Irene and I regarded Quentin Stanhope with intense interest.

"No one unusual has passed through the stations that lie behind you, or ahead of you," he said. "There is no trace of an abducted woman, of a madman, or of a group of peasant foreigners."

"The only trace," Irene pointed out bitterly, "is the dead girl at Neunkirchen."

Quentin nodded. "I find the fact that there is no trail most sinister of all. It tells me that they are good at this, at being invisible when they want to be."

Irene fell back into the seat. "Then you don't doubt that they exist?"

"No. And I have learned that there is something rotten in Prague. Something no one will talk about, but that everyone suspects like an unacknowledged nightmare. A nightmare too terrible to tell anyone about. The Rothschild agents, of course, will be more forthcoming, but I left them for you. I didn't want to blunder into matters I only half grasp."

Irene nodded, glanced at the pistol still in her hand, then shrugged and replaced it in her pocket.

"The last time I was in Prague proved very dangerous," she said.

"I think the city will not disappoint your expectations," Quentin responded with a small bow.

"I am glad you are with us."

He glanced at me, as if annoyed that the "us" included me.

"I will do anything I can," he said, not looking at Irene, "to see Nell restored to her proper place by your side."

I suppressed a shiver. Dressed as he was, as some half-wild horseman of the Wild East, I could well believe that he was eager to unseat Nell's usurper by any means he could find.

Was Godfrey Norton anything like this hard-edged adventurer? Overcivilized Englishmen made my head ache, but uncivilized Englishmen reminded me of wolves.

16.

Nell Ungirds Her Loins

~·~

As Lady Russell said, the English conclude if your
dress is loose, that your morals are also. In that case I
am thoroughly dissolute.
—MRS. SARAH AUSTIN, 1862

"I am afraid you are not at all saved, Nell," Godfrey told
me with deep regret, "but merely join me in the state of
needing to be."

I blinked, not yet being sufficiently revived to understand the fine point of accuracy that barristers are wont to
put on their simplest musings as if every sentence were a newly
sharpened quill.

Besides, as my senses returned I became aware of various un-
pleasantries. Foremost among them was the light that glared behind
Godfrey, turning him into a mere silhouette of a man. It seared my
poor eyes that had been confined to dark and close places for God
knew how long.

"Irene," I murmured.

"She is safe, well?"

"I don't know!" My voice had become a cronelike croak. "I last glimpsed her by the light of that demonic hellfire with those naked, murderous, mad things dancing around her."

"Good God, Nell! Where have you two been?"

"To *l'Exposition universelle* in Paris."

"*L'Exposition universelle*—? Your mind must be wandering. The Exposition is a place of wonder and entertainment. Perhaps I should ask *when* you last saw Irene."

"Why"—I had to think. I had to think to say anything at the moment—"on Joan of Arc's birthday, of course."

"Joan of Arc's birthday?! Since when do you mark the calendar by Joan of Arc's birthday?"

"Poor Godfrey. You have sorely lost sense during our separation, having to repeat everything I say like that annoying parrot Casanova. It was actually Joan of Arc's . . . feast day. That is it: a French Papist observation alien to Protestant Englishmen: May the thirtieth."

Godfrey sank away from me, the movement allowing the light behind him to fall upon his pale features. "May the thirtieth! But this is June the sixth, according to my best calculations. What can have happened to Irene since in so long as that?" His worried eyes returned to me. "What can have happened to you?"

"It was horrible!" I began to recall just how awful, despite my muffled, pounding headache. "Two terrible brutes trapped me in the panorama building outside the cavern. A panorama is a peculiarly French attraction, for they are always a circuitous sort. It is a circular building lined with a huge panoramic painting of a crowd scene, only this one turned like a top . . . not the painting, but the building. It was not open at that early hour of the morning, of course, and shuttered and dark inside, but some villains set the mechanism rotating, so I was quite dizzy and made even more so when a man came out of nowhere from among the wax figures and tried to smother me with a thick, sick-smelling cloth. Then I was crammed into a box—like a coffin—and knocked about for a good long time. Irene had mentioned long ago a 'vampire box' they use on stage for trick appearances, but mine was a disappearance."

Even as I recalled the circumstances of my abduction, I became more fully aware of its physical results. I ached and burned from head to foot. After so long supine in a box, I could barely take a breath deep enough to support more than a few sentences, for my corset felt like the relentless embrace of an Iron Maiden. I also was beginning to detect a ghastly foul smell, and feared that I might be its source.

"Oh, Godfrey! I have spent *all that time* in these same clothes!"

Most men would have been insensitive to my predicament or outraged sensibility, but Godfrey immediately was moved to action.

"Unthinkable! I'll return in an instant."

His shadowy figure vanished as swiftly as a withdrawn lantern shutter, leaving the blurred white daylight from the window beyond to sear my weakened eyes like live coals.

I shut my eyelids, now welcoming the dark I had feared during all my journey. Perhaps I had imagined Godfrey's comforting presence. Perhaps I was still in my jolting coffin, my mobile vampire box. No wonder every bone and centimeter of flesh on my body throbbed!

I almost sobbed, save that the breath I caught and held became a girdle of fire around my chest.

"I'm back," Godfrey announced. "We are in a castle, but all we have for servants are cats and rats."

"So like a Grimm fairy tale," I murmured. Perhaps I had awakened in one of those folk parables.

Something like a cloud floated over me.

"This is a fine lawn nightgown, Nell. It will serve as a dressing chamber for you, for no woman you would care to have touch you is available here to assist you. You say you are having trouble breathing?"

"Well, yes, my—" How should I explain my predicament with the corset to Godfrey, who was not even a physician? "I have been cruelly bounced from pillar to post and now you say I am in a castle?"

"A castle of rogues and phantoms, alas, and no very fine place at all. I think I can guess your quandary. Now don't breathe for a few moments."

While he had been talking, Godfrey had pulled the voluminous fabric over me like a tent. Then he reached within it, and I felt a strange pressure at my ribs. For an instant my pain multiplied, and I couldn't restrain a cry. But the wail ended in a relieved sigh as my tortured lungs and bones suddenly expanded, at last unfettered from whalebone and cotton lacing.

I realized that the metal hooks and eyes at the corset front had been pinched together until they burst apart. Only a man's great strength could accomplish this instant unbinding. I was very glad then that when Godfrey wed Irene he had assumed some of my former duties as ladies' maid. And I recalled another instance when another man in other circumstances had so loosed me. I would have blushed, but I was too weak to do so.

Every new breath came more deeply, and more painfully, so I felt both relieved and yet more tormented than ever.

"Now." Godfrey's fingers were working at the many horn buttons fastening the front of my coatdress. "You must permit me some liberties. You have been cruelly confined, in every respect, for days."

Although I trusted the motives and refinement of Godfrey above that of all men on earth, his attack on the buttons reminded me so vividly of the demented creature with the pale, mad eyes pawing at my bodice in the panorama building that it was all I could do to keep still and avoid screaming.

Yet as the heavy wool gown came away like a husk, I again felt such welcome relief that I could not stop myself from weeping.

"If you were taken in Paris," Godfrey was saying, "and confined to a box, you must have been a prisoner for almost a week and have traveled by coach, boat, and railway train. Did they feed you, give you water?"

"I can't remember. I don't know what they did to me, or who they were, save that I was always very sick and a sweetly medicinal smell hovered over me the entire time."

"Some drug, possibly chloroform. We are at least fed here from time to time. I will try to get you some broth or soup."

"We?" For an insane moment, I hoped he would tell me that Irene was here with us after all and that it was all a nightmare that was over and the Rothschilds expected us to dinner at eight.

"I am speaking of you and I. There. The dress is off. Perhaps you can manage the other things as you gain strength."

My arms had not yet fought their way into the nightshirt's full sleeves. I sought to pull the loosened corset from under my body, but the effort was too taxing.

I became aware then that the sweet, sickly odor which had been my constant companion, almost a guardian angel during my ordeal, was finally fading. In its place rose some extremely impolite odors that I realized to my horror came from me, odors common on the debased streets of a district like Whitechapel, no doubt, but utterly foreign to a decently reared female of any sensibility at all.

After all I had survived, I could have now gladly died on the spot.

"And I will order the makings of a bath from these savages," Godfrey said. "I cannot provide a maid whose aid you would deign to accept but perhaps after some soup and water, er, soap and water and soup, you will be stronger and can manage to tend to yourself."

At that he withdrew like the gentleman he was, leaving me to take inventory of my truly lamentable state and to wonder where on earth we were and among what unutterably savage monsters that cats and rats should seem finer housemates than human beings.

17.

Sterner Stuff

Our sons are made of sterner stuff, but less winning are
their caresses.
—EURIPEDES, *THE SUPPLIANTS*

⊰ F R O M   A   J O U R N A L ⊱

"First, Quentin," Irene told our new and quite illegal fellow
passenger, "I believe you need to explain to Pink your current garb and headlong method of boarding trains."

"Really, no!" I demurred. Quentin Stanhope did not
look like a man who was pleased to explain himself to anybody.

At the moment, however, he was engaged in deeply regarding
me. Taken aback, I closed my journal and inserted my pencil in
the silver tube mechanism that was both its holder and a lock for
the book.

"It's simple," he said at last, stretching his booted legs toward
the empty side of the seat opposite where Irene sat alone. He had
chosen to sit alongside me, perhaps the better to discourse with
Irene across the compartment. I found his presence most oppressive.

"This eastern part of Europe is a string of petty principalities, some long ago knuckled under to the Austro-Hungarian Empire, some maintaining a precarious independence. Each duchy has its officious tyrant, and the tyrants in turn have their gaudy military forces. My current guise combines the features of a dozen over-bearing uniforms common to the region. Wherever I go, I am taken for a pompous, garlanded popinjay from the neighboring satrapy. So I go unchallenged but not much respected, an ideal position for a spy."

"In addition," Irene said, having long before returned her pistol to Nell's innocuous pocket, "you may leap upon any operetta stage in Europe and melt into the chorus at an instant's notice."

Mr. Stanhope stroked his false mustaches, perhaps horsehair, and smiled. "On occasion the best disguise is the most extravagant, a lesson you learned long ago, Madam Diva."

I could not restrain comment. "Then I must stick out like a sore thumb in my checked wool cloth and cap."

"A charming ensemble," he said with a bow. "I wish I could wear something as lightweight, neat, and practical."

Somehow those words did not cheer me.

"Pink's garb is more than practical," Irene put in. "It resembles the clothing Nell was wearing when last seen. We have but to use her as a living reference point if we wish to question persons along the way."

"I chose this myself, at *Le Bon Marché*."

"And a brilliant ploy it was." Irene went on while I reflected that I had all unthinking managed to duplicate Nell's manner of dress. "We are also equipped with a cabinet sketch of James Kelly, the demon upholsterer of the Rue Caron. Its presence has already borne fruit."

"Then this mad upholsterer is responsible for the sad death behind us?" he demanded.

Irene nodded. "The ticketmaster identified him as a man lacking money for passage . . . and returning later with the fare in fistfuls of coppers."

Quentin frowned as if he would like to have James Kelly in his own fists.

"Such a death as met the flower girl at Neunkirchen," Irene said as gently as she would address a child, "was merciful compared to what the victims in London and Paris faced, when the killer had more time and less obvious motive."

"Tell me about that," he said. "Tell me about Nell."

Irene stirred uneasily on the plush train upholstery. I thought she would produce her smoking case and lucifers, but she didn't.

"Godfrey was abroad," she began, "on Rothschild business. Had he been in Paris, would Baron de Rothschild have called upon him instead of me? I don't know. However, murder is not beyond my ken, and murder is what needed investigating: two women at a bordello patronized by the leading men of Europe. Inspector le Villard of the Paris police, whom I know, came to fetch me, along with his superior, the Prefect himself."

"You could hardly refuse such a summons."

"I never would refuse such a summons. Unfortunately, Nell insisted on accompanying me, despite the demurs of two very insistent police authorities."

"There is no one as adamant as an English governess."

"As a former governess," Irene corrected. "And she had been a shop girl and typewriter girl by then, as well as an instructress of a foulmouthed parrot and my shadow at two death scenes. But what we found at that *maison de rendezvous* was brutal beyond anything we two could ever have imagined."

"Oh, come now!" I couldn't keep from saying. "I was the first one to spy out that scene, and stomach-turning as it was, Nell was not the unprepared innocent you portray. She'd followed the newspaper reports of the Ripper case last autumn like a three-year-old overdosing on sweets before Christmas, as she herself confessed. 'Had a weakness for ghost stories as a child.' Was as bloodthirsty as a little Apache, more like it. I'm sorry, but it won't do her any good being painted as a swooning ninny. I don't see why you two always have to tread on eggs about her."

While I believe in plainspeaking, I'm not at all surprised when it's not well received.

Quentin Stanhope regarded me as coldly as only an Englishman can, but I had withstood the icy eye of Sherlock Holmes when he was ordering me what to do and that was a chillier regard than any I had met on earth thus far.

"Who *is* this woman?" he asked Irene in a way meant to put me in my place: nonexistent.

Irene joined him in discussing me as if I were a butterfly pinned in a specimen box and quite deaf, not to mention dead.

"She is a blunt, American newspaper reporter who goes by the pen name of Nellie Bly. She has masqueraded as an inmate in sweatshops, madhouses, and brothels. She is a brave woman but perhaps has forgotten that reading about murderous thrills and chills is quite different from encountering them personally. Yet she is right in one thing, Quentin: Nell, the most peaceful and domestic of female souls, has always had a great interest in the gory, the frightful, the sensational. It was she who quickly educated me to the depredations of Jack the Ripper in London, down to the disembowelings."

"Nell?" He remained smugly disbelieving. "You'll forgive me, Irene, but a child may pretend to a certain swagger as a matter of self-protection. You should not have allowed her to follow you along this brutal path, particularly these—what do you call them now?"

"Lust-murders. And it is not I who named them, but a certain German aristocrat, Baron Richard von Krafft-Ebing."

"Lust-murders." Quentin Stanhope's frown became a glower, and given his current costume, he truly looked as ferocious as a Hun. "It would be like exposing my dear niece Allegra to a tour of Bluebeard's castle. I can't condone it."

"She insisted! You know how adamant Nell can be."

Again I intervened. "I recall she was quite boastful about having visited the Paris Morgue before, when you found the drowned man."

"Drowned man?" Quentin's alert gaze bored into Irene's face again. "I'd not heard of that."

"You've not heard of many of Nell's and my adventures, perhaps because you never stay in one place long enough for a good story-telling session. Nell is not the sheltered miss you knew in London more than ten years ago, Quentin, any more than you are the coddled young gentleman-about-town. You know that there are stories of your life on the steppes and in the Hindu Kush that would whiten our hair to hear. Give us poor sheltered European ladies credit for having a few adventures of our own."

"American!" I put in. "You and I are American, and I have never been sheltered."

Quentin Stanhope ended the discussion by lifting his gauntleted hands in a gesture that was both surrender and a command for peace.

"We should not argue when dear lives are in the balance. I had thought one reason I was facing those maddening brutalities in the far corners of the world was to keep the wolves from the doors at home. But Saucy Jack and his ilk have clearly broken down the barriers." He glanced at me. "You can't realize what a shock it is to see Irene traveling hand-in-glove with a woman not Nell."

"Oh, don't worry," I reassured him with a grin. "We are far from hand-in-glove. It is more like hand-in-shackle."

My bitter undertone made him raise his eyebrows at Irene, but he didn't pursue the subject, at least not while I was present.

"What you both are saying," he summed up, "is that Nell is made of sterner stuff than I think. That may be some comfort as we fumble our way to finding her, and Godfrey, but how are we to be sure that following the killer of these women in London, Paris, and now Neunkirchen will lead to our companions?"

"Exactly!" I put in.

"I don't doubt it from what you told me of the deviltry afoot in those two great cities," he told her. "Still, it goads me to be but a step behind such a killer. And there is more troubling news."

Irene said nothing to encourage revelations, just watched and listened. It was odd to see her ceding center stage to another. Then I realized that danger had made more or less equals of us all, and she did not have an audience of her betters whose attention and assistance she needed to cajole and command.

"What is it?" she asked quietly.

"My sources among the Rothschild and British government agents, who have given me carte blanche thanks to the hidden aid of persons whose identity and high office I can only guess at, have all found disturbing traces. There was a party ahead of us, ahead of Kelly, all the way from Verdun, with luggage enough that some was loaded into the baggage car, from Verdun to . . . a final destination. Prague."

"Prague. I cannot say I am surprised. This was Godfrey's most recent posting for the Rothschilds." Irene managed to look both hopeful and troubled.

"So you said," Quentin pressed. "Do you know what his mission was?"

Irene shook her head as if irritated by her own ignorance. "It was a private commission between him and them. What sort of trusted agent would tell his wife the details, even if she was so thoughtless as to ask? I would no more ask you what your instructions from the Foreign Office were. Are."

His smile made the dangling mustaches bracketing his mouth into wry parentheses. "Discretion is a rare virtue in a wife."

"Discretion is a rare virtue in anyone, I have found. However," Irene added with a raised eyebrow, "I have concluded some things about Godfrey's assignment."

"Excellent! Deduction is an established facility in wives."

I sat forward myself to learn if Irene had withheld matters from me that she would share with an old friend.

"I believe that Godfrey was engaged upon vital but extremely dull matters of international property and political concerns," she said, most disappointing me. "National alignments in this part of the world shift like chessmen on a board and have for centuries. Godfrey's approach to any legal entanglements arising from this chronically volatile condition would be an impeccable blend of foresight, tact, and unexpected daring. He adores the red tape and fine points of legal discourse, yet is quite willing to turn them on end for his own purpose, or perhaps for a perceived greater good. I admit that such cerebral skirmishes bore me, but if Godfrey encountered trouble on such a mission, it would be because he was more than certain parties expected."

"Including the parties for whom he was acting?"

Irene sighed and smiled at the same time. "Especially the parties for whom he was acting. He demands a certain standard of himself, and of his associates. It is, at times, annoying to one and all."

Quentin Stanhope laughed. "Still, they hire him."

"As the Foreign Office continues to employ you: they know they can find no more honest agent. Your refusal to accept the official version of events at the disastrous battle of Maiwand eventually exposed two dangerous spies in the region: Tiger and Sable."

"But only years later, when everyone had forgotten the unnecessary deaths caused that day."

"The dead remain so. Tiger and Sable remain alive and dangerous."

He rested his forehead in his hand, stroking his sunburnt brow as if it throbbed. "We've heard little from or of them. They may be pretty toothless by now, or dead of their schemes and counter-schemes. Old battles, Irene; hoary foes. I have made an ancient land my home and myself into an anachronism."

"How lucky, then, that an anachronism is precisely what I need at the moment. Godfrey mentioned a murder in one of his letters, in passing." She smiled again, ruefully. "To Godfrey bloody murder will always take second place to the thrilling crimes of international appropriations, treaty violations, and legal atrocities involving state seizure of property."

"These are the matters you think have led him astray into deep personal danger?"

Irene nodded. "What do you think, Pink?"

I was startled from my intense mental recording of this exchange for later entry into my journal.

Nell was so right about one thing, and one thing only! "Think,

Pink" indeed! Still, my lowly opinion had been sought, and I would give it, even if it was not what my hostess wanted to hear.

"I think that James Kelly is laying the trail to follow and that the gory murder of a young woman in Prague, as mentioned by Godfrey himself as noteworthy, is the obvious incident to investigate next. As for this Golem man-monster of Prague that is suspected of reviving just in time to do this latest dirty deed, he sounds like a fantastical scapegoat to me. Still, he does remind one of those nasty sayings found in London and Paris about the Jews not being the ones who will be blamed for nothing, or whatever phrase that so contradicted itself. Follow the Ripper and we will find Godfrey, and Nell. If they're still alive to find. That's my opinion."

My forthright views may not have won instant seconding, but they certainly silenced Irene and Quentin for some time.

18.

A Lukewarm Baptism

After Godfrey's departure, I found myself plunged into a troubled stupor I certainly could not describe as anything so refreshing as "sleep."

I also found myself starting awake, as though the thought of sleep itself had become a torment. Yet a moment later I would again plummet off the cliff of consciousness into this uneasy waking dream.

In one vague interval someone had come and gone without my noticing. I gazed during one of my instant waking periods at a huge tub that now sat atop the thick turkey rug, steam rising from its rolled copper lips.

I had managed, in my linen-wrapped tossings, to unbutton and work off my petticoats, which now coagulated at my ankles in a gray froth of much-abused ruffles. I still half-lay on the rigid corpse of my split-asunder corset, too weak to work it out from under me. Only such hard goods as my walking boots and the many chains and charms upon my silver chatelaine were salvageable. At some time during the long ordeal, the checked cap that matched the coatdress had been shed like an autumn leaf.

The sight of the steaming tub inspired me to action beyond my current strength. I arranged to slide off the bed, leaving my under-clothes behind in an unappetizing pile like a skin-shedding snake. At least I was still shrouded by the nightgown Godfrey had brought me. I remained snakelike despite my dislike for the creatures: I had to crawl rather than walk to the oasis of cleanliness that awaited me like a desert-heated mirage.

I thought of Quentin Stanhope fleeing the slaughter at the battle of Maiwand in Afghanistan, half-conscious, crawling through end-less dunes of rock and sand.

With such a stalwart example in mind, I finally came to the warm copper vessel. I knew I needed an attendant, but believed Godfrey when he said that I would not care to suffer the assistance of anyone native to the place.

The windows, two arched Gothic panels flung wide like an an-gel's wings on a vista of heavenly blue sky, told me that my chamber was at some great height only a lizard could escape, else why taunt prisoners with unguarded openings?

Lizards. I shuddered. Why was I thinking of miserable crawling things? Perhaps because I had been reduced to their low animal form of animation myself?

I was able to get to my knees and gratefully inhale the hot clean mists rolling off the water. At least someone had heated it royally.

Finally I trembled my way upright, or half-upright. My lower limbs shook with the effort, and my poor ribs burned as if goaded by hot pokers.

Lifting the gown's voluminous skirts around my knees, I stepped into the shallow end of the tub. Slowly I immersed myself, arranging the copious folds of my gown over the tub's edges as a sort of tent.

I would not stand unclothed before those open windows, even

if only clouds and hawks could peer in. I felt no security in this aerie of stone and wood, and in this most abysmal moment of my life could bear having no witness, not even a mouse from a hole in the wall.

The water was warm and enveloping. At first it stung my abused skin in a hundred places, but soon it comforted. I glanced at the huge copper ewer intended for rinsing. Beside it on the carpet lay a sharp-edged block of yellow soap, big enough to fill the hand of a giant.

Even from where I sat, I could see a slick of black-edged bubbles on the bar of soap's surface. Who knew what filthy sort of person had used it before me? Yet my numerous stings and cuts needed cleansing, and the inherited dirt would soon dissipate in the fresh water of my bath. So I leaned over—ouch!—to seize and baptize it in the untainted water.

It rose up cleaner. I began to rub it on my extremities, wincing at the clumsy shape and sharp corners. Soon my once-pristine water was cloudier than the sky outside my window.

I slipped the nightdress over my arms and left it draped across the foot of the tub. Then I closed my eyes, held my breath, and submerged my head and face, hair and all.

Milky water closed over me like warm silken sheets. A gentle shroud, it sheltered me from any unkind eye. I surfaced and lathered my sadly tangled hair once, twice, three times, producing a fleecy blanket of bubbles on the surface of the water by the time I finished.

Examining the floor again, I discovered a large, rough oblong of pale linen. My towel, I supposed.

This I dabbed at my hair and face, then my arms, until I was able to wrap it around myself, rise to my unsteady feet in the rapidly cooling tub water, and pull the nightgown into service again.

Not much later I was dripping on the rug but decently covered, and theoretically cleaner. I paced back and forth, hoping the motion would dry me more. In so doing, I discovered a dressing table jammed into a dark corner, with a mirror hung above it.

The still-stinging wounds aggravated by soap and water tempted me to the mirror. Once before it, I saw the surface glowed with the reflected light of the window. I discreetly elevated first one portion, then another of my gown, examining myself. I gasped to see the red-purple blotches left by the corset stays and huge bruises as gruesome as a bloody sunset all over my body.

No wonder I ached and burned so!

Worse than that actual discomfort was the uneasy suspicion that intrusions more foul than mere knocking-about might have been performed upon my unconscious form. I closed my eyes. Behind them a man's rapacious figure came streaking for me like a bird of prey, all gleaming, focused eyes and reaching talons . . . who knew what had happened to me during the captivity that was but a blur in my memory?

James Kelly had held a blade to my throat in his mean lodgings, and I had escaped. But who knew what he had done during all my unremembered days and nights of captivity?

Someone knew, I told myself with a shudder. Several someones. All of my unknown abductors, for more than one man had participated in my capture.

When Godfrey knocked at my door an hour or two later, I was mostly dry and sitting with my feet tucked up under me on the bed.

I had kicked my discarded clothes into a pile beside the cold bathwater.

"Nell. Good. You look better."

He eyed the malodorous pile by the copper tub. "Perhaps we could, er, wash these things in the cooling water."

"Godfrey, 'these things' are not worth the washing. I do not even want to contemplate what they went through, much less myself. I wish them burned."

"But . . . unlike myself you were not traveling with luggage. What will you wear?"

I inspected him, aware for the first time of my companion's dress.

It was perfectly ordinary: his own tweed lounge suit so suitable for traveling, as my yellow-and-brown checked coatdress had once been. . . .

"Nell! What is it? Have I said something to upset you?"

"Nothing. I merely . . . mourn the much kinder past. I want these things burned."

"Possibly the . . . people who serve here might produce some apparel you could wear, but it would not be . . . conventional."

"Filth is not conventional either. Burn them."

I had not meant to sound imperious. Indeed, I had never before sounded imperious in my life but apparently my extreme distaste for any souvenir of my awful captivity had convinced Godfrey. He swept the things into a bundle and deposited it in the head-high hearth on the chamber's inside wall. A long match soon scratched the stone, and I watched the past week succumb to a slow fire.

Someone knocked at a door.

I started and huddled back into the pillows. My bed was huge enough to host Napoleon and most of his marshals. The tapestried curtains hung down like locks from a powdered wig, accented along the fold with pale swathes of dust.

I sneezed.

Godfrey went to his bedroom chamber door. I glimpsed a tray supported by bare female arms.

He spoke, an odd combination of English, German, and a bit of Bohemian, I think. He returned with a silver tray covered with cracked and crude pottery.

One such piece held a thick sort of soup in which floated a few deep red husks.

"I've eaten here for more than a week, and survived." Godfrey sat at the foot of my bed to lay the tray before me. "They favor highly spiced fare wherever we are, but it is hearty. I asked for broth, and you see that I have gotten stew."

"And dead red worms," I added, peering at the offending particles.

"Those are peppers, Nell. Don't eat them if you don't fancy fireworks on your tongue. But they appear harmless. If our captors had wanted to poison us, they could have done it by now."

"Our captors! Have you any idea who, Godfrey?"

"Gypsy wagons visit the yard far below, but Gypsies are as common as cows in Poland, Bohemia, Austria, and Transylvania, where I think we now are."

"Transylvania? It sounds a pleasant, forested land."

"It is a mountainous, remote land, as much of Europe is the farther East it goes. We are almost on the edge of the mysterious East."

"There is nothing mysterious about the East except why Englishmen should be enchanted by it."

"Not I. I am enchanted by the West. And how is she, our Irene?"

"I don't know, Godfrey, that is what torments me! I left her surrounded by the Baron de Rothschild's agents and Buffalo Bill and Red Tomahawk, as well as a coven of the most debased witches and warlocks a good Christian woman could imagine in her worst nightmares."

"This is not reassuring, Nell, Rothschild agents or not. 'Buffalo Bill?' 'Red Tomahawk?' "

"Famous scouts from the American Wild West. They were our allies, fierce as they were, and we sorely needed fierce allies in that place. I will never forget Red Tomahawk's bloodcurdling war cry as he leapt to his hide-covered feet to hurl his battle-axe across the fire-lit cavern and into the man who was . . . well, doing something he shouldn't have been to this poor, demented woman, but then they were all demented and leaping about like demons."

"Witches. Warlocks. Demons. Given what I have seen here at this castle, I am more likely to believe in demons than I once was. But try some of this soup, or stew, Nell, before you lose what little appetite you have."

"Why do I feel so . . . lost? I have lost time, memories, some sense of my self—"

"The drugs they gave you were disorienting. I suspect that you were shipped across half of Europe like so much hard goods."

"My head still aches! Everything aches. I have never understood why someone would willingly take such drugs."

"What do you know of people willingly taking drugs?"

"I? Nothing. Only that I have read . . . things. Oh, my head throbs so! Do not tax me, Godfrey."

He responded by lifting a large pot-metal spoon, somewhat dented, to my lips. In its bowl congregated an assortment of alien vegetables and some stringy strands of chicken.

"You must recover your appetite, Nell, if we are ever to escape."

"Escape?" The word so cheered me that I slurped some of the mess into my mouth. It was impossible not to slurp.

"Indeed. We are kept like a fallen prince and princess in a tower so high and remote we might as well be set like a cap on the widow's peak of the world."

"Oh, dear! And where in the world is this widow's peak located?"

"In an obscure chain of mountains known as the Carpathians. They are the barrier that kept the bloody Turk from running rampant over Austria and Germany and Poland and France and even England. I have been using the dusty library shelves in my bedchamber, not having much else to do. There is quite a range of languages, including English. A charming chap named Vlad the Impaler turned the tide by literally crucifying the invading Turks by the thousands."

"Oh," I said, thinking how useful Vlad the Impaler would have been in the cavern under *l'Exposition universelle*. Ordinarily I am not in favor of barbarians, but having seen the barbarous acts performed in that cave, I was ready to call up Lucifer Himself to our defense if need be.

"Irene must be all right," Godfrey declared.

"How can you be sure?"

"Because Rothschild agents would fall before Irene would fall, and I do not think they did. And you mention how successful the fierce Indian of the American West known as Red Tomahawk was in throwing his axe. You are vague about the misdoings of the barbarous persons in the cavern but I suspect that Wild West fighters, Rothschild agents, and Irene were sufficient to handle them. Did she bring her pistol?"

"Yes."

"Well, that settles it then."

"I must admit that Irene forced me to run from the field of battle and that I did not see its conclusion."

"Why did she do that?"

I shuddered and sipped more soup to warm my courage. "There was a dreadful man we tracked. Mad and a murderer. James Kelly. Irene thinks . . . we all think, thought, he is . . . was . . . Jack the Ripper."

"Jack the Ripper!" Godfrey drew back, and withdrew the warming soup as well. "Jack the Ripper. That was in London. Months ago. What has Jack the Ripper to do with you, and Irene, and Paris? And this spring?"

"Oh, Godfrey, that is such a tale! If James Kelly is truly Jack the Ripper, then I have had his knife-hand at my throat. . . ."

"Nell! That is not an achievement."

The soup was placed upon a bedside table, forgotten. Godfrey's pale gray eyes were blazing like polished sterling silver. He was the wisest, most handsome, and kindest of men. I had almost forgotten that he, too, could be very fierce.

"I rather thought it was. I stuck him with my hat pin."

"You stuck Jack the Ripper with a hatpin?"

"If any of those poor women in Whitechapel had been wearing a more fashionable hat as opposed to a mere bonnet that ties on, they would have needed a hatpin and would have been better equipped to defend themselves."

"I, er, suppose so. In fact, I wish I had a hatpin here."

"We do!"

"We do?"

"I fished it out of the tangle that had been made of my hair during my . . . ah, ablutions." ("Bath" seemed too forward a word to use with an unrelated male.) "I wore a cap with my coatdress, but it lacked ribbons and was not of a mind to stay put, no matter how jaunty it looked, so I skewered it with my twelve-inch hatpin, on an angle from front visor to back chignon, so it would not be noticeable."

"I see," said Godfrey, who clearly did not. "Apparently it escaped the notice of your captors. Where is this redoubtable hat pin now?"

I tried to avoid glancing down at my *poitrine*. (Which is also called a *decollétage*. Sometimes French words are very useful. But not often.) "This nightgown you provided was quite voluminous, but the front placket was mysteriously . . . deep. I was forced to affix it into some semblance of modesty with the hatpin."

"The placket was designed for a male wearer. So you have a foot-long hatpin holding your nightshirt together?"

I glanced down at my modestly closed gown. "It works perfectly."

"So long as you do not toss and turn in your sleep! Nell, I must have it."

"I cannot remain modest and give up my hatpin."

"You cannot remain breathing and not."

"It is as serious as that?"

"We are in the hands of Irene's worst enemies."

"Not ours?"

"We are mere pawns, but the game is deadly. Think of the enormity of arranging the abduction of us both, one in Paris and one traveling from Prague. It took planning. It took patience. And it took nerve."

"But why?" I asked, surrendering the pin and clamping the gown together by hand in its place.

"If we knew why, we'd be on our way out of here. And if Irene knew why, she'd be here, shortly. But we cannot rely on distant aid. We are in the soup together, dear Nell." He glanced at my crude bowl. "We must first survive, and then we must escape."

He finished by stabbing my hatpin through the lining of his jacket where it could not be seen, like an invisible sword in a fabric sheath.

A sword big enough for an elf, and we would have to fight ogres.

19.

Sentimental Journey

~ঃ৮চ~

*She isn't much for style, but what she has to say
she says right out.*
—GEORGE MADDEN, EDITOR OF *THE PITTSBURG DISPATCH*, 1885

◁ F R O M   A   J O U R N A L ▷

Quentin Stanhope proved to be less of a traveling companion than a uniformed jack-in-the-box.

At each stop, he would hasten off the train. While Irene
and I availed ourselves of comfort stations and ate lunch—
when there was time—or purchased food from station ven-
dors for the journey, Quentin had better business to be about. He
sent cablegrams, interrogated station workers, and roamed even farther afield.

Sometimes he rejoined us in our compartment for the next leg
of the journey. Sometimes he did not join us until the next stop,
or several.

Like a lady on a ballroom floor anticipating a waltz, Irene
seemed content to allow him to lead. She spent the long hours
jolting along the tracks and through the hilly countryside studying
Nell's notes and drawings of the Paris attack sites.

"Why is Sherlock Holmes so intrigued by cork and wax droppings?" she would mutter. "Obviously spirits were used to excite the—" She glanced up at me. "What shall we call these cave people, Pink? You are the wordsmith. We need something accurate but apropos."

" 'Demons' seems a little excessive."

"Nell tends to see things in extremes," she agreed, "but what else would you call participants in a drunken, dancing, yammering Roman orgy that ends in mutilation and possible death?"

"Crazy?"

"Madmen, then. It served for Jack the Ripper. Madman. Then why were women among these crazed . . . celebrants?"

"I guess women can go as crazy as men, given half a chance. Maybe more so. When I was in the madhouse, most of the inmates were female."

"As are most of the inmates in a brothel, unless the house happens to be among the minority devoted to unnatural acts. From the populations of madhouses and brothels, one could conclude that women are more insane and immoral than men are."

"Not me! The women don't hold the purse strings, that's the thing. When you don't have the money, you have to beg, steal, or starve . . . or sell your work or yourself. And then the poor things, even the sweatshop girls I worked among, what do they do on their rare days off but get drunk and let the mashers have their way with them and then they end up in the homes for fallen women. I also put in some time there in the service of a story."

Irene gazed my way, seeing inside me for a change, as if the urgency of her quest had eased off a bit. "How did you become a girl reporter, Pink?"

"The way all the best things happen. By accident."

"That's an interesting theory of life. How so?"

"Well, when I was twenty a man who called himself the Quiet Columnist wrote in *The Pittsburg Dispatch* that girls aren't good for much of anything but managing a home. Nice work if you can get out of the sweatshops and the boardinghouses and stay away from men who'll beat you as fast as look at you. He said that a woman 'outside her sphere' was a 'monstrosity.' "

"A woman's 'sphere' being—?"

"Married to a man and safe at home. He completely overlooked women who must earn their bread, like my mother and myself. I can quote the worst of it, for I carry a clipping in the front of my journal to remind me always: He wrote that 'women, who have an insatiate desire to rush into the breaches under the guise of defending their rights, but which is in reality an effort to wrest from a man certain prerogatives bequeathed him by heaven, are usually to a degree disgusting to womanly women and manly men. There is no greater abnormity than a woman in breeches, unless it is a man in petticoats.'

"That column made me so mad, I can't tell you!"

"You don't have to."

"I suppose you've been told to stick to the domestic arts a time or two as well."

"Even by no less than Sherlock Holmes. Your Pittsburg columnist seems to have gotten his 'breaches' and 'breeches' mixed up, not to mention a lot of five-dollar words that add up to nothing. You didn't find that our evening stroll in trousers made us into instant 'abnormities,' did you?"

"I do believe in gracious female dress, but admit I found wearing trousers a terrific lark."

I was eager to continue my recital of Pittsburg indignities, caught up in telling my own story for a change.

"Anyway, I sat right down and wrote a long letter telling Mr. Quiet Columnist's boss, the paper's editor, that I could so do those things and seek work, and indeed had to. I signed it 'Lonely Orphan Girl.' Q. C. seemed to think we girls all had a choice in life, when most of us don't."

"And you got a letter back."

I managed to look shame-faced, like the green girl of twenty I had been five years before. "I didn't use a return address. Women don't do that, put their names out in public like that. Even Bessie

Bramble, the one woman columnist on the newspaper, uses a pseudonym."

"I have never found anonymous indignation very satisfying," Irene said, harking back to my earlier comment.

"Anyway, Q. C.'s boss got my letter."

"His 'boss.' Such an American word," she mused. "We forget what a colorful slang we have, and so individual. 'Dear Boss.' "

She was quoting a letter attributed to Jack the Ripper, but I was off on my own story. I told the stories of others so much I had forgotten how much my own meant to me.

"I didn't say anything colorful in my letter, although I could have. Anyway, next thing I knew, there was this request in the letters to the editor column to 'Lonely Orphan Girl.' " I recited the words I would never forget in all my life. " 'If the writer of the communication signed "Lonely Orphan Girl" will send her name and address to this office, merely as a sign of good faith, she will confer a favor and receive the information she desires.' "

"That is certainly an ambiguous invitation."

"Oh, that is just the way they talk in the newspaper business. Most roundabout. The very next day I put on my best outfit, a chic little fur turban and a long, black, Russian silk cloak, and went to *The Pittsburg Dispatch* offices."

Irene had launched me on recollecting a key moment of my past. I could feel myself reverting to a raw, idealistic girl of twenty. Propelled by indignation, I had stood up in court at an early age to swear an oath and accuse my stepfather of brutality toward my mother in a shocking divorce action that saw me declared a "ward of the Armstrong County Court." Yet six years afterward, it was still hard to stand up for myself to *The Pittsburg Dispatch*.

"My, it was a big building. I had to walk up four floors to the editor's office and was so out of breath when I got there I could only whisper. The newspaper office was large and filled with men in shirtsleeves and eyeshades, all busy about their tasks, all too important to cast me a glance or ask my business.

"That very girl-blindness saw me unchallenged right to the office of the editor himself, Mr. Madden.

"The office boy pointed out Mr. Madden, who was only a few feet away. I was so relieved I said, having regained my voice, 'Oh, I expected to see an old, cross man!' "

Irene laughed so hard and long that I couldn't continue my account and fretted while she indulged herself. "Unintended flattery is always the best," she finally sputtered out. "Do go on."

"Was he surprised to see me! But he called me 'Miss' and bade me sit down and asked me about my letter and my family and all. I spoke right up and told him how I had been supporting my mother and me. Why come all this way and not?

"Well, Mr Madden was quite a jolly young man, and he asked me to submit an article on 'The Woman's Sphere.' Of course I did. After that he asked me to do another article and what topic would I like? So I said, 'Divorce.' "

"You did not take the safe route even from the beginning."

"Not talking about divorce seemed more dangerous than talking about it, especially since my mother's was one of only fifteen divorce cases in Armstrong County that year and only one of five brought by the wife."

"So an angry letter launched your career."

"No, a silly, wrongheaded column did. And I must say that Mr. Madden was ever so helpful to me, and even Mr. Erasmus Wilson, who was indeed an old man but not at all cross despite my taking issue with his column, for he was the 'Quiet Observer' and always very kind to me in person."

I paused, and had to add in all honesty, "Though they both said my style was poor and I could not write."

Here Irene shook her head. "The men are 'generous' enough to 'let' you do the work but must console themselves that you are not very good at it. *Hmmm.* It strikes me that your forthright writing style suits your subjects far better than their orotund pronouncements, from what you've quoted of them, and that you have indeed 'conferred a favor' on the journalism profession by joining it so energetically."

Her unexpected praise made me live up to my name again and blush like a stove, cherry-hot. I forgot my growing impatience with her indirect way of approaching puzzles, for I saw that she understood what I had been through to get where I am and that it took constant thought and struggle.

Quentin Stanhope was not the only one sending cables from the station. I "paid" for my secret absence by sending stories back to the *New York World,* anonymous tidbits of my brief time in a *maison de rendezvous,* including chatty reports of Buffalo Bill's encounter with the Prince of Wales and Sarah Bernhardt's tea with the Baron de Rothschild and Bertie as well. I did not mention the hostess or purpose behind these last gossipy items, nor did I tell my bosses what story I was really pursuing, only that it would be a real "corker" if I could get it.

With that fact preying on my mind, I glanced out the train window, surprised to see red tile roofs making a small mountain range below us.

"The City of a Hundred Spires," Irene said, her voice hushed.

I did indeed spy several spires thrusting like decorative thorns from the lower ridges of the red roofs.

"The last city in which I performed grand opera," she added, her tone so low that it took me a moment to interpret the words. "A city I last visited with Nell and Godfrey." These words were a whisper I had to lean nearly cheek to cheek with her to hear.

She roused from the reverie with a sudden shake of her head, as if throwing off cobwebs of paralyzing memory.

I jerked away, feeling I had crossed a forbidden threshold.

"Prague," she informed me in her ordinary, dispassionate voice, indeed a lecturer's tone, "is the most interesting city in Europe. It is, in fact, the very navel of Europe, sitting as it does at the exact center of the continent."

"I have not heard much of it," said I.

She smiled at me, with pity. "I can't decide whether Prague is blessed in that its virtues are hidden, or cursed in that the world so underestimates it and its people."

"Who are its people?"

"Who indeed? The city is built on five hills and at the juncture of several races and three great world religions: Judaism, Catholicism, and Protestantism. I list them in the order of their appearance on the world stage, so as not to play favorites."

"Isn't Prague just a part of the Austro-Hungarian Empire now?"

"That is politics. I am talking about the soul of the city. You will see, when you have spent some time here."

"How much time are we to spend here? Don't we need to catch up with Jack the Ripper quickly? If he has in fact come this way, which I don't think is very likely."

"You can't anticipate where someone will go unless you know where he has been."

"And you think Jack the Ripper has been in Prague? Just because Godfrey mentioned a brutally murdered girl in his letter? There are brutally murdered girls to be found the world over and most are not victims of Saucy Jack. Some say he has escaped to America. I'd be better off on home ground, chasing rumors, or in London, annoying Sherlock Holmes, than accompanying you on a pilgrimage to the scenes of your earlier triumphs and tender memories."

"Rumors don't make for sensational revelations on the grand scale required by a daredevil reporter," she said coldly. "And Sherlock Holmes will do more than express irritation if you interfere with his new investigations in Whitechapel."

"You overheard his last admonitions to me in the Paris hotel room," I accused.

"Is that a crime?"

"You were . . . demolished at that time, in despair."

"I still had ears, and will use them."

"You said you would use *me*, whether I would or not. How?"

She sighed. "I have become used to a companion, a wall off

which my speculations can ricochet, even if it is a crooked wall. There would be much you could learn on this journey if you would be less impatient and more trusting."

"Patience and trust have gotten my kind nothing but abuse."

"And what is your kind?"

"Female."

She shrugged, not arguing.

"Here," she said, "is my case for this journey. Red Tomahawk followed the Gypsy caravan east. The party then switched to a train from there. Going east. The party's belongings were bulky enough to require passage in the baggage car. A girl was murdered near Neunkirchen, with similar wounds to the women in Paris."

"But . . . such travels do not seem the work of one man. Jack the Ripper was a single phenomenon."

"Was he?"

"You're saying the mad members of that strange cult killed the women in London? That it was a communal crime?"

"Yes and no. I'm not sure yet, but I am certain that Prague is a key element in the puzzle. Godfrey was lured from this city into . . . what, we don't know yet. Our prey in Paris scattered and yet headed in this direction."

"So Sherlock Holmes is wasting his time in London?"

"I sincerely hope not. In fact, I am counting on him not wasting his time. I doubt that he permits that, anyway."

"Then why not join forces with him?"

"Who says that I have not?"

"But . . . he has no notion of it."

"Sometimes the best ally is the one who thinks he is completely independent."

"You speak in riddles and contradictions, like the Sphinx!"

"The Sphinx. Part feline, part female. I am not offended."

"Will you ever be frank and open with me?"

"When you are so with me."

"Oh! You are impossible."

"Thank you. Now that you have expressed your frustrations, would you like to meet the King and Queen of Bohemia?"

"Really? The top royals? I could get quite a nice face-saving item from that and buy myself a bit more time to practice your 'patience and trust.' Will I have an exclusive interview? And do we have time to spare for a society-page jaunt?"

"We can't afford not to."

Why was I not surprised at the Prague station that our train was greeted by a brass band and a set of toy-kingdom soldiers in uniforms that made Quentin Stanhope's quaint coat of many nations look restrained? In fact, I expected him to be lurking among the local color guard but couldn't detect him.

In moments we were escorted into a true Cinderella carriage—six white horses and four big gilded wheels. Then we were driven through the city streets past the populace's wondering glances and up a steep road to a huge castle on a hill, from which protruded, of course, a quiver of truly towering spires.

"The towers belong to St. Vitus Cathedral and a few other ancient churches that share the prominence with Prague Castle," Irene said, still serving as travel guide.

It was hard to tell what was wall and fortification and what castle or cathedral or palace. Irene told me that many buildings made up this man-made cliff-face of architecture dating back to the sixteenth century and as early as the tenth, although a great fire had destroyed almost all of the oldest sections four hundred years earlier.

I was indeed impressed by this massive fortress on a hill . . . really, half a city by itself.

Liveried footmen saw to our descent from Cinderella's former pumpkin in Hradčany Square and escorted us through the wrought-iron gates of two courtyards, one magnificent and filled with marching guards in uniforms that further paupered Quentin's fanciful improvisation, the other modest and therefore older. A third court-yard confronted our party with the St. Vitus Cathedral.

I say "confronted" because this enormous, towering stone edifice bristles with a lacework of decorative splendor in gilded wrought iron and stained glass and mosaics.

By the time we had tramped past a fountain and up a flight of stairs into the castle proper, I felt like a girl who had gotten too much rich candy from Valentine's Day admirers.

Our footsteps echoed through rooms of marble and rare woods and gilt as we passed into an enormous chamber lined with forty-foot-tall pillars that dwarfed the furnishings of innumerable sofas and tables and chairs. It was even more lavish than the *grande promenade* room for the girls at the *maison de rendezvous* in Paris. The comparison made me realize just how fancy that Paris brothel had been and how cannily it catered to men like the one awaiting us before a fireplace mouth even taller than he was.

At a distance, his height and girth reminded me of Bram Stoker. I wondered for a wild moment if the man I had met as "Bram Stoker" in Paris had been the King of Bohemia in disguise. Many royal persons in Europe traveled incognito.

But as Irene and I approached our royal host, I saw that his fair hair was more gold than crimson and that, although he wore bristling side whiskers, it was not the full beard Bram Stoker cultivated.

This man also wore military uniform, a magnificent ensemble of red-and-black wool so swagged with gold medals and braid that it made Quentin's all-purpose uniform look a thing of poverty and pity.

"Do I bow, curtsey, or swoon?" I hissed to Irene with my lips not moving as we approached His Royal Highness. The King of Bohemia was a far more handsome and formidable figure than England's Prince Bertie!

"He is Germanic, so formality is always welcome," she answered, sweeping into a floor-dusting curtsey worthy of a Russian prima ballerina. She had opened the revers and drawn up the skirt flaps of Nell's plain black "surprise" dress before we had left the carriage, so she now had some fine embroidered pink-silk "feathers" to flaunt.

I followed suit as best I could in my prim, checked coatdress and matching cap, wishing I wore the furred turban and Russian silk cloak I had on my first interview at *The Pittsburg Dispatch*. While I don't believe that clothes make the man, I do believe that being suitably well-dressed makes the woman more successful at whatever she undertakes. It is good to reassure the male sex that we are just women and too decorative to be taken seriously. When they don't pay us more than superficial attention, we can get a lot more work done. At least I have always found it so.

"Irene!" the King said in English, bending forward in his stiff attire to raise her upright. "You visit my city and country again in the guise of a busy and not-too-gaudy bird of passage, and your constant companion is also one who dresses for all business and no chatter."

"This is not Nell," Irene said quickly, "but a young American friend we call Pink."

"Pink. Most extraordinary." He gazed at me through narrowed blue eyes, as if not believing their testimony. "The other one was called—?"

"Nell," she reminded him again, patiently.

"Nell. That's right. Did you enjoy your musical welcome?"

"I loved it! I felt almost like Sarah Bernhardt, although in only a small way. Only Sarah herself can feel like Bernhardt in a large way."

"I like your ways, whether small or large, far better than the Divine Sarah's," he said laughing, standing back to gesture to a pair of huge brocade-covered armchairs.

We took our seats as he occupied a third gigantic chair.

"And Clotilde?" Irene inquired as she drew off her gloves—pink, I saw, to match the interior trim on the surprise dress.

"Ah, she will be here shortly. Much as she adheres to your every word and whisper, she does not wish you to spend too much time alone . . . without her."

For an instant I had thought the King was about to say "too much time alone with me," but that couldn't be.

"You two are still inseparable then?" Irene asked.

"Ah. How dare I not be devoted to my lady wife? She has been to school with a paragon and never lets me forget it."

I was certain that a great deal more was going on here than I might guess, but before I could determine what, I heard the click of a distant door, then the further clicks of shoes moving across marble floors.

A thin pale woman approached us, her hair the white-gold satiny sheen of the far North. She was clad in a changeable green-lavender tea gown of exquisite design that could have only come from where we had last been, Paris.

I rose with Irene and we curtsied again.

Again a royal person reached out her hands to Irene and elevated her at once to her own level. "My dear Irene! I was delighted when Willie mentioned that you would be traveling through Prague. And my dear Nell—!" She turned to grasp my hands and extend me the same astonishing royal favor when her pale blue eyes blinked as if facing too much sunlight.

"Why, Nell, you have changed—"

"This is not Nell, though her mode of dress may be similar. This charming girl's name is Pink and she is American, as I am."

The Queen's almost invisible eyelashes flickered like falling snowflakes, seeming to melt off her face with the motion. "Not Nell. Yes. I can see that now. I simply expected—I'm so sorry, my dear."

I had the oddest impression then: that the King would hardly know Nell if he fell over her and that his Queen had a deep and abiding attachment to her.

Once again the Mouse from Shropshire had divided and conquered, or, rather, half-conquered.

"And where is the ever-charming Godfrey?" Queen Clotilde inquired conversationally, sweeping to a proprietary place beside her husband. "I assume you have come here to join him, so why is he not with you?"

For a moment Irene faltered. This simple social inquiry struck her like lightning and turned her to stone. For the long awkward seconds of a missed stage cue, Irene Adler Norton had no answer. Or perhaps she had too much answer.

I was always quick with my tongue. "That is what we have come here to find out," I said forthrightly. I have always been forthright, and I supposed that royalty could stand it as well as anyone.

I glanced at Irene, who was still well and truly pale. "As you know, Your Royal Highnesses, Godfrey was visiting Prague on business. You may not know that he was called away and has mysteriously never been heard of since."

The King looked at once to Irene. The Queen instead eyed me with sudden, deep interest.

"Godfrey? Missing?" she said. "He paid his respects at the Castle only a fortnight ago."

She seemed utterly unaware of how much could go awry in a fortnight, much less a day. Perhaps that is a condition of being a queen. On the other hand, Clotilde, royal or not, struck me as something of a dull Dora.

"What may we do?" the King asked at once, still watching Irene with a strange blend of anxiety and expectation.

I could see her stage persona reassembling after the shock of Clotilde's unanswerably innocent question. Her breath was expanding her lungs, her chin rising as if she were preparing to sing . . . only now, simply speaking was a feat. To be standing here, among these people who were both powerful and ignorant, knowing what we knew of Paris and Jack the Ripper and Nell's abduction and Godfrey's frightening disappearance. . . .

"My dear friends," she said, slowly becoming herself again, "Pink is right. This is no social call. We come fresh from Paris, where the populace would be terrified by the rampages of Jack the Ripper-like murders, did they know of them. Godfrey has apparently been lured from Prague to a destination unknown, and this disappearance seems connected in some mysterious way to the Paris events. What I need is whatever aid I ask for, which I won't know until the need is immediate and dire."

The royal faces had grown sober as her words mounted up. Clotilde turned a shocked and beseeching face to her husband half-way through the narrative.

He patted her hand that rested on his huge forearm like a bear reassuring a child, but he never looked at her. His eyes were only for Irene, which is a powerful testimony to her natural presence even when rattled, and I must say that she rattled rarely. And it testifies to her beauty, I suppose. One can never underestimate the potency of that among certain impressionable men. As Paul Bunyan and I like to say, "The bigger they are, the harder they fall." And Paul Bunyan ought to know.

"You shall have whatever you wish," the current Paul Bunyan in our presence promised.

I was uncertain which woman he was placating the more, Clotilde or Irene. Perhaps both. Men prefer any concessions they have to make to women to be doubly advantageous.

There was something unspoken in the room, among the three of them, that I would have given my best sterling silver garters to understand.

Unfortunately, I could have bent down to take off these scandalous items in full public view and have thrown them down on the marble floor like dice amidst these three at this moment, and no one would have paid me the slightest attention.

"The Rothschilds," Irene began, her voice sounding hoarse and unused. She cleared her throat and her voice came clear as the cathedral bell when she spoke again. "Of course the Rothschilds will do all they can to assist me, since Godfrey was looking into matters pertaining to their property."

"In Bohemia?" the King was quick to ask.

"No. In Transylvania."

The King nodded, mollified. Apparently he expected to be made aware of the Rothschild actions in his land. The Queen clutched his arm tighter.

"Transylvania! That is such a wild and backward land," she complained, "overrun by Gypsies and wolves and superstitious peasants. There is no great city there, like Prague, only crumbling walled castles and hamlets of ignorant peasants. Whatever would the Rothschilds want with property in that Godforsaken land? Whyever would someone as civilized as Godfrey go there?"

"Such backwaters, my dear," said the King, "are where vast fortunes are to be made swiftly and without interference. Look at the American wilderness."

"I do not wish to," Clotilde answered. "This is a wild enough part of Europe for my taste. Prague is the last civilized city before the uncivil East unrolls its not-so-magic carpet and controls all the wild wastes of the world."

Irene answered before I could rise to my country's defense. "Your Highness's Viking forebears were no doubt a bit superstitious and wild, to hear tell. Today's Scandanavians are known for exporting delicate fairy stories and pastries, but their history was raw and bloody, like that of any nation in the making."

"But we did all that during the Dark Ages!" For such a colorless woman she was true-blue patriotic. "You Americans are still shaping the borders of your land, often by conquest. I only remark that Translyvania is a place no one of refinement or culture would care to visit."

"I doubt we could argue with you," Irene answered with a smile, "but since a person of refinement and culture I value very highly is likely there, perhaps not by his own will at this point, there I will go, once I have satisfied myself that no clues to his whereabouts remain in Prague."

"Of course you must go whither your husband goeth," Clotilde replied with what I consider truly simpering and annoying docility.

Not that I didn't share her sentiments that anywhere a husband went a wife could and should go, and vice versa. Only there was no need to be submissive about it.

"I can provide escort," the King said.

Irene bowed her head. "That is very generous and may be necessary, but first I need to explore Prague, and particularly this case that one of Godfrey's letters mentioned. A young woman was found dead in a way that revived rumors of the Golem."

"Oh, not that again!" The King's ruddy face grew as red as Old King Cole's. Though he was a young man, barely past thirty, and sturdily made, I could see him becoming quite fat and tyrannical in his later years, rather like Bertie.

"The Golem is myth!" he went on. "Yet one that does much harm, to Bohemia and the Rothschild interests for that matter. I imagine you will be meeting with representatives of those interests. There was some such meddling during your last visit to my hapless land."

"Your Majesty is not suggesting that I am an agent of the Rothschilds—?"

"No, but you know who is. Damn it, Irene! If Godfrey has gotten himself into some mess because of those banking politicians—"

"Godfrey is but a barrister, Willie, you know that. And who got Bohemia into a mess last time, if not rescued by those banking politicians and their . . . assistants?"

My eyes caught Clotilde's. Suddenly the King and Irene were talking like old friends, or enemies or . . . *hmmm.*

Clotilde remained clinging to his arm like a sack of Paris silks by Worth, but her pale blue eyes took my measure as a disinterested party. She shrugged ever so slightly, for my eyes only, as if to say we supporting players must keep our own counsel, and our eyes and ears open, while the lead actors hold the stage, but afterward . . . surely there would be time for a French scene or two between she and I. . . .

Of course I resolved to cut her out from the herd and have a nose-to-nose with her as soon as possible.

"You will stay for tea?" the King inquired abruptly. "I will send for the Rothschild representative so you may consult with him here, away from prying eyes in the town. And there are some paintings I have acquired since your last visit, that I should like your opinion of."

I had the sense of a spat diverted into a social occasion.

I was impressed. I was not on spatting terms with any royal persons . . . that I know of. Yet. But I am young.

20.

Of Corsetry and Atrocity

❦

They were real instruments of torture; they prevented me from breathing, and dug deep holes into my softer parts on every side.

—A VICTORIAN LADY

The clothes they have left for me are entirely improper.

"At least they are clean, as I insisted," Godfrey said, handing them over with the awkwardness of a good man confounded.

I find it most bitter that he was abducted with his luggage intact and can remain a gentleman even in durance vile while I have been stripped of every outer vestige and left only my inmost self.

It is just my ill luck, I understand, but I cannot reconcile it.

Then I think. Once, when I was young and foolish, and indeed I once was, I had cherished hopes of a sentimental alliance with an ungainly young curate in my father's parish. I had almost forgotten his name but now I have much time for reflection and the memory returns to me like a favorite book that opens to a signed flyleaf in a familiar hand: Jasper Higgenbottom. He went to be a missionary in darkest Africa, which was entirely appropriate, given the unfortunate elephantine appearance of his ears. But he sang quite well. I had supposed I might perhaps marry and accompany him.

If I had . . . I should be poor and holy and wear whatever castoffs were available to me.

So . . .

I will pretend I am in darkest Africa, although I will not pretend that I am wed to Jasper Higgenbottom. I have outgrown such ambitions. If I were to pretend I were wed to anyone nowadays, it would be . . . well, I would not so pretend. A woman of my age, past thirty, does not pretend. She accepts.

So I accept these clothes, that no doubt Godfrey has humbled himself in ways I cannot comprehend to obtain for me. My eyes blur with sadness. Godfrey's every thought is for my comfort, and by God's grace I shall be comforted. No woman could have a doughtier champion, and he himself in worrisome captivity! Taken first, and for no more reason than I. For no more *known* reason than I. I find my jaw setting in a most uncomfortable way.

Is it possible that I am angry?

Anger is a cardinal sin, but I think in this instance that it is justified.

I shake out the garments, more puzzled than before.

There are several cotton petticoats and a skirt of many yards of fabric, but oddly short. There is a shirt, or blouse, of coarse linen, with sleeves full enough for an acolyte on Easter Sunday. And there is a laced buskin of sorts, like a truncated corset.

The boots are the oddest part of the ensemble. They are low-heeled, of red-dyed leather embroidered fancifully all over the leggings. I am enough a maker of fancy-work to admire the skill that has decorated their gaudy surface.

The stockings are striped red and green. Oh, dear. And will at least not be seen.

Of course there are no civilized undergarments. I regret my Belgian laces sacrificed to the fire, but they were ruined beyond redemption.

I resolve to think no more on my unremembered journey here.

In less than an hour, I am finally attired in something more than a nightdress.

The linen and cotton scratch my skin. I had not realized that fine lawn and silk could be so pleasing. The blouse has no decent collar, but a drawstring neckline, like a shift. I pull the strings taut within an inch of their lives, but still cannot cover my throat. And the bodice . . .

Godfrey knocks at the door, and I must open it.

I step behind the heavy wood to let him enter my quarters. Far behind it.

He bends to gaze at my incredibly wide but short skirts, which plainly reveal every serpentine embroidery on my boots up to almost my . . . knees. Of course I am covered by the leather.

"Boots that Irene would envy," he pronounces.

I am strangely relieved.

"Indeed. She is fond of boots?"

"She is fond of all apparel," he says with a grin, "but boots particularly."

"Now that is something we have not discussed."

"Are you going to come out from behind that door?"

"I don't know, Godfrey, quite honestly. No disrespect to the garb you obtained, but it is rather . . . odd."

"It is worn by the Gypsy women who service the castle."

"Gypsies! No wonder. I cannot come out."

"Why not?"

"The, um, corset laces. I cannot reach behind to tighten them. I realize that you have performed this service for Irene in the role of husband, but I cannot ask you to perform such an intimate service for myself, who am not even a relation, so I shall have to remain behind the door."

Godfrey takes a long step back and appears to think. He covers his mouth with his hand, at least, and looks most cogitative.

"You are right, Nell," he says finally. "I cannot help you."

Despite myself, my spirits sink. It is my impression that Godfrey can always help anyone with anything, even Irene when she is being her most difficult, which a performing artist can indeed be, especially when she has lost her performing art.

"I can point out," he adds, "a purely objective observation. The women about the place do their own laces."

"They must have arms as long as an ape, for I have tried for almost an hour!"

"You may be right about the length of their arms," he says, his hand over his mouth again, as if he were expecting a cough or perhaps concealing a smile. "But they manage it because the, er, corset actually laces at the front, not at the rear."

I take a long moment to reconsider. "Oh. Then perhaps I can come out from behind the door, after all. If you would be so kind as to step into the hall for a moment—?"

He speedily obliges.

I wrestle with the annoying corset and finally draw the strings into a droopy bow that wilts at the front of my waist.

The mirror tells me that this is not much better than before. Much as Irene and her friend Sarah Bernhardt rejoice in going corsetless, I cannot help but feel undressed though dressed, a most bizarre state.

However, my sole witness is only Godfrey, and he of all people can understand the lengths to which I am forced to go.

I invite him back in.

"I must say, Nell, that is a rather charming ensemble. I recall an operetta or two that Irene appeared in during her apprenticeship days. Did she not wear some such garb?"

"Yes, but she was portraying a peasant!"

"That might be just the disguise we need to escape this castle."

"Disguise? Escape? You have a plan?"

Godfrey pinches the bridge of his nose and shuts his fine gray eyes.

"My dear Nell, I have thought of nothing else since I found myself abducted to this remote place. I have concluded that climbing free is not possible. Therefore, we may have to escape by subterfuge. Since the Gypsies are the only souls to routinely visit this godforsaken spot, you have just the outfit to make your way unnoticed out of here."

"Not you?"

He looks as uncomfortable as I had felt a bit before. "Not I. I had hoped to climb my way out some moonlit night, but—"

"But?"

Godfrey goes to the open shutters and I follow.

We looked down together, down on a great green plunge of forest and valley, the gray walls of the castle like some frozen, dirty waterfall barely visible beneath us.

"I had perceived a route by which I could at least visit chambers on the lower level," Godfrey says. "See that gutter? And the fenestration running horizontally from it? Then the crack in the stones on an angle, and the window far below? I think I might make my way there."

I gaze upon the projected route with horror. I see the slight stepping stones he indicates, but can also see that every step along the way is a possible plunge to instant death far below.

"It is too dangerous."

"So may be staying put."

"You really meant to take this path?"

"Yes. Before you came."

"Irene would be furious."

Godfrey smiles. "She is good at being furious but she is not here."

"I am!"

"I know. And thus I have renounced the route."

I look down again, for a long time. I do not like to think that my presence would hamper Godfrey's efforts to escape. If there is a choice between which of us must return safe and sound to Irene . . . it is he. I know that the steel bonds of friendship must bow to the unknown (on my part) steel-and-satin bonds of love.

So. Would I serve Irene best by allowing my female weakness to keep Godfrey from risking himself to obtain freedom . . . or by allowing him the freedom to risk himself on his own account, and hers?

It is a more puzzling choice than the proper way to don a Gypsy corset.

I realize I cannot decide on the spot.

I am saved by a knock on the connecting door. Instead of Godfrey, I find a sullen Gypsy delivering dinner.

It is a manservant, and he winks at me when he leaves.

Or is it my short skirts and embroidered boots?

Or my inside-out corset?

I would never have had to contemplate such mysteries had I gone to Africa as the missionary bride of Jasper Higgenbottom.

Godfrey and I shared our first dinner in the castle.

He pulled—I pushed, but not very much—the round table from the center of the room to the window, then dragged two of the heavy wooden chairs over.

They are carved, high-backed affairs, fit for bishops to sit in. The furnishings of the place smell of mildew and wood rot and dust.

A battered brass tray held our food, a strange mix of peasant fare and more extravagant bounty.

Yet more thick soup and bread, cheese, beets, some sort of meat stew. And a bottle of red wine that Godfrey assured me was a very fine vintage.

Since no water was served, I had no choice but to drink some wine in the tall metal chalices studded with bizarre stones.

Given the princely chair and the drinking material, I felt rather like a Papist prelate.

Beyond the window, the sky underwent the subtle changes of day becoming dusk becoming twilight. As the setting sun tinted the view rose-red, birds called and wheeled past in the distance like dark embers whirling up a chimney.

Had our circumstances not been so dreadful, it would have been a rather pleasant repast. There was even some kind of heavily fruited cake for dessert.

"You look like the heroine of an operetta, Nell," Godfrey commented in the mellow tone of one who has eaten and drunk well. "Irene would be most taken with your ensemble. I believe she would order a matching one."

"Indeed, she relishes dressing me up like a doll in the kind of clothing that is least natural to me. Well, she need only be kidnapped by Gypsies, apparently, and this ludicrous outfit would be hers."

"I doubt the Gypsies are our kidnappers. They are mere attendants."

"It is not every abductor who has a castle for a—what is that word that Pink used once, so American—a hideout."

"You must tell me more of this 'Pink' person that Irene took under her wing in Paris."

"I do not think that I must, Godfrey, but I will. Her real name is Elizabeth, a solid, old-fashioned name that might give one a confidence about its possessor that is entirely misplaced. She is utterly American and most forward for a girl in her twenties who should know better and besides that she is, well, no better than she should be."

He frowned to consider my words while turning the chased silver goblet in the dying light to watch the sunset tinge the pale stones bloody.

"Can you not be a trifle more blunt, Nell?"

"We encountered her in a *maison de rendezvous*! She may have found the bodies of two slain harlots, but she was no different from them, save that she was still alive."

"A significant difference, you will allow. So Irene was interested in her as a witness to the discovery of a crime."

"I do hope so! What other reason would she have for insisting the girl move into our Paris hotel rooms? She even took her to the Paris Morgue, without me."

"Obviously, as a witness," Godfrey hastened to point out. "Irene will do many unusual things when pursuing an enquiry. You must tell me the whole story of these Paris murders, and what they have to do with Jack the Ripper."

"Oh, I will. I have, in fact, the small notebook from my chatelaine with me to serve as reference, though I have had to write very small and succinctly."

"That must have been extremely difficult."

"Writing small?"

"No, succinctly." His gray eyes twinkled as he sipped the wine.

"Well, first I wish to know how *you* were kidnapped. Did a man with mad eyes come rushing at you?"

"Luckily, no. I simply followed instructions. The Rothschild interests had been contemplating a loan to a Transylvanian nobleman wishing to use this castle as collateral. I was to travel here to assess the property and ensure that man's agents were able and honest."

"And once you arrived here?"

"It was made plain that I was not to leave. In fact, I believe the entire transaction to have been a ruse. I have met no Transylvanian nobleman, only Gypsies and guards. And the cats and rats, of course, which I do not believe add value to the property. In fact, a decaying castle in this remote forest has no value whatsoever. The count, unless he is totally fictitious, which is distinctly likely, will have to look elsewhere than the House of Rothschild for underwriting."

"Obviously this Transylvanian business was a complete ruse to get you here. But I cannot imagine why, or why I am here also. Perhaps your secret mission for the Rothschilds in Prague would better explain matters."

"Perhaps it would, but I am sworn to silence."

"Since I am the walking dead, perhaps you can confide in me."

"Nell! Do not refer to yourself that way."

"Godfrey, I have spent nearly a week in what amounts to a coffin. I feel quite resurrected. What can be so secret that you cannot break silence in such dire circumstances?"

"Baron de Rothschild himself demanded secrecy."

"Yes, I know, and Irene was not too pleased about that."

"She was annoyed to be kept in the dark but in a perverse way she was also proud that I was the one man on earth the Baron trusted with this mission."

"Now she must be merely frantic. I shudder to think how our mutual disappearances may affect her. She is a performing artist, after all, and her emotions are always finer tuned than those of less imaginative persons, such as myself. She may not yet know of your predicament."

"I pray not! The Rothschild interests in Prague expect me to be gone for some time and knew that communication would be slow and unreliable."

"Are we really so remote as all that, Godfrey?"

"We are in the back garden of Nowhere, dear Nell. These regions are quite uncharted by all but the natives."

I sighed, too abstracted to refuse more wine.

"It cannot be this assignment regarding Transylvanian real estate that was so secret," I said finally. "It must have been a matter much closer to Prague."

"You are right."

"Don't sound so impressed. I am familiar with your ways of thinking and acting since I was your typewriter-girl in the Temple years ago. And"—I could not resist getting back at him a tiny bit for presuming that I should not be a full confidante now that our fates were conjoined—"I have apprenticed Sherlock Holmes since last I saw you."

He set goblet to tabletop with a thump. "Holmes! What was he doing in Paris, and what were you doing associating with That Man?"

I was much amused by Godfrey referring to the creature in the same capitalized tone that I took, so I speedily answered his question. "It involves those very macabre matters I so unwisely referred to earlier. I, too, was sworn to secrecy by the Baron de Rothschild, along with Irene, of course."

Godfrey's mouth made a grim line. "I see that the House of Rothschild has been exceedingly busy with both sides of the House of Norton and Adler. Not to mention the House of Huxleigh. Clearly, we must make a clean breast of things hitherto secret. Shall I go first?"

"Please." Secretly, I dreaded having to describe the cruel and gruesome scenes Irene and I, and sometimes Pink, had confronted since Godfrey had left us gay and innocent in Paris.

First he rose and found a candelabra, lighting the stumps of several yellow tapers. By now the sky was almost dark. The birds had become silhouettes that still called and dipped and rose far away, looking more like bats.

Godfrey set the candelabra on our impromptu dinner table, where the flames flickered in time to the last visible flights beyond our window on the world.

He poured more ruddy wine into each of our goblets.

The darkness falling both inside and out, the candlelight, the vast but deserted castle setting, all these reminded me of the most deliciously terrifying ghost stories that had gripped my mind as a child and never let go.

I rose and fetched my nightgown from the bed, using it as shawl over my overexposed arms and shoulders.

Once I had seated myself again, Godfrey began.

"The Baron enjoined secrecy because the matter touched on the one issue that frightens him: a violent uprising against the Jews. The site was again Prague."

I nodded, having seen this fear of the Baron's for myself only recently, but then involving his home city of Paris.

"Irene and I had been in Prague, along with you," I pointed out, "when rumors of the revived Golem in the Jewish Quarter threatened the civil peace there last year. Why could we two not know of the problem now?"

"The Golem was merely a legend, an animated clay man-monster capable of killing. That was . . . child's play"—for some reason the phrase made Godfrey wince as soon as he had employed it—"compared to the latest manifestation in Prague. Quite frankly, the Baron thought female ears far too delicate to hear the circumstances."

"The Baron," I said indignantly, "drew Irene and me into matters in Paris that involved murder and mutilation and *maisons de rendezvous*."

"He must have grown desperate, then, after I left."

I decided not to take offense. "I suppose he was. It took Sherlock Holmes too long to come over from London. He had to rely in the nonce on our fine female ears."

"And this led to the dancing naked demons and Red Tomahawk's battle axe?"

"Yes. But do go on about your more shocking case in Prague, Godfrey, while I try to think of terms genteel enough to convey to a gentleman all that we three women have been through in Paris in the past three weeks."

"Irene, you, and this Pink person?"

"Yes."

Godfrey stirred, then took a cigar case from his inside breast pocket. Only one smoke remained. "Do you mind, Nell?"

"I always mind but on certain occasions I keep quiet about it. This is one of them."

He half-rose to lean over the candelabra and draw one candle flame into the already lit and extinguished cigar-end. I realized that the poor man had been husbanding his supply of cigars and would soon be out.

In moments a noxious blue plume twined up toward the window.

As with Irene, smoking was a process that aided thinking, and then led to talking.

"You know, Nell, how volatile the peace between Christians and Jews is in all our great cities."

"Indeed, since I have delved so deeply into the murders of Jack the Ripper I learned that it has been of grave concern to the leaders of London and Paris as well as Prague. It seems that the first instinct with these murders has been to blame the Jews."

"And in Paris you say there were Ripperlike killings of women."

I nodded. "Two courtesans destined for the Prince of Wales and a poor woman near the Eiffel Tower whose profession may have been innocent, or not. And another woman, not to mention the interrupted mutilation in the cavern."

"Courtesans, the Prince of Wales, mutilation. I am rather astounded to hear you use such terms so easily."

"I could not help knowing what was really going on, though I tried very hard not to. Perhaps you see that you need not spare my 'delicate' ears."

"The Baron did think this was too much grue for women. A body was found in Prague as well."

"You mentioned the death of a woman in one of your letters, and that the Golem was suspected again."

"Did I? It seems a lifetime ago. No, that woman's murder was ghastly, but routine compared to another more unthinkable murder, involving a mutilation—"

"Of a second woman!" I cried in excitement, for if multiple women had been slain in Prague, then the Ripper had been at work there before Paris. London to Prague to Paris, it made no sense. Kelly couldn't have gone as far as Prague, could he? Would he?

Godfrey shook his head, speechless.

"Not another woman dead?"

He shook his head again. "Not this time. A baby. An infant."

"A baby? *Murdered?*"

I had thought myself beyond all shock but now I grew suddenly speechless. My arms were wrapped around each other holding my makeshift shawl closed over my bosom. Let my arms open out, just a bit, and they could cradle a child. A baby. An infant. I had not held a little one since visiting my father's flock in Shropshire. During my years as a governess, my charges had always reached the age of the schoolroom.

Yet I remembered holding these small, sometimes squalling, often hairless bundles of soft pink skin and wide, wandering blue eyes.

That someone, anyone, could slaughter a baby—!

"Nell. I feared it would be too much for you."

Godfrey's hand on my wrist made me jerk my arms apart. The phantom babe in my arms vanished safely into the past.

"Yes, it is," I said, "but tell me anyway. Only three weeks ago I would have never dreamed of such infamy in a sane world, but I have since seen for myself the kind of fiend who might do such a thing. It is as Irene said: if we do not work to stop him, who will?"

"There were rumors of forbidden Jewish rites at the old cemetery," Godfrey said as total dark descended on the world outside and the room within, except for the fluttering of the candelabra flames in the air from the open window, which sounded like the hollow whoosh of bat wings, and the emberlike glow of his last cigar.

"There are passages and caverns beneath that area," I pointed out, "as Irene and you and I found on our last visit to Prague."

He nodded. "The conspirators who needed a prison found that lost underworld first. This time another breed of cave rat had infested the area.

"The King sent in soldiers on information that had been given by some mad Gypsy beggar raving about the Infant Savior dying while still in His manger."

"When was this?"

"In April."

"So Kelly could have come to Paris after . . ."

"It is hard to imagine a man named Kelly, Nell, taking part in the debased ritual the soldiers interrupted. It was a sacrilegious enactment of a painting of the Virgin and Child they found: a young woman with her newborn babe lying in a manger. Only no magi came to offer gifts, only madmen who speared the infant through the heart and drained his blood as the mother looked on.

"The men the soldiers found escaped, all scattered like rats through the passages, knowing every turn as a snake does its coils. The so-called mother remained, along with the tiny corpse.

"Pottery jugs of some strange liquor lay all around. And cups. There was some evidence that the men had drunk the baby's blood."

"And they escaped, these cannibals?!"

Godfrey nodded. "The soldiers had not been prepared for what they found. Shock struck them to stone at first, battle-hardened soldiers. So all they had was the mother, who claimed she was the Virgin Mary, and the poor, white, limp body. The child was only days old."

"Horrible! Even Paris was nothing like this. Do you suppose, Godfrey, that it is possible that the rumors were right? It has long been said that the Jews kill Christian babies. Could this have been some hidden Jewish ceremony to deny the Godhood of the baby Jesus?"

"The mother was Moravian, not Jewish. The men who ran wore hooded robes and girdles; no one could say if they were Jews or Arabs . . . or Druids, for that matter. Allegations of Jews killing Christian babies have never resulted in proof, although they resulted in the killings of many Jewish men, women, and children in the ghettos. Baron de Rothschild's representatives insist that no Jewish ritual, however old, sacrificed anything but animal flesh."

I shook my head in disbelief. How could I have expected to have encountered an atrocity even worse than the insanity in the cavern beneath *l'Exposition universelle*? And so soon after? Was the entire world awash with madness and brutality and pointless death? Perhaps so. . . .

Godfrey went on, reluctantly, but caught up in witnessing to the case he had encountered. "The mother—woman, though she was just a girl herself—could or would say nothing, save that she was the Virgin Mary. She, too, had suffered." Godfrey looked away. "Certain . . . parts had been mutilated."

"What parts?"

"Nell, I'd rather not say."

"I must know, Godfrey."

"There is no polite way to describe it."

"You are a barrister. I trust you to find a way to convey your meaning in the subtlest possible terms."

"We have never spoken of such matters. Most men and women do not."

"Most men and women are not imprisoned in deserted castles in the wild Carpathian Mountains with Gypsies and cats and rats. You must understand, Godfrey, that Irene and I interrupted just such a wild, vicious scene in Paris. There is perhaps a connection. Tell me."

"That poor girl. Someone had . . . removed . . . certain attributes of womanhood, apparently months before. Before the baby was even born."

"Certain attributes?"

"The ones considered most feminine."

I thought I knew what he meant, but must be sure.

"Can you be more specific?"

"I can, but I . . ."

I had never seen Godfrey so at a loss for words. He took a long draught of the dinner wine, then spoke, suddenly as brusque as a surgeon.

"Her left breast was missing, for one."

I gasped.

"You see, Nell! I should have kept silent."

"You do not understand, Godfrey. I am not so much shocked by the brutality of the deed, God help me, as by the similarity of it. That was why Red Tomahawk threw his battle axe. It was to stop a man who had cut off a woman's breast from doing further damage. There seems to be only one explanation. I had spoken of demons and witches in trying to describe that scene in Paris and the atrocities we traced from one end of the so-called City of Light to the other, but now I have a better description. Devil worshipers. These sorts of things are the work of devil worshipers."

"You're not saying that Jack the Ripper was a devil worshiper?"

"Why not? Whyever not? The things he did, the mutilations . . . it was suggested that his abominable . . . excavations into the bodies of his victims was for wombs to sell to physicians. What if he was looking for unborn babies?"

"Nell! I cannot imagine you even imagining such things, much less suggesting them to me."

But Godfrey had not been where I had been and seen what I had seen, nor had he once eagerly read the dozens of gruesome ghost stories that had seasoned my young imagination.

"All I can say is that just after that unthinkable act of mutilation, when I rejoiced to see Red Tomahawk hurl himself and his axe at the man who performed it, another man emerged from that writhing, debased crowd.

"I saw James Kelly burst from the mob of robed figures, running right for me as he recognized me from our first encounter. He meant to make sure that I did not elude him again."

I shook myself free of the dreadful memory, whose shadow had followed me to this remote castle on the edge of Europe, and to Godfrey.

"I was captured shortly after, and brought here. I wonder what they want of me. Women do not seem to fare well in their hands."

"She was very young, this girl they found in Prague," Godfrey hastened to reassure me. "Perhaps sixteen, no more."

"If you mention my great age to relieve my mind, I would point out that most of Jack the Ripper's London victims were above forty and I am just past thirty."

My best tone of umbrage accomplished what I had intended: distracting Godfrey from the bad news he had borne and his own dismay that I had seen too much in the past three weeks to pretend shock at the news of it.

"I did not mean to imply that you were too old to be a victim, Nell," he said.

"I should hope not. Nor am I too old to contemplate escape

from a most unpleasant circumstance. I propose that you attempt your route across the castle walls, only I will braid our bed linens into a rope so that you have some safety line."

He glanced doubtfully at the hulking darkness of my gigantic, drapery-hung bed. During our talk I had realized that neither of us dare linger at the castle, no matter how apparently deserted, to see what our captors meant to do with us when they arrived. And they would arrive soon, the entire coven, no doubt.

"I assume you have a similar resting place?" I prodded. Dear Godfrey, he had glimpsed a bit of the horror, but not its full outline.

He nodded, still puzzled.

"The sheets for these behemoths of beds are the size of sails, Godfrey. I need an instrument sharp enough to start a tear along the weave of the linen, and of course they bring us no knives to eat with. Luckily they did not notice nor think to take away my chatelaine, which was in my pocket. My embroidery shears are just the thing. I shall shred your sheets and mine. Once I have strips to braid I can produce a rope long and strong enough to take you halfway to Warsaw. Our current captors will never notice that the linens are missing beneath these heavy brocaded coverlets, and, from what you tell me, they are far too slovenly to want to change our bed linens."

"This will take much time, Nell."

"Leave me the candelabra, and I will begin tonight. You will see that it will go faster than you think."

Any practitioner of the needle arts knows that one stitch, in time, will amount to thousands.

Godfrey had left me for the night—whistling, I noticed, after the door leading to his rooms had closed. Men, I had concluded, were simply large boys: deny them exercise and derring-do and they become quite ungovernable. Allow them their boyish enthusiasms, with suitable strictures, and everyone will be happy.

Of course it takes a clever woman to allow them enough rope, so to speak, without them breaking their necks.

So now I allowed myself to consider the enormity of my self-appointed task. The linens were large, but exceedingly tough. The worst part of the process was creating the strips; braiding them was simple.

I felt a bit like a trio of fairy tale heroines: the poor girl left overnight to spin straw into gold; the loyal sister who wove nettles into shirts to turn her seven brothers from swans into men again; and Rapunzel whose infamously long locks sufficed to make a ladder to and from a prison tower.

I pulled the first sheet from my bed. Every fabric has a way it will resist tearing and a way it will more easily rip. Finding the weaker weave in this fabric was a puzzle. My tiny embroidery scissors nibbled at the hemmed edges until they had parted enough for me to grab the fabric with both hands and pull with all my might. The sides of my small fingers were abraded raw, and the candle wicks were swimming in the last pools of liquid wax before I gritted my teeth and gave a mighty, Samsonlike pull . . . at last the tightly woven cloth came rending apart with a shriek like a cat having its tail stepped on.

I stared, panting, at the single yard of separated fabric.

Rolling my fists into the fabric where the rent ended, I gave another mighty tug. And another yard of fabric finally gave up the ghost. Again. And Again.

By dawn my arms and back and sorely tried ribs were aching, but I had a mound of two-inch-wide strips high enough to hide a yearling sheep. These I bundled back into the bed and spread out to resemble disarranged linens. The entire outer sides of my hands were raw and oozing, and I had no ointment. I used part of one sheet strip to bind both of my hands around the palms, so Godfrey should not see the damage, then admonished myself for being the silliest goose from Shropshire! Of course I should have used "mittens" during my previous tearing work. Certainly I would from now on, and spare my skin.

I surveyed my room and my deception, weary but proud.

I had little doubt that the few servants I had glimpsed in this vast, deserted castle would be the last souls to go probing around in my bed linens.

And the rats and cats would not care what nests I made, if only I would share them!

I quieted a shudder. Better rats and cats for company than devil worshipers.

21.

The Queen and I

When a charming young lady comes into your office and smilingly announces she wants to ask you a few questions regarding the possibility of improving New York's moral tone, don't stop to parley. Just say, 'Excuse me, Nellie Bly,' and shin down the fire escape.
—PUCK MAGAZINE, 1888

❧ FROM A JOURNAL ❧

"How is it you are called 'Pink?' " the Queen asked.

We sat in another lavishly painted and gilded withdrawing room, the Queen and I. She presided over a porcelain tea set as intricate as a miniature city. In fact, I began to see that the significant pieces were covered in bas-relief landscapes of local Prague scenes.

"First," I returned, "how is it that you speak English?"

Here, she blushed, instantly endearing herself to me. "Madame Irene encouraged me to learn Bohemian and English and French to aid my husband the King in his enterprises. Forgive me, but your bluntness in asking reminds me of my dear Miss Huxleigh."

My warming sense of endearment chilled. Irene had not mentioned her friend's dire circumstances, and I could see why. The
King barely registered the Admirable Nell's existence, but the Queen
was seriously attached. How had such a situation come about? Ah.
The Queen had not always been the Queen. Perhaps Irene and Nell
knew the King previously to Clotilde's entrance on the scene. But
then the King should know Nell very well. What a mystery!

"I believe my bluntness, as you call it, is American energy, not
British bluster."

"Ah. You do not like the British."

"Not very much."

"And have you met Godfrey?"

"I'm afraid not."

"He does not bluster."

"Then he is an exception."

"Oh, yes," said the Queen, with a small sigh that made me raise
my eyebrows figuratively. "My husband is not British, but he can
bluster. However, I am learning to . . . direct it."

"Did you direct it just recently into the *grande promenade* our
. . . associates are taking together at this moment?"

She blushed again. "I am obligated to Madame Norton for a
great personal service she did me. Part of it was learning to be
diplomatic, which most distresses me because it seems that dissem-
bling is a key part of diplomacy."

"It is indeed," I said with a smile as I sipped tea from a Meissen
cup as fragile as a newborn's fingernail. "I am not very diplomatic
I fear, though I can dissemble in a good cause."

"And what do you consider a good cause, Miss . . . Pink?"

"Why on behalf of the poor and the weak, the meek and mild,
the women, the children, the workers, the lost."

"Gracious! You sound like an anarchist."

"No, like an American reformer. We are all over the place over
there, and quite harmless, as no one ever much listens to us."

"I suspect they listen to *you*," Clotilde answered with a shrewd
sky-blue glance over the eggshell lip of her cup.

Strange thing about delicate porcelain: it can hold boiling water and not shatter. I figured Clotilde might be one of those types. And I guessed that I was not the first American woman she had consulted.

"They called me Pink as a child," I admitted suddenly, "because I blushed so much. It stuck, the nickname."

" 'Nickname.' What a word. It means an endearment?"

"I suppose so."

"Then may I call you 'Pink,' since my dear Miss Huxleigh is not here? I would never dare to call Miss Huxleigh by her given name, I cannot say why."

I found myself speechless for a spell. It was not my intention to usurp Nell in anyone's regard, and I found it rather sad that the people who most genuinely liked Nell called her Miss Huxleigh.

"You may call me Pink," I said finally, "but I will call you Your Highness, as I am an American and not used to titles and will forget if I don't use them, and besides, we Americans are secretly knocked sideways by them, so my calling you Your Highness is akin to your calling me Pink."

Clotilde sat still for a moment as she translated this speech both literally and emotionally.

"How refreshing you Americans are! No wonder Willie . . . well, that is the past. But you must promise to give me a 'nickname' someday. I would dearly like one."

"No one has ever used a diminutive for you?"

"I was a Princess Royal born. No one dared."

"Well, I will dub thee one. Let's see. It will be American, I warn you."

Clotilde laughed and clapped her hands. "You cannot guess how much I would like a touch of the American about me. I am already half-French, thanks to the gowns of Monsieur Worth."

"But he is English, I hear."

"Not anymore."

"All right. Clotilde. Tilde. That's an accent mark, but it's not right for you. I know! Matilda. Very American and with a French twist: *ma Tilde*, you see?"

"Ma-til-dah?"

"Great American frontier name. You could wear gingham and buckskin with that name."

"Ging-ham?"

"A cotton checked material. Very practical."

"No one has ever called me practical. I like it! Er, checked?"

"Like my coatdress. Checked and practical."

"And American?"

I hated to admit that I had adopted the style from Nell. "And a bit British."

"Then I shall be a little like all my friends."

It made me sad to think she thought I was her friend. A reporter can be friendly, but she daren't start thinking of her subjects as her friends because she has to tell the truth about them. Odd; I had subjects, just as Queen Clotilde did, come to think of it.

"Well, Matilda, now that we are on nickname terms, you must tell me about how you got to be Queen of Bohemia and met Irene and Nell and all that."

"How I got to be Queen of Bohemia was destiny. Willie and I were betrothed when we were eleven."

I nearly swallowed the Meissen cup with my last gulp of tea.

"But how I met Irene and Nell and what we three did afterward is quite a tale."

"I am like an ewer, all ears," I said.

So she told me, more than she should have of course, but it was all very useful.

Et tu, Pink.

22.

Lone Wolf

It was well to forsake the train, as we had the caravan, and let my other minions see the baggage to its final resting place.

My beast and I travel on together, on horseback with a rogue band of Gypsy men who are half-Magyar, half-Cossack, and all animal. We have joined a different and far less visible train.

So much for our enemies in pursuit.

Oh, the traveling is far rougher: the nights raw and the food barely edible, and then barely cooked. No silk and no sherbet, no star, that is for certain.

But Gypsies travel in packs, like wolves and dogs, and he craves the society of others. I cannot say that he craves the society of "his fellows," for there are none like him.

This he seems to have known from a very early age. I sometimes wonder if he seeks crowds so that he may assert his natural place above them.

Yet he is a man of the people still. He wolfs down the abominable food along with the strange, strong liquor the Gypsies find for him somewhere.

I am tolerated in their midst, a freak with moneybags. I pay for their missions to the caravans and other camps, from which they return with haunches of raw meat (whose source it is best not to ask) and the heavy pottery bottles that look as old as the Crusades.

They offer my beast first taste.

He drinks down half of the first jug in one endless draught, his head thrown back like a wolf howling, only this beast swallows the howl, again and again.

They would never offer me to drink from that vessel, and I don't protest. I do not wish to see the beast in myself, but in others. One's own beast is always too predictable.

The violins moan like a woman in heat, and the great bonfire in their midst sizzles like burning skin.

The night is chill. The violins skitter up and down the scale of tortuous sound. Smells of spilt wine and vomit conjoin into a strange Gypsy sacrament. At night we momentarily link with the passing caravans. Then the women and girls join us to stamp their bare feet on the icy ground, at one with grime. The gold coins on their wrist and ankle bracelets spatter like grease on a hot skillet.

Swarthy faces grin in the ebbing and flowing firelight. Eyes are ebony set in mother-of-pearl.

His eyes, though, are aspic-clear, a pale, eerily bloodless silver-blue.

Remarkable that one so dark should have eyes so light.

Opposites war in him more openly than they do in the rest of mankind.

I am rapt in it, the crude and the exalted, the holy and the inhumane. Perhaps it is my heritage from a harsh land that also spawned great wealth and beauty. I am bound to my earth, my dirt, my mortality. My feet are peasants, but my soul soars like royalty. My shod feet can't feel the hard earth, but I sense its slow, icy heart beating beneath my slightly numbing toes. It reminds me of other music, other dances.

I could sit here. Turn to stone. Grow deaf to the cacophony, blind to the raucous stew of sights, cries, and smells. I could become a mountain, an Alp or a Caucasus, a Hindu Kush. I could become a graven image, a god. I could become a monument.

Once I so aspired. I masqueraded as an artist then, and all artists are mad. Or should be. I know this Woman. And I do not know her. She was an artist once, but lost that rank, like a deposed queen. She lost her kingdom. Can a Queen lose a Kingdom? In a just world, yes. But there is no just world, only many worlds that can be twisted and spun and tossed from universe to universe like balls.

So I have become a Juggler. And sometimes I toss lives instead of balls.

Hmmm, balls.

Quite a metaphor. Our world but a ball. A celebration but a ball. A manhood . . . but a ball, or two.

It can all come tumbling down if the Juggler wills it: the world, the glitter, the power.

I sit here, a supportive player. The King in disguise. The Queen in retrograde. Everything burns with cold. Skin and illusion peel away.

Play, Gypsies, play! The music defines the dance, the dance the play, the play the climax.

Death.

Death is the greatest choreographer, playwright, scrawler in history.

He has very pale blue eyes, and He is Mine.

23.

Rapunzel in Ash-blond

~∿∽~

*15 May.—Once more have I seen the Count go out in
his lizard fashion. He moved downwards in a sidelong
way, some hundred feet down, and a good deal to the left.
He vanished into some hole or window.*

—JOHNATHAN HARKER'S JOURNAL, BRAM STOKER'S *DRACULA*

The brass bathtub so mysteriously imported to my bedchamber also mysteriously remained in place, though
empty.

I began to realize what force Godfrey had exerted to
obtain for me an article of a domestic scene far less grand
and far more comforting than this vast, mostly unpeopled old castle.

Since the few servitors the castle boasted only entered Godfrey's
chamber, I took to coiling my lengths of braided linen in the dry,
red-gold giant's bowl of the bathtub.

Godfrey always brought our meals in to me on the tray by which
they were delivered to him. It didn't matter the hour—morning,
noon, or night—we broke fast, supped, and dined on similar dishes:
stews that blended unidentifiable meats with unidentifiable vegeta-

bles. Our only libation was wine, a dry, sour yellow wine that reminded me of certain wolf leavings in the snow.

Our nightly entertainment was the distant howl of these wild creatures. Much as I publicly approved Godfrey's plans to survey our prison with a mind to escaping, I couldn't imagine fleeing the safety of old stone into the cold teeth of wolf packs.

We spent our evenings huddled in our heavy tapestry bedcovers by my fireplace. At least wood was plenty, as well as great wooden lucifers as long as tapers.

"I think the common link is Gypsies," I often began. "There was a troupe in Paris that disappeared before we discovered the meeting ground below. And you say the courtyard teems with the creatures here."

"Sometimes," Godfrey amended. "At other times the areas surrounding the castle are as deserted as its interior."

"But the few people you have seen in the castle are Gypsies."

"They are dark-favored and colorfully dressed, but I don't think that makes them Gypsies in this part of the world. There is one woman, sturdy enough to chop wood should she choose, and two men I have seen. None speak English, although I can make myself understood with a combination of German and English, especially English pantomime, if I work hard enough at it."

"How odd it is! That you arrived at that quaint little village as advised and that the moment you took the coach to the castle you became a prisoner."

"A tacit prisoner, Nell. I was never bound, simply led to my chamber and locked in. The coachman actually toted up my luggage before lowering the latch on my door from the outside. I didn't even discover that I was a prisoner until I decided to 'go down' for breakfast the next morning."

"I wish *I* had suffered such a genteel abduction."

"My dear Nell, so do I! I would have changed places with you a thousand times over. I cannot explain why I was treated so gently. It infuriates me!"

"Did you do nothing in Prague to irritate the Gypsies?"

"I think the Gypsies are not an end but a means, Nell. Colorful they may be, but it would be a mistake not to look beyond them."

"Or smell beyond them! The food we are afflicted with reminds me of something one would leave out for the castle mastiff."

"Given the wolves' chorus we hear each night, a castle mastiff would be a welcome brute. Still, food means our captors intend to keep us alive."

"For what? Another bloody ritual? I would rather be eaten by wolves."

"Yes, Miss Riding Hood?" Godfrey leaned across the distance between our two chairs to tug playfully on one of my braids that had come unpinned from atop my head.

I found myself blushing in the hot halo of the flames. Deprived of even a comb, I had concluded that my unkempt hair could benefit from the same rigorous interweaving that I was accomplishing with the bed linens. So I had braided my hair and coiled it on my head. Godfrey claimed I looked like a Swiss mountain maid, and indeed, the cloudy mirror in the corner revealed a figure from one of Irene's more cloying operettas. I doubt my own father would have known me, had he returned from the grave to ascertain the doings of his only daughter.

"I no longer wish Irene to rescue us," I announced as soon as my burning cheeks had cooled a bit.

"No?" He seemed amazed.

"I could not bear to be seen like this."

"I think it rather charming."

"You have been alone too much in a deserted castle," I admonished him in my best governess declaration.

Godfrey cast off the bedcover like a cocoon and stood. He was wearing only his shirtsleeves, most irregular for a gentleman in the presence of a lady, even if she is got up to look like a milkmaid.

"The clamor in the courtyard has died down. I'd a mind to try out your climbing rope tonight."

I turned to regard the bathtub with its burden of twisted linen. Would my braided ropes hold?

I rose also, forsaking the warmth of my brocade tent, and went to study the yards and yards of pale coils like a headless snake in the bathtub.

"Will they be strong enough?" I wondered aloud.

"That depends on the knot we fashion at the turret window. A pity that the bed linens weren't filthy."

"A pity! Not for us."

"I meant that this white rope will be very evident against castle walls."

The flaw in my scheme came home to me like a knife in the ribs. My vaunted safety line was a betraying trap should anyone observe his expedition.

Imagine feeling deprived because one has only clean sheets to work with! While I stood there gaping at my handiwork, I heard Godfrey rustling and scraping behind me like a giant rat.

A giant rat. It was possible that what I heard was not Godfrey, but exactly such a creature the size of a Shropshire calf. I turned, afraid of what I would see.

Godfrey was on his knees by the still-crackling fire, digging ashes up like a dog.

His mad actions had covered his shirt in a pall of gray, and his hair and face as well.

He looked up at me, laughing. "If you dry the stew bowls, we can carry the ashes to the bathtub."

"Have you gone mad? Bathing requires water, not ashes."

Godfrey rose, his cupped hands filled with ashes that he carried to the bathtub and emptied atop my lovely, white-linen ropes. It was as if a storm cloud had opened above them, raining gray.

After that we shuttled to and fro with our empty wooden dinner bowls until the ropes were the dull color of a moonless night.

Our evening's labors were hardly begun.

Godfrey coiled the gray loops over both shoulders and still there were uncounted coils left in the tub. I had no idea that I was being so industrious during my long, sleepless nights.

I looped what I could over my arms and trailed him to the

window, still open, as it always had been. That open window was the one element that kept my mind from turning on itself during these endless idle days and nights. That and the act of tearing and braiding.

Now my labors were to meet their test, and Godfrey's life would be the proof of the pudding.

He leaned perilously far out of the window to loop one end twice around the stone support in the window's center. Then he made a series of mighty knots the size of fists.

"Would I had been a seafaring man," he noted with a shrug, wrapping his hands in linen bandages as I had done when working.

I tied them off.

Godfrey had left a long tail of rope free. This he now knotted in turn around the legs of a trestle table we both wrestled to the window.

"Would I had been a mountaineering man. If my knots slip," Godfrey added, "the table will crash into the window. Being too wide to pass through, it should act as a stopgap. If the wooden boards don't give."

"And if my braidwork gives?"

"On that score I have no fears." Godfrey jumped up on the window frame and balanced there like a large monkey, certainly a seafaring man's trick. "The knots are the key to success, and they are all my doing, not yours, Nell. Remember that."

"Do take care, Godfrey. It is quite chill out there at night without a coat."

He nodded and occupied himself with inching down the wall on my line.

I leaned over the sill. A waxing moon cast light like caps of snow on the high point of every brutal rock littering the sharply sloped meadow far below.

The air beyond the open frame was surprisingly icy. My huge fireplace had done more to warm that cavernous room than I credited it with. Wind tugged at my entwined braids and chapped my cheeks.

"Where are you going?" I finally thought to ask. The goal of being able to go somewhere had obscured what could be gained from it.

Godfrey nodded to a point at the left and below. "A trio of window arches. I thought I'd start small and close to home."

At that he pushed his feet against the stones and swung sideways like an ape. When his feet touched stone again, he was at least a story lower than before, had this towering castle anything so modest as mere stories.

I grew quite dizzy from following the arc of his descent and was forced to draw back inside. The quiet countryside so far below looked as peaceful as an eiderdown comforter. I almost cherished the illusion I could fly, that I could lean out and waft featherlike below to the cool snow banks waiting to cushion my fall.

Delusion! I had eaten too much Gypsy stew for too long. It was bad enough that Godfrey was bouncing from stone to stone like a monkey on a string. Barristers should never let their feet leave the ground. How could I ever tell Irene that Godfrey had hung by a thread of my construction?

I leaned against the cold stone wall and shut my eyes and listened for the inevitable sounds of disaster.

I awoke sitting on the floor, my limbs so stiff that I had to unbend them by inches and wait for the fires of Hell to desist burning before I could unbend another inch.

The actual fire across the room had become a shadow of itself, as if a mastiff had shrunk into a Pomeranian.

The moonlight had shifted to cast silver pathways on the stone floor and the threadbare carpets.

I finally forced myself upright against the stones and leaned to peer out the open window.

A great gray loop of braided rope disappeared into the castle wall a dreadful distance below. Except for a tremor in the wind, it sagged motionless, a pendulum without a weight.

Godfrey was gone!

24.

Irene and the Gypsy Queen

~···~

*She could not detach herself from the idea that the
supernatural played a part in all her doings, and she clung
to the use of gestures and passes and words in the exercise
of her art....*
—UNORNA IN F. MARION CRAWFORD'S *THE WITCH OF PRAGUE*, 1891

⊰ F R O M   A   J O U R N A L ⊱

 "How soon will we meet with the Rothschild agents? To-night?"

Irene and I had been established at the hostelry of her choice, an ancient inn near what was called the Old Town, for half the day.

I presumed we were so near the Jewish quarter because of her Rothschild connections.

But I was wrong.

"Tonight we will seek a fortune-teller," she pronounced, as if just making up her mind.

"A fortune-teller? If I wanted to expose such a fraud I could have stayed in New York City. Is this why we're not enjoying a grand hotel near the Charles Bridge?"

"We are not enjoying a grand hotel near the Charles Bridge because there is nothing to learn there."

"And there is something to learn from a Prague fortune-teller?"

"Given that she predicted my marriage to Godfrey and my getting a tattoo that I have not yet acquired, yes."

"A tattoo? You wouldn't!"

"Apparently I will."

"Where?"

She withdrew from the cupboard into which she was hanging her sparse pieces of clothing to stare at me. "Where?"

"Where will you get that tattoo?"

"In Tibet."

I found myself momentarily speechless. I didn't recognize a portion of the anatomy known as "Tibet."

"And she correctly predicted that you would marry Godfrey?" I repeated.

"The allusion was veiled, to be understood afterward, but, yes, which was remarkable, as I despised him at the time."

"You despised Godfrey at one time?"

"Well, he was an Englishman."

"You don't like the English?"

"*Ummm*, sometimes."

"You are surrounded by them!"

"As Buffalo Bill once was by Indians, but they all get along now."

"Maybe."

Irene paused in folding delicacies into drawers. "Why do you so dislike the English, Pink?"

"They act so superior."

"Well, they are. They are our mother race. We are mere offshoots and upstarts. Interesting offshoots and upstarts, I grant you, but—"

"Nonsense! We Americans are coming up in the world. We don't need the Old World. The New World is better, brighter, richer, smarter."

Irene shrugged. "The Old World still has its influence. We pursue the Ripper through the dark heart of it. You cannot underestimate it. You make the same mistake they did about us once."

"Gypsy fortune-teller," I repeated, sighing and holding my head.

Irene only laughed. "Come and see, then tell me what you think. 'There are more things on heaven and earth—' "

She had sounded quite spooky intoning those words, but I would be darned if I would play Horatia to her Hamlet. So I said nothing, only put my few sparse belongings away and complained of the accommodations no more. I was no Oscar Wilde on tour in the U.S., but meek as a lamb shorn of velvet breeches and lovelocks, just a girl reporter in a checked coat and cap.

Obviously Irene had intended to test my mettle all along.

I was awakened around midnight by the flicker of a lantern.

I almost leaped up from the trundle bed I occupied when I saw a shadow cast large on the opposite wall.

The soft cap turned out to be my own, borrowed, but the men's trousers and jacket were hers. The mustache was either an absent animal's bristles or theatrical crepe hair.

"It is a good thing that I don't pack a pistol," I told her as I dressed hastily in the dark in my one warm gown, my game checks now badly in need of a dampening and brushing. "I might have shot your shadow. You looked exactly like a burglar."

"Good," she said, lighting a small cigar and holding it in her teeth at a jaunty angle. "I am eager to see how my local seeress does predicting my future as a man."

We slunk down the inn's backstairs, feeling our way along the rough plaster walls. Irene used the glowing ember of her cigar as a very faint light. She held her husband's sword-stick in one of her black-leather gloved hands. I was glad I had worn gloves, and not just because Miss Nell would approve.

The streets were lit by old-fashioned candle-powered lamps that flickered as if moths were dancing a mazurka around their lights. The cobblestones were rougher than any I had trod in Europe. Despite wearing sensible-heeled boots, my ankles wobbled like unicycle wheels as I walked.

Irene strode, her boot heels striking the ground hard and accurate. Was she also a wire-walker in her spare moments? I considered another skill I had recently seen her demonstrate, Mesmerism. Was I perhaps being hypnotized into thinking we were taking an outing even now? With so mercurial a companion, one never knew.

When we arrived at a wider street, she transferred her cane to her left arm and threaded my left arm though her right.

She was escort. I was . . . lady.

The muffler that concealed her delicate chin and neck steamed with a combination of night mist, breath, and smoke.

Bright rectangular doors into beer parlors fanned open and shut as drinkers came and went. We walked past unhailed and unchallenged. I glimpsed our shadows from time to time. A man and woman. Man and wife? More likely man and paid companion.

I smiled to myself. A harlot in a demure checked coatdress? Not likely!

The paving stones grew rougher, the ways darker and narrower. I had not seen the congenial flash of a tavern door opening for some time, and the thick, heady scent of dark beer was only a memory.

"Will a fortune-teller be working this late?" I whispered, wondering if our outing was doomed.

"Perhaps not, but she will wake up for us."

"Are you always so inconsiderate?"

"No, but I wish her muddled with sleep. You'll see. Enough money and she will sing for her supper at 2:00 A.M."

"It is surely not that late—early?"

Irene didn't answer but paused at an intersection of alleyways to look up. Various signs paraded down the byways in the faint, flickering lamplight, indicating shoemakers, pig-sellers, apothecaries, all the varied small enterprises of a large city.

"Ah." She pointed to a large sign of a white hand divided into portions like plots of land, covered with numbers and other arcane symbols.

"The Sign of the Severed Hand?" I murmured.

"Sometimes you are as acerbic as Nell."

"She has been this way before?"

"Yes."

I wasn't about to hesitate then. I followed Irene down a narrow, weaving byway smelling of urine and worse.

I realized that Whitechapel was a good deal like this, narrow, choked, both deserted by turn and crawling with nightlife.

Behind us I heard the soft trod of footsteps sticking to damp pavement, a sound like octopus suckers pulling loose, I imagined.

Lights flashed down other alleys.

I heard snatches of voices. Song. Cursing.

A sudden faint cry of "*der Mord!*" Which I recognized as "Murder!" in German from skimming Krafft-Ebing's book.

Such cries in English had sounded more than once when Mary Jane Kelly was being severed skin from vein from muscle from bone in a tiny Whitechapel rented room unpaid for except in flesh and blood that night.

"These shouts are common in such quarters the world over." Irene's hand tightened on my wrist to reassure me. "Here. One more narrow way to go."

We were entering a passage, not a street, that smelled of sauerkraut and beer and something far more exotic.

We breeched not a door but a heavy damask curtain.

The room beyond was as chill as the night outside, lit only by the dull flicker of a bowl of live embers making a centerpiece on a rug-covered table.

A woman's face hung like a red moon above the low-burning bowl.

Gold glittered at her ears and forehead and wrists—all I saw . . . those tinkling, shifting chains of gold coins, as regular as sausages.

Irene spoke in German, a question.

"English will do," the woman said, her voice thick with the taste of another tongue, "for the sake of the girl."

Although I had presented myself as nineteen years old only recently, I felt my twenty-five-year-old spine stiffening in resentment.

"Do not deny yourself," our hostess told me, "I know you are older than you wish people to think." She leaned further over the embers until the eerie red light reflected from every crevasse in her time-curdled skin. "Sit."

I saw nothing to sit upon, but Irene's hand upon my arm forced me down until a pile of dusty rugs became my divan. I tried mightily not to sneeze, not sure what such a great wind would do to the embers.

An ember elevated from the bowl like a reverse comet. It touched a taper end, and we had candlelight.

Illumination was no kinder to the fortune-teller's face than utter dark. I can't say what it did to ours.

The woman spoke. "I have the crystal that never lies. I have Tarot. I have the future in the palm of your hand. What method do you wish?"

Odd, the fortune-teller only addressed Irene, perhaps because she took the role of a man.

"What method speaks to you tonight?" Irene replied in English in the same unnerving basso she had used in German.

A pair of knotted knuckles intertwined beneath the woman's age-corroded chin. She wore long, heavy, dangling earrings like a girl, but now they seemed anchors pulling every line in her face down to the bottom of a sea where death waited.

"Palms," she said.

At first I didn't understand the word, not in that goulash-thick accent. *Balms*, I thought she said, thinking I could use one.

Instead I saw a claw of hand curving alongside the ember-hot bowl, empty and hungry.

"Ladies first," Irene said, her deep voice dipped in irony.

I removed my glove and placed my bare hand, my right hand,

palm up in the woman's. She immediately began intoning a litany of my life.

"You offer the hand you make of your life yourself. The left is what history and your parents gave you. You are self-made, and not a fine lady."

I nodded.

"You offer your hand openly, like a friend, but you are not what you seem."

"Who is?" I managed to interrupt.

"Some are. You not. You have traveled a long way to deceive, but you fool yourself most of all. You will live long and not prosper."

"Not prosper! Shame on you." I tried to jerk my hand away. "The Gypsy fortune-teller articles of incorporation must require news of prospering and tall dark men."

"You will have bad fortune with men and money. You will stand alone in the world. Your name will be forgotten, but your fame will last forever."

"I don't like this," I told Irene, again attempting to jerk my hand free of the clawlike vice that held it.

"You have not paid me yet," the crone observed, "so I need not tell you lies."

"Money buys lies?"

"Money buys what looks like truth."

Irene reached into her coat pocket. I expected the appearance of the third of our party, the pistol. Instead she spread a scimitar of silver coins across the figured cloth.

The fortune-teller drew my hand nearer.

"You consider yourself a huntress, but now you are the hunted. You seek fame, but you shall win it in other enterprises than the one you follow now, if you survive to win anything. Your life is in danger."

She released my hand, pushed it away, threw it aside, and scooped Irene's silver into the dark with her.

I heard it clinking together in one mass, then no more sound.

"What about my tall, dark man?" I demanded.

"He is several and none of them very good for you. I would suggest a convent."

She turned to Irene, who quickly said "I prefer the crystal," and placed a single gold coin beside the bowl of embers.

I understood that Irene couldn't unglove her hands without revealing her masquerade. The Gypsy woman didn't argue. She lifted the glowing bowl in her two hands and set it aside.

I gasped audibly as her hands touched the metal container, but she didn't even flinch.

Instead of being impressed by her apparent imperviousness to heat, I wondered how she managed the illusion. These purveyors of the secrets of the universe are all tricksters.

She rose and twisted toward the table in the shadow behind her, turning back with another object in her palms, a slightly misshapen clear globe of such cheap manufacture that I could see the wavy green quality of the glass from the dim spot where I sat. Crystal ball readings were even more of a fraud than palmistry.

The woman quickly set the object, which had a flat bottom so it wasn't a complete ball, down between us.

The eyes so dark that they seemed all pupil glanced at me as she spoke several words in another language.

Irene translated in her smooth basso. "Natural rock crystal eons old from the Ural mountains of Russia, tinged with malachite for the green shade the lady so obviously admires." Irene conveyed even the Gypsy's taunting tone as she answered my unspoken skepticism.

I was not impressed. Like myself, or a performer like Irene for that matter, these carnival hucksters become adept at reading the smallest change of expression or posture. Ordinary, unguarded people give away at least half their thoughts without even thinking about it.

I forced myself to widen my eyes with surprise like the greenest girl.

The woman ignored me and hunched over her crystal ball with its supposed exotic ancestry . . . more like cheap, green, wine-bottle glass from Czech factories that also produced so many of the faux glass gems called Rhinestones, after the German river. Poor Bohemia, always an imitation.

The globe was fashioned so that the sparse candlelight that lit the chamber was amplified into a universe of tiny stars within its curves. In this regard, it made a pretty curiosity.

The Gypsy gazed into the orb, then into Irene's eyes.

"The gentleman," she said, "is well traveled and will travel farther still soon."

Irene's mastery of languages alone could tell a dolt that.

"There is a woman paramount in his mind, a foreign woman for whom he has great love and concern. She is not a beauty, but I see another woman as well, who combines great beauty and ugliness. She too is foreign. Seek one and you will find the other, but you will not like it."

"Ridiculous!" I grumbled in English to Irene. "I get the usual tall dark men, who elude me, and you get . . . what, the short, fair women, who elude you?"

"I see a third woman," the Gypsy went on in her suspiciously fluent English. "She is not what she seems. I see her fate entwined with that of a tall, dark man. No . . . two tall, dark men! Both are far away, and one is in terrible danger of his immortal soul."

Did Gypsies believe in souls? I wondered. It was an interesting question. What religion did they follow, if any, besides the Great God Manna?

Irene had leaned forward, the walking stick upright between her leather-gloved hands. She acted as if she was actually interested in what the woman had to say.

"You have visited me before," the Gypsy suggested, her words half-assertion, half-question.

Irene shrugged, an answer as ambiguous as the Gypsy's comment. The woman's seamed palms caressed the globe, shaded the dozens of tiny points of flame dancing deep inside it.

"You visited me before with another woman," the Gypsy said, more strongly, "yet your heart is true. Most interesting. I have never seen within my globe a soul so surrounded by great danger. Yet you yourself may truly be impervious while all around you fall. You walk like the undead, casting no shadow but an illusion."

"The undead?" I challenged.

Black Gypsy eyes drilled in my direction. "My words may be wrong in this language that is native to you, Lady. The undead are deathless, ancient."

"Vampires," Irene intoned in a truly spooky baritone like a bad magician casting a phony spell on stage.

"Vampires?" The Gypsy echoed the word. "Many words, many languages. Always the same ending. They live, and others die. They are deathless, though they grant death."

"A living, walking corpse," Irene explained to me. "She is right. The tradition exists in many countries."

"The Golem?" I wondered.

Irene nodded solemnly. "I hadn't thought of it that way, but yes, in some ways a vampire."

My words had silenced the Gypsy, who made a series of signs that set her gold coins ringing like miniature bells.

Irene leaped into the evidence of her superstition. "The Golem has walked in Prague, has it not?"

"So it is said."

"Centuries ago."

She nodded again. "Rabbi Loew, a great magician of the city, is said to have created it."

"And before rabbis with magical powers," Irene said, "there were alchemists in Prague."

"Prague is a magical city."

"And Gypsies were in Prague then, at the time of the alchemists?"

"Gypsies were in Prague always."

"Gypsies are older than the Golem, the medieval alchemists?"

The old woman nodded, her fingertips caressing the crystal. I wondered if it felt cold, as crystal should, or hot, like fevered flesh. Almost I extended a gloved finger toward it.

The woman's quick warning look froze me in midgesture. She was as sharp and lethal as some hawk guarding her eyrie. I did not doubt that a dagger lay concealed somewhere about her person or the room.

"There are other walking undead," Irene said, almost dreamily.

I saw that she was speaking in a measured, almost Mesmerizing way again. She spun the head of Godfrey's walking stick between her hands, the clouded amber carving seeming to absorb light and then move within itself.

This was fascinating: the duel of one charlatan with another!

"Death is alive in Prague," Irene continued.

"Death rules all cities."

"Death in brutal, violent guise."

"Death is always brutal."

"But death is most often natural, however cruel. I speak of Death as murderer."

The woman drew her hands back from the crystal as if they suddenly had become too hot, or too cold. "A murderer is a criminal."

"Unless he cannot be caught. Then he is something else, maybe he is a cousin of Death, of the undead you mention."

Another flurry of signs, as frantic as Catholic crossmaking in a cathedral. These motions were not Christian, though. They were older than that. I had never rubbed shoulders with the Old World in all its truly ancient garb. For a moment the Gypsy woman in her drooping skirts and blouses and golden coins seemed some goddess of untold ages. Through my dazed mind passed images of Chinese conjurors, of temple dancers and Mongol concubines, of everything exotic since the beginning of the world. Oddly enough, the semblance of Red Tomahawk crossed my mind like a warding gesture. I thought of Indian medicine men and of how little my fellow citizens had plumbed the ancient roots of the races we were so good at driving into the wastes and even to the raw edges of the Continent, and killing one way or another.

I wished I had a fringed shawl like the old woman to wrap

around myself, for warmth, for remembrance of the past that wove it.

But all I had was my secret mission.

For an instant I wondered if that was all that Jack the Ripper had, and perhaps even the Gypsy woman's legendary "undead." And the Golem of Prague. We were all "undead," weren't we, because we were the living? Or at least the waking and walking. Was someone who had succumbed to a Mesmerist temporarily undead? There were many ways to sleepwalk through life, I decided.

"Your people," Irene was saying in her deepest, lulling voice, "wander by their own will. They love music and laughter, and the joy of shifting reality in other people's eyes."

Her one gloved hand juggled an invisible ball so real that I thought for a moment the Gypsy's crystal had leaped into her fingers. She was not hypnotizing the woman, I realized, she was performing for her!

The old woman blinked away from her. "You have done this, too," she accused. "You do it now."

"It is not owned by the Gypsies."

"No. But we are best at it."

"Are you as good, too, as serving as tools for other people's illusions?"

"We serve ourselves only. No people in the world are so free."

"But you are free because you appear to serve others . . . to mend pots; to tell fortunes, for fortunes; to play music; to give young girls to old men."

The woman whisked out a scarf and draped it over her crystal, as if protecting it from Irene's words. Her eyes couldn't darken, but they sharpened.

"The pots crack," Irene said, ruthlessly. "The music ends. The fortunes become true or false as the clients make them so. The young girls are not virgins, and they take more than they are taken."

The woman said nothing.

"Still, as you say," she went on, "the Gypsies are free. Why then would they accept the yolk of the non-Romany? Why would they conceal madmen and murderers?"

"Who is to say who is mad? Who is to say what is murder? We take gold and go our own way."

Irene reached into her jacket pocket. I feared the revolver. She brought out another coin, this one gold, elevated it between forefinger and thumb, then snapped it away. It landed on the thick cloth, next to the slightly green rock crystal.

"Gold." Irene produced another coin and snapped it away again. They thumped to the cloth, one after another, a rain of old coins, a Gypsy ransom.

The woman snatched one up, clamped her teeth on it, hungry as a wolf.

"Not gilded tin," Irene said. "Ural mountain gold, mined millennia ago by trolls and Tibetan monks." She was grinning at the extravagance of her claim.

The Gypsy woman's eyes narrowed to thick black lines in her lined face. She pointed a witchlike finger, knobby with arthritis, curved like a scimitar.

"You are Romany now." She produced the dagger I had feared from some part of her person . . . up a blousoned sleeve, from under a full skirt, who knew where?

With a gesture too swift to stop, she pierced her misshapen fingertip. A drop of blood fell onto a Tarot card she had thrown to the tablecloth.

She seized Irene's gloved hand. The dagger tip slashed through thick leather into skin like a needle through silk. Irene never winced, not even when the woman pinched a ruby drop of her blood onto the card to mingle with hers.

"Show this pasteboard to any Romany whose aid you need. This is the Three of Swords, the card of revenge, which we understand as no other. Now. What else do you want for your gold?"

"A woman has died, brutally, in Prague. Where, and by whom?"

"Many women die brutally. Look for where Kings hide and

ghosts of the undead walk. I say no more, for you have come to me before and know I see true."

"And what of the outcome of our endeavors?"

The woman drew back the cloth to glance into the crystal ball.

It was like a wobbly planet pulled from its orbit into public view. A poor thing. A lump of glass, or, if she told the truth, crystal from the hidden heart of the earth. Either way it told no truths nor answered any questions.

The Gypsy woman shrugged, her grand gestures done. "It is up to you, as it always is."

She swept the gold coins into the clanking custody of her swagged skirt, blew out the candle, and vanished.

We stood there for a moment, both of us having risen during that bizarre ceremony of blood and gold and Tarot card.

"It means nothing," I said.

"Nothing always means something," Irene answered.

We listened. For the clink of coins. For an exit of footsteps. Nothing.

"She is good," Irene said in the dark. I could hear a smile in her voice.

"You gave her a king's ransom."

"My King is missing, and my Queen. Now I must find the Jack."

25.

Alone

❧

Deep into that darkness peering, long I stood there wondering, fearing, Doubting, dreaming dreams no mortals ever dared to dream before...
—EDGAR ALLAN POE, "THE RAVEN"

At first I kept vigil, wrapped in the tapestry bedcover, huddled on the floor beneath the window like a loyal dog who awaits his master's return.

Every few minutes I would struggle out of my enveloping cocoon and, as the room's chill air encased me like ice, lean as far out over the gulf as I dared.

Nothing changed. My interwoven strand of rope hung slack. Jerking on it didn't dislodge it from the window into which Godfrey had vanished hours before, but neither did it result in an answering pull.

At last white-fingered dawn crept over the dark mountainsides, as ashen as the Wednesday beginning Lent.

I finally tottered on my numb feet to my sheetless beds and burrowed into the coverlet, sitting like a snail in my fabric shell, yet feeling no security. My heart was as cold as my feet.

Something had befallen Godfrey. Perhaps he had tried to return up the rope, slipped and fell to the rocks below. I had seen nothing among the rocks and brush beneath the pines that encroached upon the old castle like Burnham Wood on the march, not even when dawn's thin light puddled on the ground like spilt milk.

Or . . . he might have fallen inside the castle, perhaps on a staircase of rotting timber.

Or . . . he may have encountered some of the savage Gypsy men, who took it amiss that he had gone a-roving. . . .

Or wolves may have taken shelter inside the castle's lower regions, and had fallen upon him in a pack and eaten him alive—!!

The longer I thought, the more dire the possibilities became.

I was shivering like a nervous lapdog now and moaning softly to myself.

I stopped suddenly.

Another moan had reached my ears. The wind sawing through the pines and then through the open window? Or . . . an interior moan? The echo of distant voices in the castle kitchen, perhaps, traveling far and faint and thinning into what might seem a moan to a suggestive mind?

Kitchen! I deluded myself. The meals we ate required no cook and no kitchen but were Gypsy campfire fare, was that not obvious? Ergo, no Gypsies need reside in the castle, or even work there, and from what I had glimpsed of their wildwood lives, a stone ceiling would be an abomination to them.

Speaking of ceilings, I glanced up to the one in my bedchamber, which I had ignored until now, when every detail of my prison room had become sharpened like a stick in my eye, reminding me of Godfrey, now gone, reminding me of my helpless condition, stranded like a princess in a tower, her rescuing prince having fallen off the glass mountain.

A moaning sound again!

Either there were wicked people about trying to frighten me or . . .

Or a ghost.

I pulled my icy toes under the folds of my nightshirt. Of . . . Godfrey's nightshirt. My features twisted as I realized that this might be his final bequest to me.

Did ghosts walk at dawn? Perhaps in Transylvania they did, especially in the midst of this thick, dark, cold, scowling forest. My room still harbored pools of night-shadows in the corners.

And what else?

I heard a scrape. Possibly the screech of claw on stone. Cats? Or rats stirring one last time before the pallid daylight beat back the night and its denizens for another twelve hours.

The hinges on the huge wooden door that led to the hallway squealed like a dying rat. I had never seen it opened, never dreamed that it did. Everything came to me through Godfrey's chamber.

Surely this door had been locked?

Not now. It was so wide, perhaps five feet, that it took a long time for even a slit of hallway beyond to appear.

When that tall needle of darkness appeared, I stared into its black heart. Slowly my eyes made out a lighter figure etched against it, almost like a stone statue to be found in a Catholic church.

While I stared, wondering who would set a statue on guard outside my door and what saint this figure was meant to represent, a bit of warming daylight from the window reflected from two tiny glittering points—the eyes! Like quartz stone set in gray marble they glimmered, moist, vivid, alive, seeing me!

No saint, but a *ghost* hovered outside my door.

It was my worst nightmare come true, and I must face it alone. So I did the only sensible thing an Englishwoman in such straits can do.

I screamed until I had no more air in my lungs, and then I swooned.

✦ ✦ ✦

I really cannot recommend such behavior, however time tested.

When I awoke, I was in a most uncomfortable pile on the floor.

However, as I looked around for the horrid figure on the threshold, I discovered my scream had raised, not the dead, but the dear person of Godfrey!

He bent over me like a concerned doctor, sprinkling water on my wrists and temples.

However, we did not have water, so it must have been wine he sprinkled on my person.

I sat up, shaking off the bloody drops.

"Are you all right, Nell?"

"Are *you* all right? I saw the rope hanging limp against the castle and assumed the worst."

"What worst?"

"Several variations. Thank God you are here. The place is haunted. I saw the most horrible revenant with icy burning eyes in the doorway."

Godfrey's head turned while he examined the threshold. "I just came through that door. No one was there."

"Of course not! Ghosts can vanish in the shake of a demon's tail. It was awful, worse than anything from Sheridan le Fanu."

"That is what results from reading too many ghost stories at a tender age, Nell," he said, assisting me to my feet and dusting me off most considerately. "What did this ghost do besides appear?"

"That was enough. I have never seen such evil eyes, so light you could look right through them, as through water."

Godfrey nodded at the arched windows behind me. "Light can play tricks, especially in such a Gothic pile as this. In fact, I reached the doorway as you were screaming. Perhaps your eyes had created an illusion from the light and shadow of the hall and I stepped into it."

"Your eyes are quite a light gray, Godfrey, almost silver at times, but I have never had the experience of seeing evil incarnate in them, and that is what those ghastly eyes from the hallway were."

I shivered and could not stop. "It is true," I admitted, "that your ash-stained clothing could have seemed like the stone garb of a statue."

"There, you see? Easily explained." Godfrey examined his clothing and began dusting himself off. "Ashes and then stone dust from all that climbing and wall hugging."

"Then you reached your goal?"

"Indeed, and I returned with booty."

"Booty? What of value could reside in this decrepit castle?"

Godfrey began pulling items from the front of his shirt, while I looked correctly away.

"Books. The bay of windows is in a vast library with books even older than what sits on the few shelves in my chamber. A fascinating collection dating from several eras, some as old as the Dark Ages, I think, and many in foreign tongues."

"Evil tongues, no doubt."

"Unlike Irene, I am no linguist, but many were filled with the thick consonants that betoken eastern European languages, and others were in strange letters both like and utterly unlike European languages."

"So what did you bring back?"

"Something to divert you. In English I found a volume of the American author, Nathaniel Hawthorne—"

"I have never heard of him."

"Now you have," he said, handing me the dusty book. "And . . . perhaps I should not hand this one over. It is too inciting of the imagination for you now."

"What is it? Godfrey, let me at least see? Oh! Poe. You remembered my fondness for his works."

"I don't know." Godfrey opened the first few pages and frowned at the title page. " 'The Masque of the Red Death.' Much too morbid for you to read, Nell." He tsked like a governess withdrawing a treat presumed too rich for a child's appetite.

"I have read most of them anyway, Godfrey. Let me have it, or I shall . . . shall scream again."

"We can't have that. Your scream is piercing enough to injure even ghostly ears. It is a formidable weapon, if you could manage to remain conscious long enough to use it twice."

"I am afraid I emulated a fitful child too well. I meant only to scare the ghost away, not to use all my breath doing it. My next screams will be more of the staccato sort, I promise you, Godfrey, so I shall stay awake for hours to scream every villain in the place deaf."

He let my eager hands claim the book of Poe, and grinned.

I realized that he had thoroughly distracted me from the issue of the evil-eyed "ghost."

"Is it not strange," he went on, "that books as relatively recent as these should occupy shelves in a remote Transylvanian castle's library?"

"Everything about this place is strange. I would not be surprised to find *Psychopathia Sexualis* in that library."

Godfrey immediately grew alert. "A barrister has more than a passing acquaintance with Latin and that title is not one I would expect a parson's daughter to be bandying about. What book is that?"

"An exceedingly nasty one that Henry Irving and Bram Stoker and the theatrical set pass around their men's club meetings. It is full of the unimaginable deviltry that men may commit, so I am told. Irene had found a copy at the Left Bank book stalls. She thought it shed light on the acts of Jack the Ripper, as if anyone would care to see what the light would reveal in that case."

"I shall need to have another look at the contents of the library. Perhaps we could visit it together tomorrow night."

"I am not about to swing from my own rope, Godfrey. However odd my borrowed dress, it is still not suitable for exercise."

"That's the point, Nell. Don't you realize that I climbed my way down, but found my way back up by normal means, and I did not encounter any ghosts?"

"Did you encounter anyone more solid?"

"Now that is odd. There were signs that someone had been using the library recently. The dust was disturbed. But the tales of my explorations must wait. First we need to make like sailor-men and pull the rope back up before someone on the ground sees it in daylight."

"Of course! How could I have forgotten about that?"

"I suspect you were worrying about my whereabouts and the ghost outside your bedchamber door, which may have been me. Besides, you would never be strong enough to manage such a task by yourself."

While he talked, Godfrey made for the window and leaned far out to look for witnesses. Satisfied that none were visible, he nodded at me and seized hold of the braided linen. A mighty tug brought a loop of the stuff inside the window.

I picked it up from the floor and joined Godfrey in tugging. He had been right. This was hard, menial work. I pulled on his command of "heave" and released the rope on the "ho." Like navvies we struggled, and after ten or fifteen minutes of frantic labor, the last length of the stuff finally lay heaped on the floor.

"No rest for the wicked," Godfrey said jovially. "We must arrange this pile under your coverlet."

The conjoined coils were heavy enough that the two of us made several trips to transfer the bulk from the floor near the window to lumpy rest under what remained of my bedclothes.

I couldn't help wondering why we bothered to move the rope. "If you can find your way unmolested inside the castle, what do we need with the rope?"

"First, to hide the fact that it ever existed from our captors; second, we may indeed need it again, especially if locked in our quarters. Third, I did not say that I was able to explore the castle unmolested."

"You seem none the worse for wear!"

Godfrey's expression grew wry and secretive at the same time. "There is wear . . . and there is wear."

"What do you mean?"

Godfrey sat in one of the overbearing high-backed chairs that populated the castle. "Since I had the opportunity, I explored the lower regions of the castle."

"And?"

"It is built upon and into the mountain. I moved down into storerooms that reminded me of the system of tunnels beneath the Rothschild country estate at Ferrières. Do you remember that, Nell?"

"How could I forget that underground trophy room with all the mounted heads of beasts upon the walls and the odor of cigar smoke penetrating everything? Although the tiny train to bring food hot from the distant kitchen to the main dining room was rather innovative."

"No miniature trains here, would that we could escape on one! Only storerooms mostly empty of everything but dust and dead spiders. Yet each time I discovered a stone stairway, I was able to go lower into the foundations of the castle, which quite literally are the foundations of the mountain.

"As I went down, guided by a bit of candle I had found, I began to feel the rush of cool, damp air."

"Air?"

"I was far below the level where windows were possible."

"Then . . . there might be a tunnel of sorts, a way out of the castle."

Godfrey didn't answer me directly. Instead his eyes narrowed as he probed his memory.

"That's what I thought, hoped. I was surely on the last habitable level before solid stone was all that remained. The area was vast, although relatively low-ceilinged. It reminded me of what might lay beneath the burial vaults of a cathedral. Low Gothic arches stretched out in all directions, but the ground was that strange combination of stone and packed earth that makes one think one is standing on the very bones of earth. It was oddly reminiscent of some forgotten chapel. A few wooden shipping or storage boxes were lying about as if tossed up on some dry seabed. I had the strangest sense of being below, not sea level, but below the level of ordinary life."

"How eerie it sounds! And still you felt the rush of air?"

"Not a rush. Perhaps more of a . . . an unseen current, like the cold, dry breath of the mountain. The place seemed utterly deserted, my footfalls the only sound. Then, from behind one of the massive pillars that supported the arches, I glimpsed a movement."

"Oh!"

"I don't mean to frighten you, Nell. Obviously, I returned un-hurt."

"It is so like the best of ghost stories. Is that what you saw, a ghost?"

"Would that I had. A ghost could not betray my expedition."

"Who was it then?"

"A Gypsy girl."

"Even there!?"

"Even there. And more than one."

"No! How many?"

"Gradually, I detected three. They were as shy as wood nymphs, and very young, wearing no jewelry, nothing that would chime as they moved. That is when I realized that they must have entered the castle from . . . outside."

"Outside!"

"They were trespassing as much as I was. They circled me at their shy distance, drawing nearer but still darting behind pillars. I felt the center of some bizarre Maypole dance. I racked my brains for some way to bribe them, dupe them, follow them out. But they obviously spoke only Romany, and our mutual silence seemed a conspiracy of sorts. I feared that if I broke it, I would break some spell, would somehow give their muteness voice, and they would then betray me as I could betray them.

"So we watched and moved in that soundless minuet and finally they faded away, and I retreated to the higher regions. I don't think they will report my presence, for then they would reveal their own, which was as unlawful."

I shivered. "They could have been ghosts. Murdered Gypsy girls trying to show you a way out."

"This much I know. There must be a way in, and out, from far below. We have made much progress in moving about the castle's exterior and interior. Now we must decide how we can use what we have learned."

" 'We' nothing, Godfrey! You have done all the dangerous part."

He took my mittened hand in his. "We, Nell. It is both of us, or neither of us, that I swear."

26.

Foreign Activity

～υℓℭ～

Well, well; what a broth of a boy he is!...
He's like a breath of good, healthy, breezy sea air.
—WALT WHITMAN ON BRAM STOKER, 1854

⊰ F R O M   A   J O U R N A L ⊱

By the next morning I was speaking in Irene's deep basso of the night before, thanks to almost catching my death of cold and damp on our expedition.

While I coughed and honked like a San Francisco fog-horn, Irene pored over maps of Prague the Rothschild bank had sent to our rooms earlier at her written request. Why a visit to a Gypsy fortune-teller should inspire urgent study of city maps was beyond me. Irene was dressed for a day at home, at least, in soft slippers, a long burgundy faille skirt, and a ruffled pink shirtwaist that would do very well under the surprise dress.

"You have been here before," I commented about the maps, "twice. I'd think you would know your way around by now."

"Not by foot among all these narrow byways," she commented absently, her forefinger tracing one, then another, serpentine route on the map.

"I hope you're not detecting another complicated pattern, as in Paris, behind all the evildoings in Prague, perhaps in the shape of an Egyptian Ankh. Say, I bet the word 'Gypsy' comes from Egyptian."

"The ankh is a religious symbol, true, and you're probably right about the origin of Gypsies, but I don't have enough information yet about any recent murders in Prague to discover grand patterns. I hope Quentin can remedy that when he comes."

"Quentin is coming?" I sat up in my humble trundle-bed. "I must dress then."

"You are ill and better off staying snuggled under the quilt."

"Not with strange men visiting the rooms."

Irene cocked a dubious eye over her shoulder. "You have, as you assert to all who will hear, resided in brothels on two continents. Why the nicety now?"

"I am not masquerading as a *fille de joie* now."

"Nor would you do well at the profession in your current state," she added with amusement, still mooning at the map like a lovelorn cartographer.

I sneezed, violently, in answer, but struggled out of the entangling linens nevertheless.

"You surely do not think," Irene added, "that Quentin cares whether you are attired for the street or not? I'm sure that his spy work has required him to visit a brothel or two hundred in the performance of his duty."

"How that would shock Nell," I said while I struggled into my clothes behind the curtain that sequestered our washstand area from the room proper. "I do believe that being shocked is one of the joys of her life. I myself am, of course, long beyond shock."

"I wonder," Irene murmured, but perhaps I misheard her.

I finally emerged from behind my makeshift dressing room wearing a soft cream-colored shirtwaist and long black skirt, the only other outer garments I had allowed myself on this sudden and dangerous journey.

Irene glanced at me with a wry smile. "I would suggest a bit of powder on your nose."

I rushed to the round mirror over our fireplace. My nose was as scarlet as the fever. My nickname should be not Pink now, but Cerise.

"It's in my traveling case," Irene suggested.

I'd been dying to rummage in this glorious puzzlement. It was the centerpiece of her carpetbag, with all other items surrounding it like padding. The burled wood was fitted with myriad drawers and compartments, hiding a glimpsed hoard of sterling silver bottle caps, so I hastened to the object in question where it sat.

I was like a child ransacking my mother's dressing table, save no child had ever had a mother like Irene, and I wondered if one ever would.

The cosmetic carrier reminded me of a silverware chest, every niche lined with emerald-green velvet, all holding in tight custody enough intriguing bottles to release a caveful of genies. I found the wide glass jar of powder and used the soft fur of a rabbit foot to stroke it over the blazing nose revealed by a mirror set into the case's top lid.

I then ran my fingertips over the satin-smooth fronts of the tiny drawers, not daring to explore further, but memorizing the rare fittings as a blind person might.

Imagine my shock when a portion of the case's bottom pushed out as if on a spring, and I saw a drawer of various paper money and gold coins open before me!

Irene arose at once to stand guard above me, shaking her head. "You have managed to trigger a release that has baffled the border guards of six nations." She shut the drawer.

"I thought it was only a vanity case."

"That was the idea. Feminine fripperies are the last suspected of serious content. That can apply to people as well as cases."

My apologies were interrupted by a knock at our door, which Irene rushed to answer.

Quentin Stanhope stepped in, but I hardly recognized him. He was dressed as a man about town in dark city suit and homburg, with no exotic mustaches. Other than his weather-darkened skin, he looked like an ordinary Englishman, or Frenchman, or German.

He immediately removed the hat to quirk a smile at Irene and me in our demure lady-clerk garb, looking as uncomfortable as I felt. Given his newly civilized aspect, I was glad to have dispensed with my tiresome checked coat . . . and my shining scarlet nose.

"I may not look it," he said, "but I've had quite a night of it."

"I am not used to gentlemen who boast of such a fact to ladies," I returned.

Irene stared at me, no doubt because I had made quite a night of it many times during my undercover assignments in houses of ill repute. Still, I felt we were all appearing as our proper selves at last, and much preferred pretending to the sane and safe society in which we gave the (temporary) appearance of being staunch members.

"We had quite of a night of it, too," Irene answered, "consulting a Gypsy fortune-teller in the old quarter of the city."

"Nothing so arcane for me," Quentin said with a grimace. "I paid my compliments to one of the moderately regarded Prague brothels, where I am sorry to say another woman has been killed. I have brought back an interesting suspect, though I had a devil of a time extracting him from the police."

Irene held her breath for a long moment, then said, "You haven't caught James Kelly, have you? He'll require stern handling. Why would any police force let him go? How did you get him away from the authorities? I admit I long to question him under the proper circumstances, which is any time before the police do. This miserable man was last seen in pursuit of Nell, by my very eyes. Where is he?"

"I don't know who the fellow is, but he's waiting below. He could be a Kelly. There's an Irish look to him. The Rothschild agents helped me convince the police that he was a mere blundering Englishman who had happened to visit the place, like myself, and had no link to the atrocity so recently discovered."

"Another woman killed." Irene began pacing. "This is an epidemic! I do not like deceiving the police, but they could hardly understand the larger implications and the critical issue of . . . Nell."

Quentin, who had been trying to get another word in, in vain, glanced at me and shrugged his surrender. "I'll have him up," he said, leaving our chamber.

"Another murder." Irene practically ground her teeth with frustration. "Last night! When we were out." I knew what she was thinking. We might have prevented it. Yet I doubted we would have happened on the right brothel at the right time even if we had been searching them for James Kelly.

Footsteps sounded outside our door.

Irene rushed to pull the door wide open. "What—?"

Quentin entered, a sheepish red giant in his wake: Bram Stoker.

"Bram!" Her tone was neither accusing nor welcoming, simply announcing.

He paused outside our threshold, hat in hand, wiping his forehead with a huge white square of Irish linen.

"My dear Irene, once more you find me in an awkward position, and I find myself most shamed to see you again."

"Shame is a pointless emotion that has its origin in the attitudes of others, not anything we have done ourselves. I don't much subscribe to it."

Still he hesitated to cross our doorway. "Are you sure you want the company of such a blackguard as I might be? Had this chap not taken my part, I would be undergoing a police interrogation even now, and these fellows here do not speak a drop of English."

"Come in," she urged him, impatient at last. "You certainly have a tale I would like to hear."

As he entered our chambers, nodding ducklike in embarrassment, I noticed at once that his beard was not as sharply trimmed as in Paris and that his clothes were rough-and-tumble tweeds more suitable for country lanes than city thoroughfares. All in all, Bram Stoker resembled a shaggy auburn-haired bruin that had charged through a very large bramble patch.

"Sit down," Irene ordered. Mr. Stoker responded like a tame bear in the circus and sat, saying no more. "Quentin, go down to the dining room and order up breakfast . . . everything hearty you can think of, with pots of tea and coffee and lots of cream for both."

Bram had sat upon the nearest possible object, a leather-covered ottoman. To see such a huge man perched upon such a low stool made him look an oversized youth being kept after school for bad behavior.

Despite her vaunted disdain for shame, Irene immediately capitalized on this advantage and began striding back and forth before him, in apparent agitation. "I sent you on ahead to find Godfrey. What are you doing in Prague still? Prague is where Godfrey's journey into obscurity began, not ended!"

"I know, I know." Mr. Stoker patted his forehead again. Like most large men, his nerves showed up on his face in the form of perspiration. "I have, in fact, tramped over half the Carpathians in the past few days and only yesterday returned to Prague to seek out more specific information on the area."

"Which you expected to find in a brothel?"

Mr. Stoker flushed as readily as I do. "That earlier murder in Prague that Godfrey mentioned in his letter to you? It had occurred outside of a brothel, which I discovered on my first swing through the city, before I took the train to Transylvania and from there went on foot. I learned much in the mountains." He seemed to gather himself, anxiety fleeing before the greater excitement of news. "Much. There has been a good deal of foreign activity at a particular village near Sigisoara, near the old castle that hangs over the settlement like some crumbling church from a forgotten religion."

He rubbed his hands together in relish even as his huge frame shuddered with delicious distaste. "The region reeks with bizarre legend and folktales. I have never encountered such an elaborate history, though I have never visited this eldritch part of the world before. I tell you, Irene, it makes the bare, witch-haunted heaths of Macbeth's Scotland seem like a South Sea island paradise compared to it. This bitter land's name means 'over the forests,' and it consists of a plateau surrounded by mountains, often iced over with snow. The forests are thicker than thorn bushes. Every height is crowned with a fortress, and the whole region is one impenetrable mass of stone and tree, except to the man on foot, of course, and he must venture alone. The only carts I saw were a few Gypsy caravans drawn by lone sway-backed horses, and they went singly. Otherwise, it is all peasants and travel by shank's mare, which suits me. These rural folk seldom venture from their villages and have not done so for hundreds of years."

"No wonder even the Magyars have kept their greedy paws off of it."

This was Quentin Stanhope speaking. He had finally followed his charge into the room and now lounged against the fireplace mantel in the way of the lord of the manor. So like an Englishman!

Quentin nodded at Mr. Stoker but looked at Irene. "Not your Mr. Kelly, I presume?"

"No." Irene sounded momentarily disappointed. "This is Mr. Bram Stoker, a respectable man of the theater."

"I thought that there were no respectable persons of the theater," Quentin retorted.

"You have been listening to Nell too much," Irene answered, and then caught her lip between her teeth, as if dearly wishing to listen to Nell too much right now.

Not I! I stole another glance at Quentin Stanhope. He looked quite dashing in his current street guise. I could see why even meek little Nell had developed a sentimental attachment to such a man, especially one with the same chameleon tendencies as her pal Irene. Nell was, of course, far too prissy for the likes of Quentin Stanhope. He would require a more adventuresome woman. I had never met the absent Godfrey, but couldn't help wondering how a pasty-faced barrister in an idiotic lambs-wool wig could possibly compete for female hearts with a sunburnt spy in Arab robes.

Quentin Stanhope intercepted my gaze and winked at me before turning an absolutely bland expression back on Irene and her theatrical friend.

Well! At least someone in this company realizes that I am a keen
and useful observer and no mere Sancho Panza to some female Don
Quixote.

"Getting back to Transylvania," Irene said to Bram, sounding
troubled. "You describe a difficult, rugged terrain."

"No doubt!"

"And this is the place where you think Godfrey was sent?"

"I am no confidante of the Rothschild interests." Mr. Stoker
aimed an accusing look at Quentin Stanhope, who obviously was.
"I am a mere walker and wanderer, but I have learned to absorb a
great deal from my solitary tramps. I sense . . . some ancient evil
brewing in those whited sepulchers of mountains. Should I have
encountered *Macbeth*'s three witches over a boiling pot in the forest,
I would not have been surprised."

"Or a single witch over a bowl of burning embers," Irene murmured to me in a stage aside.

I could see that she allowed for a theatrical sense of exaggeration
in Bram Stoker's account. Her comment to me both mocked that
tendency in him, and in herself.

And in me? And Quentin? Perhaps. We all played larger-than-
life roles in the world. In a sense, we all performed stunts. How
ironic that the only two apparently endangered members of our
circle were the most conventional among us.

"So, Bram." Irene changed subjects as an orchestral conductor
might initiate a new movement. "Why *were* you at the brothel?"

Bram Stoker bristled, quite literally with that red beard of his.
"Why was Mr. Stanhope there?" He looked at Quentin.

"For the same reason, I suppose," Quentin said. "I was investigating the earlier deaths of prostitutes in Prague. Unfortunately,
another occurred while I—we—were in attendance. Irene had told
me that you had gone on ahead, but I didn't realize who you were
when I extricated you from the thick-skulled Bohemian authorities,
who are utterly innocent of the international implications of these
murders, and should remain so."

Bram looked a little dazed. "Quite right. I'd returned to Prague because I was at a loss on how to proceed in Transylvania. Rein-forcements seemed called for, though my military strategy is usually deployed for the stage and in my stories." He sighed heavily. "The truth is, Irene, I am at my best tramping around a new scene meeting residents and gathering stories. Storming the castle was never my bailiwick."

"You believe you have found a castle that needs storming?" she asked.

"Perhaps. Meanwhile, we are now enmeshed with another of these brothel-house murders. It is most confusing."

"No," said Quentin, thrusting himself away from the mantel that had been his prop. "It is appalling, but not confusing. I have been in Prague long enough to discover that the city has been plagued by a series of prostitute murders."

"How many?"

"Perhaps four or five. They were over a series of months and prostitute murders are common, but these were uncommonly violent."

"When?" Irene asked.

"Before the killings in Paris."

"And last autumn, in London?"

"After London."

"So . . . London. Prague, then Paris . . . and now Prague again. Why would a lust-murderer, a man obsessed with a particular type of woman, usually a prostitute who can be found in plentiful supply everywhere, shuttle back and forth across Europe like a train on schedule? Is that it? He traveled by train?"

"What," I put in, "of your discoveries in Paris? The saints' days and the geographical pattern of the murders?"

"Indeed. What of it?" Irene's gold-brown eyes burned as red-hot as Russian cherry amber. "Quentin! I need a map of London, of Whitechapel, with the Ripper's killing sites marked upon it. Can you get that?"

He raised his now manicured hands. "Specific demands mean swifter need, no doubt."

"No doubt. You can contact a man in the Foreign Office for aid. One Mycroft . . . Holmes."

Quentin Stanhope paled beneath his bronzed complexion. "*In* the Foreign Office . . . my God, Irene, M. H. *is* the F. O. It's worth my neck to irritate that gentleman with an unwelcome or trivial behest."

"I have it on good authority that he will be helpful. You might mention the name 'Sherlock.' "

" 'Sherlock.' *Hmmm.* Interesting. I will wire at once."

He snatched up his homburg and was out the door with only a terse nod of farewell.

I was taken aback by this turn of events and demanded of Irene, "Do you really want Sherlock Holmes to know in what direction you are heading?"

"No, Pink, I don't, but it can't be helped. Besides, he strikes me as far too devout a man of science to wander far into the swamps of religious symbolism. He offered me the aid of his highly placed brother, and I will take it. Besides—" She smiled ever so slightly. "If he thinks I am intruding upon his homeground by drawing on Mycroft Holmes's resources, he will be less likely to look abroad for my inspiration and leave us alone to do our rescue work. His interests are not personal as ours are. I will not sacrifice Godfrey's or Nell's safety for the easy-resting of any royal head in the world, nor anyone's ulterior purpose."

I felt that she cautioned me against self-interest as well.

Bram Stoker had finally risen from his place of reprimand and now hunkered over the Prague maps Irene had used as a tablecloth.

"Fascinating," he murmured. "If Stanhope were here to tell us the locations of the murders, I imagine we could also plot the similar crimes of Prague. Here. This spot is the brothel where Stanhope and I, er, discovered each other. And there is the old Jewish cemetery, only a few streets away."

"So it is." Irene had come over to stand beside him, looking like a porcelain doll beside some great stuffed friendly bear.

I watched them warily, not forgetting Irene's identifying the cosmopolitan Irishman as a Ripper suspect: he worked late at the theater, had been in London throughout the Whitechapel Horrors, was to be found in Paris this May when women again died, and could have easily slipped away to Prague on his solitary walking "vacations" to remote and unusual places. And Prague had just provided the *second* brothel in which he was to be found the very same night as a dead woman was. Add to this his obvious fascination with occult and gruesome matters and . . . Bram Stoker was still a very formidable suspect. The Krafft-Ebing book made plain that lust-murderers were people you'd never look at twice in that regard. Besides, I could better imagine an intelligent man like Stoker escaping unseen from the several Ripper murder sites, whereas James Kelly might be too madly erratic to play quite the clever fiend the world called Saucy Jack.

Irene produced Nell's artist's case from her carpetbag and drew a sheet from the many papers it guarded.

"There is a man we had encountered in our investigations," she told Mr. Stoker, "who was in Paris at the same time we were. I was able to describe him to an artist friend in Montmartre."

"Not Toulouse-Lautrec?!"

"No, Henri is a fine caricaturist but too much of an artist to permit people to resemble themselves overmuch in his work, other than through a wicked line or two that is far too subtle for the literal observer." Irene's smile at memories of the artist's vivid posters of Paris nightlife faded. "Nell and I encountered him during our first sojourn in Paris. She was most unimpressed by his work."

I bit my tongue to keep from saying that being unimpressed was something of a religion with Miss Penelope Huxleigh. In the States we would have called her a wet blanket.

Bram Stoker lifted the sketch into the light from the window. "I don't know this hand, but—" He squinted at the paper. "By God, that is the servile fellow I saw slinking around the brothel last night. I took him for some laundryman who liked to sniff the dirty wash!"

He turned scarlet and glanced at me with horror, not realizing that I knew instantly the type of brothel hanger-on he meant. Our genial Irishman was more intimate with the cast of characters in bawdy houses than he liked to admit.

"You saw him? This man?" Irene demanded.

"Briefly. He was leaving when I noticed him."

"This was after the woman's dead body was discovered?"

"No. Only moments before. I should remember, for I was soon herded into a small room filled with large policemen in very gaudy uniforms and put through my paces. That's how I met Stanhope. He was brought in to translate. I say, what makes him exempt from suspicion, when I am not?"

"He is in the British foreign service, and you are not."

"A spy? Really?" Mr. Stoker eyed the closed chamber door, as if he would rush out to catch up to Quentin Stanhope and instantly interview him. "Fascinating! Seemed a rather trivial chap."

"That is the point of spying. But you must tell no one."

Mr. Stoker looked insulted. "I keep many eminent persons' confidences in my position as manager for Irving and his theater."

"Nell's life may depend upon it, and Godfrey's."

"I swear, Irene," he said, hand on heart. "I would never do anything to harm a hair on either of those heads."

That I believed. But then the Ripper never killed anyone he knew, did he? Only anonymous prostitutes that the world would little miss or long remember.

The two of them stared down at the map for some moments after this sober turn of the conversation. Then a knock on the door announced the normal world going about its daily business. Irene literally shook herself into a more normal mood to admit the waiters. She lured Bram away from maps and missing friends by sweeping the table free of papers she transferred to the nearby desk. In moments the surface that had been the center of gruesome speculation became a centerpiece of a breakfast feast.

After some persuasion, Bram finally tucked into the piles of eggs and sausage and fried potatoes like a starving wolf. I suspect that if what he said was true, he had arrived at the brothel too late for dinner. In any decent foreign brothel, dinner was a lavish affair that marked the beginning of the night's entertainment.

Irene rearranged the food on her plate with the tines of her fork, as she often did nowadays, seeming to design the meal rather than consume it.

I joined Mr. Stoker in eating hearty.

"Yes, eat up, Bram and Pink," Irene said. "We will be taking a walking tour of the more unsavory parts of Prague tonight, but first I hope that Quentin will return with the map of Whitechapel. I suddenly crave more than eggs Benedict."

The tines of her fork carved a parallel pattern in the white arctic waste of our tablecloth. When Irene thought, her fingers often pantomimed musical motions . . . piano playing, the curlicues of a musical clef. The fork tines were perfect for scribing a musical staff, but that is not quite what she sketched so absently.

After tilting my head, I recognized the strange figure: an "X" through the staff of the letter "P." A Chi-Rho. Before unknown to me, this ancient Christian symbol would ever after bring to my mind the Christ . . . and Jack the Ripper.

27.

Auld Acquaintance Not Forgot

❧

I asked you for a violin & you did not refuse me but (to me weak mentally & bodily, & who wants something to keep him up) did worse than that by putting me in a state of anxiety & suspense.

—JAMES KELLY TO A BROADMOOR ASYLUM OFFICIAL, 1884

"If I eat much more of this overseasoned Gypsy goulash, I shall soon be playing the violin," Godfrey said, pushing the bowl away.

I would die before I would admit it, but I had grown accustomed to the pepper-spiced meals that were our daily lot. It was ever so much more palatable than French cuisine.

"This imprisonment of ours makes no sense, Nell!" he added. "No one cares that we are captured, and the Gypsies certainly can't be behind it. Unless . . . they are acting for forces that oppose the Rothschilds."

"What forces oppose the Rothschilds besides Christians?" I asked.

Perhaps I had been meant to be a missionary, I daydreamed over my battered metal spoon as I dragged it through the dark, meaty

sauce. Perhaps I had been destined to eat unknown dishes in undiscovered corners of the world, converting pagan souls to the Lamb
of God. . . .

"If I eat another morsel of lamb I shall *baaaa!*" Godfrey exclaimed, throwing down his spoon.

"Lamb? It is lamb?"

"Surely a Shropshire lass would know lamb if she ate it."

"Shropshire lamb is not so highly seasoned. Besides, I never ate
the lamb."

"Well, you have been consuming lamb by the bowlful now."

"Oh." I pushed my food away.

"Christians don't generally oppose the Rothschilds," Godfrey
said, returning to political speculations, "only small factions that
wish to foment political upheaval and use the Jews as a striking
point. That is why they might try to create an atrocity to fix everyone's attention, such as this murdered infant."

"Someone would . . . arrange such a dreadful death merely for
political reasons?"

Godfrey sighed. "I need only point you to the New Testament,
my dear Nell, to find a death arranged for political reasons."

I sat stunned. As well as I knew my New Testament and stoutly
would have argued its eternal import for modern men and times, I
truly did not expect to find parallels in current events.

Godfrey was odiously right. Not only had Our Savior died at
the convenience of warring Jewish religious factions and the Roman
officials ruling Judea, but much earlier His Holy Family had to flee
to Egypt with the baby Jesus to avoid an infamous occasion of
infanticide: Herod's attempt to foil the prophecies of a Jewish Mes-
siah by ordering all first-born Jewish boys under two years of age
slain, known to history as the Slaughter of the Innocents.

"It that why people ever since then are so ready to accuse the
Jews of killing Christian babies?" I asked with dawning horror. "Because they know that the case was the opposite so long ago?"

"People do tend to reassign their own demons to other people, persecuting what they hate in themselves in someone else, usually someone completely innocent."

"That is such a cynical observation, Godfrey."

"I am a barrister and now a prisoner. I have seen a great deal to make me cynical."

"And your father," I said, recalling bits of his unhappy family history. "He persecuted your mother for leaving him, charging her with being unfit to mother her children, when in fact he was the intemperate, irascible, irresponsible one."

"Intemperate, irascible, irresponsible." Godfrey repeated my trinity of adjectives as if every word were a personal blow. "Fair enough, and I suppose he did try to have her named a public sinner while he remained a private one. Hypocrisy did not die out with the Pharisees, Nell."

I hardly heard him. Ideas . . . no, *revelations!* were knocking at doorways in my mind I had never known were there.

"And Jack the Ripper," I said, just as suddenly. "James Kelly, rather. He detested discovering that he was born out of wedlock so much that he hated his mother—though not his father, that is odd—for the fact of his irregular birth. Once he found out, even though his father had left him money and opportunity, he hated all women because he might create another bastard like himself with one. Even when he was married, he called his wife a whore and killed her. And then he set about killing prostitutes."

Godfrey was sitting as if turned to stone, staring at me.

"What? Have I hit upon something?"

"I cannot believe what has happened to you, Nell, using such words."

"What words?" I thought back, then sighed. "There is no other way to express such facts, Godfrey," I said in my sternest governess tone, "though I blush to resort to such terms as I must use. I also beg your pardon, but once one has really understood what Jack the Ripper did there is no retreat to polite terms. Nor can there be when a babe in arms is a pawn in some disgusting savage ceremony.

Irene said that if we three did not move to find and stop Jack the Ripper, he would go on and on and on."

"You *three*? Was Irene including me, even though I was at a distance? Or—" Godfrey's face darkened. "Was that man Holmes in the picture as well? Is he the one who lured you and Irene into such dark and dangerous matters?"

Godfrey was so close to the facts that I actually flirted for a moment with telling an untruth, for his own peace of mind. But Sherlock Holmes had never been included in Irene's more recent version of the three musketeers, and in this case, for once, the true facts were less frightening than the imagined ones.

"No, Godfrey, I am afraid we were an all-female cast: 'we three.' Irene chose to rescue a young American woman from the brothel at which the first two murdered Parisian prostitutes were found."

"Rescue . . . ? This American woman was a would-be victim? Some innocent maid or laundress?"

"Alas, no, that would have been far more suitable than the facts. She was a . . . lady of the house."

"A lady? You mentioned that aristocrats patronized the place, but not female ones." Godfrey was looking more confused and appalled by the moment.

"I am trying to remain delicate of expression, Godfrey. She was one of the . . . damaged goods for sale."

"And Irene rescued her? How."

"She, er, moved her into our hotel suite."

"With you? This harlot?"

"She actually was fairly presentable for an American girl . . . and a trollop. She was possessed of some wild idea that she must learn life through the back alleys. I believe that Irene thought I would be a good influence on her."

"I fear the influence has gone the other way, given the shocking words that fall so easily from your lips."

"It is hard to be chary of only words if you have seen the deeds that we have witnessed in the past fortnight, Irene and I. And . . . Pink."

"That is the American trollop's name?"

"*Nom de guerre*, I suppose? She was christened Elizabeth, which bespeaks some hope for her."

"I am not as reassured by birth names as you are, Nell." Godfrey sighed and put his forehead in his hands, seemingly intent on scrubbing off the new wrinkles of worry. "At least Irene has not been consorting with that man Holmes. I find his interest in her rather suspect."

"Oh, don't worry about that, Godfrey! Irene has said that he is hopelessly adrift in these cases of lust-murder; that a confirmed bachelor like him hasn't the faintest idea of what is at stake."

"And you do?"

"Well, no. But it doesn't matter because Irene does."

"I am not reassured."

"I wish you would be! I am doing my best. You must understand that I have been in the presence of the Prince of Wales and the Baron de Rothschild in recent days. These eminent personages asked, nay, beseeched our help."

"I thought that you did not think much of the Prince of Wales."

"I don't, and now that I know of his *siége d'amour* I think even less of him. Vile appliance for a naughty, naughty, greedy boy!"

"I think that I do not wish to hear the specifics."

"But this ignoble two-tiered couch does link James Kelly, the unhinged upholsterer, with Jack the Ripper, so we must be grateful even for that unwanted knowledge."

"I believe I could use less unwanted knowledge right now, Nell. This . . . case you and Irene and this Pink person have been involved in strikes me as far too sordid for any investigative force but the police. Worse, from what I have gathered, you have been exposed to and identified by some murderously insane elements. If what you say is true, this brutal conspiracy of slaughter extends from London to Paris to Prague."

"I haven't even gotten to the plot against the Jews," I interjected.

Godfrey held up a beseeching hand. "Later. For now I must

think. If Prague is a link in this hateful string of crimes, then my abduction may not be as arbitrary as it seemed."

"You were not taking your abduction seriously, Godfrey?"

"No. I thought of it as a forestalling action to keep me from finishing the Rothschild business. An extreme measure, to be sure, but customary in this territorial and rather primitive part of the world where bandit kings and warlords rule every mountain pass."

"So you expected to be released unharmed when some preordained time period was over?"

"I suppose. Of course I would have escaped the castle before then, if . . . if things had been different."

"I believe, Godfrey, that my arrival is the 'thing' that has put the period to your plans to escape. But don't you see? My arrival changes all your assumptions?"

"How so?"

"If I have been spirited from Paris to Prague, I presume, and thence to this forgotten castle, both our imprisonments have more to do with me than with you. I can see only one reason for my presence here: I am to be a future victim of Jack the Ripper, otherwise known as James Kelly, rogue upholsterer."

"Your pardon, Nell, but this is a political scheme, and I am the unwitting victim."

"*Your* pardon, Godfrey, but you are apparently an afterthought, kidnaped perhaps to distract Irene from tracing my movements. I am the prime unwitting victim. As soon as that dreadful James Kelly creature escapes his pursuers and finds his way here, I will be meat for his mania."

I shuddered at the thought of the death that awaited me, worse than boiling in water at the hands of any unconverted cannibal I could have ministered to so sweetly but ineffectively in Africa.

"I regret to say that you are both wrong," said a voice that had no right joining in our argument.

We looked up to the doorway, at one in our gestures if not our opinions.

The voice had been female. It had spoken in English, though rather heavily accented English. And it was vaguely familiar.

We had been alone for so long in the castle, with only the rare and taciturn Gypsy for company, that just hearing English words made our hearts leap up. At least we both leapt to our feet to confront the visitor.

She entered fully, revealing a traveling cape of hunter's green velvet touched with soft ridges of red-blond fur that complemented her hair color.

That hair was curled and dressed into a Parisian edifice as artificial as the Eiffel Tower and almost as high. She might have stepped out of the Worth Salon on the Rue de la Paix, save her ensemble had a savage simplicity that even Worth would decline to duplicate.

She set a matching sable muff the size of a Pomeranian lapdog down on the end of our trestle table.

Godfrey bowed, gentleman that he always was. "If you are truly our hostess, I must commend you on the consistent quality of the stew."

Tatyana, the Russian spy once known as Sable, smiled, an expression that emphasized her foxy pointed chin and her long, swan-like neck. I had lived in the country and knew that foxes could smile.

"I will convey your compliments to the chef," she said. "I would be grateful to the Gypsies, if I were you two." She eyed me with denigrating smugness. "I see your mode of dress is much more amusing these days. You remind me of a shabby chorister from some nonsense by your Gilbert and Sullivan. Still, you should be grateful. The Gypsies spirited you away from great danger at the hands of a man all England fears and soon all Europe will, too. And perhaps, later, the entire world."

"At your behest?"

She shrugged. "I have used the Gypsies before. They make an excellent spy network: they are everywhere, though often invisible, and they will do anything for money, particularly if they think one is paying too much. It is not hard to pay too much for Gypsies. They are surprisingly loath to rise in a world they despise."

"I suppose I should thank you," I said tartly, with what I hoped was irony, although I become hopelessly awkward whenever I try irony.

"Indeed you should, for you have given me leverage."

"Over Irene?" I asked, my breath catching in my chest.

The name brought a subtle change to her otherwise inscrutable expression. It was as if I had said "poison" to a queen cobra.

"Over your partner in custody."

I glanced at once to Godfrey. What could she mean? The expression on his normally genial face told me that he had understood her meaning all too well.

"You should be glad of my arrival," she added, nearing the table again to stroke the sable muff as if it were a pet. "The food will be better. There will be . . . amusements to pass the time. You must, however, allow for my retinue to, er, occupy the building.

"It has been neglected for centuries," she explained, "thanks to foolish local superstitions, so it makes a perfect retreat from the rushed and ugly day-to-day world of the rest of Europe. You may now encounter servitors other than Gypsies, but I advise you not to speak to them. They are more primitive in their own way and less gregarious than the Romany; besides, they know very little English."

With that she retrieved her muff. Her sable hem swept over the stone floor to the door with the soft sound of a departing wave. In a moment we saw no more of her. Her recent presence seemed as unreal as a dream, except that a strong spicy scent floated in her wake as if she were a China clipper loaded with exotic teas.

Godfrey sat down and applied the wine goblet to his lips for a good half a minute.

"Tatyana," he said at last, voicing our mutual recognition of a mortal enemy as if declaring the subject of a hellish toast. It did not resemble a toast to anyone's good health, least of all ours.

"Quentin knew her as a spy over a decade ago in Maiwand. Afghanistan," I added at Godfrey's blank look.

"Quentin—?"

"Quentin Stanhope," I repeated patiently as to a sick child. "You remember! The uncle to my dear former charge Allegra Turnpenny. He had turned to espionage in the service of the Crown in India over a decade ago and got caught in a game of cat and mouse and betrayal with a turncoat British agent called Tiger and a Russian agent named Sable. Quentin was called Cobra," I added with pardonable pride, for a striking cobra may easily topple creatures as clever as a sable or as ferocious as a tiger.

"Of course I remember your acquaintance and our exotic house guest, but I doubt even Quentin Stanhope can do us much good here." Godfrey's monotone was part despair and part determination and part grumble.

"Irene will—"

"Irene will not, I hope, come anywhere near here, for this Tatyana woman is her worst enemy. You will remember she attempted to poison Irene once in Prague, and long after the game was over. She is a treacherous, vengeful creature. No good can come of either one of us being in her hands. With both of us captured . . . barristers are supposed to be unimaginative by profession, but I confess my speculations are both lurid and extremely pessimistic."

"Nonsense! I have faced Jack the Ripper and survived. One overdressed Russian woman is not enough to daunt me. She must have a purpose and it is probably political. She is a spy, after all."

"That was a long time ago, Nell. Just because Quentin Stanhope continues to work for the foreign office it doesn't mean Tatyana has remained loyal to her Russian roots. She struck me as someone devoted to her own cause above all others."

"And that is?"

"I don't know," Godfrey admitted, a troublesome "V" of worry lines settling between his dark brows like the furled wings of a raven in residence. "All I know is that it bodes no good for either of us.

Or for Irene, wherever she is. Which I devoutly hope is nowhere near us and will continue to be so.

"It is now even more imperative that we contrive to escape, for if we remain we are nothing but bait for those who most love us and whom we most love."

With that he began worrying again, overlooking the fierce, un-flagging blush that racked me with panic and delight when I realized that Godfrey's use of the plural "us" could imply someone else besides Irene whom I most loved, and . . . who most loved me?

Ah, no. That was a delusion Tatyana would most enjoy my cherishing. So I resolved never to think of such an impossibility again.

28.

"X" Marks the Spots

And the crew were very much pleased
when they found it to be
A map they could all understand.
—LEWIS CARROLL, *THE HUNTING OF THE SNARK*, 1876

⊰ F R O M   A   J O U R N A L ⊱

That afternoon Bram Stoker was replaced by Quentin Stanhope as we huddled over a map of London in our hotel room in Prague.

The influence of Mycroft Holmes was not in the power to move mountains, or to transmit a map upon a beam of light. It was in mobilizing the sources closer to hand.

Within hours of Quentin cabling the foreign office and mentioning the magic word "Sherlock," we had a modern, pristine map of London's Whitechapel district in our hands, courtesy of the Prague royal library.

We also had a cable Quentin had received back, listing the crossroads where the women of Whitechapel had died, and including the location of the "Juwes" doggerel.

"This is incomplete." Irene stared down at the map and the

cablegram that lay atop it. "Sherlock Holmes made quite a point to Nell that murdered women and Whitechapel are synonymous. They have been so long before Jack the Ripper appeared on the scene. The crimes that are attributed to the Ripper by the British police are arbitrary at best, and severely underestimated at worst."

"This is what we have to work with, Irene," Quentin said. "However unconvinced Nell might be, she would not quibble to use the tools at hand were it another's life in the balance."

"No. Nor shall we. All right. Mary Ann Nichols, known as 'Polly,' is designated as the first Ripper victim, though she may not be. She was slain here at Bucks Row, just off Whitechapel Road on the high, eastern end of the district."

Irene made a large "X" to mark the spot.

"The next victim was Annie Chapman at Hanbury Street. Look! Almost on the same east-west axis as Mary Ann Nichol's death scene, but dead center of the district."

I winced at the unintended aptness of her American usage, "dead center." Irene drew another "X" on the map.

"Third. Elizabeth 'Long Liz' Stride, at Fairclough and Berner Street."

Irene marked the third "X" and drew back from the map to study it. "These three points make an upside-down pyramid, almost an equilateral triangle. What is the fourth location, Quentin?"

He read from the cable. "Catharine Eddowes, on Mitre Street, near Aldgate."

Irene drew a double "X" there. "And near here the chalked lines about the Juwes were discovered. Look, the Eddowes site is almost across from Stride, as east-west goes, but a long, long walk. Eddowes was the Ripper's second victim that night, before he presumably turned to scrawling ambiguous statements about Jews." She frowned at her series of "X"s. "Four points now, and if you connected them, you would have a rectangle, a skewed rectangle, although I believe there is exactly such a construction. I don't believe that geometry is Jack the Ripper's field, however."

She shook her head, disappointed. "Number five."

Quentin consulted map, cablegram, then map again.

"Dorset Street. Mary Jane Kelly. Almost directly northeast of the Eddowes site, although a shuttlecock of confusing streets lay between them. Kelly? Wasn't she the one that was cut limb from limb?"

Irene nodded. "In the privacy of her room. The Ripper had all the time in the world and disassembled her like a *Les Halles* piglet."

"Now we have five points on the map," I said, "and they still make no sense."

"Points on a map never make sense until they are linked," Irene mused. "Quentin? You have puzzled over a map or two in your time."

He nodded and shrugged at the same time. "Four of the key sites are clustered to what I would call the left of center, three of them being locations of victims. They are Annie Chapman, the second . . . Mary Jane Kelly, the fifth . . . Catharine Eddowes, the fourth . . . and finally the Goulston Street graffito. Eddowes is the farthest point east of the four. But look how far west the first site, Nichols, is. All off by itself, as is the Stride site, yet Stride and Eddowes were attacked in the same night."

"And no straight, easy path between them," Irene noted.

"That and the graffito that night almost argue for more than one man," I noted.

"More than a James Kelly, certainly," Irene said grimly.

"Six sites," I said, "if you count the Juwes graffito as a separate one. Four of the six to the left of center. There is no reasonable pattern. Just as Paris is laid out in neat geometry, thanks to l'Enfant's elegant redesign, London remains a postmedieval jumble. Make sense of it if you dare."

My comment seemed to spur Irene to prove me wrong. She seized a pen from the letterbox, dipped it in a crystal inkwell, and used the edge of the cablegram as a somewhat insubstantial ruler.

In a moment she had drawn a bold black diagonal line from the first murder site to the fourth. Spinning the cablegram edge, she drew a second diagonal line from the fifth to the third site. It was Nichols to Eddowes, Kelly to Stride.

I could not deny it. Her lines created an giant "X," just as they had in Paris.

"Points on a map can be manipulated as 'X's into eternity," Quentin objected. He had never seen the map we had drawn of the Paris murders, an "X" intersecting a giant "P." This Chi-Rho symbolized the Christ figure, the very same marking we had found scratched in some of the Paris cellars and catacombs where the secret cult associated with Kelly had met.

Irene nodded, grim-lipped, noncommittal. She set the edge of the cablegram at the top of the map, on the second Whitechapel murder site, Annie Chapman's final resting place on Hanbury Street.

Next she spun the edge of the paper left, then right.

"Where shall we draw this last, vertical line? There is no southern point to fix its axis. If I draw it straight down, it crosses the diagonal lines off center, creating an empty triangle between them." She frowned, unhappy with the figure her calculations would draw.

"If, however, I . . . cant the vertical line to the right, along the strong angled street lines of Brick Lane and Osborne Place . . . if I permit the vertical to curve slightly as in a cursive letter, the downward stroke intersects the two diagonals at their jointure and . . . and I have isolated above Whitechapel High Street a section of byways that makes the top of a 'P': Hanbury Street east curving into Great Garden Street and bounded on the bottom by Old Montague Street thence meeting Brick Lane to make a closed circle."

We stared at her construction of ink and lines, Quentin Stanhope and I. We consulted each other silently. He had not seen the same pattern laid on the map of Paris, as I had, but the resemblance was uncanny.

Irene reached into the folder and withdrew another map, another city. Paris, with the Chi-Rho laid over it by Nell's hand.

"Good God!" Quentin leaned in with the sort of fascinated distaste that implied a literal body lying on the table. "The patterns are close enough to send chills up my spine. What kind of debased being would kill so savagely by the rigorous rules of geometry?"

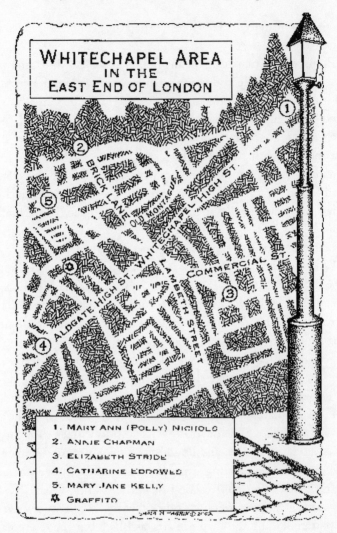

WHITECHAPEL AREA
IN THE
EAST END OF LONDON

1. MARY ANN (POLLY) NICHOLS
2. ANNIE CHAPMAN
3. ELIZABETH STRIDE
4. CATHARINE EDDOWES
5. MARY JANE KELLY
卐 GRAFFITO

"The geometry is incidental," Irene said, her voice muted, "as it is to most of life. The question is who would kill by a symbol of God?"

I could think of only one answer, but did not say it for fear of sounding foolish, though Nell would never have hesitated to name names for a minute.

The Devil.

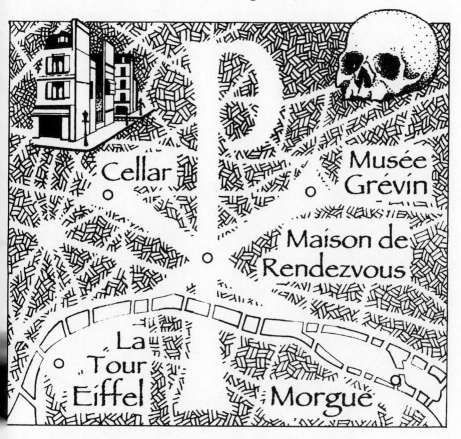

Cellar

Musée Grévin

Maison de Rendezvous

La Tour Eiffel

Morgue

29.

Game for Dinner

At the present moment you thrill with the glamour of the situation and the anticipation of the hunt.
—SHERLOCK HOLMES TO INSPECTOR MACDONALD,
ARTHUR CONAN DOYLE, *THE VALLEY OF FEAR*

What a tantalizing dilemma!

Would I rather have the hand of James Kelly with a clasp knife at my throat, or would I rather be the prisoner of the mysterious spy-mistress who called herself Tatyana? Perhaps I was facing both.

I did not ask Godfrey to resolve my quandary.

He had become quite grim after realizing that Tatyana was our captor. Though I breathed many prayers of thanks that it was not that madman Kelly who had darkened our door, I must admit that I found Tatyana intimidating. Godfrey clearly considered the Russian woman to be the greater foe, but he had never walked the path Irene and I had in Paris.

While we were still engaged in debating the dangers of our situation, there came a knock on my door.

Our discussion stopped while we gazed startled at each other.

Tatyana surely wouldn't have returned, knocking, where before she had ambled in unheralded like the Queen of the May (although it was now early June).

Godfrey, of course, took matters into his hands and rose to answer the knock. I was momentarily disturbed that someone should witness Godfrey's and my closeting and make unpleasant assumptions about his presence in my room. On reflection I concluded that it was quite natural for prisoners to conspire and only a demented mind would misconstrue our close association.

Then again, Tatyana was clearly demented.

While I debated with myself, Godfrey returned, leading a petite, brunette woman wearing the plain dark dress and servile white collars and cuffs of a personal servant.

She curtsied to me, this dark-favored sprite, and spoke English with a French accent.

"Madame Tatyana say that you will take care to dress for the dinner, and Monsieur as well. This are for you. Dinner at eight."

What I had taken for a pile of bed linens apparently was a gown. Of sorts. There was no point my spurning the things in the presence of the messenger, so I nodded to the long bench at the foot of the bed.

"Thank you—"

"Mignon." Offered with another curtsy.

She turned to leave.

"And how long," Godfrey asked, stopping her as if he held a pistol on her, "have you been with Madame?"

"Been with?"

"How long have you served her?"

"*Deux ans.* Two year." She held up a pair of fingers lest we still be uncertain.

"In London, too, then?" said I.

"*Oui.* Since Buda-pesth."

With that she curtsied again—apparently Madame Tatyana required frequent obeisance—and departed.

"Well done, Nell!" Godfrey smiled for the first time since Tatyana had announced herself. "So our hostess was in London previously, and the French maid betokens a sojourn in Paris as well."

"What is a French maid doing in this forsaken castle?"

"Apparently what she did in London and Paris. What has she brought you?"

"Oh, I'm not even going to look at it. I am not going through any mummery for Tatyana's benefit."

Godfrey had gone over to prod at the clothing. "It might be to our benefit, though, to appear as docile captives. I say, these look more like draperies than clothing."

"Revolting pattern. It reminds me of the Girl Who Trod on a Loaf in the fairy tale and sank down into Hell twined round with spiders and snakes and other crawling things."

"Ah, I see. The pattern is dragonflies and reeds, all in peacock blue and emerald green and gold threads. A costly fabric, to be sure."

"It looks like something barbaric she would wear herself, all the more reason I should shun it as if it were sackcloth and ashes."

"Perhaps not, Nell. Tatyana likes to pretend to elegance, even here. We may learn more by humoring her manias than defying them."

"You will wear formal dress, as she demanded?"

He shrugged. "Why not? All my baggage was captured with me. Methinks a woman who imports a French maid to a half-crumbled castle in the wilderness has pretensions that may be turned against her."

"She certainly has too much time and money on her hands," I grumbled, lifting the heavy gown. I might as well have been handling the carapace of some huge, exotic bug, I shivered so at the cold metallic touch of the glittering weave.

"I don't know how to dress my hair without my comb and brush," I explained, "but I will try to do it up so as not to embarrass you."

"The entire point is not to enrage Tatyana. The more we play into her charade that we are her guests, the more we may learn how many henchmen she has brought with her."

"Perhaps they're all as harmless as French maids."

"I fear not." Godfrey glanced at my dimming window and consulted his pocket watch. "We have an hour. I suggest you do what you can before the daylight fades and you are dependent only on candlelight." He paused on the way to the door. "Your injuries . . . you are able to dress yourself? I have assisted Irene. I can always do laces through a crack in the door."

"A most sensitive offer, Godfrey, but I believe I can manage by myself."

I did not mention that I had observed Tatyana before, by her account a former dancer with the Russian ballet. It had appeared to me that she habitually dispensed with corsets, as Irene did herself from time to time. I doubted that this heap of clothing would include anything so restrictive of movement. But of course I could not tell Godfrey that. It was best that gentlemen not be encouraged to speculate on the exact elements of a lady's underlayments, no matter how dire the situation, even if they knew all about them, as apparently Godfrey, and Quentin, did.

I found my face hot with shame as I untangled the garments.

A camisole and drawers, but no corset. I glanced down at my peasant blouse, skirt, and wide, laced felt belt. Perhaps the belt would serve as a corselet beneath the gown. I would very much like to present Tatyana's gown back to her with a much smaller waist than her own!

Although I felt like a rabbit assuming a discarded snakeskin, I must admit that the fine silk and lawn of the borrowed linens were far kinder to my abused skin than the rough peasant weaves I had been wearing.

If I ever got back to Paris . . . *when we* got back to Paris . . . I believe I would shock Irene by visiting Worth on the Rue de la Paix for some outrageously expensive fripperies.

The gown was as I had expected: one of those Sarah Bernhardt, tartar-style robes banded in costly gold braid and held shut by a heavy brass and copper belt that would look magnificent in an Alphonse Mucha poster. I only thought what a fine weapon it would make unclasped.

I had to light the candles from the flames we kept going in the fireplace. I stood before the mirror and reluctantly unbraided my coiled hair, a necessity that I had found deliciously unencumbering and practical.

I gasped my dismay at the result of loosening them after several days. Every hair was crinkled like strands of hemp. I wore a snuff-brown haystack. How could I tame such a clutter without a comb?

A discreet knock at the connecting door to Godfrey's suite undid me.

"Go away!" I burst out in panic.

"What is wrong, Nell?" he called back, alarmed. "You are still alone?"

"Yes. No!"

That "no" brought him bursting into the room, looking for villains to engage.

"It's only me," I said meekly from my corner by the mirror. "I am not a vain woman, but I do not know what I shall do with this dreadful hair!"

He approached me gingerly, like a man well used to a woman at war with her own annoying image, as I suppose most women are. Except, one would think, Irene.

He stood behind me in the mirror and leaned left and right to seek out my face amid this explosion of unbridled hair.

"Why do anything at all with it?" he said at last. "You look like one of Burne-Jones's medieval maidens, which seems oddly appropriate for the gown."

"That shows you what you know of women's dress, Godfrey. We are not all actresses. I have not worn my hair down since I was sixteen. Only loose women and children do so, and I have no desire to masquerade as either one."

"Only loose women and children wear their hair down?" Godfrey mulled that. "An odd juxtaposition of innocence and sin for the same act. Irene—"

"It does not matter what Irene does. I do not approve of half of it, and you do not approve of one-quarter of it, and don't deny it."

He chuckled. "That's quite true, but that is what makes life with Irene so interesting. If she were here, she would suggest you forget your hair and concentrate on what we wish to learn at our dinner tonight. It may be that your . . . ungoverned hair is the very thing to distract Tatyana from the danger we pose to her. She enjoys putting people on strange ground and then watching them stumble to overcome it. You will offer her amusement. I suspect she is most dangerous when she is bored."

"You think that my disgraceful hair could function as a ruse, then?"

I frowned at myself in the mirror. I looked like a hedgerow with a face peeping out of it. An elfin face. A faery face. They were both treacherous races, fey and unpredictable. Could I be fey and unpredictable? It would be a first, but it might be useful.

Godfrey rested his hands on my shoulders, like a comrade in arms. "I am sure of it."

"You certainly look quite dashing and not at all disheveled," I said, taking in for the first time the diplomatic grandeur of his white tie and tails and the subtle glint of gold studs and cufflinks.

"I was supposed to conclude the Rothschild transaction in Transylvania at a formal dinner party. I believe that tonight is that occasion. Shall we find our way downstairs to whatever room has been designated as the dining chamber?"

He offered me his arm, which I took.

The weighted hem of the brocade gown brushed the toes of my bright leather Gypsy boots, which I found quite comfortable and light to wear. So I was Romany at head and toe, Russian in between, and utterly English underneath.

Perhaps Tatyana had never yet encountered such a formidable foe as I after all.

After we had descended a huge curving stone staircase unnoticed, Godfrey, who had managed that clandestine foray through the castle in the dead of night, steered me in directions that might lead us to another part of the castle.

Each time he was foiled. A Gypsy with a greasy leg of roasted fowl in each hand blocked our way to the kitchens, from whence floated exotic odors and came the clang of many pots.

A return to the staircase and a charge straight ahead found the front hall . . . which was occupied by more Gypsies sitting on empty wooden food crates, tuning their battered violins.

Again we swept left of the staircase, through a series of rooms fitted with rotting tapestries and broken furniture. A bay of shattered glass windows promised a way to the outside . . . save that two grizzled men in tattered uniforms were playing a game of dice on the stone floor, a pottery bottle of spirits making a third between them.

We circled back to the stair and the mammoth hall that surrounded it like a chapel, all lofty stone arches lost in the dark above. I was struck by how much castles and cathedrals resembled each other: vast, forbidding, formal, cold buildings built to elevate God and man above the common throng in a medieval society where one was either peasant or aristocrat.

From the smaller front hall came the screech of slaughtered violins. From the kitchens the clang of the brass cymbals. I could not hear the percussion of rattled and thrown dice from the solarium, but from another room not yet seen I heard the murmur of human voices speaking a language other than English.

Godfrey heard that, too. He looked at me, shrugged, and turned us in that direction. It was now time to face the music and join Tatyana's bizarre dinner party.

The room was the library Godfrey had told me about, a long, narrow space with three stories of books reached by a series of spiral stairs.

Lighted candelabras made the old gold bindings glisten like rich veins of ore along the dark shelves. It felt like being in a dwarves' undermountain mine or on the stage set of a Wagnerian opera. I admit to being charmed, and charmed also to see the sturdy library table laid with a tsar's ransom in table linen, porcelain, and silver.

A massive stone fireplace at one end of the room was high enough to hold a complement of guards at attention with pike staffs.

The fire that blazed in it was strong but seemed a puny thing in comparison, and the room remained chilly. Despite the spring season, these high mountains hoarded their winter cold like old people did memories. No wonder Tatyana wore such heavy gowns. She was used to such chill climates.

A huge brass samovar, or urn, sat beside the fireplace and beside the samovar stood . . . a tiny man, handing out chalices of some heated cider. He was dressed in a starched white ruff and red velvet knee breeches and coat, rather like a Spanish court dwarf.

He beckoned us over like a conspirator, and spoke English when we got there. Cockney English.

"Oid 'ave a bit o' this, Miss. Warm the cockles and the knuckles at the same toime."

My pen chokes at recording the exact mispronunciations he offered with the warming liquid, but it was good to hear an honest English voice, no matter how garbled.

"How long have you served our hostess?" Godfrey asked affably. (No one was more affable than Godfrey when he wanted to know something without letting the subject know that he wanted it.)

The stunted creature was eyeing my wild hair with alarming approval. "Summer last. Quite a traveler, milady, to some strange plaices, but the grub is good and the pay is foine. 'Ave a good cupful, Miss. It'll straighten the hefforts of yer curlin' iron, all roight."

"I do not resort to such implements as curling irons," I said indignantly.

"Natural, is it? Quite a wonder."

And he winked. Only men of the lower orders wink at women, so I turned away without answering and sipped the warm drink, which slid down my parched throat like heated honey.

The fire (and the dwarf) at our backs, our goblets clutched at our fronts like weapons, Godfrey and I surveyed the persons in the room.

They ignored us, which was rather disconcerting.

Tatyana herself sat in the high-backed chair at the far end of the library table, although it was rude to sit at a dinner table before the guests were summoned.

She wore a gown with a high starched halo of gilt lace around the bared shoulders, her yellow-red hair piled into coarse clouds atop her head. She reminded me of portraits of Queen Elizabeth: richly and exotically garbed in an embroidered fabric dripping jewels the size of dewdrops, imperious.

Behind her chair stood a rude servitor, and with a start I realized I had glimpsed him before, during Irene's midnight confrontation with this very woman at her hotel in Prague, when we had visited there but a year before.

He seemed to be wearing the very same dusty, dingy blue peasant blouse, with its set of buttons on the single shoulder and the waist belted in by a scuffed brown leather belt. I was sure that equally dingy pantaloons were below the blouse, stuffed into equally scuffed brown leather boots.

The international cast of characters for this charade amazed me: a French maid, an English dwarf, this Russian oaf, the Gypsy caravan, the hungry Russian peasants guarding the kitchen, the Bohemian soldiers gaming in the solarium . . . and of course Godfrey and myself, fresh from London and Paris save for diversions to Bohemia and a portable coffin.

Tatyana was talking with a new figure, a tall, cadaverous man in a narrow black robe, rather like that effected by Mr. Sherlock Holmes when he impersonated a French clergyman. I can think of no more odious combination on earth than that of Sherlock Holmes and a French clergyman. Luckily, it was a disguise and temporary.

"A village elder, I gather," Godfrey leaned inward to whisper to me. "I doubt he speaks English, but I know some German. If you will divert our hostess, I will try to get him aside and see what I can learn . . . see what he thinks Tatyana and this castle are all about. He seems to be the only local guest here."

"Divert our hostess! Godfrey, that would require me to speak to the monster."

"It would be a great help if you could manage it," he suggested gently.

I sighed until my shoulders were squared with determination. "I can't imagine how I shall chitchat with the woman."

"Just pretend that she is Sarah Bernhardt."

"Another person with whom I have nothing in common. Very well."

Together Godfrey and I approached that end of the table.

I needn't have worried. Like Sarah Bernhardt, and sometimes like my great and good friend Irene Adler, it seemed Tatyana was most taken with appearances.

"Why, Miss Huxleigh, you look quite . . . Serbian in that old gown of mine."

I wasn't sure what a Serbian was, probably a breed of dog, but I was quite sure it was far below a Russian.

Pretend that she is Sarah Bernhardt. Godfrey was an adept diplomat indeed. The Divine Sarah, my friend Irene, and this woman had one thing in common: all were performers, or former performers. As long as I played their game—as Our Great Bard so perfectly put it, that assumption that all the world's a stage—we should get on famously.

I did a mocking little curtsy like Mignon. "Serbian?" I said. "I would think that I was more Shavian."

"Ah. You like your Socialist Englishman?"

I detested Shaw almost as much as I detested Wilde, but the play's the thing.

"I like the gown," I said, diverting her again to her play and the part I was to act within it.

I realized my role now: she was queen, I was courtier. But there is much conspiracy in royal courts. I noticed that Godfrey had edged next to the cadaverous figure in black and was directing his attention to the elaborate sterling silver centerpiece as big as a barrel, representing a battlement besieged by warriors on horseback.

Tatyana was watching him out of the corner of her eye, always, but she leaned her rouged cheek on her beringed fist and commented, "You do not look English any longer."

"I have traveled far from home, and in . . . rough company."

"Nor do you look Romany, as you did this afternoon." She laughed and quaffed from a metal goblet like Godfrey and I held, only I guessed it held something cold and searing, not hot like our cider.

I sipped, savoring cinnamon and other less-known spices, not sure what to say.

"We wait dinner upon one last guest," she announced. "Mr. Norton!" Her voice rang out like a challenge. "You will sit at my right hand."

Godfrey remained very still. I could see him debating obedience.

"And you, Miss Huxleigh, will sit opposite, to the right of the seat at the table's other end."

I glanced down at the other empty, high-backed chair, fit for a queen, or a head of household. Who was to occupy it? Not Godfrey. Surely not the dwarf?

I heard the crack of a door in the anterooms, almost felt the slight inrush of chill night air.

"Ah. Our party is complete." Tatyana stood before her throne, lifted her glass. "He is here at last. My dear . . . guests, my loyal servants, what can I say? Enter the Tiger."

We all turned as we had been programmed to do, like supernumeraries in the Lyceum Theater production of *Macbeth*, to welcome the leading man into our midst.

In walked another Englishman in evening dress: sturdy, bald, mustachioed, completely at home among this international circus of characters; a man I had last seen gripped in a death-lock with Quentin Stanhope above the Thames on Hammersmith Bridge. This was the heavy game hunter and spy and mortal enemy to Quentin, Godfrey, Irene and myself, and to Mr. Sherlock Holmes . . . Colonel Sebastian Moran.

I wondered if Godfrey would consider swooning a sufficient diversion under the circumstances.

30.

Digging Deeper

⊰•⊱

*Decadent literature spread perfumes too dark and heady,
its exuberant blood-flowers breathe suffocating air.*
—FRANTIŠEK XAVER ŠALDA ON PRAGUE'S HAUNTING *FIN
DE SIÈCLE* MYSTIQUE

⊰ FROM A JOURNAL ⊱

We gathered again that night in our hotel room: Irene and myself, Quentin Stanhope, and Bram Stoker.

We were all garbed in black, as agreed. Irene and I wore the men's clothing we had donned during one expedition in Paris and that she had resurrected for herself during our visit to the fortune-teller. Bram's frockcoat did not button quite high enough to obscure his white shirt front, but Irene ringed his neck with a dark muffler to finish the job.

Quentin's clothing made him into one solid charcoal stroke on a piece of white paper. He affected the same black jersey beneath the jacket that Irene had, as well as a soft, dark cap pulled low, muffler and black leather gloves like a coachman.

He even produced a pot of bootblack in case we should wish to darken our faces, but Irene felt that hats and scarves would be sufficient.

We assembled in that humble hotel room like a slink of burglars, surrounding the table clothed in a map of the streets of Prague that would soon be our stalking ground.

"No police, no Rothschild representatives?" Bram Stoker asked, eyeing our unconventional party a bit nervously.

For all his great size, the writer of lurid tales and theatrical manager preferred a cast of dozens for the battle scenes. He hadn't realized we were mounting a new production of *Joan of Arc* with the leading lady and her understudy playing half the invading force.

Irene produced her revolver from a pocket. "We are better armed than we look." Quentin, nodding, allowed the butt-end of a pistol that Buffalo Bill Cody would be proud to flourish to emerge from one pocket.

Naturally Bram Stoker looked to me and my jacket pocket.

Firearms were not in my armament, so instead I hefted Godfrey's sword-stick from its resting place against the bureau and withdrew enough of the haft to show a grin of bared steel. I felt rather like Jean LaFitte the pirate.

"I am not armed," Mr. Stoker said regretfully. "I travel with nothing more lethal than a walking staff for the moors and mountains, and have never encountered trouble or troublemakers."

"Your size alone is a weapon," Irene said. "And I hope that we won't need any of our 'equalizers.' At this point, I am only looking for a trail, not the ones who made it."

"Ones," Quentin pounced. "Then you are not trailing the Ripper. Or do you believe he has partners in crime?"

"I don't know," Irene admitted. "I only know that if we can find some pattern here in Prague, we will have half a chance of understanding why Nell and Godfrey are missing."

Quentin pulled something out of his other pocket . . . an innocent scrap of paper.

"I've noted the locations of the murdered women found recently in the city, at least the ones that are made public. I find it rather interesting that the Whitechapel murders are news the world over but that these Prague killings and the more recent but no less horrific slaughters in Paris remain a well-kept official secret."

"I'm not surprised," Irene said. "The London panic taught the authorities discretion. Public furor only made the task of tracking the killer harder. And," she added, "no sensible government wishes to unleash the anti-Jewish sentiment that always lurks beneath the surface of European civil unrest."

I put in my professional opinion. "Certainly the repetition of the Goulston Street graffito in Paris would have raised a few international eyebrows, discretion or not. I wonder if you and Godfrey have been used throughout this latest outbreak to obscure the truth, rather than seek it out."

I had expected to unleash operatic fireworks of denial at my implication that the Rothschild motives might be self-seeking. Instead Irene merely nodded.

"There is always that danger in accepting work from people with power, Pink. Isn't that true, Quentin?"

"The trick is to be of use in a good cause without being used to advance a bad one," he agreed. "I take nothing for granted. It is even possible that Godfrey was abducted by the Rothschilds for some larger purpose of their own that he had ceased to serve, especially if his investigations into the Prague murders led in the wrong direction."

"It is also possible," Irene added, "that the Paris murders were orchestrated to divert attention from the Whitechapel killings. If so, some faction may be angry that the officials have so successfully kept them out of the public press."

"Then maybe," I said quickly, "the public press is exactly where they should be."

Again Irene surprised me by nodding agreement. "Such a sensational revelation would best be made public in an uninvolved country."

I admit my heart began beating with a vision of what might very soon be. I had known, and resented, that I was accompanying Irene because she wanted to control me and perhaps to somewhat replace Nell. Now I saw that she might at any moment find it useful for me to wire the whole sordid Paris episode to my newspaper, just to keep the powerful people for whom she sometimes worked from totally obscuring the truth for their own safety.

My initial admiration for her, dampened by recent uncertainties, came roaring back. Like myself, she ultimately served what some might call the public interest. Of course, it was necessary to see somewhat to one's own interest so as to be properly positioned to rise in defense of the public good at the exactly right time. . . .

"Anyway," Quentin went on, "I can't offer the tidy illustrations you . . . and Nell have marshaled for London and Paris." He waved a gloved hand over the map of Prague. "Like London and Paris and most great cities of the world, Prague is bisected by a river. Unlike the much larger capitals, Prague is lopsided, with only the smaller Mala Strana and Prague Castle districts sitting across the river from the sprawling districts of the city's western and southern sections."

We stared at the areas he indicated, and nodded sagely at the obvious.

"The Whitechapel murders," Irene said, "were confined to a very small area of a notorious but quite small site within the equally notorious East End of London. In Paris, the murders kept to the right bank, but involved the entire city on that side."

"Here they do not cross the river either," Quentin said, "only here the river is not the Seine, but the Vltava. And they have so far been confined to the crowded section in the crook of the river, northeast from the Joseph Quarter in the Old Town to the New Town Hall district, and southwest from the Old New Synagogue to the museum. These streets are dense and old, narrow and dirty, easy to disappear into . . . and out of."

"Like Whitechapel," I said.

"Were any of the bodies moved from the place of death to be displayed elsewhere?" Irene wondered.

"Nobody's considered that," Quentin said. "Certainly they were readily found, openly left on the street as in London. Why? Was it different in Paris?"

"Some of the bodies were moved to the Paris Morgue for identification. Although the Whitechapel bodies also swiftly found their way to city morgues, the Paris Morgue is a showplace as well as an official mortuary. So by the very fact of being killed in Paris, the victims were on display, if anonymously. While one body was held back even from that public acknowledgment, another was deliberately brought into a famous Paris wax museum and substituted for a corpse on display."

"Nervy!" Quentin said, almost admiringly. "But you know, perhaps the Whitechapel bodies were also put on display, just less obviously so. Civil murder isn't my bailiwick, but weren't the bodies found quite soon after the killings, in the open, stumbled over, in fact, by the usual Whitechapel residents whose jobs start in the wee hours or go past midnight?"

"Yes," I said, eager to join the discussion. "Everyone assumed the victims had been dropped in their tracks, but they could have been dragged around a corner into a more public view, at the least. Often a bobby was due to pass by the sites within minutes, or no more than half an hour."

Bram Stoker spoke again, as our speculation finally touched on his area of expertise. "You're saying the Ripper always set the scene, whether on Hanbury Street or under the shadow of the Eiffel Tower in Paris, much as a stage direction might call for a body to lie by the footlights at the beginning of an act."

There was a silence. No one had quite conceived of the Ripper as a stage manager.

"Quentin," Irene asked, "where were the bodies found here?"

His forefinger danced over five points on the east side of the Vltava: "Here, by the New Town Hall and diagonally opposite at the far northeast corner of the *Staré Město* district."

Irene seized the pen and the ink-stained edge of the cablegram from Mycroft Holmes and drew a line.

"And here," he went on, "at the Old Town Square, and diagonally down near the museum."

"And that was the order of the crimes?"

"Yes." Quentin watched the dark slash of another line intersect the first, forming the telltale "X."

As he had said earlier, drawing "X"s on maps was arbitrary

child's play. Finding a Chi-Rho at the heart of them was harder.

Irene's pen point tapped one location on the map, leaving a cluster of black dots. "As we noted, the ancient Joseph Quarter is in many ways a shadow of Whitechapel, an ancient tangle of streets where the poor and the outcast have always huddled. And the spiritual center of the Joseph Quarter is the old Jewish cemetery. Nell, Godfrey, and I found it a useful place to visit once before. That is where we will begin tonight."

"At the cemetery?" I asked. "What can dead people tell us?"

"People go all the time to that cemetery to leave notes on a dead man's tomb," she said, "notes full of questions, pleading, prayer."

"You speak of Rabbi Loew," Bram Stoker said eagerly, "the prominent rabbi of Prague who purportedly raised the Golem. But, you know, Irene, that is like most legends, pretty far-fetched. The rabbi was dead two hundred years before those Golem rumors became common in the city."

"Two hundred years!" I cried. "Just when did this rabbi die?"

Irene turned to Bram Stoker, who leaped into the breach like a happy schoolboy with just the right answer when he is called upon.

First he smiled at me. "You are an American. One hundred years is an aeon in your young country. Europe is older, and the farther east one goes, the older and deeper the roots drive if you can but find them. When did this rabbi die? In the sixteenth century and the Old New Synagogue was already in use then. Yes, even the New Town is very old here. Prague is haunted by some of the most charming legends, including its history as a seat of medieval alchemy." Mr. Stoker shrugged his massive shoulders. "Some legends are not so charming, and I like those even better as a source for my stories."

"Tell us some," Irene requested. "It's a bit soon to go prowling."

I have heard a few first-class lecturers in my time, including Oscar Wilde and Buffalo Bill Cody, but Bram Stoker could have held his own with anybody. No wonder he had entertained steamship passengers with a magic act during the Atlantic crossing!

We sat on the sofa and chairs arranged for tea, Mr. Stoker barely perching on a tapestry-upholstered side chair. As he spoke, his face and arms became animated. At times he leapt up from the chair to enact a point.

"The business that has brought me to this city of a hundred spires is sad indeed, but I am glad indeed to have made its acquaintance," he began. "Prague is not a city known for murder, but rather for the mysterious and mystic, yes. And it has been much contested through centuries of war and religious conflict.

"Irene, you mention the precarious position of the Jews in these modern times. You speak of political scapegoats. It has always been so, and in Prague particularly so. I speak of the distant fifteenth and sixteenth centuries, when the European quest for westward exploration was rivaled by the East's fierce pounding at the continent's back door. The Ottoman Turk pressed hard at this string of countries that were being drawn into what would become the mighty Austro-Hungarian Empire. And religious differences proved fatal for many. Land on the wrong side of the eternal Catholic-Jewish-Protestant triangle, and you could be burned at the stake and tortured first."

"It sounds like our Wild West Indians are just a last gasp of what has been going on in the world for centuries," I said.

"The evil that men do is bottomless," Mr. Stoker agreed, "no matter their race or creed. So Prague was a prize that was tossed back and forth between Polish kings and Hapsburg kings, and always the Turks with their eyes on it, until in the late fifteen hundreds a Hapsburg youth of twenty-four was made the first King of Bohemia to nobody's satisfaction, including his own."

Irene interrupted the story. "The Holy Roman Emperor Rudolf II."

"What makes Rudolf interesting is that he did not while away his life at the court in Vienna, but actually moved his court to Prague, along with artists and goldsmiths and precious stonecutters and scientists and astronomers, which during that time included alchemists. Tycho Brahe and Johannes Kepler were among the brilliant scientists who worked in the city, but the most notorious of Rudolf II's guests were two Englishmen, John Dee and Edward Kelley."

Irene shook her head. "Yet another Kelley! The infamous Dee and Kelley, alchemists, occultists, frauds. Antonín Dvořák toyed with composing an opera on the subject, but could think of no way to include female voices. I was singing in Prague at the time, and he was seeking subjects that were both Bohemian, yet suitable for my very difficult dark soprano voice. He even suggested that I could sing Kelley, the younger man."

"Really?" I asked, astounded. "The great Dvořák wanted to compose a part just for you?"

"Once," she said shortly. "Before I dallied in Bohemia, I had a European operatic career that was not considered insignificant."

"Well, I never heard of you."

"I should hope," Quentin Stanhope said a trifle sternly, "that a young person of your limited background and great distance from the European centers of culture would have 'not heard of' a great many important matters and persons, for what is life but an opportunity to learn one's limitations."

"Irene is a sublime singer," Bram Stoker added to the chorus descending upon me. "She is to the musical stage what Sarah Bernhardt is to the dramatic stage, and it is a true tragedy that circumstances have limited her performances of late to circles of close friends."

I really hadn't given a moment's thought to Irene as anything but a lady detective of sorts, so there was nothing to do but subside into silence.

After a long pause, Bram Stoker filled it.

"Dee and Kelley are fascinating, but can hardly have anything to do with contemporary killings, here or elsewhere. In fact, it seems almost as unlikely that we sit here more than theoretically concerned even with such a modern monster as Jack the Ripper." He eyed Irene, looking doubtful and wary.

"You are sure," Bram asked, "that Nell and Godfrey vanishing is related to the Ripper case?"

"Nell was last seen in Paris being pursued by the leading candidate for the Ripper, and Godfrey—" She paused, sighed heavily, then spoke again. "No one but Pink knows this. And Sherlock Holmes. A lock of Godfrey's hair had been left on my pillow in the Paris hotel when I returned from our raid on the barbaric rites of the cult where Nell vanished."

"You are certain—?"

Irene didn't allow Quentin to finish. "What can I say? That Nell and Godfrey may be lost? That we may all be too late?"

He paused, then pounded one fist into another with such violence that we all held our breaths.

"Quentin!" Irene stepped to him, caught his hands in her own. "Don't you think that I have imagined every awful eventuality? A thousand times. So are we to be frozen by our fears? Are we to be what these monsters wish? Feckless. Fearful. Unable to move? No! There is evil in the world. Sometimes it is aimed at us, very personally. Then is when we must surmount the usual. Then is when we most must be unpredictable. Then is when we must dare! And succeed."

"You believe this, Irene?"

She waited a long moment to answer and then it was anticlimactical. "Usually. When I am not feeling so utterly useless and hopeless."

What a tactician! She was forging an alliance from the uncertainties we all feel at times. From beneath her dark jacket she lifted the locket on a long chain she had used to mesmerize the Paris victim of those same barbaric rituals we had been discussing. She opened it to reveal the poignant comma of dark hair. "I know the color; besides, why lay another's hair upon my pillow? Especially since Godfrey was found to have gone missing shortly before the Paris raid."

The men kept silence but I could not.

"Who would do such a thing? A clever person who saw you were close on the Ripper's trail may have wanted to distract you, but I'm sure travelers in the lands beyond Prague often lose touch with civilized outposts. It must be like the Wild West before the railroad: a long time between mail runs."

Irene remained unconvinced. "Anyone who knew enough about

my personal circumstances and was clever enough to want to deceive me with a false lock of hair could have easily managed to obtain the real thing. I sense a larger game than find-the-Ripper being played, which is why I wanted you, Quentin, among our party."

"And me?" Bram asked. "What good can I do? I am a world traveler, yes; a good arranger of stage and other business; a sometimes scribbler."

"You are also a member of Henry Irving's Beefsteak Club and are familiar with our guidebook on this hunt for the Ripper, Krafft-Ebing's *Psychopathia Sexualis*."

"I am not proud to admit to that knowledge. Among artistic folk there can be a fascination with the basest forms of human behavior."

"Not only 'artistic folk,'" I put in. "The reading public laps up that sort of thing like oatmeal with cream in the morning. The fortunate love to hear how sadly the other half lives. Ordinary folks in London weren't interested in hearing about what they called those 'unfortunates'—the women who lacked even brothels in which to ply their underpaid trade but had to use the public streets. Once they had attracted the attention of the Ripper, everybody gobbled up all there was to know about them, from just how their innards were shredded to what few worthless remnants were found in their sorry pockets."

I do not often give speeches, but I had not had a chance to write a good indignant article in too long.

"That's why I like living in so-called uncivilized countries," Quentin said, eyeing me with both surprise and sympathy. "Some of the practices may be savage, but starvation, forced labor, and slavery are out in the open, not hidden away in city byways so nice folks won't notice."

Irene shook her head. "The world should be better than any of that by now, but I know it isn't. Even grand opera appeals to audiences with madness, scandal, suicide, and murder, all sung in perfect pitch, of course. I am but a singer and must follow the syllables and staffs as they are composed, but why do writers revel in the darkest side of humanity?"

She was asking Bram Stoker.

"A taste for the fantastic is inborn, I think. My son Noel began having nightmares at the age of three. The demons are always in our earliest dreams. It is better that we let them out during daylight."

"If these bad dreams are let out to play," Irene suggested, "do you mean that it is less likely that one will enact them in real life?"

"You have played parts, I am sure," Bram said, "that mimic acts or represent ideas you would never endorse in actuality."

"And someone like James Kelly, reared to follow a strict sexual morality he could not, will he replay his guilt in nightly private performances on the streets of Whitechapel? According to Krafft-Ebing, this hatred of women, the entire sex and each innocent individual, is a common feeling among such men."

"It is slightly more understandable," Bram said, "when you consider that women are chosen by society to be our strictest judges of morality, the mother, the wife. I agree that man is a feckless being, full of raw, unworthy needs he cannot control. No wonder his ravening soul turns good women stern and makes them ready to send him away. No wonder he will find bad women."

"If some women were not so 'good,' then, other women would never have to be 'bad'?"

Bram looked puzzled, unsure how to take Irene's comment. "A good woman is an angel on earth," he finally blurted out. "A man is a fool and a lout for causing such a one any trouble. The man must live up to the natural goodness of women."

"And," I wondered, "the women in brothels? What has happened to their natural goodness, sweetness, and light?"

He realized, as if struck by lightning, that I had first met most of the present company in a brothel. If his presence in the same brothel was open to charitable interpretation because he was a well-known man of respectable reputation in his profession, my presence there was unequivocally damning. I was a fallen woman, period. He was, as the Scots rule in court, not proven: though we both had been found in the same place on the same night at the same scene of a crime. And of course, he did not know then nor did he know now my true professional purpose in being there.

This time Bram Stoker paled instead of blushing, as I usually did. During the days and nights after my debut in the Paris brothel, I had been absorbed into Irene's immediate circle. I had behaved as the respectable young woman I knew myself to be. Bram Stoker had forgotten that I was supposed to be beyond redemption. And if I was not worthy of redemption because of my presence at the *maison de rendezvous*, then what did that say for him?

"So," Irene said, "how does one rank sin and crime? Had the Ripper only paid the women to do what dozens of other men did and gone on his way, who would have accused him of wrongdoing? Oh, the police, if they had to make an arrest now and then for what went on anywhere and anytime in Whitechapel."

"It's not just Whitechapel," Quentin said. "And not just women."

"What do you mean?" Irene grew suddenly alert.

Quentin shook his head. "I have seen treachery unparalleled in Afghanistan. MacLean dead, nearly beheaded at Tiger's and Sable's damned conspiring that came to naught. I have lived on the uncivil side of the blanket, and reveled in it. I have seen things south of the Carpathians that would make Jack the Ripper pause."

"Perhaps that is what Jack the Ripper *has* seen. You must not hold back, Quentin. You must tell us what the world holds for those who look it in the face. What were you thinking of just then?"

"Many things. Many things I vowed to forget." He waved a hand in front of his face as if pushing away cobwebs. "We are mixed company here."

"No. We are one company." Irene was as grimly resolute as I had ever seen her, which was saying something. "Nicety has no place among us. We can't afford to mince after a galloping maniac merely because there are ladies present. Tell us what you know; why else have you learned the opposite side of civilization except to educate?"

"All right. These mutilations of the Ripper that appall so many. They are not unheard of. In Africa, in Arab lands, it is even common practice to mutilate young girls in their female parts."

Irene and I listened with masks of iron. To show revulsion might stop this grim recital.

"Mutilate how?" Irene asked.

"Excise . . . parts. The girl feels nothing afterwards but pain. The husband knows he is the only father."

"Ah." Irene glanced at me.

I nodded. I knew the intricacies of this and that more than most, thanks to my having to learn how to hoodwink the madams in the brothels as to the state of my virtue.

Bram Stoker avoided looking at us, but was listening with utter fascination.

Quentin also avoided looking us in the eye. He stared out the window, as if seeing all those foreign countries with foreign ways.

"Arab brides? Also very, very young. In some tribes they are first excised of their responsive parts, then they are . . . sewn shut." His words were clipped. "On the wedding night, the virile groom will achieve consummation with the sheer power of his masculinity. The less virile groom will have to use a knife first."

Quentin stared out the window. Bram Stoker gazed at the map of Prague as if struck to stone.

Irene and I remained silent, each feeling the savagery of the practice, which would make of pleasure an eternal agony.

"Who does the cutting, the sewing?" Irene asked.

"The married women of the tribe."

That was perhaps the most shocking fact of all.

We said nothing and could suddenly hear the mantel clock tick. I had never noticed the clock ticking before.

"Dear God," Bram Stoker said at last. "It beggars all the lurid turns of my imagination, or anything the world's greatest playwrights, even the ancient Greeks who blanch at nothing, have put onto the tragic stage." His voice was shaking slightly. "I can see why women even in our civilized age and country might wish to avoid the marital duty."

"To lie back and think of England," Irene asked, "as the Queen advised her many royal daughters on the occasions of their many politically advantageous royal weddings?" She turned to Quentin. "What of the Arab concubines?"

"You mean—?"

"Are they also surgically altered?"

"There is no need. They will bear no heirs."

"What difference does it make if the surgery is physical, or mental? The effect is the same."

"You are saying," Bram Stoker said, stumbling his way through points of view he had never encountered before, "that we are as uncivilized in our way as the Arab tribes."

Irene nodded. "And that Jack the Ripper, in his own mad way, is merely exercising a twisted version of the prerogatives of other men in other places."

"But . . . the Ripper wasn't trying to safeguard heirs." Mr. Stoker was still blinking at the enormity of this line of thought.

"Are you sure?" Irene said. "Some suggest that the Ripper had contracted a venereal disease from a Whitechapel whore and killed these others out of revenge. A man with a venereal disease might pass it on to his wife and through her to his children. Was he not then, in his maddened mind, protecting heirs?

"Some suggest that the Ripper was hunting a whore who was pregnant by him and that he found her in Mary Jane Kelly and took away the foetal material, as he had the wombs in the other victims, unnoticed in the bloody carnage of that scene.

"I suggest that the attacks on the very womanliness of these women in Whitechapel and Paris and Prague, from excised wombs to severed breasts to slashed faces, is not so different from the systemic mutilation of some women in Arabia or elsewhere."

"And what is the common key?" I asked.

"With the Ripper, insanity is foremost, but behind it are motives that have become customs elsewhere. It has to do with hobbled wives and concubines who are good for only one thing: what is denied the wives, pleasure."

I could see Irene drawing the patterns even as she spoke. She walked back to the map and stared down at its enigmatic lines, at the confusion its very attempt at clarity spawned, as all maps do.

She traced the lines of the Chi-Rho. "And God is in it, whether He is called Allah or Yahweh or Christ because so often men who sin say that God gives them leave to be so inhuman."

"Religious mania," Mr. Stoker said, "it was often mentioned last fall in London, but never that seriously pursued."

"It will be seriously pursued now," Quentin said grimly. "You are right, Irene. The Koran is cited that men are to have concubines on earth and in heaven, but wives must be faithful conduits to many sons on earth, hence they are conquered and subjugated through the very acts of generation. I merely thought the practice an inexplicable foreign barbarity, but it is worse: it is a wholly self-serving strategy."

"As good a definition of evil as I have ever heard, Quentin," Irene said.

Quentin Stanhope suddenly took a deep breath. "You were right to force me to speak so frankly, Irene. I find I can now tell you the full truth about the worst atrocity here in Prague. I uphold your cause, Irene. I would give my life to recover Nell and Godfrey. Yet I found myself tongue-tied when it comes to detailing everything I have uncovered in Prague until you insisted I testify to what I have seen elsewhere, and told no one."

"You must tell us all," she said, "especially about Prague."

"The last death, or the last until the one at the brothel last night. No one knows but two Rothschild agents, Godfrey, and now myself. They only told me because Baron de Rothschild in Paris had demanded full cooperation with you and your agents, and I was the first to reach Prague. Even then it took a cable to the Baron to convince the agents to talk to me." Quentin laughed bitterly. "Would that the members of the Queen's army had such unswerving loyalty and obedience."

"Some do," Irene said.

Quentin shrugged, as if dismissing himself. "The woman was found alive. Alive and . . . defaced. But"—he glanced from Irene to me and back again. I realized it was because we were Bram Stoker's "good" women who were to be spared lest we judge too harshly.

"An infant was with her."

"Unhurt?" I asked. I had taken care of my many younger brothers and sisters from an early age, and a tale of youthful suffering never failed to fire me up.

He shook his head.

"An infant?" Irene repeated, as shocked as myself.

"Days old. The child's throat had been cut, and he had been drained of all blood."

"Vampires!" Bram Stoker said . . . cursed. "Modern vampires!"

"Drained of all blood," Irene repeated, "but he must have been alive when. . . ."

Quentin nodded. "It rivals anything I have heard of in the brutal East, but now I understand the murder scene of the perverted Madonna and child."

"What of the mother?"

"Young, perhaps seventeen. Only a trusted physician was allowed to examine them. He was not a young man, and suffered a small stroke afterward."

"Was the woman by any chance mutilated?" Irene asked as dispassionately as a physician who would *not* suffer a small stroke.

It struck me again that often women are better suited than some men for the gory details of life and death.

Quentin nodded. "Her left breast had been cut off recently and . . . there were other cuts in her generative parts."

Irene nodded brusquely, unwilling to probe more deeply as much for Quentin's sake as our own. We had been on this trail longer and had begun to expect the obscene.

Then she looked, stunned, at me. "Pink! The woman we saw in Neunkirchen . . . the cuts. They made an 'X,' didn't they? And here in Prague?" She glanced wildly back to Quentin, who nodded with obvious distaste.

"Has anyone thought to look, to see . . . if there is a vertical cut, surmounted by a half-curve?"

I gasped right out loud, despite priding myself on my fiber. The men stood stunned into silence at the very thought behind her question.

We had been drawing Chi-Rhos on maps of three capital cities. Had Jack the Ripper been drawing them on women's flesh all along, and had they been obscured by the blood and thunder of the grosser dissecting acts he had committed?

Was it all just a religious mania, as some said? Jack the Ripper was "down on whores," as written in one of his purported letters, and he thought he was doing God's work?

I can't say that I ever put much faith in God after all the woes my poor mother and we children had faced after our true father, the judge, died and left us destitute. But I sure didn't think much of Him if he would allow such things to keep going on in His name, or at least under His sign.

In a way I was glad that our poor, sheltered Nell, wherever she might be, was not here to confront such brutal acts by fiendish men.

31.

In the Soup

*But I cared a great deal for the much more formidable
person behind him, the bosom friend of Moriarty....*
—HOLMES TO WATSON, ARTHUR CONAN DOYLE,

THE EMPTY HOUSE

I didn't swoon, although I had long hoped the man was
dead.

On second thought, it seemed better to not draw attention to myself so I could be taken for granted, as usual, and
thus have a chance of seeing and hearing something that
someone thought I shouldn't.

After all, Colonel Moran could hardly have paid me very much
attention, even on the fateful occasion where Quentin had battled
him in my presence. He was a hunter and used to "heavy" game,
like African lion and Bengal tigers and Russian bear. I was Shropshire rabbit through and through. Yet rabbits have very big ears.

And indeed, it was Godfrey he glowered at, though why he
should, I can't imagine.

Godfrey recognized him at once also, but acted as if this man's
presence and identity did not matter in the slightest. I decided to
take my cue from him.

So when Tatyana nodded to indicate I should take the seat she had decreed for me at Colonel Moran's right hand, I wafted that way like an agreeable dinner partner.

I didn't like the way the man stood behind my heavy chair and pushed it toward the table, so I was not so much seated as "scooped" and shoved.

Still, I remained as serene as Irene playing a scene with a leading man who can neither talk nor walk well, which she has informed me was often the case when performing in grand opera.

The lean man in black sat on Tatyana's left, or sinister, side. *Hmmm.*

Although only four or five feet separated us from the trio at the table's other end, I could tell that the English colonel felt he had been assigned a chair "below the salt."

I couldn't help thinking that Tatyana regarded all women as rivals and wanted to keep them well beyond arm's length. Hence my banishment. Also, she wished to upset Godfrey and myself by separating us.

Colonel Moran's short fingernails gleamed as they strummed the wooden tabletop. His blue eyes were as icy as an arctic sky, as I recalled, his white hair having retreated like some glacier to expose a gleaming bald forehead and skull that was as bony as his bearlike jaw. He seemed to have become some human icon of the massive beasts he hunted and killed: Indian tiger and albino Russian bear. His baldness reminded me of the tonsured sleekness of a fanatical medieval monk, the kind who would put perfectly innocent men to the stake. And women, of course. One sensed a rigorous, keen intellect married to the self-importance of a saint . . . or a sensualist. He had met me, and Godfrey, at one of Sarah Bernhardt's crowded soirees. I could only hope neither of us were sufficiently memorable when the Divine Sarah and Irene in full fine feather shared the room. Again this renegade fellow struck me as a man who was a law unto himself.

"*Parlez-vous français?*" he suddenly barked at me, and I do mean "barked."

"*Un peu*," I answered with utter honesty. A little.

He rushed some other foreign words out next, thick and brusque.

I shrugged.

"English?" he asked.

"My language or my nationality?" I asked back.

He laughed then. "Is there a difference?" He frowned at me, a formidable expression on that high forehead. "You are known to me?"

"I think not."

"What are you doing here?"

"I don't know. Do you?"

"I should," he said shortly, and leaned back from the table as the surly servitor from the other end of the table came to pour a stream of red wine into his empty silver goblet.

I watched the servant, not the colonel. There was something familiar about him, just as the colonel had sensed something familiar about me. That meant we had seen the familiar person in a place and at a time when we were concentrating on something, or someone, else.

I knew what had distracted the colonel from recognizing me: the presence of Irene, who could dazzle a blind man into overlooking braille, and, later in our accidental acquaintance, his life-and-death struggle with Quentin Stanhope on Hammersmith Bridge.

But what kept me from recognizing the lumbering servant? Other than the fact that he was unkempt and his shirt was stained with things too disgusting to think about, of course. How could Tatyana keep such a clod in her retinue?

I glanced to the fireplace, where the Gypsies from the hall were now gathering like hounds at a medieval banquet, quaffing nameless spirits from pottery jugs and still tightening their miserable violin strings as if it mattered whether they were in tune or not. Three swarthy young girls had joined them, tambourines dripping as many gold coins as their dingy articles of dress.

Tatyana enjoyed having these low creatures do her unconventional bidding, that is why they were here.

I tried to dissuade the slow-moving servant from filling my gilt-lined goblet with the bloody wine, but he would have poured it right over my fanned fingers, so I jerked my hand away from the cup just in time to avoid a burgundy bath, or whatever variety the wine was. I couldn't help noticing that the fellow tried to stare down the front of my gown. I pulled my shoulders back like a soldier to prevent any unintended gap. The man grinned before moving on.

"I have seen that chap before," the Colonel said after drinking deep of the wine. He was looking at Godfrey.

So the Colonel was present, but had not been informed of who we were or why we were here!

"I feel I should know him, too," I said, deliberately looking at the tall, thin, old man instead of Godfrey. Anything to divert the high-tempered Colonel Moran from Godfrey. Quentin had been a seasoned foreign-office spy, and still struggled to fight the man to the death. How would a barrister like Godfrey be able to defend himself against such a formidable foe?

Having chosen the lean old man as diversion, I was forced to contemplate him. Quite frankly, he still looked remarkably like Sherlock Holmes in disguise as the French *abbé* in Paris not two weeks ago, except that this man's hair was iron-gray, not white. Of course his black garb was not a cassock, I saw, but a frock coat so old-fashioned he more resembled a liveried servant than a guest.

"Some local official," Colonel Moran said with a dismissive snort as he took in the fellow's age and garb. "It is the younger man she is really interested in."

"Then I do not see why we are here," I said forthrightly.

He turned a sudden and awful grin on me. "Obviously, you are here to amuse me. I seldom share a table with an English female these days. I am trying to decide if she has chosen to surprise me by partnering me with a nun or a whore."

"I am Episcopal," I said quickly, taking a false sip of the wine to hide my confusion.

"She is never predictable," he muttered as much to himself as to me. "She likes turning foes into allies and allies into foes. It will cause her trouble one day."

"It seems that she is only arranging some business," I noted, for Godfrey and the strange man in black were in animated conversation, much punctuated by gesture, indicating that they did not fluently speak each other's language.

"She is always arranging some business. She promised me a superb hunt tonight."

"What game?"

"Wolves? I have heard them howling. But I do not hunt pack animals. They are too pathetic. Weakness makes them band together. The only worthy game is a beast that walks alone, like a tiger or a lion. I am hoping for bear. Or . . . something else unexpected that can rise up on two legs."

Another serving man, this one garbed in worn livery, glided by to place saucers of soup on our golden charger plates.

This was not Gypsy stew, but true broth with exotic mushrooms floating within it! I lifted a sterling silver spoon, then waited to see Tatyana served from the same tureen.

She caught me watching, and lifted a not disapproving eyebrow in my direction.

The next instant she gestured the wine steward, if such a clumsy sort could be called that, to take an empty place along the side of the table and seat himself as though a guest.

He, too, was served several ladles of broth, save that he picked up the low flat dish and drank from it like a dog!

I looked away, carefully skimming my spoon to gather a polite serving, and sip it.

Colonel Moran laughed, and lifted his wine cup in a mock toast.

"To your health, Miss or Ma'am. I see that you will not let manners desert you no matter the company."

He put down his wine to attack the soup with the same *politesse* I had used, as if welcoming a civilized example.

I confess that the soup was delicious, the broth light and flavored, the ingredients tender yet filling.

At the table's other end, Godfrey was sketching patterns on the linen with the tip of his knife, the old man leaning forward intently to follow the invisible symbols.

It did indeed look like a business discussion. Could this be the person he had expected to deal with on the Rothschild matters? He paid no attention to me, but I could sense that his attention from the corner of his eye never left me, and Colonel Moran.

"Damned if don't know that fellow from somewhere!" The Colonel drank deeply again.

"London?" I suggested, knowing that the two men had first glimpsed each other in Paris.

"London? Perhaps. Is that your home?"

The darks of his eyes expanded with curiosity.

"It has been, although I am originally from the country."

"The country! You don't say. How would I ever have guessed? And what name do you go by?"

"I was christened Penelope."

"Penelope!" He chuckled. "What a different world from mine you must live in, Penelope. No doubt that is why Sable has invited you. She adores contrasts."

"Sable?"

"A pet name of mine for her." He leaned very close, and I think he leered. "Do you have any pet names?"

"I'm afraid not, but I do have some pets."

"And what sort of pets do you keep?" he jeered.

"A very lazy, large black cat."

He snorted despite scooping up another spoonful of soup.

"A parrot."

He rolled his eyes.

"A mongoose name Messalina."

He looked up from the soup.

"And two serpents that I have not yet named."

"And why have you not yet named them?"

I pretended I was Sarah Bernhardt playing some doomed, pagan empress. "I am not quite sure which shall survive yet."

The colonel stared at me. "Definitely not a nun," he muttered to his soup as he finished the serving. "Are you sure you don't keep a monkey?"

"A monkey? Certainly not. Why?"

The moment I spoke I regretted my question. I did not want Colonel Moran connecting me with a monkey of any sort. He was recalling a fortunately brief encounter we had at Sarah's Paris party that included a piano and a monkey. I could only hope the monkey was more memorable than I had been on that occasion.

"I don't know," he said. "A monkey suddenly came to mind. I have lived in climes where they are common as pets, as are mongeese. However did you acquire one of that breed?"

I could hardly answer that his mortal enemy Cobra had given it to me. Luckily, the sole liveried servant I had seen came 'round again to collect soup bowls and the resulting stir distracted my interrogator from monkeys, if not me.

"So what are you in England, an artist's model?" The colonel was gazing lasciviously on my unbound hair.

No doubt he expected me to be flattered instead of insulted. And no wonder he could not recognize me! I'd forgotten my frothy hair made an entirely new woman of me. Glory be! But an artist's model? They were hardly better than harlots.

"No, I am a—" What could I say I was? A retired governess and typewriter girl? Tatyana was right: it was vital to keep one's enemies off balance. I remembered reading some American newspapers that Godfrey occasionally bought for Irene, remembered especially a brazen female correspondent with the unforgettable name of Bessie Bramble. "I am a . . . daredevil lady reporter for the newspapers."

"The devil you say!"

"*Dare*devil I said."

"You?"

"Well, there aren't many of us, so we don't have to dare much."

"I haven't seen women writing for the British papers."

"I . . . don't. I'm the London correspondent for the *New York World*." There, let him do me harm at his peril. The entire globe would hear of a missing daredevil lady reporter! Eventually.

32.

Caught Mapping

≈≈≈

All these eastern European lands are caught in a crossfire of religion, race, and a brutal taste for conquering their neighbors... Shrines to Christian saints still decorate roads throughout Poland, Transylvania, Moravia, and Bohemia, yet the people placate pagan gods, demons and superstitions.... They still see vampires on the threshold and werewolves among the trees.
—GODFREY NORTON TO NELL HUXLEIGH, CAROLE NELSON
DOUGLAS, *ANOTHER SCANDAL IN BOHEMIA*

⊰ FROM A JOURNAL ⊱

Dusk has forced us to light the lamps.

In that artificial light, Irene plunged her pen into the crystal inkwell again and began tracing a familiar figure on the map of Prague.

The curving street of *Vaclavs nemesti* ran from the museum toward the Old Town Square, where it looped to the right around the ancient Jewish Joseph Quarter to complete the letter "P" that intersected the "X" made from the sites where murdered women had been found.

"It's hard to believe," I said, "that a maddened killer would select his victims from their nearness to certain streets so that their death scenes would provide a pattern on a map, should anybody have the wit to see it.

"Sacrifices, like all rituals, call for specific places," Quentin said. "God told Abraham to take Isaac up the mountain."

"I don't argue that point, Quentin," I said, calling him by his Christian name for the first time. It was ridiculous, after all the horrors that had been so plainly spoken in our midst, that we should cling to formalities in addressing each other. "I am simply saying that it is odd that Jack the Ripper, the man everyone presumes to be a killer, should oblige religious ritual with the placement of his victim's bodies."

"I agree," Irene said.

Before she could go on, Bram Stoker added his opinion. "It does not strike me as at all odd. Remember, the Ripper killings involving the ritual laying out of the dead women's few poor possessions . . . and the worst expression of this was the way he 'arranged' their entrails around the body, over a shoulder and such."

Irene supported Bram as well. "That is one fact that made the Jews suspect of the crime: they perform ritual sacrifice of animals, and so were favored suspects because the women were killed as if in a ritual."

"Masons found suspicion clinging to them, too," Bram said, "for much the same reasons. Like the Jews and their mysterious Kabbalah that Christians regard with both fear and fascination, they have ritual secrets that spawn rumors of conspiracy and violent orgies."

"Yet the Chi-Rho is a Christian symbol."

"Useful," I put in with a flash of insight, "if the Jews wished to discredit the Christians."

"Usually it is the other way around," Irene objected.

"Which is why," I retorted, "that would be such a brilliant plan."

"I find this religious linkage most troubling." Quentin tented his hands and tapped his forefingers against his lips. The prayerful gesture was most at odds with his words, but he seemed unaware of it. "According to the work of this Krafft-Ebing to whom you directed our attention, Irene, a man who kills women, or children, from some sort of religious mania that judges them befouled, acts alone. Yet every indication since London has been that many are involved in these killings, even if it is only Gypsy caravans spiriting away the wrong-doers."

"And Gypsies aren't religious, are they?" I put in. "We don't have many in America, although some have begun showing up with immigrants from eastern Europe."

"They believe in God, whom they call Del," Quentin said, "and the Devil, whom they call Beng. I suspect that is enough to make them religious. But their deepest beliefs are in the clan and predestination."

"Now I see where Gypsy fortune-tellers come from. How do you know so much of them?" I asked quickly.

I had not meant to sound challenging, but Quentin Stanhope appeared to know everything about anything exotic there was, and I doubted even an Englishman could be such a know-it-all.

"It is very simple, Pink." He smiled, pronouncing my name with such la-di-dah precision that it sounded like a mockery. It was indeed an absurd nickname for a grown woman and a daredevil reporter at that, but I liked people to underestimate me. Except, at the moment, Quentin Stanhope. "The Gypsies, or the Roma, as they call themselves, originated in the particular region of the globe where I have misspent my youth, India."

"India! That does not seem very likely."

"What is likely has nothing to do with the Romany, Pink. For a time Europeans who encountered them and saw they came from the East, like the three wise men, decided they were from Turkey or Nubia or Egypt. In fact, I have conversed with some and I find basic words, numerals, kinship terms, and names for body parts, and actions, to be Indian.

"That said, they were never solely Indian, but part of a ragtag military force India assembled in the tenth century to fight the Muslim armies determined that Islam should dominate Buddhist India and even beyond into the edges of Christian Europe. In fighting to hold back Islam, the mercenary Roma soldiers were pushed into the fringes of Europe. The Gypsy people spread deeper into western Europe in our own century, and, now you say, are emigrating like the Irish, the Poles, the Russians, and the Jews to the great gleaming shore of America, indeed a melting pot for the melting-pot people of India and now Europe."

" 'Bring these, the wretched refuse of your teeming shore, to me. I lift my lamp beside the golden door,' " I quoted from the poem Emma Lazarus wrote about the statue in 1883 to raise money for the pedestal it would rest upon three years later. "We could do with a bit less 'wretched refuse,' if you ask me. But I only wanted to know where the Gypsies came from."

"Ah, you can't know where anyone came from unless you know where they are going, and vice versa." He turned to Irene, who had barely concealed her impatience during his lecture-hall answer to my simple question. "And it might interest you to know that in the course of their centuries-long movement westward the Roma were kept as slave labor in one part of Europe." He glanced at Bram. "In that same quaint neighboring region that so fires your imagination. Transylvania."

"Slave labor? But that was ages ago. Is slavery still possible in this day and age?" I demanded.

"More than possible," Quentin answered, "and in more places than you would believe."

Before he could enlighten me further, and I did wish to be further enlightened, as I saw a story in it, Irene leaped to direct the discussion back to more relevant matters.

"So the Gypsies could indeed be forced to do some master's bidding?" she said. "That makes their appearance in Paris all the more suspicious and establishes a direct link to Transylvania, where Godfrey was sent on his last mission."

"The Romany are too diffuse to summarize. Even in slavery they would cling to their tribal ways, and there is no way more difficult to change or challenge than that of the tribe. So I would guess they are shrugging off any remaining servitude and moving on, as they always have, absorbing what they call *gajikané*, or foreign, bits of language and custom into the eternal constant of their clannish lives."

"You admire them!" Irene charged.

"I admire all who defy definition and who survive the centuries."

"Have you moved among them?"

He nodded. "They are the most difficult to know, to trust, or to give trust to. One must regard them as a pack of wild dogs. They may invite you to share their meat, or they may make you their meat. It depends upon their mood."

"So they would be united foes but unreliable allies?"

He nodded.

"And dangerous slaves or servants?"

He nodded again.

"Yet the Chi-Rho would mean nothing to them," Irene mused. "I have met but one Roma, and her only twice. She is part fraud and part Sybil, and it is always up to me to decide which part is speaking. And she gave me a gift of great price when last we met, although I paid well for it, in gold . . . and in blood." She glanced at Bram. "I would hie us all to your mysterious Transylvania, Bram, now that I know Gypsies point that way also and certainly Godfrey was lured there. But . . . do we risk abandoning Nell somewhere in-between?"

No one answered. No one could.

"The trail of murders begins in London, where there are few Gypsies save their native Tinkers—and there were no Gypsy suspects in Whitechapel—and goes to Prague, *then* to Paris. All are great metropolitan centers. Why would Nell be dragged to the wilds of Transylvania?"

We were silent, all too aware that there was one good reason why Nell would not be "dragged" to Transylvania or anywhere else: her lifeless body lay somewhere between the exposition site in Paris and the path James Kelly took, which Irene and I knew for a fact went as far as Neunkirchen at least.

None of us would say this. The decision must be Irene's.

She stood and stared down at the map of Prague. "Sherlock Holmes lost the Ripper in Whitechapel by a matter of minutes," she muttered as if to herself. "He is back there now, retracing his own footsteps. We both scoured Paris until we turned up James Kelly. Prague has not been subjected to the same search. That is what we must lay to rest: Prague's role in these events, and the only place to do it is here."

Her finger stabbed a point on the map.

She looked up at the rest of us, resolved.

"We will continue with our expedition tonight, and if it proves unenlightening, we will move on to Transylvania and Quentin's Gypsies and Bram's sinister village with all speed."

33.

Cryptic Doings

﹏☙☀❧﹏

The oldest grave is that of a poet and physician who died in 1439. Avigdor Kara was a rare survivor of an Easter pogrom in 1389 that slew almost the entire Jewish population of Prague, some 3,000, killed by the city's Christians after local priests accused them of desecrating the Host used in giving Holy Communion.
—TRAVEL GUIDE ON THE OLD JEWISH CEMETERY

❧ F R O M A J O U R N A L ❧

The streets of Prague echoed with the sounds of any city: the creak of wheels and constant slap and jingle of harnesses, the click of hooves sharp as sleet, and the distant rainlike patter of footsteps.

And, of course, because this was Prague, where silver, crystal, and beer ruled long before King Wilhelm occupied Prague Castle, a never-ending tune was the off-key celebrations of men leaving beer parlors.

We went on foot, Bram Stoker and I taking up the rear because

Irene and Quentin knew where we were going, and presumably why.

Night mist slickened the rough cobblestones. Bram Stoker had to restrain himself from reaching out to support my elbow when my boots slipped on the uneven surface. But I wore men's clothes as he did, and, unless I wished to disguise myself as a sot, there was no reason for me to lean on his support.

I think it half killed him not to play the gentleman, though, and I much liked him for it.

In fact, I so relished this outing! Much more fun to pass as a man among men than among three women disguised as men. No one glanced at us, or noted our progress.

We passed a lone woman now and again, obviously seeking business. They were mere shadows, hesitant to break into the knot of four "men" to find one who might patronize them. Four men might simply take their wares for nothing.

They reminded me of lost dogs in the city: wary, hungry, needing recognition but fearing it will come as a blow. I shuddered at the notion of the thousands of these lone, dark ghosts haunting the byways of every great metropolis hoping to attach to a living body for a few minutes and thus earn the illusion of warmth one way or another . . . with money for beer or for a bed out of the weather.

I let my walking stick hit the stones sharply, rhythmically. I was not one to be stopped for foolishness, the sound said. The lurking women hovered but came no closer to our party.

I realized then that it was not enough for me to write of women in brothels. I must write of women with no brothels to call home. And I felt anger at how unchallenged I could be at night on the street in my male garb, among men, while these homeless souls could be arrested and abused merely for being out here at this hour unescorted. Even respectable women were sometimes caught up in the net, despite their protests, and then their reputations were so soiled that they might as well join the nightly sisterhood in truth.

The ways grew narrow and deserted, although the merriment of the taverns could always be heard tinkling at a distance, like echoes from another world.

So narrow grew the streets that the constant faint odor of horse dung vanished. I smelled instead . . . lilacs. The scent reminded me that the world in general—not the dim, murder-haunted world I had chosen to inhabit these past four weeks—was easing from spring into summer.

The lilac smell grew so strong that I realized we were bearing toward it. A park? We moved between two tall buildings and saw an open space gaping. Not large, but occupied only by low walls, much crumbled. This was a park of tilted stones and scrawny maple and sycamore trees with a few lavish lilac bushes scenting the air until it hung heavy and sickly sweet, like something not quite wholesome but no less attractive for that.

A lantern was unshaded ahead of us. I blinked as the light blazed off gray and reddish stone blocks tilted this way and that.

Irene and Quentin were threading their way through the ruins, so Bram and I followed suit, less gracefully, stubbing our boot toes on the fallen stones. I grew quite dizzy from looking down while moving over the shifting ground and obstacles, from inhaling the thick, sweet odor as cloying as chloroform. . . .

"What is this place?" I asked Bram, who shrugged his own confusion.

So we stumbled, half-blinded, after Irene and Quentin, until they stopped by a large low building in the middle of the ruins.

There we caught up with them, and caught our breaths. At first I thought that Irene was smoking, but then I realized that I saw the faint wreaths of our breaths unfurling in the light of Quentin's lantern.

I also saw the general shape of the construction before us: a stone "house" of sorts, but barely higher than a tall man's hat. And it had no windows!

The others were also noting the trail of their breaths in the chill and damp night.

"At least that proves that none of us is a vampire," Bram said jocularly. "A vampire would not breathe."

"Charming!" said I. "I understand why you write fiction. Once set upon a theme, you never let it loose."

"Bram's thought is apt," Irene answered me. "We are, after all, in the place of the dead."

"We are?" I gazed uneasily at the dark around us.

"This"—Irene lay a gloved hand upon the stone structure as one would touch the arm of an old friend one was introducing to strangers—"is Rabbi Loew's famous tomb."

"Tomb! Quite a sizable one. Then this place is, is—"

"The ancient Jewish cemetery in which Rabbi Loew's tomb is located," Quentin said.

"And the broken walls we were dodging all the way here—?"

"Ah!" Bram Stoker sounded delighted. "That was the centuries' deposit of gravestones. A pity we did not come by daylight. I understand they were piled up over the decades to twelve levels, until they tilt atop each other like cards in a badly shuffled deck. One might almost think the deepest dead eager to push all their fellows out of the earth from below."

"Or your walking undead pushing upward to rise again," Irene said sardonically. "But this site most reminds me of the living," she added, patting the smoke-grimed stone of the rabbi's tomb. "The last time I was here Godfrey and Nell accompanied me, and Nell accidentally tripped a mechanism that opens a door to the tomb's interior."

"Why should we wish to join the ancient rabbi in his tomb?" I asked. "Surely he has nothing to say after so many centuries."

"It is never wise to underestimate one credited with resurrecting the Golem," Irene answered me. "What we found on our previous exploration were stairs down into and through the tomb to an underground network of tunnels."

"Underground! Like Paris!"

"Perhaps," Irene said. "On my last visit they were a well-kept secret used to further a political plot, one in which rumors of the

Golem's walking again was an important factor. I'm wondering if their presence is still such a secret, or if they have been put to evil use again."

"So," said Bram Stoker, sounding cheerful, "we may encounter the legendary Golem below?"

"I can attest," Irene said with an enigmatic smile, "that we did indeed glimpse the Golem himself during our last visit. But tonight I am most hoping that we will find traces of the same sort of secret society that we uncovered in Paris and, perhaps, even find our missing ones, for this place has served to hold a very special prisoner captive before."

"Wait!" I cried. "That Gypsy woman you consulted; she hinted something about this place before we left her."

"Indeed, Pink, she did. Not even gold will get a direct answer from one of Quentin's Roma, but I believe they delight in riddles as much as the Sphinx and will say just enough to lead one in the right direction, if you are wise enough to see the clue."

"You are dealt with as you deal," Quentin agreed. "Those whom they hoodwink have been misled as much by their own greed as anything. Those who deal straight with them will be rewarded with an honest answer, can they but recognize it."

"A very two-edged people," Irene commented. "Our problem now is not Gypsies but duplicating Nell's utterly instinctive discovery of the tomb entrance. As I recall, she was working her way around to the other side, complaining of the ungiving stone—"

For this I could not blame Nell. The ungiving stones of the cramped graveyard had butted against my boot toes many times on the way here. Quentin handed the lantern to Bram, whose great height allowed him to cast the widest beam of light. We all began feeling our way around the tomb, tapping the stone for hollow sounds like the three blind mice in the nursery rhyme.

Irene and Quentin used the butt ends of their pistols to rap the stone. It sounded like we were attending an open-air séance. With all the talk of vampires and Gypsies and Golems, I admit I was as uneasy as a cat in a roomful of rocking chairs, especially when my hand inadvertently rested on a sort of stone knob. Surprised enough to slip on the dark ground, I was forced to grasp my makeshift handhold even harder and started to feel it escape my grasp.

In a moment I was stumbling forward, the ground falling away from me with every step. My feet were stuttering into the hard, cold dark. I was only able to give one shameful startled squeak before I was silenced by the struggle to keep myself upright.

Luckily, that miserable squeak was heard.

A shaft of lantern light fell upon me from above. I saw that I was in a narrow stone passage. The sharp cliff I had been rushing unwillingly down was a crudely hewed set of stairs.

"She has found Nell's route," Irene crowed softly from above. "Quick! We must follow before the secret mechanism lets the door fall shut on us."

I heard the welcome sound of boot soles clattering down behind me and stopped myself only by running directly into the end wall below with both my gloved hands.

Stronger hands plucked me away from the wall and supported my elbows while I caught my breath. Bram Stoker.

"That so-called stairwell is narrower, darker, and steeper than the below-stage exit beneath the vampire box at the Lyceum," he said, patting my shoulder before he released me to stand on my own power again.

It was hard at such a moment to imagine Bram Stoker as a Ripper candidate.

Quentin and his lantern had managed to bypass us all in the narrow space. Now he stood waiting to lead our party into the unknown dark.

"I can't believe," Irene said, shaking her head at me, "that you were able to duplicate Nell's entirely accidental entry to this secret crypt."

"Crypt?" I asked, looking about uneasily.

"There are burial niches in the walls, but they are mostly empty," she answered.

Mostly?

We spoke in whispers, for the hard stone surroundings echoed our every breath, it seemed.

The light from Quentin's lantern beamed both backward and forward in odd, shattered swaths. I glimpsed our party's faces eerily lit, familiar features drawn down into gaunt and sinister shadows, and glimpsed the arched penumbra of a niche here and there.

At last we moved forward on level, if not smooth, ground, our shoes shuffling over stone and packed earth and loose bits of . . . gravel, I suppose. Or bone.

I could not imagine Nell moving down here without shrieking her lungs out, but then realized I should be very glad to hear her shrieking, as it would mean she was alive and we had found her.

The notion that our quest might soon be over made my fingers itch for pen and paper, but it was better that I carried the cane. I held it before me at a diagonal, so its top or bottom should warn me of any impediment in the dark.

At last the passage widened into what could be termed a room.

We all stopped and let Quentin take a soft-footed tour of the space, sweeping his lantern high and low to illuminate the details of the space.

Of course there came the chilling screech of tiny nails over the stone and earthen floor. The light caught the flash of pointed snake tails whipping out of sight . . . not snakes, but the furless extremities of rats.

The lantern also passed over a surprisingly familiar form: a simple wooden table.

The table proclaimed human occupancy, and that was a more chilling sight than the retreat of a legion of rats.

Quentin quickly shuttered his lantern until only an illuminating sliver remained. Its thin thread of light drew swiftly but silently near us.

"It's best I scout ahead," he whispered. "We don't know who, or how many, may be down here. You say the tunnels are extensive, Irene?"

She nodded, her face barely visible in the faint light.

"We'll be left in the dark," Bram objected in a careful whisper.

"I have lucifers," Irene replied, "but I'd rather Quentin came back safe and sound with the lantern. Go ahead, but be back in five minutes, or we will have to raise a clatter looking for you."

He nodded and moved away in uncanny silence, the crescent of light soon dying.

"How will we know when five minutes have passed?" I asked my unseen cohorts in a discreet whisper.

"More's the point, how will Stanhope know?" Bram whispered in turn.

"He is used to estimating time without consulting a watch, as am I. In fact, I need only think myself through the first aria from *Cinderella* and I will keep perfect time."

We all fell silent then, listening for the slithering return of the rats. It was all very well for Irene to make time with voiceless arias, and I suppose Bram Stoker's stage sense might help him pass the long minutes, but I had nothing except my imagination to occupy me, and it was far too excellent a one to let loose for too long in the dark.

After more like fifteen minutes than five, of a sudden I heard a scrape right beside me.

I edged away just as the lantern shutter opened not a foot from my face.

"It's quite all right," Quentin said quickly, still whispering. "The place seems deserted now."

"Now?" Irene said just as quickly.

He nodded and I noticed that his usual genial expression had been completely erased by the lantern's harsh light, or by something else. What had replaced it was an expression of tense excitement.

"These subterranean tunnels," he went on, opening the lantern shutter wide enough to create a path for the rest of us to follow, "have been King Rat's kingdom for decades, but His Majesty has had some human competition just lately. It could be from your last expedition in the caverns, Irene."

"We didn't leave much trace," she said, watching the edge of the lantern light for any of King Rat's returning subjects.

"But surely your adventure in the place alerted others to its presence," he went on.

"Not very many, only the villains of the piece, who numbered two, with a handful of henchmen who were later captured and imprisoned in Prague Castle, which has dungeons deeper than a hundred years, and the victim."

"What would keep the victim silent?"

"The ignominy of being a victim," she said shortly, clearly unwilling to give specifics.

"I had played a bit part at the end of that act," Quentin said, "but I quite understand your need to keep the full denouement secret. I am often in the same position."

"Am I," Bram Stoker asked, "going to be defrauded of another ripping good story? I can't just make everything up, you know. True stories are a great inspiration to the fiction writer."

"Don't worry," Quentin reassured him. "The scene ahead would inspire a Verne or a Poe."

"Or a penny dreadful?" I asked. When silence greeted my question, I explained, "That's what we call sensational fiction in the States, because it can be bought for a penny and really is rather dreadful."

"Imagine what poor pay the writers get," Bram put in. "I can't say that my scribblings have earned much more than that."

"Be grateful that you have such a solid position with Henry Irving and the Lyceum," Irene advised.

"I suppose so, but it's not as solid as one might think," Bram grumbled. "Adherents of Irving are always coming around trying to worm their way into his regard, and employ."

"Then perhaps you will have a future as a private inquiry agent," Irene answered. "If you like the work."

At that moment the narrow walls ceased to contain Quentin's

lantern light, and it spilled out full width into the large chamber we entered through a natural stone archway wide enough for us four to stand abreast.

And so we stood, and gaped, our senses assaulted by a vast space that had recently entertained far more than rats.

Scents of wine and urine and something else both sweet and sour or sweet and rotten, I should say, overwhelmed our nostrils.

Our eyes fell upon dozens of candle stumps lying hither and yon in pools of hardened wax where they had been cast, their flames allowed to drown in their own melted forms.

Bottles also strewed the floor, a few tall and glass-green as would hold wine, most squat and pale, crude crockery bottles of an unknown source and containing an unknown spirit.

In the chamber's center charred logs resembled the ruins of a miniature cathedral. Other, unburnt logs lay around the edge of the roughly circular space, almost like seats for an arena. A pile of the same logs was heaped a few feet away from the remains of the fire.

All in all, one imagined a crowd of people gathered around the fierce and immense flames that had charred such mighty logs to blackened splinters. One saw smoke rising and filling the room with its murky fumes before choking the several tunnels that led away from this chamber.

"It looks like they spilled more wine than they drank," Bram said as he moved behind Quentin over the uneven ground. "Look at all the drops sprayed on the stone, the ground, the logs."

Irene had bent down to pick up one of the crude pottery bottles. She lofted the jar like some rare amphora from an ancient civilization.

"There was red wine in those bottles, too?" Bram asked.

"I don't think so." Irene wafted the narrow open mouth beneath her nose and sniffed delicately, as if it were a rare and costly Paris scent. "Red Tomahawk mentioned this on the exposition grounds in Paris. A 'strong firewater' he did not know. Quentin, have you ever seen or smelled the like?"

He came over to grasp the empty bottle and inhale its vanished essence. "Something spiritous still soaks the pottery, yes. But I have been too long in the land of Islam, where alcoholic beverages are forbidden. It is beyond me."

"Bram?" Irene offered him the lowly pot.

He, too, imbibed the odor, then shook his shaggy head. "I usually indulge in the local ales when I travel. This is stronger stuff."

"If only Sherlock Holmes were here," Irene mused. Her thumbnail picked at the lip of the bottle and a bit of candle wax flaked off and fell on the floor.

"Well," said I in some umbrage. "Aren't you going to let me in on this sniffing party?"

Irene gazed upon me as if she had forgotten my presence. "Of course, Pink. The bouquet is all yours."

I took the clumsy thing in both gloved hands. Unlike the rest of them, I bet I had seen its like before, though not on this continent. I closed my eyes, tried to shut out the ugly reek of the wretched acts that had gone on in this cavern, and passed the opening under my nose, back and forth, sniffing. The remaining odor was faint, but stringent, raw.

I finally threw my head back. "I don't know what they call it in civilized places like Europe, but where I come from it's called rotgut and moonshine and, to Red Tomahawk's people, firewater. It's homemade raw liquor, the kind that will never get a label for anything but making a man drunk fast and hard."

The other three just stared at me.

"What would all these crude bottles of American spirits be doing here?" Bram finally asked.

Irene took the bottle from my hands and gazed upon it. "Because, like myself, it is—and it isn't—American, perhaps?"

34.

Dance for Your Supper

❧

My heart used to jump in my dancing days when Bram asked me for a waltz. I knew it meant triumph, twirling, ecstasy, elysium, giddiness, ices, and flirtation!

—A DANCING PARTNER OF BACHELOR BRAM STOKER, 1873

Once again I was unsuccessful in discouraging the loutish servant from spilling more red wine into my goblet, but despite the scanty attendants the dinner continued to be almost worth the dreadful company.

The chef himself appeared from the kitchen to serve the main dish, braised venison in brandy bechamel sauce, as he announced in French-accented English. He was the expected portly fellow, of late middle age, with an unfortunate sprinkle of dandruff in what was left of his dark hair, which made me nervous of the salt.

Yet I must admit that I attacked the main course with a will. After the days of Gypsy stew it was heavenly, and I managed to devour it, in a ladylike manner, without my usual qualms for the poor deer sacrificed to our appetites. It is so hard to eat hearty when one is constantly thinking of the once-living source of the food.

The salad featured roots and leaves I was entirely unfamiliar with, and I only picked at that, aware of how common herbal poisons are.

The servant seated at our table did not trouble to use implements but caught both meat and vegetable up in his hands as if eating them in the field where they had been harvested.

By now Godfrey's fevered conversations with the old man were done, and he was forced to attend to Tatyana's comments.

Colonel Moran watched their conversational duet with unmistakable ire. Seeing Godfrey from a distance, especially looking past the peasant lump that sat two seats down from him, reacquainted me with his great physical attractions, as well as with the true nobility of his manner and expression.

My heart sank. Not only would Colonel Moran but hate Godfrey the more for his very virtues, but they would make Tatyana covet him the more.

There. I had named the greatest danger: Tatyana and her covetous infatuation with Godfrey, which I had first witnessed in Bohemia more than a year ago, but had been too thick to quite understand.

I thought back to my recent conversation with Godfrey, when I glimpsed how evil can arise out of supposed good, how love can turn to hate, how one can come to despise and destroy the very thing one most craves because that is the only way to own it forever.

Tatyana, I saw, desired to own Godfrey forever, perhaps because he was the one man least likely to be owned, least of all by her, unlike her fine French chef and her brutal servant and her Gypsy thugs and her half-tame heavy game hunter.

And, I saw, the game of winning Godfrey, of controlling Godfrey by coercion, would soon lose its zest. Then her game would be to see that no one else on earth could aspire to know and love him. That meant Irene, first and foremost, but it also meant myself, to whom he was the dearest brother in the world and all I had left of the one parent I had ever known, my kind and gentle dead father.

It struck my overwrought mind that the library table had

stretched as long as a medieval banqueting table; that Tatyana and Godfrey and the strange old man were far figures in a crystal ball that looked equally to past and future.

I had never felt so helpless, not since I had lost my position and housing and very soul in London years before. Then Irene Adler had noticed my plight. She had plucked me from the streets of the city and into the theatrical whirl of her endless optimism.

Despite all this, I was just a dismissed Whiteley's girl, a failed governess, an orphan, a fool who thought I had learned a thing or two of a world I did not much like in the past decade.

Would that I *were* a daredevil girl reporter, that I were Irene or a Pinkerton and could pull a cocked pistol from my pocket, could overturn the table with a flick of my wrist, could do something, anything, to change the moment and its inevitable outcome.

Somehow I found myself standing.

A chair leg had caught in my trailing robes. My abrupt motion flung the heavy chair backwards. The sound of wood smashing to the stone floor still reverberated.

Everyone, startled, stared at me: the chef, the colonel, the old man, the peasant, Godfrey, Tatyana. Even the Gypsies, whose bows were wavering into silence on their catgut strings. I myself seemed to be some vibrating string, frozen forever in making the wrong note. As usual.

I have no idea what I would have said or done next, save that I was as incensed as I have ever been in my life. Then the wild screech of a single Gypsy violin echoed to the high stone ceiling like a animal in its death throes . . . like a woman screaming in a back alley in Whitechapel or Paris or the Old Town of Prague.

How eerily a violin can evoke the human voice! This one ran up and down the scale of inhuman agony until other tortured chords joined it. Finally the tempo picked up, and the atonal racket of tattered vocal cords became a raucous, unfettered melody reeling around the huge room.

Someone seized the fallen chair behind me and swept it away. I felt the tug on my train as a cat might a pull on its tail.

Before I could turn to look, Colonel Moran was standing before me, his bare hand extended. "A dance," he said, not asking, but ordering.

I looked immediately to Godfrey, who had risen to my defense.

The awful Tatyana was standing, too, making herself his dancing partner even as I was pulled into the room's empty center by the spy once known as Tiger.

It was a wild waltz we embarked upon. I had never done more than take a sedate turn around the schoolroom with my older girl charges.

Now I was the center of a maelstrom, whirled in a constant eddy of music and motion by the naked hand of Colonel Sebastian Moran at the waist of my gown.

Godfrey had not been given time to don his gloves after dining, like a gentleman, either. Tatyana's hand rested in his bare palm, and he had no choice but to pilot her through the great galloping steps of a frantic waltz.

At least Godfrey set the pace and direction in his enforced dance. I was swept to and fro, the room spinning around me like the panorama building I had been so anxious to see at the world exhibition in Paris and that also had been my swift undoing.

Worse, my unbound hair slapped my face like both blindfold and whip. I remembered playing an inadvertent game of Blind Man's Buff with Allegra's Uncle Quentin a decade before and wished I were in his gentle hands here instead of the relentless grip of the Colonel, who was staring at me with bulging eyes, his teeth set in a fierce gated grin.

All the while the only music was the grinding and wailing of the cursed violins and the dull chime of a few listless tambourines.

I could see Tatyana playing a trick I had witnessed before, pulling the pins from her hair as she danced until it was as loose as a Gypsy girl's. Like mine.

Before I had been frightened. Now I was mortified. I glimpsed the old man and the dwarf sitting alone at the table as I was spun past again and again.

This was worse than my captivity in the box, for then I had been drugged into submission. Here I was to be danced to death.

The music stopped without warning.

The Colonel released me as suddenly.

I still swung, like a bell on a rope, and finally stopped, watching the floor spin beneath my feet, afraid to look up and see the chamber rotating like a top seen from the inside out.

I heard a pair of hands clapping.

"Medved!" Tatyana cried. "Dance, Medved, dance! Play, fools, play!"

Just as I heard shuffling footsteps approach, the violins leaped into bow-bending action again. I swear the bagpipes of Scotland are as melodious as a flute compared to Gypsy violins in a frenzy.

Bare, hot hands seized my left hand and my waist. I jerked my head up, fighting the dizziness, glaring at the Colonel . . . and saw instead the inhuman hulk of a servant Tatyana had invited to swill among us like a hog.

Bits of soup and meat dotted the front of his crude shirt. His dark and dirty brown hair was an uncombed tangle far worse than mine. I felt my gorge rising before he even jerked me left and then right in a bearlike pantomime of a waltz.

The moment reminded me so much of the awful, seasick instants inside the nautical panorama, when the sweet thick scent and taste of chloroform masked my mouth and the demented killer James Kelly had come staggering toward me with his mad eyes gleaming with unholy light. . . .

This brute servant's eyes held that selfsame mad gleam, as intent as two candle flames burning blue with intensity.

At least he did not whirl me in tight, swooning circles as Tiger had. He stomped first left, then right, dragging me with him, his huge boots pinning my hem to the floor now and then and threatening to topple me over in a heap.

I tried to slip out of his hot-handed grip, and it would loosen for a moment as he stared down at his booted feet as if they belonged to someone other.

"Dance, Medved, dance!" Tatyana urged from some unseen distance.

The violins rose higher and higher in some frantic Gypsy tune. The oaf suddenly put both hands at my waist and lumbered us around and around.

Then he stopped, let me go, let me stagger backwards a few steps and leaped to capture me again. This time there was no semblance of a dance. He was grinning and nodding, lifting my hair from my neck, his greasy hands touching my unprotected skin, pushing the neckline of my gown down, fumbling at the front of my bodice as if I should accept it.

Again I was back in the panorama, trapped and mauled, sinking into a sleep that had lasted almost a week.

No! My arms lifted up and out, not so much to strike him as to ward off evil.

The gesture surprised him. He began laughing and made to push closer.

I heard a terrible crash, metal clattering and glass shattering. Tatyana's raucous laughter echoed like an out-of-tune aria performed by a banshee.

Another hand seized mine, spun me, drove me almost to the end of my wits. I was so tired of being on a planet that turned like a top at every opportunity.

Godfrey had me in his dancerlike grip and slowly stepped into the pattern of a box waltz. We moved back and forth like Austrian automatons, scribing a docile square on the stones underfoot.

The lead Gypsy violin descended the scale, slowing as it went until it was dragging out a mocking slow-motion waltz. There were no turns, no gallops, just step side-back side-front. One-two, three-four, like a march of very tired soldiers.

Gradually, my vertigo faded. The funereal pace of the violins calmed my racing heart. I kept my gaze on Godfrey's calm gray eyes, on the slight smile on his lips.

Without my noticing it, he maneuvered me back to the table again, and pulled away when I was close enough to rest my trembling hands on the wood and stand long enough for him to retrieve my chair and seat me.

"You English call that a dance?" Tatyana taunted. "Come, Medved. We shall show them a dance."

She led the revolting servant onto the floor, his hand still grasping the neck of a pottery jar he swigged from again and again.

Godfrey was less interested in Tatyana and her untrained ape than in Colonel Moran, whom he finally spotted sitting in his own former chair. So he leaned against the table beside me and cast a comforting glance my way.

I was glad to be off my feet and anchored once again, but I did turn in my chair to watch the exhibition Tatyana was about to make of herself with her "Medved."

She had been a ballerina, or so she had claimed when we had first encountered her in Prague. Ballerinas were such ethereal, graceful creatures that it was hard to imagine this woman of fire and earthy contempt ever emulating a dying swan.

Now she mimicked some Gypsy fandango, circling around her drunken swain, shaking her coarse, flowing blond hair at him, leading him close to her, then leaping back to let him founder.

He was openly reaching for her now with huge, greedy hands. I shuddered to picture those grimy fingers on my neck and shoulder and knew I should have to rub my skin raw in my room tonight to banish the memory. Grasping hands. What had they done to me during the days and nights I was drugged? Was this ghastly man among the retinue then, free to rummage about my person?

The lack of memory was maddening! I would never know what had happened to me, or what had not. My teeth started chattering, but couldn't be heard over the violins, which were keeping pace with the drunken lumberings of the great uncouth fool in the center of the room.

Tatyana danced at him like a teasing blade in a duel, drawing him forward, then driving him back. After a few minutes of this, the creature finally toppled over, bottle clasped in his hand, like some traveling company Caliban drunk almost to death on Prospero's island that had once been his.

Laughing, Tatyana leaped over his fallen body and came striding toward us.

She shook her unbound hair like a mane. "Your business is done here," she told Godfrey. "Take the little Englishwoman upstairs to her room. At least you did not marry such a milksop as this. Go!"

Godfrey shepherded me away and out into the entrance rooms of the castle.

The revelers slumped in their chairs or on the floor, except for the thin old man, who remained oddly erect in his seat. The violins played on, more slowly and fainter. Medved slumbered like a fallen Satan in the center of the room, his unbroken bottle beside an outflung hand, leaking liquid that darkened the stones like blood.

I didn't speak until we were making our weary way up the grand stone staircase, Godfrey's hand supporting my elbow while I dragged my heavy skirts up riser after riser.

"What did she want? What was the purpose of such a travesty of a dinner?" I asked him.

"For one thing, the old man was Count Lupescu, who owns this forest and its castle. It was my assignment to purchase the lot for the Rothschilds."

"So it was legitimate business you did here?"

"If that old fellow was really Lupescu and he really does own this estate. Madame Tatyana is quite capable of stocking the castle with her own cast of characters, all serving her whim and her twisted sense of amusement, as we do."

"We serve her? I do not!"

"We are prisoners, of course. We dance to her tune, as the evening demonstrated quite literally."

"Godfrey, I have been thinking of Irene."

An expression of pain crossed his face. "It may be better not to do that until we have put this place behind us. We must escape before she is lured into following us here. She is the true target of this elaborate plot."

"Why?"

"Because she is Irene, and Tatyana is not."

"That is cryptic."

"A woman like Tatyana is driven by all she is not."

"Not a dancer anymore, but Irene isn't a singer anymore."

"Tatyana is also not active in the Great Game as she knew it anymore; she must create her own game."

"The Great Game. You mean all the European nations fighting over bits and pieces of India and the Orient, that Quentin has been drawn into for so many years?"

"The Great Game is one nation trying to control another and another and another. Tatyana regards herself as a nation unto herself, and she will try to control anyone who crosses her path, or who she can trap into her path."

"Why would she be so evil?"

"Because it is easier than trying to be good."

"Now that is simplistic, Godfrey. That would work to quiet a schoolroom charge, but I am a grown woman and less likely to swallow it."

We were by our rooms by now. Godfrey loosed my elbow. "Evil is very simple, Nell, almost childlike. I suspect it's mostly utter selfishness. You had best go in and wash off what of it you can."

"I do wish I could bathe again!"

"I fear the Gypsies will be far less biddable now that Tatyana and her minions are here."

"I wouldn't care to disrobe in this place with some of the residents it has now," I added with a shiver.

"Most wise." He looked very worried as he gazed down at me. "Remember. We do have an escape plan."

"We do?"

He nodded and kissed me good night on the forehead, as my father used to.

"We do, and we may have to use it soon."

I opened the heavy door into what I regarded, perhaps optimistically, as my room, and watched him enter his adjoining chamber. I knew that Tatyana would send someone fast on our heels to latch us in from outside. At least Medved was now too drunk to manage this duty.

Godfrey had not allayed my fears. Our chances of escaping this castle were even dimmer than before, and now there was obviously something to escape: Tatyana, Colonel Moran, and the trained bear of a man Tatyana was encouraging to become an even more terrifying beast.

35.

Bloody Words

~∞~

*I saved some of the proper red stuff in a ginger beer bottle
over the last job to write with but it went thick like glue
and I cant use it. Red ink is fit enough I hope ha ha.
Yours truly,*
—JACK THE RIPPER

❧ F R O M   A   J O U R N A L ❧

I must admit I liked making a sensation.

For the next ten minutes I was quizzed on the locales
in the United States where rotgut and moonshine could be
found, and of what and how it was made.

I was no expert on this topic, but pointed out that
homemade spirits have long been the privilege of the common folk
in every land and that the so-called government interferes with that
process at its own risk, although it always does.

In fact, I pointed out, the British insistence on a whiskey tax
was a greater influence than a tea tax in encouraging the American
rebellion.

While I stoutly explored this topic, Irene was walking through the ruins of the activity in the chamber, picking up two or three of the pottery jars, the ones with gobbets of white wax still clinging to their open lips.

"This isn't wine spill," she noted casually, staring at the earthen floor beneath the old Jewish cemetery of bodies piled twelve generations deep.

Slowly, the men's attention returned to her.

"What is it then?" Quentin asked.

"Blood."

"Blood?" Bram Stoker paled, then hurried to her side. "These drops, all blood? What makes you say such a thing?"

"Because we"—she glanced at me—"have seen such quantities of blood spilled at an underground site in Paris."

I hastened to her side as well, quite ready to give up my role as fount of all knowledge of things alcoholic.

Under the sweeping examination of Quentin's lantern, the spray of drops did look very bloodlike. I finally identified the sickly sweet odor of the cavern: not lilacs, like above, but blood.

"Have you examined the walls?" Irene asked Quentin.

"For what?"

"More blood."

We all followed him to the perimeter of the cave, trooping behind as his lantern light washed up and down on the crudely hewed stone.

Under our feet lay burnt-out candle stubs, dried kernels of rat leavings, and more burgundy drops turned almost black except at their very centers, which were as rich as a bloodred rose.

"Good God!" Quentin had stopped, the lantern swinging slowly from his hand.

"What is it?" Irene demanded, rushing up behind him.

"Writing. In mostly consonants. That damned Czech. . . ."

"Let me see! I have sung in that language. I recognize some words."

Irene seized the lantern and moved along the wall, peering at a faint black pattern that looked vaguely foreign, like an Arabic or

Cyrillic alphabet. Were we to add Arabs and Russians and Czechs to our Gypsies and Indians and Transylvanians for a truly exotic stew?

Irene sighed and let the lantern droop at her side.

"We have seen these words before, in another language. I can't make out every word, but one particularly is clear. I believe that when we get this phrase translated it will read: 'The *Gypsies* are the men Who Will not be Blamed for nothing.' "

I gasped out loud. I had seen the strangely feminine-case French version (*Juives*, which read in English like a misspelled "Juwes") on a cellar wall in Paris not two weeks before. An almost identical phrase so mentioning the "Juwes" had been scribed in chalk, supposedly by Jack the Ripper, at Goulston Street in Whitechapel on September thirtieth.

The men in our party, knowing less, were less impressed.

"What a strange sentiment," Bram said. "It makes no sense. Grammatically, it is a nightmare."

"Nightmares do tend to be ungrammatical," Irene said, still bending over the faint letters. "The last phrase of this type we saw had been inscribed in blood. Sherlock Holmes theorized from the evidence that a man had been whipped along the wall and forced to write those words in his own blood."

"Sherlock Holmes never theorizes," I corrected her. "He declares."

"Thank you, Nell," she said sardonically, glancing at me, both acknowledging the tart common sense of her lost companion, Nell Huxleigh, and the fact that I was known as Nellie Bly in the wider world.

Perhaps she was also acknowledging that in my own inimitable way I was serving as a useful compatriot in the act of confronting and solving crime.

Quentin glanced at me with a puzzled frown, a look of loss upon his ill-lit features that it was impossible for a daredevil reporter to miss.

Irene sighed. "This scene is too similar to the Paris locale to be coincidental." She pointed to another mark on the cave's wall. "Even to the ancient symbol of Christ, the Chi-Rho, which combines an 'X' to represent the cross of crucifixion intersected by a 'P,' which represents the Savior. I can think of only one sensible course."

"What is that?" Quentin asked.

Irene sighed again, loud enough to be heard in the first balcony, had we been in a theater. As it was, rats skittered away at the deep, theatrical regret audible in that sigh of defeat and resolution.

"Mycroft Holmes must be contacted immediately. We need his brother Sherlock here to examine the scene as soon as possible."

She glanced around the disordered environment that screamed mute violence not long past.

"And most severely cross Mr. Holmes will be with us all about the mess that we and the rats have made of everything."

36.

Alone at Last

❧

They threw their heads back and poured the pure liquid,
which had a sweet, slightly narcotic smell . . . straight down
their thin throats. When satisfied they wiped their hairy
mouths on their sleeves. . . .

—V. P. KATAYEV, *A MOSAIC OF LIFE*

 Who would dream that I would ever welcome the privacy of my grandiose cell? Not even the nightly thump of the exterior latch falling to entrap me within could dismay me.

I did indeed find myself breathing more easily once alone in my chamber.

The fire was low, so I piled stick after stick on the embers glowing like hungry wolfish eyes until the black mouth of the mantel roared like a red-hot lion.

Then I went to the basin where the water would form a thin crust of ice by morning, wrung out a cold cloth, and patted it over my face and shoulders.

I quickly undid the borrowed gown's fastenings and stepped out of all of Tatyana's things, soon sheltering under the comforting volume of Godfrey's nightshirt. It felt like exchanging filthy Gypsy garb for an angel's robe.

Then I wrapped myself in the bedcover, sat in a chair by the fireplace, and allowed my mind to sink into the exhaustion it welcomed.

Soon I dreamed, for upright wolves played the violin in the corner of the castle, tongues lolling, while Tatyana's peasant servant tore off his face, and I saw the pale blue eyes were indeed James Kelly's, and Godfrey turned into the old man who turned into Sherlock Holmes, and I became a bird who fluttered up to the rafters and tried to warn everybody about what was happening.

I beat my wings and beat my wings, but nobody heeded me, and I couldn't fly anymore. . . .

I awoke to the fire beating flaming wings of heat against the stone walls of its prison. It sounded like an entire flock of crows imprisoned in the chimney above.

I heard another flutter that had been tickling my awakening senses: voices rising and falling nearby.

I pushed my heavy hair behind my ears to hear better—I would have to rebraid it in the morning, for I certainly didn't want to emulate Tatyana in any respect.

One voice was low-pitched, a basso Irene would call it. Godfrey. The other voice was more erratic, ranging from contralto to soprano.

I unbent from the chair, aching all over, and tiptoed to the door that connected with Godfrey's chamber, dragging my warm coverlet with me.

"It is the finest French brandy," one voice was saying.

Hers.

"I don't need it," Godfrey said.

"Ah, but you should want it. Need is for peasants."

"I am of peasant stock."

"Not I. So I will have the brandy you refuse."

I heard the gurgle of liquid into a cup or goblet.

"Are you not interested in my forebears?" she asked.

"Not particularly."

"You English! You always modify everything. You always understate. Is that because you're afraid of losing everything?"

"It's because exaggeration leads to self-deception."

"And how do I self-deceive?"

"I don't know you well enough to say."

"You are so self-contained. So distant. Is it possible you want to be a barrister, to transact boring business for the kings of commerce? To live in Neuilly and drive to Paris occasionally to see the sights? To assist an unemployed opera singer in matters of a trivial nature? To escort a prim Miss Nobody from a dance floor?"

"You see what you want to see, say what you think will wound. Can you truly wish to live like this? To play doomed games of spymanship in lost causes? To cultivate the crude because you have lost your one grip on culture and are an unemployed *danseuse*? To consort with criminals and Gypsies? To hold a Mr. Nobody captive because you have nothing better to do?"

"You are jealous of Sherlock Holmes."

"You are jealous of Irene Adler."

"A strange way to refer to your wife."

"She is more than my wife, and I think you know that, and it maddens you."

"You have no idea what worlds I could maroon you in."

"I do, and I suspect this is only one of them."

I leaned closer to the door, listening through the generous crack near the ancient hinges, hardly daring to breathe.

This was a duel. I had seen them skirmish before, Godfrey and this wild woman who called herself Tatyana. I had seen Irene duel her as well, in the dark of night, by surprise.

What did she want, this woman who would not, could not leave us alone?

I listened to their voices rise and fall, to the insults exchanged, the offers tendered and refused.

She wanted us all where she stood: alone, hating, powerful for having no boundaries that others observed. Like Lucifer after the fall.

I realized that if anything happened to any one of us, to our strong and honest trinity, Irene and Godfrey and I, she would have won.

If I were harmed and Godfrey was there, yet unable to prevent it, . . . she will have won.

If Godfrey were forced to bow to her will to save me or Irene, . . . she will have won.

If Irene risked all to reclaim Godfrey and I, and perished in the attempt, . . . she will have won.

She was indeed envious of Irene, not for *what* she had, but for *who* she had. And now Tatyana had us.

My nails dug into the soft flesh of my palms, that had been tainted by the touch of Tiger and Bear, and perhaps worse, beyond the safe gate of my damaged memory.

She claimed to want Godfrey as a woman might want a man, though I know little of that emotion. What she really wanted was what Lucifer desired most, a soul, a will.

And what was it that Jack the Ripper had wanted on those bloody nights? Not a woman as a man wants a woman, that I knew now. He wanted a soul, a soul ripped from a body, a body ripped from humanity.

I sometimes have been mocked for my religious nature, even gently by my friends, a nature that is, well . . . natural in a parson's daughter. But such early lessons teach a sensitivity to good and evil in their most elemental forms. The more sophisticated world does not wish to admit their existence.

I could live with what *might* have been done to me while I was unconscious and a prisoner. I could not live with what would certainly be done to Godfrey, and Irene, and myself, should Tatyana be able to manipulate us further.

I listened to the murmur next door. It was like overhearing barristers in court. The game was enjoined, the preliminary fencing launched. It had not yet come down to win or lose, good or evil, life and death.

But it would.

I cannot say how long I crouched there like a child on a stairway eavesdropping on adults, fearing the worst but determined to hear whatever I could.

Perhaps the sin and strain of eavesdropping had deafened me to all else.

How else can I explain the sudden shuffle of boot on stone and turning to find my room also occupied by an intruder?

I would have screamed had I not known that it would put Godfrey in danger if Tatyana knew I'd been listening.

I rose slowly, my knees resisting after such a long while bent.

Had I suspected that anyone else would have intruded on our quarters, it would have been Tatyana's old partner in espionage, Tiger.

But this unexpected guest was far worse than the intimidating Colonel Moran—the dancing bear she called Medved.

He was dancing now in his beastly way, swaying slightly from side to side on his booted feet, a pottery jar clutched against his filthy shirt front.

He grinned at me, showing a full set of teeth at least, but he was young yet and could be expected to loose them in carousing later.

"Eat," he pronounced in English as if it were an achievement. "Drink."

"I have eaten," I said, moving away from the door so he wouldn't barge through and betray my listening post. I hoped he was too drunk to even hear the murmur of neighboring voices, particularly his mistress's.

He followed me as obligingly as any distraction could wish,

stopping only to tilt back his head and drink from the unstoppered jar.

I felt the windows at my back, the chill night air raising goose-flesh on my neck and arms. It was shocking how cold the room became once away from the hot-throated fireplace.

I began to shiver.

He came lumbering and grinning after me, humming some simple Gypsy tune.

I had backed us into a dim, cold corner, away from all the noise and warmth of the crackling fire. It was as if I had left a friend behind at a time I most needed one.

At least I could hear nothing of Godfrey or Tatyana, but that may have been because my heart was beating too loudly to permit any kind of eavesdropping at all, except on my own frightening situation.

"Cold," he said, this one-word wonder. It was amazing that he spoke any English at all, but I suspect that Tatyana relished teaching him the occasional nugget of European knowledge, much as one would enjoy tossing a bit of meat to a hound.

I wondered if his mind was whole, and if he was Gypsy or of some other exotic tribe of pariahs, perhaps one of Quentin's Afghans or Turks.

He frowned as if noticing my shivers. "Drink." His greasy fingers splayed and then came behind my head. Together his hands forced my face to meet the lip of the crude crock. Bitter cold yet strong acid poured into my mouth, down my throat, down my chin and neck, burning like liquid fire wherever it touched.

I sputtered and choked, bucked away like a force-fed lamb, struggled to breathe, and inhaled some of the corrosive stuff up my nose.

All the while he laughed and nodded, and released me only to apply the same bitter medicine to his own mouth again.

I was revolted to the brink of vomiting.

But he was singing again, and swaying, staring at me.

Though his hair was as dark as a bramble bush, I suddenly realized that his eyes were as light as water, that I was seeing right through them as through an open window. Some strange, cold, pale fire shone behind them, like a thin curtain of ice. I had never seen such a transparent gaze, utterly unreflective, drawing me into an oddly sweeping empty world behind them, like the misty countryside you glimpse over the Mona Lisa's shoulder, past her smile.

He was smiling. And swaying from side to side. Singing. Gruff nonsense syllables a bear would mouth. For a moment I wondered if a man could transform himself into a bear . . . if Buffalo Bill Cody's Wild West Indians could do it. They were like Gypsies, weren't they, Indians? The men dancing around a fire, chanting, swaying. The internal fire of the mysterious liquid still tingled on my tongue and all down my throat and chest and stomach.

It was as if I had swallowed acid, but felt no fear.

He came crooning closer, his eyes growing as large as full moons in the daylight sky, white and milky, cool as silk.

I couldn't seem to concentrate hard enough, or long enough, to notice his food-encrusted tunic and greased-matted hair. The eyes were clean and as hot-cold as the liquid in the bottle he lifted again to my teeth.

Almost I would have lost myself to this strange lethargy so like something else I had known. A dream, perhaps.

But then I felt his fingers tugging at the bosom of my nightshirt, pawing, trying to rip the fabric apart. Suddenly the scene was familiar. Myself trapped by the velvet curtain that divided the close, artificial scenes of the panorama from the freedom of the outside world. Hands reaching for me. A strange soft pillow of forgetfulness pushed against my mouth and nose. Staring blue eyes unblinkingly absorbing my sight, my sound, my self.

I pushed it all away, the memory and the man-bear intruding on my very soul.

The next thing I knew I had fallen to the floor and the pottery jar came down hard beside me, spilling its contents and rolling sideways across the Oriental rug.

A triangular piece had fallen away.

The wounded bear was roaring silently up on two feet, blood running from a corner of its mouth. It wiped a crimson paw on the already abused shirt front, leaving a dark swath of liquid and blood.

I think he left, taking nothing with him but a brute surprise.

It was morning when I awakened, damp and dirty and confused, as if from an artificial sleep.

I would have thought I'd dreamed my night visitor, but I awoke stretched out like a Gypsy on the rug. My mouth had a dry, stale taste. The fallen jug lay just beyond one outstretched hand.

The fire across the room had gone out, and the front of my nightshirt was still wet.

I sat up, shuddering with the cold that aggravated the severe stiffness I noticed next.

My first thought was Godfrey. Was he safe? I had no idea how last night's "debate" had ended. I was afraid to find out.

While I lay there, huddled and uncertain, I heard a gentle knock.

Even that startled me like the thwunk of an executioner's axe. (Not that I have ever heard the thwunk of an executioner's axe, but one can imagine how it would sound. And if one likes ghost stories, one does.)

I pushed myself upright and hobbled to the connecting door like a beldame from a fairy tale.

I pulled the door open a crack and placed an eye to the crack.

"Nell!" Godfrey was dressed and looking quite normal. "What has happened?"

"I need a coverlet."

"Your own is—" He appeared to realize that I would have to expose my nightshirt-clad self to retrieve my coverlet and vanished for a moment, returning with the coverlet from his bed. I pulled it through as narrow a width of the door as I could manage, recalling the rich man and the eye of the needle from the Scriptures, and wrapped myself up in it like an Indian squaw.

Only then did I step back and admit Godfrey to my chamber.

"Obviously you have had a fright, Nell," he observed, stepping over the threshold to survey my chamber. His eyes fell on the fallen jug at once. "Oh, no! Tell me it was not that drunken oaf from Tatyana's table below!"

I nodded, clutching his coverlet.

Godfrey took me by the shoulders and guided me to the fireplace chair, where he deposited me. Then he fanned the last dying embers and teased them into flames with slender sticks peeled from the piled logs beside the mantel.

"I heard Tatyana last night," I finally said. "What did she want?"

Godfrey paused in building sticks into fire enough to ignite logs. "Nothing honorable. Or sensible. But she enjoys resistance, at least for a time. I could overpower her in an instant if I decided there was any profit in it." He turned, his forehead wrinkled with worry. "But you, Nell, alone in here with that brute—! What happened?"

"He came in shuffling and swaying and singing."

"Drunk on whatever fills that pottery jug."

"He made me drink some, pushed the thing against my teeth."

Godfrey came over and patted me on the shoulder, rather awkwardly. "If you had called out, Nell, I would have come."

"And what would Tatyana have made of that? She does not like being forsaken for another."

"Better you should have called out. She wouldn't have liked her trained beast devoting attention to you. Better they should quarrel among themselves. Is that all he did, force liquor down your throat?"

"He, uh, tried to assault your nightshirt, Godfrey, I'm very sorry. It may have a tear or two."

"The bastard!" He peeled back my—or his, rather—coverlet to examine the state of the nightshirt. Our joint inspection revealed that sturdy British sewing had withstood the inroads of the brute.

"Nell, I am sorrier than I can say. If I knew how we could safely flee this very day—"

"It is all right, Godfrey. During this strange . . . attack I was reminded of the great similarity between this and the moment when I was abducted from the panorama in Paris. The same pawing and clutching, the same fixed, demented gaze. . . . Godfrey, is it possible that one man may transform into another? I know it was James Kelly that came at me in Paris, twice. Yet this creature here in Transylvania reminds me of him, as if they were brothers. Or the same in different form."

Godfrey sat back on his heels to consider it. I was relieved that my presenting him with a problem had taken his mind off the indignities I had suffered. One does not wish one's indignities long contemplated by others, no matter how near and dear.

"I suppose you are talking about metamorphosis, Nell. It is a Greek idea."

"Like much that is bizarre."

"Or mythical, at least. Such notions have people turning into trees and flowers and animals, all at the intervening powers of the gods from Mount Olympus. Still, it is a strong notion, and an ancient one, so one might wonder if there was some historic basis for it."

"Perhaps I simply sensed the universality of evil."

Godfrey returned his pale gray gaze to me—absent of anything more mesmerizing than kind familiarity—and smiled. "The universality of evil is certainly a given that touches all ages and places. I am glad that you are all right."

"Of course," I said, now warmed and able to sit up absolutely straight without support of chair or corsets and without shivering.

I gazed at the abandoned pottery jug lying on my carpet.

"Irene put some significance on the wine bottles and such we found abandoned in the underground sites in Paris. I wonder if this object might be instructive. Sherlock Holmes put great stock in corks, which this container is missing, but is there something else telltale about it?"

"I don't know, Nell." Godfrey stood up and approached the object in question. "But we can look into it."

"Excellent. I can tell you it was a most potent and disagreeable libation, quite enough to turn a man into a bear."

He nodded and bent down to retrieve the homely item. A bit of pale wax fell off the top as he lifted it up.

I realized that my "diversion" for Godfrey's sake, to give him something else to think upon than my recent trials, had hit on a universal truth as widespread as universal evil.

These were traces of the same props and players—the crude bottles and cruder men, the remote locations with underground cellars—as had haunted the underbelly of Paris when the Ripper killings continued.

That is when I resolved that we must leave this place as soon as possible.

37.

Sovereign Security

❧❧❧

*Put not your trust in princes; in a son of man in whom
there is no help.*

—PSALM 146:3

◁ F R O M   A   J O U R N A L ▷

I awoke the next morning in our Prague hotel room, memories assembling around my trundle bed like dreams.

My mind tried to bat them away, but sights and smells
seeped under the door and through the window frames.

Darkness, a rain mixed of blood and wine, the reek of
the charnel house and the privy, the dry, overriding scent of old,
hard earth in which bones and rats kept company.

I stared up at the ceiling, an alabaster exercise in plaster and
gilt. It looked like icing on a cake, shockingly out of tune with what
I'd seen and heard and thought so recently.

"James Kelly," I murmured to myself. He seemed to have
slipped off the map since Neunkirchen, unless his hand was to be
sensed in every subterranean scene of chaos and revelry and implied
violence.

Why would an upholsterer be hieing across Europe merely to escape us? Our hunting party.

Irene was up, dressed, and seated at the desk, wearing the men's clothing she had donned the night before. I corrected my impression: she was likely still up from the night before and had not changed clothing.

"Awake, Pink?" she asked without looking over her dark serge shoulder to verify her impression. Sometimes her instincts were uncanny. No doubt it was from listening for cues onstage. "Better dress quickly."

"For more burrowing?"

"No, for climbing." She glanced over at me finally. "Quentin is arranging an audience at Prague Castle."

I rose and came in bare feet and nightgown to stand behind her.

A cablegram, somewhat crumpled, lay over the map of Prague.

"He cannot, will not come," she announced without looking at me, her voice taut as a wirewalker's line. "He does not say so, of course. He has a brother to convey the rejection."

I leaned over to read the message since she didn't seem inclined to stop me.

YOUR REQUEST IMPOSSIBLE. S. H. IS FULLY OCCUPIED HERE AND CANNOT LEAVE FOR ANY REASON. SURELY YOU HAVE SOME RELIABLE RESOURCES ON YOUR END. M. H.

"A rather biting refusal," I commented.

"No doubt the affair that keeps 'S.H.' in London is reinvestigating the Jack the Ripper murders, which would not have happened without our discoveries in Paris. London is a cold trail." She pushed the cablegram away. "But if Sherlock Holmes and his fuddy-duddy brother in the foreign office prefer to see his time wasted in Whitechapel . . . we shall indeed rely on our own resources here." She flashed me a friendly glance. "You slept late. It is almost eleven, and we are expected at the castle by noon."

"Goodness," I said, gathering my clothes and scurrying for the washbasin. "At least I needn't worry what to wear. It's time for my checked coatdress again."

"And time for demure women's dress for me. The King and the Rothschild representatives expect extraordinary accomplishments from very ordinary-looking people. Quentin will meet us at the castle."

"And Bram?" I asked from behind my curtain.

"He's already off to Transylvania by train. He's more comfortable in the wilderness, and I told him to investigate that suspicious castle to his heart's content."

I came from behind the curtain, tucking in my shirtwaist. "You're getting rid of him! Is he no longer a suspect?"

"Entertaining as his grue-laced stories are, I suspect him of nothing more than what the majority of Englishmen commit: pallid marriages to passionless women and some equally pallid dallying in brothels. You saw many such men in such places. What did you conclude?"

"Much what you have." I came to the desk. "It is why I have resolved not to marry. It seems such a bore for both parties and, unless there is some financial advantage in it, quite a waste of time. Besides, I don't have the leisure for such nonsense. Speaking of time, unless you have more than dried spots of blood and nonsensical graffiti to offer, I'll have to get back to London and the States."

"Still thinking you might manage to glean something from Sherlock Holmes en route, Pink?"

"One never knows."

"Marriage need not be the mockery you mention," she added. "I'd determined not to do it myself once."

"That would be my one regret in leaving before your mission is done: not meeting the remarkable Godfrey."

"Oh, I think you'd regret not being in on catching the Ripper a lot more. Be honest, Pink! And you do not believe in Godfrey, to be utterly honest, although I appreciate your assumption that we shall find him."

"Look, I'm sorry I can't stay. But you've got Quentin now and good old Bram to do your bidding. I've got enough notes for a dozen stories to excuse my absence. I would appreciate your cabling me, though, if you do catch any legendary murderer."

I bent down to snatch up the pen and scrawl the address of my New York rooms on the corner of the map.

"Come to the castle, Pink," she cajoled me. "You may yet find that the chase is worth the time."

Our hired carriage climbed the hill crowned with stone buildings and spires. Besides the huge bulk of Prague Castle, there were the towers of three major churches, the Archbishop's Palace, and other famous buildings as well, a city unto itself.

Behind and below us the sturdy Charles Bridge with its ancient facing honor guard of thirty stone saints dwindled to a dull gray strut across the sparkling pewter waters of the Vltava River.

Prague's red tile roofs surrounded the occasional blue-green copper roofs of churches like an incarnadine sea lapping at stately stones. I thought of the blood-dark drops dripping in the unseen tunnels, of Paris with its catacombs of tightly packed bones. It was as if the buildings and streets were only the skin of a city and the people that thronged them mere lice infesting the exterior while the city's true heart throbbed within and below, in the graveyards and empty spaces beneath, where death deposited its souvenirs as if all the living souls swarming above eventually sifted into dust and drained into the hidden undercurrents below.

But one could not sell newspapers with such morbid fancies, so I took out my journal and began a description of my latest visit to a royal palace. They would gobble that up like oatmeal in Schenectady.

If one did not know the evils committed in the city after dark, this day was simply one of many in a Prague spring. The scent of flowers floated on the air like a bridal veil.

When we arrived, Quentin Stanhope sprung forward to open our carriage door like a Prince Charming dressed as a diplomat in tailed coat, striped pants, and vest.

My time in Europe was accustoming me to sweeping up to grand edifices like I owned them, whether they be cathedrals or castles. I was almost ready to pay a visit to millionaire's row in Newport, Rhode Island!

I was not surprised when we were ushered into the same throne room we had visited before. The King was there, still very grand opera-ish in his gold-braided scarlet uniform, but the Queen was absent.

Clotilde's vacancy allowed me to imagine Irene in her place. Really, she was born for the role of queen of something, except she was much too independent-minded to ever make a docile European queen, as I think every American woman is, or should be.

A dapper man in striped pants, morning coat, and monocle waited with the King.

"Come sit," the King ordered as only kings can do, managing to sound both jovial and demanding.

We perched on various tapestry-covered sofas and chairs near the room's sidewall. I almost felt we should be observing a ball in progress, with dancing figures swaying in a Viennese waltz over the inset marble floor, through the gleaming marble pillars, past the empty gilt-and-velvet throne.

First Quentin introduced the dapper gentlemen to the ladies, as he was known to the King and himself.

"May I present Baron Březová of Bohemia, who is most protective of the Rothschild interests in this quarter of the world."

The Baron was in his well-fed fifties, with rosy cheeks and steelserious blue eyes. The man's affable smile pressed the gold-rimmed monocle deeper into his left cheek as he bowed to us.

I was fascinated! Would the small, clear, full moon of glass stay in place if he sneezed? Although the monocle looks like an affectation to us barefaced Americans, I did understand that many noblemen of Germanic and Anglo descent inherited monocular

vision—clear as crystal in one eye and quite blind as a bat in the
other, just as hemophilia also ran, excuse the expression, through
some of the royal bloodlines of Europe.

"Miss—?"

"Pink," Irene said decisively.

The Baron blinked, and I truly thought he'd lose his monocle.
But neither smile nor eyeglass budged.

"She is a protegé of yours, Madame Norton?"

"An associate," Irene said, smiling also.

"I must offer my sympathy on the mysterious disappearance of
your former . . . associate, Miss Huxleigh." His smile had vanished.
"But, I have good news about your husband."

"News!" Irene repeated, as if the word was foreign.

"Good!" Quentin repeated, for her benefit.

I felt a weight lifting off me like a heavy Persian lamb cape. I
hadn't realized until now that I'd feel like a dog leaving for home
with Nell and Godfrey still unaccounted for.

"Indeed." The Baron continued to bow and beam, but it seemed
automatic, mere politeness. He bent to lift a small black case like a
doctor's bag onto the marble-inlaid table before the sofa. "These
papers arrived by messenger yesterday from Transylvania. The transaction your husband was sent there to conduct, has been signed,
sealed"—here he pointed an immaculate fingernail to the great
wine-colored blob of wax imprinted with some intricate device—
"and delivered, as you see. Count Lupescu has authorized the sale
of his land for a price amenable to him and our own interests. You
see your husband's signature on the bottom paper, and the date,
but two days ago."

Irene leaned over the document, skimming tight paragraphs of
tiny manuscript in three languages: English, German, and possibly
. . . Transylvanian? That's what they looked like to me, but Irene
was now studying the two signatures at the bottom of the long
parchment page.

"This one is Godfrey's hand, his signature."

"You see, Madame. Business is transacted. All is well. He will soon be home . . . or at least back in Prague."

"When?" Irene demanded breathlessly.

"Well, when the train schedules allow."

"There was no message from him with the document?"

"The document is message enough."

"Not for me."

The Baron's smile, and monocle, drooped a bit. "Transylvania is a primitive country. Communications are not so swift or easy as in cosmopolitan cities like Prague. The paramount thing was to conduct the business and procure the document. This your husband has accomplished. Returning himself will be the easiest part of it, believe me. The Count, and all Transylvanians, are stubborn souls for having fought the Turk for centuries. To them we owe our sovereign security here. They are slow to relinquish anything that belongs to them . . . land, pride, knowledge about themselves. Mr. Norton has accomplished a difficult task. You should be proud."

"I am proud, Baron. What I am not is reassured. My husband writes frequently when he travels and such communications suddenly ceased more than a fortnight ago."

"Irene!" The King spoke for the first time. "You are not used to the slow pace of life in these backward countries. Even in Prague, we know we are not Vienna, or Warsaw, or Paris. And I understand that in America you are even faster-paced. Such impatient people, the Americans. How you slipped away from Prague and myself that time as if running from the very devil!" He almost shook an admonishing finger at her, smiling all the while. "You must allow for the tempo of the place. We are not *vivace*, we are *lento*."

She looked from the King to the Baron. I saw her always straight spine stiffening even more with suspicion. No wonder! I was getting mighty curious myself.

I glanced at Quentin, who had become as still and watchful as a polecat. He caught my eye, and his look was not encouraging.

Irene, meanwhile, had all the lines. "You say I am simply to wait and see when Godfrey will return to Prague?"

"As we will," the Baron assured her.

"Much could go wrong, if it hasn't already."

"The papers—"

"The papers merely prove that the Transylvanian Count was persuaded to sell his lands to the Rothschild interests. My husband's signature could have been imitated. I doubt it was, but I find it most alarming that he sent no accompanying letter to anyone with this document. That is not the way a barrister conducts business. That is not the way Godfrey does things. He is a . . . devout letter writer. If not to me, then to you, his contact in Prague. You cannot tell me, either of you, that you do not find this sequence of events suspicious."

They were silent.

"And what of Nell, of her disappearance from Paris?"

They both glanced at me without thinking, and in that glance came a terrible truth: that they thought she had replaced Nell with me, after all, and that one woman who served was as good as another. I felt it. Irene felt it. Quentin felt it. But our hosts did not.

I stewed in the indignation of being considered interchangeable. One woman who took notes or who took men to bed was as good as another. They were parts to be played, to be replaced when needed. That wonderful word which the British use—and I admit that the world, even I, has some use for the British now and again—says it all. Supernumeraries. Unknown, unnamed actors who play the nonspeaking roles in all the great dramas of history, expendable in battle and riot scenes, unimportant except for adding the impression of mass to the unreality of the scene. Bram Stoker knew these unsung nonentities well, having stuffed the stage of the Lyceum with them. But without them, you don't have the making of an epic for the heroes to shine in.

I was born to be a supernumerary, and Irene, but we were not willing to play the roles we were born to.

And we weren't about to do so now. It looked like I was about to extend my stay in Europe out of sheer indignation. That's all right. Indignation is a reporter's life blood. And my instincts were telling me that where the bland denials and the status quo rules, so does hypocrisy and wrongdoing.

"Then," Irene added, "there is the matter of the international links to the Jack the Ripper slayings in London. Paris and Prague have both been the scenes of similar killings of women, and in Prague an infant was slain, too."

"I'm afraid," the King said, looking away, toward his empty throne, "that I am not much involved in these sordid police matters."

The Baron nodded. "These killings that dominate the sensational press have little import on the life of the citizens otherwise. The matter has been contained in Paris and Prague. We did not allow the blood-hungry press to exploit the tragedies in these cities. London, being the first site of such heinous crimes, was lamentably slow to take control of the public's venal interest in the details. We all know that such atrocities are nothing new in the world, and such examples should be kept from the public, lest they panic."

"But these crimes are connected!"

"My dear Madame Norton, there is no proof of that. We can point out similar crimes in all these cities, recent and many years old. Man is not perfectible, alas, and—"

"And women usually pay the price," she finished harshly.

He slapped his hands together and sadly shook his head. "I suggest you concentrate on finding your unfortunate friend. I also suggest you wait here in Prague for a reunion with your husband. I pray that you will not be too impetuous to do so."

Irene glanced incredulously to the King.

He was brushing lint from the immaculate red wool expanse of his gilt-swagged chest.

"And the Baron de Rothschild in Paris—?" she began.

"He is entertaining the Prince of Wales and many others of great moment at his country house of Ferrières. I would not care to disturb him at the moment."

"The Prince of Wales and the Baron de Rothschild commissioned me to follow these crimes to their source."

The Baron shrugged. "Perhaps next week, when I can wire the Baron and your husband is back."

"Perhaps next week, three or six or ten more women will be dead, Baron." Irene rose. "And my husband will be back sooner than next week, because I will see to it."

The King stood, in both tribute and relief at her impending departure, I think. "Ah, Irene, no woman has such fire as you."

"You should know, Willie, and you should remember the outcome last time. You got your royal fingers burned."

"By the way," the Baron said as she turned to leave, "I would not put false hopes in Sherlock Holmes. He, too, has been . . . advised to leave the matter alone."

"I have never put my hopes in Sherlock Holmes, or kings and princes, Baron, but in myself and my associates. Good day."

We left. Rather, Irene left, and we followed.

Quentin walked beside me as we trailed her out through the grand halls. He looked as grave as I have ever seen a man. She never missed a turn, and we were soon facing into a Prague midday of sunshine and golden spires.

"Your husband's signature on the papers was authentic," I said finally.

"Yes. I have always believed he and Nell were alive. I have just not known where, and why. We will have to find this Count Lupescu, or perhaps Bram Stoker will do so for us." She looked at Quentin. "They obviously do not want us to investigate these Prague crimes further. So even more obviously that is our first step."

"Agreed," he said. "Where do we begin? You know more of this matter than I do."

"Your husband," I put in, "mentioned one killing of a woman in a letter to you. It was published enough in the city for him to hear of it."

Irene nodded. "They can't hope to keep everything quiet. As the King says, Prague is not a complete backwater. It is more forward-thinking than Transylvania!"

"Why would the Baron de Rothschild seek your aid in Paris and silence it in Prague?" Quentin wanted to know.

Irene gazed out over the picturesque rooftops of the city. "We can't know what the Baron de Rothschild wishes, since he is not here. And we don't have time to waste seeking his official approval. What is clear is that this particular local Baron, whoever's interests he serves—and I suspect they are primarily his own—and the King are terribly afraid of the truth, so that is what we must uncover."

"Brava!" said I.

Irene turned to me, surprise warming her deep brown eyes.

I laughed. "It's a mistake to let me know I'm not wanted somewhere. Easiest way to get me to stay."

She nodded.

"Where do we begin?" Quentin asked.

"At the brothel where the latest woman was killed, and where you met Bram Stoker."

I was stunned. "You still think he could be the Ripper?"

Now Quentin Stanhope was stunned. "Irene, if you thought that, why did you—?"

"You have not heard all the various and sundry theories on the Ripper's identity, from illiterate immigrants to the British royal family and all stations in between. But I am not concerned about Bram at the moment. He is, after all, safely out of the city and following his heart to the highlands of Transylvania. The man I am interested in is the furtive fellow who was described in the brothel only moments before the dead woman was discovered. One fact we do know is that James Kelly fled Paris and was identified en route here."

In the carriage returning us to the hotel, Irene explained to Quentin the suspicious role the one-time incarcerated lunatic, convicted wife-killer, and upholsterer by trade had played in Paris.

"The man is utterly mad," Quentin agreed when she had finished, "and could indeed be the Whitechapel Ripper. But how do his activities and whereabouts connect to those of that fiendish cult you uncovered in Paris?"

"I'm not sure," she admitted. "Sometimes I think that he has always and everywhere acted alone, and that his presence at the final cult orgy in Paris was accidental, more from his following us than us following him. He did seem to be . . . mesmerized by Nell."

Quentin's already swarthy face darkened with an angry flush. He looked quite lethal in his way. "It is unthinkable that this man or his demented cohorts could have her. Yes, let us find him if he still dares to remain in Prague, and I will have the truth out of him in no time."

"He may be unwilling to talk," Irene cautioned.

"That is of no consequence," Quentin said so shortly that neither Irene nor I wanted to ask exactly why.

All the dark and savage mystery of the East was in Quentin's face at that moment. From the tales he had told of their unbelievably barbaric ways, I had no doubt that Quentin Stanhope knew their methods well, and would use them.

I wondered what Nell would think to know she had inspired such deep but relentless loyalty. I know that I might wonder whether the defender was worse than the despoiler.

38.

Shades of Whitechapel

❧❧❧

I never meant to stab you as I sat by you asking you to forgive me and you answered no. I took out my penknife and meant to frighten you, but something seemed to come over me and I went mad and stabbed you.
—JAMES KELLY'S LETTER TO HIS DYING WIFE, 1888

⊰FROM A JOURNAL⊱

Back at our hotel Irene gathered up the sketch of James Kelly while Quentin made a smaller sketch of the Chi-Rho pattern she had overlaid on the east bank of the city.

She took Nell's portfolio with the two papers under her arm. Wearing Nell's black faille surprise dress, all its frivolous pink facings buttoned shut, she resembled a ghost of her longtime companion.

The same thought must have struck Quentin, for he paused to look long and hard at her before he opened the suite door to release us on greater Prague.

"I am not a man much attuned to female fashions, or male, for that matter, but haven't I seen that gown before, Irene?"

"It is Nell's," she said, biting her lip a moment after. "When it came to clothing that would travel well and quickly, I found Nell's wardrobe far more practical than my own. Even Pink's checkered coatdress resembles the garb Nell wore when she vanished."

Quentin bent the same unnerving stare on me and my gown, then finally nodded and opened the door for us. "I'm not surprised that Nell has served as a good model for her friends in her absence. She would be most pleased," was all he said.

I wasn't about to say that I doubt Nell and I considered each other friends. Men must have their illusions about women, or we would all go mad.

We went on foot, by design. Irene said we must see Prague as a fugitive like James Kelly would, and Quentin agreed.

It was quite the picturesque city, particularly this old section, although lamentably filthy.

"How will we represent you and Pink at the brothel?" Quentin wondered.

Irene considered while we walked, hardly noticing as we stepped around offal in the street. "Perhaps as relatives searching for some lost sister."

"And the sketch of Kelly?"

"Her fiancé perhaps, also lost. They had eloped together, unwisely but well, then had become separated by the confusion of the city." Irene was weaving her playlet now, embroidering on our story and our roles. "He fears she has been forced to support herself. You are . . . Pink's fiancé. I am her older sister. We need not be searching for one of the dead women, only a fictitious girl who is in danger of becoming like her."

"Dead?" I asked.

"A prostitute first. Then dead. I am sure the brothelkeepers and their residents are atremble at these violent deaths. They will not doubt our concern."

"And how," Quentin asked, "will you explain the fact that I am English and you and Pink are American? They can't have too many American girls seeking places in brothels here."

"You would be surprised," I told him. "The harlot of exotic background is always an asset in a brothel. Or a European brothel, rather," I amended, thinking that his experience was likely to be Eastern.

He apparently read my assumption, for his complexion darkened again. "It is true," he admitted, "that I am foreign to European espionage, and brothels. And how are you so expert in the subject?"

Before I could retort that it was my profession, Irene directed her attention to a narrow street of four-story, tall-windowed buildings. "Is this the street where the brothel is?"

I consulted my pocket watch. "Four-thirty. It is a good time to visit. The girls are just awakening from naps and getting ready for dinner later and the *grande promenade*. The attendants will be out in full force."

Indeed, the laundryman's cart was drawn up before the building, and he was trundling his bags of fresh linen inside like Santa Claus with his sack of toys.

We followed in the tracks of his clogs and found ourselves in a dark and musty hall where an old woman with a scarf crossed over her flat bosom served as a combination concierge and coatchecker.

She called some Czech words at us.

Irene immediately turned and began caroling back, only she mixed Czech, German, and English.

"Ah, some English. Speak?" Using her trilingual approach and many gestures—to me, Quentin, herself, hand to heart, she inquired after "Madame" in French. A word that seemed to be universally recognizable. The old soul's braid-topped white head nodded us within.

Irene immediately went to a door, opened it, and peered down the dark stairs it revealed.

The old woman shook her head violently and gestured us to another door.

This one opened on stairs going upward and it we took, although Irene glanced longingly back at the forbidden door to the lower regions as we mounted higher in the house.

"Information first and exploration later," she told us. "The second floor. Madame."

The second floor offered either more opportunity to climb or a short hall with three steps ending at another nondescript door.

This we approached, and Quentin knocked.

It was opened by a girl of fifteen perhaps, dewy and wide-eyed, who opened it wider when Irene murmured the magic word, "Madame."

Within was a large cozy chamber in the Viennese style, filled with lighted tapers and sparkling cut-glass droplets and very overstuffed furniture in designs like padded hearts for Valentine's Day.

Madame was plump, pretty, perhaps forty years old. Her curled reddish hair surrounded her beaming features like a Cupid's coiled mop, and she was gowned in emerald brocade like a rather attractive sofa.

I had never seen such a kindly looking madam, although all I had met were able to pretend beneficence toward their men customers.

She bade us sit and perched at the very edge of her sofa as Irene pantomimed the melodrama of our common dear one, our loss, our concern, our need to ask questions. Again she resorted to three languages. Again she made herself understood.

In two minutes the madam's expressive face was limpid with sympathy.

In three minutes Irene was rapidly whispering translated words in English to me and my ever-handy notebook. Quentin sat by, watching and reading my notes over my shoulder, nodding with sorrowful mein whenever Irene glanced his way.

Irene opened the portfolio and produced the cabinet sketch of James Kelly. The particularly clever feature of having a fine artist draw it was that it seemed quite a natural thing to have, like the preliminary sketch for a portrait. Its presence not only allowed witnesses to quickly say yea or nay to the likeness, but lent an air of legitimacy to our supposed quest. This man we sought was not a criminal, but a lost dear one.

It struck me for the first time that it was odd she had not made such sketches of Nell and Godfrey. Then I realized that she had not expected them to be seen beyond the moment of their abductions, if indeed they had been abducted.

The madam nodded at the sketch and pointed at her extravagant upholstery. Irene began to describe something. From her hand gestures, I recognized the unmistakable silhouette of the *siége d'amour* designed for the Prince of Wales upon which I had found the two Parisian prostitutes horribly slaughtered.

This two-tiered exquisitely made couch of love meant to accommodate a man whose bulk only slightly underweighed the average elephant's was apparently a device not unheard of in other European establishments. (I never ran across the like in American brothels, but then we are descended from Puritans, and not princes.)

I glanced at Quentin and saw that he had gotten the idea very well despite the foreign words used. In fact, his face betrayed a rather active curiosity, and I suspect that had we been men and not women, he could have described exotic Eastern versions of the same appliance and made all sorts of interesting cultural comparisons. It is amazing what the stuffy average Englishman gets up to away from home, which is no doubt why Bram Stoker was a credible Ripper suspect, even though he was Irish.

I must admit that these speculations gave me a great itch to see more of the world, East and West and North and South.

The sweet little Viennese torte of a madam was nodding sympathetically and spreading her arms wide enough to show off her impressive *decollétage*. I gathered we had the freedom of the house, at least until the gentlemen callers started assembling at seven or eight.

We left with nods and bows, as if departing a very pleasant tea party.

"What a lovely lady," Irene exclaimed quite sincerely as we reassembled in the hall outside. "She is most distraught at the slaughter of the innocents in Prague and bids us ask wherever we will for our lost little lamb. Why am I surprised to find cooperation in the brothels and not in the palace?"

"Innocents?" I remarked.

"She operates, according to what I gathered, an amazingly benign brothel. She sees herself as a headmistress of sorts and this as a school for the girls' betterment. Apparently several of her 'graduates' have become the cherished mistresses of men of influence."

I wrinkled my nose before I realized it was a "Nell" gesture. "I understand that you yourself were highly insulted at the notion of becoming the mistress of a man of influence." Oh, what a "Nell" thing to say! Beware of wearing prim, checked coatdresses and taking notes!

Quentin chuckled behind me, and I felt absurdly proud of myself.

Irene laughed, at herself. "All right. But she is an uncommonly *nice* madam. My beloved Prague still has its old-fashioned niceties. This tells me that our inquiries will bear fruit."

So we waltzed up more stairs and through more doors into more overupholstered suites of rooms. The girls were plump and pleasant. They giggled at Quentin's presence but managed to refrain from drawing their dressing gowns closed because of it, or keeping their lips buttoned.

Camilla had been found dead near the door to the cellar. Her throat had been cut and she herself left in a crumple of bloody linens.

Yes, this man in the sketch had been there that night, but only on the ground floor. He had come in with Tabek, the laundry man, and seen the Madame on business. He did not look like a customer, being poorly but cleanly dressed and servile in manner. He had not looked at the three girls who had seen him, but kept his eyes on the floor and his lips muttering something. Prayers? No, something in an alien language. French? Oh, no, French was not alien. French was the language of love . . . and commerce.

All these things Irene translated for me and my notebook and Quentin in her rapid *sotto voce* as she interrogated the girls in whatever bits of language that would do the job. I must admit I was pretty impressed by her way with foreign words and her method of miming when common language failed. Her theatrical history made her a superb interviewer, and I wondered how Sherlock Holmes would do in the same instance . . . not half so well, I'm sure! And she got all this without the aid of her devilish locket and mesmerizing skills. Call me a modern woman, but I don't like the trappings of séances and mentalist stage acts and had already exposed a phony mesmerist back home.

Our last stop was the first place that had caught her interest: that chill-inducing stairway into darkness.

Irene cajoled a lit candle in a holder from the ancient doorkeeper. Apparently the madam's goodwill had sifted down even to the ground floor.

"What do you expect to find down here?" Quentin asked.

He was amazingly willing for Irene to lead the expedition, unlike the average Englishman needing to be first and foremost in all things, like Mr. Sherlock Holmes.

On the other hand, Prague was Irene's territory, like New York was mine, and God-knew-where was Quentin's. There was no sense in our jousting her for sleuthing rights. Still, it's not the average man who can wait and let a woman lead.

I think he also bowed to her emotional superiority in the hunt: her husband's and her friend's lives were at stake. However much he may have cared about either, and I was very curious to know the exact history of Quentin Stanhope and Penelope Huxleigh, he had no obvious right to lead the expedition.

Irene moved one hand against the slick cellar wall as she held the candle aloft and descended.

We followed, step by step. They were wooden and poorly built, not even level.

"What are you looking for?" Quentin repeated.

"What we found before," she answered. "Ask Pink."

He did. I explained the cellar beneath the French brothel where the first two Paris prostitutes were found slaughtered in the elegant rooms above. I mentioned the spilled wine and the guttered candle stumps.

"So you believe this Kelly drank down his courage before going upstairs to wreak bloody havoc?" he asked.

"It's possible," I said, "he had a fierce drinking problem."

"It's also possible," Irene added, "that Kelly was already used to subterranean debauchery and slaughter. This is the trail that we followed through Paris. This is what we found in the tunnels under the Old Town."

"You are speaking of a secret underground . . . conspiracy." Quentin sounded doubtful. "Like the Masons, who draw on the highest in society, only this one draws on the lowest."

"Exactly!" Irene spun to face us, stopping our precarious progress. "You have put into words what I only sensed, Quentin. This is a secret society, a . . . sect of the lowliest elements. In Whitechapel the rumor soon went around that the highest in the land had met in that low district to plot and carouse and kill, but the police list of suspects always centered on the poorest, most ignorant elements in the area, and there were many. Sensation would like to believe that the rich and eminent are secretly debauched and vicious, and some indeed are. But who is most likely to resort to raw slaughter and primitive rites with candles and cheap spirits? James Kelly was mad, he was a killer of one woman that we know of; he was a lost, ignorant soul. He was not an aristocrat."

She hastened down the last few steps and rushed forward into the dark. Her candle flickered over a littered floor not unlike the tunnels leading from the Rabbi's famous tomb . . . carpeted in rat droppings, blobs of candle wax and, in the corner, one of the bone-pale pottery jugs we had found the other night.

Quentin bent to pick it up. "If we knew what spirit had filled this bottle we might know where to look for your James Kelly and Jack the Ripper."

"Spirits indeed," Irene said both ruefully and triumphantly. "What genie from what bottle do we seek? And, when released, what has that mysterious jinn made men do?"

"And women," I added. "The ones in Paris participated in their own despoilment."

"So," said Quentin grimly, "do Arab brides."

"Tomorrow," Irene said, lifting the crude bottle as if in a toast, "we visit the rail station and hopefully will let the genie out of this bottle for good."

39.

Killing the Cobra

Eye to eye and head to head,
...This shall end when one is dead.
—RUDYARD KIPLING, "RIKKI-TIKKI-TAVI"

"Godfrey, we must go."

"I agree, but how?"

"Down through the cellar you found during your exploration. You thought you saw signs of smuggling, that there may be a tunnel out of the castle."

"I saw a quantity of boxes lying about," he conceded, "and sensed some movement of air, but it merely might have been a chink, Nell."

We again huddled over the usual breakfast of stew scooped up with hard bread. Godfrey looked gaunt and tired this morning. "I saw marks in the softer areas of the cellar soil, the marks of many men carrying burdens in. The imprints were deep, as if the contents were heavy. Some boxes had as many as six sets of boot prints, so you can imagine the weight."

"Gold, do you think?"

"More likely silver, given the region. And there's the rub. Silver is not worth enough to smuggle."

"Other goods."

He shrugged. "I don't know."

"Why do the Rothschilds want this property at the end of nowhere?"

"This is a modern world, Nell. 'Ends of nowhere' will be somewhere soon enough. Look at the American West. There is hardly an unclaimed inch of it left already. Few regions in Europe remain that are remote enough to still acquire. Transylvania is one of them."

Like a barrister born, he warmed to his subject. "You wondered why the Ripper would relocate his crimes to Prague. We don't have a map, but imagine this point is London, this Paris, this Warsaw." He swiftly marked imaginary spots on the figured cloth atop the table. "Here is the Black Sea and Russia, there Turkey. You see; Prague is the navel of Europe, almost dead center. That has not been lost on the Rothschild interests."

"But the eastern parts of Europe are still mired in peasant ways. These primitive countries cannot hold a candle to England or Germany or France in any area, commerce or culture."

Godfrey smiled faintly, perhaps at hearing me link France with England among Europe's more civilized nations.

"That held true yesterday, Nell. Today's faster rail and telegraphic services make it possible for these more backward nations to catch up, and certainly those business interests first on the scene will lead the pack."

"So why did Tatyana allow you to conduct Rothschild business with the Count?"

Godfrey pushed what little he had eaten away. "It must be obvious that Tatyana desires to strip Irene of all that she holds dear."

"Obvious, yes. Understandable, no!"

"For some reason Tatyana has cast herself as Irene's rival. Perhaps it was the defeat that Irene handed the Russian interests during the last adventure in Prague. Perhaps it was Irene's ill-advised midnight visit to tell Tatyana what would be what."

"Perhaps," I put in, "it was Irene's wrongheaded scheme to send you as delegate and spy to Tatyana. I was present then as your secretary, Godfrey, and I tell you that the creature displayed an unwholesome interest in you even then. I believe that is genuine enough, and that it is the only reason Tatyana wishes Irene ill."

A faint flush of anger touched his pale cheekbones. "The woman means to seduce me, that is certain. I have never before met such a forward creature."

"Sarah Bernhardt," I said promptly.

"Sarah Bernhardt is a paragon of female reticence compared to Tatyana. If you recall, this Russian woman's spyname was Sable, after an animal native to Russia that is prized for its rich fur coat. The sable is also a relative of the weasel, which means that it is elusive but quick and lethal at the kill."

"Sable seems a much more trivial code name than Tiger and Cobra," I answered, referring to the noxious Colonel Moran and our own dear Quentin Stanhope and perhaps boasting a bit about Quentin.

"Are you forgetting another furred, lithe, and weasel-like animal, my dear Nell? The mongoose."

"Messalina!" I said quickly, remembering with an unexpected pang my menagerie left behind in Neuilly to the attendance of others and the little beast that Quentin had given me.

"A Messalina, indeed," he said, referring to the wicked and power-mad Roman empress. "An animal which always fights and usually kills the king cobra."

I felt the room fleeing to the edges of my senses. I was not swooning, but experiencing something worse, fear for another that outweighed any fear for myself. Now I understood why Godfrey's most desperate hope was that Irene *not* find us.

I could only pray that Quentin had proved impossible to find himself, that he knew nothing of our plight, and that, Cobra or not, he, too, would never venture within striking range of the treacherous Sable.

40.

Fleeing Prague

✺

*Then a quicker note to the music; the galloping hoofs of
another horse, the finest of them all, and "Buffalo Bill"
...enters under the flash of the lime-light...*
—HELEN CODY WELMORE, *LAST OF THE GREAT SCOUTS*, 1899

⊰ FROM A JOURNAL ⊱

 The ticket taker gazed morosely at the sketch of James
Kelly, and nodded.

Out of the corner of our eyes, we noticed the uniformed
guards observing our query. Irene listened intently, then
translated for us.

"The ticket taker recognizes Kelly. He took a train to Transylvania two days ago. Another train does not depart until tomorrow."

"Do you believe him?" Quentin asked.

Irene glanced caustically to the uniformed guards. "Two of King
Willie's finest. Nell and I left them in our dust the first time we
fled Bohemia. There are three more secret agents decorating the
station, possibly the King's, possibly belonging to other interests.
We are encouraged to depart, but not to depart for Transylvania."

Quentin nodded. "You travel with one carpetbag each?"

"Yes, but mine is very heavy." Irene smiled wickedly.

"We will want a warm-blood then. Can you be prepared to leave, in men's dress, in two hours?"

I glanced at Irene. This sounded exciting.

"Of course," she said.

"It will be rough and arduous."

"As long as it is effective transportation to Transylvania, I have no complaints, dear Quentin."

He smiled. "We will see what you think afterward."

I gulped after he had left. "Do you think that he has something impetuous in mind?"

"I am counting on it, Pink. It is high time we became impetuous."

We took our time wending our way back to the hotel. There was much stopping to munch pastries and poppy-seed buns. I could barely pretend to swallow a poppy seed, I was that excited.

By the time we ambled into our hotel, an hour and a half had gone by.

We reached our room and then the clothes and carpetbags flew. Irene stuffed Nell's portfolio into my bag, as her cosmetic case was essential to her packing.

Booted, trousered, capped, and mufflered, we slipped down the hotel's rear service stairs to the back alley.

Quentin was waiting in peasant dress with a pair of huge horses not accoutered in the fluttering fringes of Magyar harnesses.

I had never ridden in a Wild West Show but suspected I was about to now. Quentin leaned down to yank me up and there I was astride an embroidered saddle atop two thousand pounds of mincing, nervous horseflesh.

My heart was pounding and my trousered legs were cursing the day they had been born. Sidesaddle had never looked so sensible.

But Irene had been handed up atop an even bigger, muscular mount, and her carpetbag hooked over the elaborate saddle horn.

I felt like a rough rider in Buffalo Bill's Wild West Show. The horses' shod hooves clattered on the cobblestones as we trod the back ways of Prague, unnoticed by carriages and more conventional conveyances.

Amazingly soon we were pounding along the dirt byways leaving the city. Our bone-jarring trot escalated into a rolling lope that threatened to hurl me, at least, headfirst over pommel and horse ears into the road.

"Hold on tight," Irene urged. "Don't try to be graceful about it. Just hold on."

The best advice that I have ever heard, and a motto I resolved to adopt for my future adventures, should I live to have any.

41.

A Guest

Then worst than all last Friday...you came to me...&
spoke & looked in such a manner which has upset me....
My only hope...is that you with the power you have now
will not when before God someday be accused of not
raising & keeping up those that have fallen....I remain
Yours Truly

—JAMES KELLY, LETTER TO A BROADMOOR ASYLUM OFFICIAL, 1884

That evening as the swallows began their sunset swoops around the castle turrets, the answering wail of Gypsy violins echoed them from the courtyard.

Godfrey joined me at my window to share the spectacle. Despite our deep forebodings about everything surrounding this castle and the creatures in it, nature and music had blended to raise the curtain on a splendid sunset accompanied by the heartfelt cries of the unseen violinists.

We were so taken by the sights and sounds that we apparently did not hear the latch being withdrawn from my door, nor the knock that must have followed it.

Godfrey sensed a presence and turned, ready to attack or defend.

"*C'est Mignon*," came a timid voice, as if the French girl had detected our nerves teetering on the very brink of erratic action.

I also had turned by then, so she curtsied by rote. "Madame expect you for dinner."

"We had our dinner last night," Godfrey said.

Mignon shrugged. "It is an occasion sudden. A visitor from the village."

Of course the phrase set both of us trembling unseen like tuning forks. *Visitor. Village. Unexpected.* Had any of our dear ones . . . dear one, that is . . . fallen into Tatyana's hands? Or was this some village elder who required soothing? Either way, were we to be brought down for further torture, or would we learn some crumb of information that would serve our ultimate purpose of escape?

Godfrey had pulled his watch from his vest pocket to consult the time. We had resumed our daily garb: Godfrey in his traveling tweeds, I in my braids and borrowed Gypsy costume.

"Full dress not *nécessaire*," Mignon said hastily, curtseying again as if the gesture was a nervous tic, and perhaps it was when Tatyana was one's mistress.

We heard an indoor set of violins wailing from below like banshees.

The castle vibrated with sound and a certain nervous tremor that the shrieking birds outside the windows did little to calm.

It was as if the mountain were coming alive tonight.

"Eh . . . *trente minutes*?" Mignon suggested.

Godfrey nodded. "Half an hour."

We watched the dainty little maid curtsy one last time and mince from the room . . . and once she was in the hall, we heard her dainty hands lift the imprisoning bar back into place.

Such a bizarre blend of the civilized and the savage were Tatyana and those she surrounded herself with!

"Expect to be tormented, Nell," Godfrey said, his mouth a taut line. "Our hostess plays with those in her power as a cat taunts mice. But she knows we cannot risk being ignorant of any occasion in the castle, especially an outside visitor who might somehow aid us."

I went to the window again. In this little time the vibrant color of sunset had faded into gray and black. The birds still wheeled, too high for their screams to be heard, as we also were.

"Perhaps some Gypsy could be bribed."

"They took my money."

"But I have my chatelaine. Perhaps a silver trinket from it could be wrapped in a message to the village." I thought for a moment, then hesitated.

"Yes, Nell?"

"The man who brought our food the other day winked at me. Perhaps if I saw him again—?"

"Winked at you? You said nothing before about this."

"That is not the sort of thing one reports as an accomplishment. It was a feeble idea."

"No, it was not." Godfrey's sudden energy made me realize how demoralizing inactivity was for us both. Excitement flared in me like a fresh-struck lucifer. We were doing something, and it was my idea!

"The message should be in Latin," Godfrey decided, "and addressed to the local priest. An errand to a holy man is always taken more seriously, and he is likely one of the few village residents who can read. Also, Catholicism remains the peasant religion in these parts, as in Bohemia. I will compose a few urgent lines. You will transcribe them onto a page from your notebook and, once downstairs, will attempt to locate the local Lothario and take him aside. Show him the silver piece first. Then make the sign of the cross and say the word 'father' in Latin. And German, I think."

"Oh dear, Godfrey! That is a lot for me to master on such short notice. I don't know how to make the sign of the cross, and what is the word for 'father' in Latin and German, and what if I do not see that particular Gypsy? Besides, they all look alike . . . filthy. And I would be required to . . . flirt, I suppose, with the creature."

"The Latin is *Pater*, the German *Vader*. And surely you have seen the sign of the cross despite your Anglican background."

"*Pader, Vater*. No! *Pater. Vader*. Well, yes, I have seen it, but I have always looked away. Religious belief should be a matter of inner conviction, not vulgar public display."

"I am afraid, Nell," Godfrey said a trifle impatiently, "that vulgar public display is exactly what this scheme of yours requires. A sign of the cross is exactly that: top, bottom, and sides. Touch your middle right finger to your center forehead, breastbone, and left and right shoulder."

I frantically mimed his directions, feeling like I was striking myself.

"Do not hit yourself so hard. And murmur the word 'father' as you do it, so the man realizes you mean the priest."

Now I was truly terrified. How was I to mutter foreign words and make alien gestures at the same time? But as I went through the ridiculous motions, I got another idea.

"Before I do the cross and the fathers, I could tent my fingers like a church steeple, or for prayer. And then go into the other rigamarole."

"Excellent addition."

"But would a Gypsy understand these church symbols? They are pagans, are they not?"

"Whatever they are, they travel through many Roman Catholic countries. Be assured that they have not looked away from the common religious expressions of the street."

"It is true, I saw many old women in Prague performing these gestures. I only wish I had watched, as Irene always does. She misses nothing."

"She is an actress. Her profession demands attention to small gestures. But you shall do splendidly."

I went through my pantomime again, gaining confidence.

"But remember," Godfrey said, "your first acting assignment is to attract the attention of the winking gentleman."

"Without attracting anyone else's attention," I added. "Spywork is most strenuous. I wonder how——?"

"How?"

"How anyone ever survives it. What if Tatyana sees me with the Gypsy? She is always watching."

"She will be amused that you are behaving so atypically. She loves to force people into acting against their better impulses."

"Oh. That is right, Godfrey. There is really nobody here to shock with my behavior, so there is no reason I should not behave shockingly for a higher purpose. I begin to understand why fallen women keep falling."

"Exactly. I only hope you have the opportunity to see the same man again. I am afraid the sole person in the castle I would have a prayer of gaining anything from by flirting is Tatyana herself . . . and the price of that compromise is too stiff to pay."

"Agreed, Godfrey! Better me than you!"

We spent the next twenty minutes preparing our missive. I let the many accouterments on my chatelaine pass through my fingers like old friends, wondering which one I should sacrifice.

"We will replace whatever you lose later, Nell," Godfrey said, seeing my hesitation.

"It was your gift," I pointed out, "and I am attached to every piece of it." My fingers paused on the etui, the needlecase that had held cork crumbs for the delectation of Sherlock Holmes. The tiny scissors that had dulled themselves on our heavy bed linens so that we would have a rope to escape upon. The smelling salts that had allowed Irene and me to survive the charnel-house odor of the brothel chamber where we had encountered the first women slaughtered by the Paris Ripper.

With reluctance I selected the small vial and flicked open the ring that held it alongside its sisters. It was the closest item to solid silver, beautifully chased, and I was sure no Gypsy could resist it. I certainly could not.

Godfrey had folded the note into four tiny quarters, with the word *Pater* writ large on the outside.

This was a slim hope, dependent on a fortuitous string of un-likely events, but hope is always a tendril.

I thrust the crackling bit of paper and my sterling silver talisman in my borrowed-skirt pocket. Together Godfrey and I went down-stairs again, as unlikely a couple as was ever seen on even a Gilbert and Sullivan stage.

Our previous dinner had indeed been a formal occasion. Tonight the serenading Gypsies roamed from room to room, gathering in corners to indulge in crude liquors.

The lot in the courtyard had lit a fire on the stones. Their music played counterpoint to the interior tunes, creating a sort of drunken cacophony that perfectly reflected their state.

The great library was still the dining chamber, but all pretense to elegance had been sacrificed to haste. Although the plate and china were fine, the foods upon them were exuberant heaps of peas-ant and Gypsy fare mixed with the more elegant dish.

Even Tatyana was not attired in the European mode but rather like a woman from an earlier, ruder era. Her strawberry blond mane was worn loose until gathered in two plaits at her shoulders that then trailed down to her hips. She wore the jacket of a riding habit over some long billowing brocade skirt, and such a gleaming num-ber of amber necklaces of all colors from palest yellow to gold and orange and red as dark as blackened blood that it made a sort of chest-piece like the bones Red Tomahawk wore.

Red Tomahawk! Would that the Wild West warrior were here to help us. He would be a match for Madame Tatyana and her filthy minions!

Speaking of filthy minions, I saw the glittering eyes of her body servant gazing at me from the grimy frame of his face and hair, which was even less appetizing now that he had the beginnings of a beard.

Had I not known better, his pale, hungry, wolfish eyes were the spitting image of those of James Kelly. I shuddered at his glance, remembering Kelly rushing for me even as the chloroform put me into a bottomless swoon. I felt the flutter of his pawing hands at my bodice, saw his eyes . . . his eyes like pitiless moons.

I shook myself free of the memory as I looked away from Tatyana's tame brute. My winking Gypsy man would look like fair Romeo in contrast. I braced myself to study every Gypsy face until I found his.

Godfrey, meanwhile, had been commandeered by Tatyana. In this she unknowingly played into our plans. I took a wine goblet from the table and made my sipping round of the room, pausing to nod and tap (head and foot) at the energetic violinists.

As I really examined them for the first time, I found them no less crude and grimy than Tatyana's servant, but far less sinister. Their aspects were dark: raven-dark hair and mustaches, skin more swarthy than filthy now that I looked closely upon it, but their persons were caparisoned in brightness, like my boots of many colors.

And their dark Gypsy eyes glinted with hidden laughter and tears, not wolfish and pale and ravenous, but deep and secret and satisfied. They were lost in their music. And although that music had a raucous abandoned flavor, a deep and sensitive melancholy underlay it. Although I am abysmally untalented in the music field, my association with Irene has made me understand the art and passion of it. And once I listened, I found both art and passion in the Gypsies' playing. Their eyes held the same lost, intent expression of Irene's when essaying a Schubert étude on the piano.

They paid me no attention. This was a boon under the circumstance, a kind of freedom I had not felt since waking in this accursed castle. I sensed that could we cross the many barriers as high and wide as mountains between us, they would understand my fundamental need for freedom, now that I understood it for the first time. And, for the first time I dared hope that my wild scheme to appeal to one of their number could bear some fruit.

✦   ✦   ✦

The ringing of a dinner bell called me away from my session in music appreciation.

It was not a bell, but Tatyana's oafish servant banging a dinner fork upon a chased gilt goblet.

It brought the dinner party together, though. Godfrey, who had never left her side. Myself. The Count in his same oddly old-fashioned dark garb, rather like a Spanish aristocrat of the time of Queen Elizabeth. I did not anywhere see Colonel Moran, and was vastly relieved. Tatyana would monopolize Godfrey tonight, as she had before, making an unholy trinity of her end of the table between herself, the Count, and Godfrey. And I would be left to myself at the other end, free to surreptitiously study the Gypsy servitors and musicians, hunting my would-be admirer.

"Tonight," Tatyana announced after nodding to her "Medved" to cease his banging, "we have the opportunity of a surprise guest."

Godfrey and I eyed each other, noting the special twist she had put on the word "opportunity," taunting us with the hope that a stranger on the premises might give us some chance to grasp at freedom.

"Ah, here he comes, after performing a few ablutions in his chamber."

She glanced to the hall, from which came the sharp advance of boots. A man, then. Not Irene! Unless she was masquerading as a man. No, not even Irene, not here and now, would be so bold . . .

"I believe," Tatyana said almost coyly, a mood that did not sit well upon her long, wiry form, "that our English friends will be most pleased to meet a countryman."

Definitely a man. My heart stopped.

Quentin in some wild disguise?!

42.

A Mystery Man Indeed

❧

I bid you welcome, Mr. Harker, to my house. Come in;
the night air is chill, and you must need to eat and rest.
—THE COUNT, BRAM STOKER'S *DRACULA*

He came striding into the massive chamber, as confident as any British empire-builder. A pity he was neither actually British nor an empire-builder.

I nearly stood at my place, but forced myself to push all my emotions—amazement, disbelief, fear—deep behind the lattice of my Gypsy corselet and my thumping heart.

His confident advance stopped precipitously midway across the vast chamber. At that point, he turned his back on the dinner table and began staring up at the three stories of bookshelves, turning slowly to take them all in. I suspect that he was also gathering his wits at being confronted so unexpectedly with two acquaintances from London, and, more latterly, Paris.

"A magnificent library, Madame," he said, turning finally all the way around to pay Tatyana the necessary tribute of gazing solely at her. "Although the castle is in disrepair, I have not seen so splendid an assemblage of books since England."

"Indeed. Quite a compliment from an Englishman. We already

have two English guests, as you see." Tatyana waved a bejeweled hand, directing his attention to us and watching carefully.

"What a happy meeting," he announced back, bowing to Godfrey and myself. "A pair of doughty explorers like myself, I vouchsafe, only it is not Darkest Africa that draws our conjoined curiosity but mysterious Transylvania, eh? Mister and Missus, I presume? I seldom meet a lady in out-of-the-way places, save that she is the adventuresome wife of a man with a wandering instep. Alas, my own wife is a homebody. I envy you your stouthearted companion, Sir."

Of course the possessive Tatyana writhed like the snake she was at this misapprehension. At this so very clever and theatrical and deliberate misapprehension, which was nothing less than I should expect of our new dinner partner and canny confederate, Mr. Bram Stoker of London and most recently of Paris, France.

I giggled like a schoolgirl. It wasn't hard to feign. I was so happy to see his broad form and face and to know that he understood enough of our situation to immediately play the part of an utter stranger.

"Oh, my goodness, sir," I tittered to Bram. "I am a spinster and Mr. Norton's secretary, but I thank you for your flattering assumption that I am one of those ever so brave lady explorers. I must apologize. My luggage was lost in a river crossing, and I have been forced to wear what can be found for me."

"Then circumstance has dealt most charmingly with you. I confess that I am a frequent traveler and relish seeing every region's native dress in all its imagination and history." He again gazed around the crumbling but grandiose room and at its odd occupants with a scholar's nearsighted delight, as if nothing could possibly be wrong that this bluff gentleman would ever observe.

"Let me introduce—" Tatyana looked to the quiet figure of the Count on her left.

"We have met," Bram forestalled her, "in the village when I first came through. It was he who suggested I might be interested in seeing this most impressive example of a twelfth-century castle."

"Well, then, if the roll has been called, you may take a seat at the opposite head of the table," Tatyana suggested. "Next to Miss Stanhope."

Bram raised his eyebrows in polite compliance and nodded at me, accepting my renaming by Tatyana as absolute fact.

In truth, it was all I could do to keep from directing a lancing look her way. How cruelly she could play with those in her power, as Godfrey said. At least Quentin was not here to suffer her barbs—and worse—in person. And she would have no reason to know Bram Stoker was a friend of Irene's . . . would she?

"Well, this a treat!" Bram went on, flourishing his napkin like a white flag of truce as he sat down. "To dine in an ancestral castle dating back to the time of the Turks with the incomparably wild music of Gypsies for accompaniment and the most beautiful woman in Transylvania—possibly the world, for I have not yet quite seen all of it—as a hostess."

Bram Stoker had not spent time buttering up Sarah Bernhardt for nothing. His bow was Elizabethan and his *bonhomie* was so natural that flattery flowed off him like honey out of beehives.

Dear Bram! How could we have possibly considered him as a candidate for the Ripper? How could I even disdain his possibly inappropriate presence in brothels? He was taking command of the situation almost as persuasively as Irene could when called upon. Just to see a familiar face, hear a reassuring voice . . . danger took three steps backward and curtseyed like Mignon.

Tatyana, however, expected curtsies to be extended to her. She nodded at the clumsy "pet" always standing behind her, and he again filled the goblets with wine.

As he came to me, his coarse shirt sleeve brushed my bare forearm. I could not resist starting as if snagged by a thornbush. The creature offered me the same vile, knowing grin along with the wine before moving on to fill Bram's glass.

"Thank you, my good man!" Bram responded, still playing the part of an Englishman so hearty-natured he is blind to all around him.

As soon as our glasses had been filled, Tatyana took command of the conversation again, although Godfrey and I knew better than to try to speak with Bram.

"So, Sir, my servants and the Gypsies tell me you have been exploring the village and environs on foot for more than a week now, Mr.—?"

"Abraham," Bram said, adroitly substituting first name for last. "Oscar Abraham. And I find walking the sublimest way to travel and see the sights. I have tramped across most of England and western Europe and am now acquainting myself with the wonders of Europe east of the Rhine."

"For what purpose?"

Bram assumed a smugly modest look. "I have had a few scribbings published. *Meditations on the Midlands*, that sort of thing. There seems to be a market for the musings of the contemplative traveler. In fact, that is an ideal description for myself . . . the Contemplative Traveler. I foresee a new monthly column in some literary magazine. I thank you again, Madame, for serving as my occasion of inspiration."

If ever there was the epitome of a heedless, pompous, self-satisfied man of imagined letters, Bram Stoker was he to the fine point of a goose quill.

What a brilliant ploy! Like all people who mean ill to others, Tatyana tended to underestimate people who imagined that reasonable behavior would answer any human strife.

Godfrey squirmed in his chair at Bram's posturing, as if to underwrite her opinion of the fool who had been invited to dinner and could probably quite safely be let go again, thus giving her prisoners a tantalizing glimpse of freedom that was never to be theirs.

I took my cue from Godfrey and visibly subsided into a downcast pout, barely touching the food, but—here was *my* brilliant improvisation of the evening!—pretending to sip frequently from the wine. If later I had an opportunity to opportune my once-seen winking Gypsy, it could be laid to my tipsy behavior. Tipsy with the Gypsy. Perfect!

"And what," Tatyana inquired, "have you learned about this quiet corner of Transylvania?"

"That it was not so quiet centuries ago! Even today the villagers hush at the mention of certain topics . . . certain names and practices."

"Don't tell me that you are also a collector of ghost stories, Mr. Abraham."

"Ah, you have caught me out. There is a fierce appetite for tales of ancient evils, from the drama of *Macbeth* to the legends of Attila the Hun to this Tepes chap who may very well have resided in this very castle at one time, is that not what you were telling me?"

Mr. Stoker deferred to the Count, who stirred in his monsignorial chair. "He had several castles. Yes, this could be one. Where he lived, or died, though, is not important. What matters is that he stopped the advance of the Turks when no one else could. Vlad Tepes, known as the Impaler."

I knew better than to ask why, but feared that I should soon be told. By then the dinner dishes had been cleared, and it was time for "tales." Given the company, I knew they would be sinister. Sinister I did not mind. Bloody was another matter.

"A great Christian prince and hero of the fifteenth century," the Count went on in his soft, accented English.

I wondered why a member of the nobility in an area of Europe dominated by Hungary and Germany for so many centuries should trouble to learn English, yet it had certainly made Godfrey's assignment easier.

"And," the Count added, "utterly merciless to his enemies. We are at table and in the presence of ladies." He looked at me, not Tatyana, I noticed. "However, I can tell that you are much interested in local lore, Mr. Abraham, which I find admirable in a mere traveler through our land."

"Such interest is part of my position as a theatrical manager. Last spring the principals of my company spent weeks in the wilds of Scotland to prepare for a new and stunning production of *Macbeth*."

"I am not familiar with the name or the play."

"Macbeth is an ambitious Scottish nobleman who kills his king for the throne, but comes to a bad end. It is a tragedy."

"Ah, we have seen much of that in Wallachia and Transylvania. In Vlad's day, too. He was known as Dracul. His brother was buried alive, which may be why he settled on a slow death for his enemies."

"The impaling," Mr. Stoker prompted. "Some tribes of American Indians can be quite cruel to captives, even use spears to pin their victims to the ground while they torment them further."

"Oh, Mr. Abraham, your American Indians have not the imagination of Vlad Dracul. He impaled his victims vertically, you see, and would then thrust the stakes upright into the ground, so an entire forest of suffering souls died over the course of hours and even days. Once he impaled thirty thousand Hungarian boyars who had countered his wishes, arranged in circles around the city. When the Turks rode up to that sight, to see what he had done to his enemies among his own people, they retreated as if from a demon."

This recital earned a silence, while all present tried to imagine how these impalings were achieved, or, in my case, tried *not* to imagine it.

"It wasn't only enemies he treated to slow death on a stake," the Count continued. "He was most intolerant of village maidens who were no longer maidens, and adulterous wives and widows who did not remain chaste. These he would divest of their female parts by the knife, then impale on red-hot stakes."

Godfrey and I exchanged a glance. His expressed deep concern for what my ears were hearing, mine sought to remind him that this fifteenth-century fiend was not so different from whoever was committing murder and mutilation in the great cities of Europe. Could even the motive be the same?

"Count," Godfrey said abruptly. "You are right that such subjects are not fit table talk with women present. I am not sure they are fit with men present."

"Hear, hear," said Mr. Stoker. "Such subjects are best read of in books, rather than told among mixed company."

Tatyana stirred on her chair like an awakening lizard. "The English are so . . . what is the word? Tender? Easily appalled, perhaps."

None of us bothered to defend our nicety from the likes of her.

Tatyana's "bear" lumbered around with more wine, spilling much on the once-pristine cloth Tatyana had apparently brought with her.

As I bent to sop up the stains after he had passed, I managed to lower my voice like Irene's best onstage aside and address Mr. Stoker. "Occupy our hostess. I have an assignment she should not notice."

Bram immediately took his overflowing goblet and stumbled a bit as he pushed back his chair. *Oh, what oafs and liars we English be!*

He paced to the table's other end and proceeded to chat privately with the Count about even more of the neighborhood legends, none of them very nice from what I heard of them.

While I wondered what Godfrey could find to say to Tatyana, I noticed that the musicians from the hall had migrated one by one into the library. They had settled by the fireplace and proceeded to saw away at their instruments with such exuberance that they did us the service of making talk impossible except in very close quarters.

This was an opportunity to put my plan into play.

I stood up at the table, clasping my goblet against my chest. I strolled toward the feverishly playing Gypsies, surrounded by their bottles of wine.

I counted eight of various ages and sizes, ranging from slight to stout, from beardless youth to old men with their hair and mustaches streaked with swaths of coarse white hair as if Jack Frost had been at work while they slept.

Their skins were as brown as chestnuts and as shiny, for their vigorous motions so near the fire burnished their features with perspiration. Their garb was as bright as they were dark, with red, orange, and purple sashes prominent. The odor of leather, sweat, and strong spirits reminded me a bit of a stable, only there the alcohol is used—usually—to tend to muscle strains on the animals.

Ordinarily I would reel away from such powerful scents in the street, but here I nodded my head to what tune I could detect in the music and quaffed my wine.

I was the only attentive audience they had, and soon their black-berry glances passed over me. Instead of looking instantly away at such rude surveillance, I smiled and nodded even more vacuously to the music.

Now that I confronted a group of Gypsy men, I realized with dismay that I would never be able to identify the fellow who had brought our meal one day and winked at me. I simply had not seen him long enough to mark any individual traits.

My hand stole to my skirt pocket where the precious note and my vial of smelling salts kept company. Apparently they would stay right there.

I sighed, and forgot to pretend to sip my wine, but actually did so, backing away from the musicians.

As I did so, one winked at me!

I stopped where I stood, wondering what to do next.

A wink would be quite inappropriate, so I . . . smiled at the winker.

He grinned back and dug his chin harder into the rest on his violin, as if urged to greater efforts by my presence.

I smiled more. He was a bearded youth, I saw, with a thick shock of jet-black hair and elbows and knees that stuck out at awkward angles. Oh . . . my charges had been younger, but it was easy to see something redeemable in this raw youth, and a kind of touching puppylike friendliness in his winks.

At that moment he half-rose from the crate he was seated upon and began a soaring, aching solo that all the other violins softened and gave way to.

He was playing it for me!

Well. Apparently flirting is much easier to accomplish than I had realized. Of course I half looked like a Gypsy girl, and my short skirts and braided hair probably made me look far younger than I was.

My heart soared, partly in tribute to his soulful playing, mostly because I thought I could at least handle this clumsy young swain, whereas trying to flirt with one of the older, hardened men would have been . . . frightening.

He finished with a flourish of his bow and a shy bow of his head.

The others resumed their previous play, but my target stepped forward toward me.

I managed to clap my hands despite the wine goblet in one.

He bowed again, and smiled, his head at a bashful angle.

"Wonderful!" I said, smiling, expecting him to read my emotions rather than understand my word.

He waggled his head modestly from side to side and sat the bow and violin down on his former seat.

I put a hand to my ear. "It's so hard to hear. Can we—?" I nodded to an inglenook beside the fireplace.

Smiling, nodding like an idiot, as I was, we edged our way to the bench.

There I set my goblet down on a broad wooden arm and took a deep breath. I made sure my back was to the room and produced the silver trinket from my pocket and thrust it toward him.

His eyes gleamed as they fell upon silver, but he frowned in confusion.

I gestured: *for you.* I had never realized how much of the stage art I had acquired from my association with Irene.

He shook his head, but his eyes never left the bright gleam in my hand. Among Gypsies, acquiring things of value from other people meant wealth and worth. He pointed to his violin with a question. *For his playing?*

I nodded. "Can you speak any English?"

He shook his head, then frowned even more deeply. His fingers lifted to his lips and twisted. And then he shrugged hopelessly.

I already felt we were entered into a conspiracy, but stared at him, unable to guess his meaning.

"*Français?*" I tried. We had seen Gypsies in France, after all. Perhaps that same group had traveled here.

He shrugged and shook his gleaming black hair so like a rook's and again made the twisted gesture at his lips.

And then I understood. He locked them with a key.

"You are mute?" I pressed my fingers over my mouth.

He nodded, then lifted the silver piece and placed a hand over his heart. *Thank you.*

I smiled, but lifted a hand to bid him wait. Then I produced my small-folded paper and showed him the word printed on its surface. I went through my churchly pantomime: steepled fingers, sign of the cross (only I touched right and left shoulder in succession, which I knew was backwards the moment I did it), mouthed the words "*Pater*" and "*Vader*" and "Father" for good measure. Then I added my walking fingers at a downward angle to indicate the village below the castle.

During this entire performance my violinist nodded and grinned. When he took the paper, I put a forefinger to my lips and hissed "*Shhhhh.*"

I was reassured to see him immediately look over my shoulder and tuck the missive into the scarlet sash at his waist. Clever boy! The silver item went into the same secret storage place.

He gave me one last bow, and a wink, then moved to rejoin his band.

I turned to pick up my goblet from the settle arm.

No one seemed to be looking my way at all.

Strolling slowly around the bookshelves that edged the room, I made my wine-sipping way back to the central table. If I had seen myself upon a stage, I would not have recognized a particle of my behavior or my appearance.

And yet, I thought I deserved an inaudible round of applause. I had accomplished my aim without demeaning myself with some drunken Gypsy. In the morning I was sure my Gypsy serenader would make his way to the local church to present the priest with the paper, feeling well paid by the silver trinket in his sash.

If someone official from the village came to the castle to inquire after Godfrey and I, surely not even Tatyana could afford to ignore it. She could not imprison an entire village! And who could contain Gypsies, even with free-flowing chests of silver?

The thought of her imprisoning more people made me regard Bram with an anxious eye. What would she do about him? Surely she had no suspicions that we were known to each other. Still, he had happened upon her private preserve. I hoped he would leave with the Gypsy violinists tonight.

"Ah, Miss Stanhope," he said as I approached. "I had hoped to bid you good night before I leave."

"It was a pleasure to have met you," I said with more fervor than I allowed to show.

"Oh, but Mr. Abraham," Tatyana interrupted us. "I cannot allow you to walk back down to the village alone in the dark. Not after all the tales of wolves and vampires you have told."

"Tales, dear lady. I do not believe such legends."

"Still, you have too effectively chilled my blood tonight. I will provide you with a bedchamber. The upper regions of the castle are not in the best repair, but they should suffice for a man who so loves walking through the out-of-doors. Nonsense! I will not take no for an answer. My servant will conduct you and Mr. Norton and Miss, ah, Stanhope to your rooms."

She nodded at the brute, who seized a candelabra off the dinner table. I doubt he spoke much English, but he seemed to understand the gist of it. I would our escort was my gentle and mute Gypsy youth, but it was better that he packed up violin and bow and left the castle with my missive.

"I have no kit with me," Bram objected to his sudden residence here.

"Mr. Norton is fully accoutered," Tatyana said with a slow, mocking glance at Godfrey. "He will lend you anything you need in the morning. It hardly would be a razor, would it? After all those stories, you would not want to shed a drop of blood in this castle. Who knows what creatures it would call . . . the undead? The wolves? Miss Stanhope with a bandage at the ready? Miss Stanhope strikes me as a person who will always have something useful at the ready."

Another odious, knowing smile, this time in my direction.

Did she know?

No, I would not lose faith in my evening's effort. News of our imprisonment would soon reach the village and from there, one could only imagine who else. I knew that Irene and our friends would not be idle in our absence. Was not Bram Stoker's presence here more than mere coincidence? Somehow on our way upstairs we must find out. At least the Oaf spoke little English.

Medved preceded us, the candelabra casting his shadow back on us, so I had to be mindful of the steps I couldn't see. Godfrey and Bram each took my elbow once the stairs had turned us out of sight from below.

"The note?" Godfrey asked, his brow furrowed.

I nodded. "A most winning young Gypsy. I'm sure he'll follow through."

Bram frowned at us as Godfrey explained in words as short as he could manage.

Our guide plodded up the stairs ahead of us, apparently oblivious to everything but his task, like some great ox.

Bram's frown became deeper. "The note was directed to the village priest?"

"Yes. He would read Godfrey's Latin and has the authority to organize a rescue party."

Bram stopped for a moment. "But . . . that other man at the table, in unrelieved black. I met him the first time I came to the village. He *is* the village priest."

43.

Before the Dawn

The next night he tested me again, becoming excited and obligating me to acknowledge his excitement. I had to conclude that I must be very dirty, impure and given over to passion since he clearly felt it necessary to subject me to perpetual testing.

—MADAME X

No blow is harsher than that which removes all hope.

The supposed Count was the village priest?

Was everything in this accursed castle and its neighboring village a mockery and mummery?

Godfrey and I exchanged a horrified glance. My feet forgot to keep moving. I almost would have tumbled backward in numb shock had not my escorts had me firmly by the beribboned elbows.

And my charming Gypsy lad? He must have known that the village priest was in the room even as he scraped away at his miserable violin and bowed and winked and pressed his palm to his heart and took my sterling silver smelling salts and Godfrey's laboriously composed note.

My first flirtation for a clandestine purpose had been an utter disaster. Mute, indeed! If I ever encountered that treacherous fiddler again, I would break his violin over his lying head until he screamed to heaven for mercy.

Now the stone stairs to the castle's upper reaches seemed insupportably high and long. Every riser brought us closer to confinement again, with no hope of release.

Tatyana's servant stopped beside a door and nodded at Bram Stoker.

Our friend never for a moment abandoned his pretense of innocent stranger. He bowed and kissed my hand in farewell, and shook Godfrey's.

"Most pleasant to meet fellow travelers in these mysterious regions. Most pleasant," he said, turning to face the black hole that was his chamber.

Without a by-your-leave, he hoisted a lit candle from Medved's many-branched holder and vanished inside.

Medved lifted the exterior latch and let it bang into position, locking Bram in. He made no secret of the act.

He moved along the dark corridor, stopping at the next door, which Godfrey recognized for his cell. Godfrey took my hand and squeezed it. "Be of good cheer, Nell. It is always darkest. . . ."

He forbore to finish the truism, but paused to strike a lucifer and light his last bit of cigar before vanishing into his assigned darkness, where I knew a few candles awaited lighting.

Medved threw the latch shut and immediately went shuffling down the stones to my chamber door. At least I had the comfort of knowing an interior door linked Godfrey's room and mine. He had mentioned nothing of another inner door. Bram Stoker was locked in alone, with no chance of exchanging information with either of us.

While I was fretting over the disposition of our only ally in this place, I had neglected to note that my guide had paused to lean against the cold stone wall and pull something from the pocket of his full pantaloons.

It was a crude pottery bottle from which the lower orders who staffed the castle drank. I watched in disgust while he took a long swallow of its contents, then wiped his mouth on a shirt sleeve that obviously had played napkin for some time.

His eyes slit in sleepy content before he pushed himself off the wall and moved to my door.

I rushed through it into the welcome privacy of my own dark chamber, turning to shut the door behind me. It did not budge.

Neither had my guide, who stood like a wind-shaken tree on the threshold, swaying until the flames of his upheld candelabra swept wildly left and right.

"Good night," I said, pushing on the door with all my might.

He pushed back without visible effort. The door banged back against the wall as I retreated before him.

"You must leave," I said. "Tatyana—"

Invoking his mistress's name had no effect. He set the candelabra down on the nearest horizontal surface, the dressing table in the corner, and went lurching into the center of the room, swigging on the bottle as he came, my recurring nightmare.

During my entire stay in Castle Tatyana, I had feared my fate: an unwilling sacrifice in a bloody ritual similar to the one Irene, Pink, the Rothschild agents, Buffalo Bill Cody, Red Tomahawk and I had interrupted in Paris. I had not feared for my virtue, for it struck me that a virginal sacrifice might rank higher than otherwise among these demented devil worshipers. But either Medved was not a member of the cult, or my assumption was wrong. From the drunken, clearly lecherous look upon his face it appeared that I might very well face a fate worse than death before facing the death that was supposed to be a better end. Although, having witnessed the bloody tortures the cult inflicted on its own, I was no longer so sure that there was any fate worse than death at its crazed hands.

Medved's relentless advance was herding me toward the huge bed. Now I felt the racing anguish of another fear. Beneath that tapestry bedcover lay a lumpy coil of braided linens, our escape rope. Not only did I risk rape, but in the course of it the revelation of our literal last thread of hope that we might escape this place by our own efforts.

This realization made me end my retreat. "Stop!"

He did, but his smirk told me that he only paused because he took my standing my ground for capitulation. What kind of women was he used to? Gypsies, no doubt, who are wed at an unconscionably early age and who are also offered to non-Gypsy men for a price. The ill-begotten Gypsy servant threw his head back to drink again, liquid running through the bristles of his infant beard, down his grimy throat, and into his shirt collar.

A moment later his hand seized the back of my head and the hateful pottery jug butted my teeth. He used my tightly bound braids to jerk my head back and pour the horrible burning liquid down my throat. I could not believe the man I had repulsed before would assault me again!

I choked and coughed, feeling my very lungs corrode from such a bolt of acid. An icy dampness ran over my chin onto my chest while my eyes watered until even my tormenter became a blurred image much more merciful to behold than his real self.

I could tell the monster was smiling! He began prating at me in some thick-tongued language I couldn't name. I could tell that his voice was as soft and persuasive as that language could allow and that terrified me all the more. It implied that he thought I should, or would, cooperate in his disgusting notions, that I liked the fiery spirits spilling down my throat and blouse front, that I liked his presence in my room. Or soon would come to.

His voice had grown singsong, and his right forefinger waggled back and forth before me like an admonishing pendulum, moving with the rise and fall of his voice.

The spirits must have been stronger stuff than I had ever imbibed before because I was growing dizzy and seemed to see two fingers waving before my eyes.

And . . . his eyes blurred as did his form, so that for a moment he did not look like himself but like James Kelly rushing for me in the panorama building just before the inhaled drug took my senses. Would I ever forget those mad, glassy, pale blue eyes? Not with them before me again! Perhaps my weakened perceptions had laid over this creature called Medved a deluded image of James Kelly. His eyes never blinked. I was reminded of the bottomless eyes in the little green snake I kept at home, but those were as dark and bright as a jet button. These eyes were windows, pale stained glass windows into a very stained soul. I understood that this man expected to have his way with me; he expected that I would bend to his will in this, but if I did not, it would not matter to him.

I felt something hard at my back, like a wall. It took my befogged mind a moment to realize I had been backed up against the massive bedpost.

No, the hidden rope!

He pushed the container to my face again, and I received another drowning in spirits. My spitting and coughing only earned a laugh as if he watched a kitten whose face he had pushed into a milk dish. What a brute!

I used my Gypsy sleeve to scrub my face clean of the unclean liquid, but he captured my wrist. Something tugged more than fear at my midsection. . . . He crooned now in that rough language of his as one would soothe a wild animal, pushing my arm behind me . . . behind the thick trunk of the bedpost.

Though I could no more take my eyes off his loathsome lulling gaze than a robin could break the hypnotic swaying gaze of a cobra, I understood the tugging at my middle. He was undoing the laces of my corselet, one-handed, a man used to undoing women's dress, whether drunk or sober. He would soon have a rope of his own to tie my hands behind the bedpost, and then he would not need even his eerie serpent's eyes to control me.

I remembered what Irene had said of the women of Whitechapel, earning their bed and beer money in ugly moments against a wall, standing up. They agreed to that tawdry exchange and were usually drunk enough to hardly know it.

I was suddenly no different than they . . . drenched in spirits, compelled to do some stranger's will.

Another observation from Irene surfaced: that she had mesmerized Bertie into thinking he'd had his way with her so she would never have to repel his advances again. *If only I had her gift to mesmerize this man who seemed able to mesmerize me!*

And I remembered what fought cobras, Quentin's tough little mongoose, a creature of thick fur and wiry, muscular swiftness.

Medved roared as my trio of memories helped me break his poisonous gaze and I screamed, as my Gypsy boot kicked out and up, unhampered by heavy, long draped skirts, powered by all the panic that was in me.

I heard the connecting door bang open against the wall.

"Nell!" Godfrey cried, reaching inside his coat jacket for the hidden hatpin as he ran toward me.

But even a makeshift weapon was irrelevant. Medved was writhing on the floor in a coiled ball like the filthy snake he was, groaning.

"What happened?" Godfrey demanded in horror.

"He forced himself in with me. He forced himself upon me. His eyes were so evil I couldn't look away. He forced his filthy liquor down my throat. He, he undid my laces and soon would have bound me."

"No," Godfrey interrupted my breathless report, still gazing at the man on the floor, "I can see what happened to you. What did you do to him?"

"I finally broke his satanic spell and screamed."

"And that plunged him writhing to the floor? I admit it was an alarming scream, but—"

"And I lashed out with my foot. I kicked him."

Godfrey's face cleared. "Ah. Do you know where?"

"Wherever my foot would go high enough and hard enough. I don't know, Godfrey! What does it matter?"

"You are right, Nell." Godfrey gazed upon the recumbent form with a grimace of knowing satisfaction. "All that matters is that you were able to repel the wretch. I'll get him out of here."

At that he bent to pull the fellow up by the scruff of his shirt and one arm. He pushed him stumbling to the door and out into the hall.

Godfrey leaned against the wood, one ear pressed to it. "Perhaps he is muddled enough to leave without locking us in."

A mighty thump from beyond the door ended that hope.

I began shivering. "I was so afraid."

"I know, Nell." He came to me and stood befuddled, as if sensing that male comfort needed to keep its distance at this moment.

"And I was also afraid he would discover our hidden rope."

"That, too, was a grave risk."

"The worst thing was that the creature acted as if I would agree to his advances. He seemed to regard them as a treat or a boon. Isn't he aware what a revolting creature he is? I'm sure not even a Whitechapel unfortunate would agree to his attentions."

"He is truly a barbarian, Nell, more animal than man. That's why Tatyana keeps him in her retinue. She believes that every man is no better than he is, and every woman no better than she."

"Is that why she holds us prisoner, to make us desperate enough to betray our better natures?"

He nodded. "That is the whole idea, beneath whatever political games she is playing. The political games are a pretext, I think, for her need to show up the civilized world and its people as utter hypocrites."

"What would make such a savage woman?"

"Savage circumstances, Nell. Is there anything I can do for you?"

"No. First I must wash my face free of this foul liquor."

While I moved toward the basin and ewer, Godfrey bent to retrieve the fallen bottle.

"Odd stuff," he said after a moment. "It is clear as water yet has a faint but unusual odor."

"So Red Tomahawk said about the empty bottles we found on the Exposition site. He called it 'firewater,' I believe."

"Indeed, rightly so!" Godfrey said after a moment, sputtering.

I turned from patting my face and shoulders dry. "Godfrey! You didn't drink from that foul bottle?"

"I am not sure whether I drank from it or swallowed fire like a circus performer. This is an extremely potent and raw liquor, Nell."

"I know! I am still reeling on my feet from the small amount that Medved creature was able to pour into me. Please put that awful bottle down, or, better yet, throw it out the window! I wish no reminder of my recent ordeal."

But Godfrey did not heed me, instead standing in the middle of the room, staring at the homely object in his hand. "It must be home-made, brewed secretly in a primitive area where commercially distilled liquors wouldn't reach, or would be too princely to pay for."

"What else would you expect from a creature like Medved? I can't imagine why even Tatyana puts up with him. Please destroy that devil's brew, Godfrey. Hasn't it caused us enough grief to-night?"

He weighed it in his hand, as if considering throwing it away, then shook his head firmly. "We can't destroy it, Nell. Don't you realize that this is the one thing, the one object that connects you and I and where we are now to where you were? To the Paris murders that seem the continuation of the London murders of last autumn?"

I stared at it with mounting horror, not at the bottle itself and he who had abused me with it, but at my own incomprehensibility.

How had I allowed my natural repulsion for spiritous liquors to blind me to the similarity between this pottery container here and the remnants of similar bottles in the subterranean secret places of Paris?

I rushed to Godfrey, seized the bottle, and carried it to the candelabra. I supposed, belatedly, that Medved had been forced to stumble back downstairs in the utter dark. Perhaps he might have broken his neck, but sots always seem to fall without consequence.

I pushed my farsighted eyes to the very rim. With a shiver of horror I found a bit of pale wax clinging to the edge, wax that was the very twin to the tiny crumbs Sherlock Holmes had been collecting in the cellars and catacombs of Paris.

44.

Dangerous Explorations

✧

*For all these, and a great many more thrilling details, we
must refer our readers to the pages of Mr. Stoker's clever
but cadaverous romance.*

—REVIEW OF *DRACULA* IN *THE SPECTATOR*, 1897

I leaned as far out of Godfrey's window as I dared. A length
of my woven rope stretched along the castle wall, horizontal
to the ground.

At the other end of it was Godfrey. Or so I hoped! The
dark night was lit only by a full moon that played hide-
and-seek with an ever-changing curtain of cloud. Only the occasional tremor of the rope reassured me that Godfrey was still inching
his way along the wall to the window of Bram Stoker's adjoining
bedchamber.

Now . . . if only Bram had not so thoroughly lived up to his
role of unflappable Englishman that he had fallen asleep!

After our realization that the drinking vessels used in Paris were
also common to the inhabitants of the castle, or some of them,
Godfrey and I had resolved that to stay was folly. Especially now
that Bram was virtually a prisoner as well. If we could rouse Bram
and get him to Godfrey's room, we would be three.

So I waited on this end of the rope, hoping that soon both men would be making their way back to safety before we took an even greater risk in a bid for freedom.

What an eerie night it was! In the courtyard not visible from this part of the castle I could hear the distant wail of Gypsy violins. From the surrounding mountains came the piercing howls of wolves, sometimes singly, sometimes in chorus as they appeared to harmonize with the oddly human wailings of the Gypsy violins.

I thought of my treacherous lad among them and cast a Gypsy curse his way.

There must have been a mighty conflagration in the courtyard, a fire like that the Gypsies had careened around on *l'Exposition universelle* grounds only three weeks before. I could hear the flames beating like great bird wings and glimpsed a glow like dawn at the far bottom wall of the castle visible to me.

Apparently the smoke rose so high it disturbed the vermin in the turrets high above us, for there would come every so often a high keening chitter like a banshee, and I would look up to see a dark cloud burst forth against the lighter clouds of night and break into waves as hundreds of bats deserted their high perches to fan across the night sky.

This disturbance among the animals that haunt the dark made me even more uneasy. Some event of great moment seemed to be building to a climax all around us, as in a play. I, for one, had no intention of staying for the curtain call.

The rope jerked and then trembled and jerked again.

I watched its pale length until a pair of black-gloved hands came edging along it like crows. Then the full dark figure followed. Godfrey, at least, was making his perilous way back. Was Bram with him, or had he been unable to face this circus high-wire stunt in the dark? I could not blame the man, if so. That was a very high price to pay for being the friend of my friend, Irene Adler Norton.

Then I remembered the despicable Tatyana calling me "Miss Stanhope" in that snide, mocking tone and thought that I would harness wolves and bats if I had to in order to escape her.

Godfrey's strained face was soon peering around the window frame, then he got his feet on the broad stone sill and leaped down into the room again.

"Bram?"

He jerked his head behind him and leaned out to assist our sturdy friend as he fought his way through a frame barely wide enough for him.

Bram sat for a moment on the sill, swinging his feet like a child and catching his breath. He withdrew his handkerchief and swabbed his brow.

"Was the journey too arduous for you?" I demanded anxiously. "It is a frightful distance down, and cold and dark against the castle stones, but the rope seems secure enough."

Bram leaped down to the floor and stamped his booted feet on it.

"My toes were going numb in that wind, but that's minor damage. I haven't embraced sheer rock so hard since I encountered that rough bit of cliff-climbing in the Highlands. To answer your question, Miss Huxleigh, I am an enthusiastic hiker and a happy clamberer. I'm pleased as punch to do our murderous hostess out of a prisoner this night."

He turned to Godfrey. "Why was the village priest introduced to you as a so-called Count?"

"I was supposedly sent here to deal with the Count who owned the castle and surrounding lands. It must have been a fabrication from the first. Hence the local priest, as the most educated Transylvanian at hand, was persuaded to sign and seal a property agreement I had drawn up. What puzzles me is why a legitimate priest would participate in such a charade."

"That question is only one of many that have been at high boil around the village. The Gypsies have been pouring into the region and are gathering in the castle courtyard as if it were a Wild West powwow of Indian tribes. The lady who occupies the castle has drawn many servitors from the Gypsies and many from the young folk of the village. Why this ruined castle is now bustling with so much activity is the greatest mystery of all, although the villagers like the money that flows from her coffers to theirs."

Bram Stoker finished his analysis by glancing at me in puzzlement. "Your garb at dinner was charmingly atypical, Miss Huxleigh, but your costume now quite confuses me."

I had become hardened to unconventional dress and so glanced at myself in reminder. It was indeed a "costume." I had borrowed a pair of Godfrey's trousers and suspenders and rolled up and basted the pant legs to suit my height and incidentally to reveal my gaudy Gypsy boots. I found the loose blouse and corselet too comfortable to relinquish, for Godfrey's jackets had proven far too roomy for me to wear.

"Our only way to freedom is by the rope," I said. "I will not remain behind while you and Godfrey climb down to another entrance into the castle and seek to return in order to free me. I have already been accosted twice by a madman in my own chamber and do not intend to remain here alone."

Godfrey reported the most recent, forcible ejection of Medved. After that, there was no argument nor further comment on my mode of attire.

Of course I was far more worried about my attempted feat than I would say. My hands, abraded by the task of tearing apart the bed linens, were not entirely healed. While they were useful for most daily tasks, I could not say that the strain of using them to cling to the rope would not try them beyond my ability to hold on. And I have never been the sort fond of heights. Even leaning over the window sill, solid stone two feet thick that it was, made me slightly giddy.

Confessing such weaknesses would only hamper my gentlemanly companions' own efforts to save themselves. I would simply have to go through with it. Irene would imagine herself some dashing mountaineer and embrace the courage that went with the role. I had no such training, and no such convenient capacity for imagination.

My imagination was wont to dwell on the great height, the

biting wind, the overwhelming dark, the impossible distance, the likelihood of there being something rotten in the weave of my rope that would suddenly unravel thread by thread until, with a shriek of fiber from fiber to rival the howling of a lone and starving wolf, the rope would give, and we would all plunge to our battering death upon the rocks below like so many sailors whose ship had shattered into toothpicks beneath them. . . . There, that was a sufficiently dire example of an imagination gone berserk.

Perhaps it would help if I imagined Tatyana and her henchman Medved only feet behind us on the castle wall, crawling after us like loathsome spiders or lizards. But such a vivid picture might make me hasty, and instead of being goaded to greater efforts, my grip would slacken, my feet slip, and I would go crashing to a slow, bruising, tumbling death below like a rock cast loose from some alpine peak and jostled until it dispersed into tiny bits thousands of feet below. . . .

Perhaps I should not try to use my imagination at all.

"We will link ourselves together," Godfrey was decreeing, having been studying the practicalities of our attempt while my imagination was running amok. "There will be enough give between us that we won't hamper each other's motion."

"And if one should slip?" I asked. "Myself, for instance."

"Oh, that," said Bram Stoker quickly. "You are such a light weight that we will hardly notice, and will haul you back up directly."

"And if you should slip?"

Bram hesitated not a moment in drawing a clasp knife from his pocket. "I will cut the rope."

"I have no knife," Godfrey complained.

Only a man would compete in means of noble self-destruction.

"Besides," he added. "That would only save us if you went first. I have made this climb before, so I should lead."

"There's only one sensible order," Bram said. "Miss Huxleigh must go last, because if either or both of us fall and we must cut the rope, she will still be fixed to an anchor. You must go second, as if you slip I am strong enough to draw you back up. I will be first because my greater weight makes me a liability, and I can cut myself loose if necessary. But it will not be necessary, my friends! You will be behind me and can advise me on the route. What could be simpler?"

"Breaking our way through a door and finding some stairs," I put in.

"Have you taken note of the thickness of these doors?" Godfrey asked.

I had, and our climbing expedition was by far the quieter escape . . . unless one or all of us fell and then our voices would no doubt join the howls of the wind and the wolves and the screech of the bats and the Gypsy violins.

So we queued up at the window and looped my handiwork around each of our midsections in the order decided upon while Godfrey secured the end of the rope around the stone support pier of the window as before.

Would it hold three where it had one before? Time would tell.

Bram Stoker shook hands solemnly with each of us and climbed upon the sill. I had the strangest feeling that matters of relationship or sex or size or age made no matter here. We were embarked on a common enterprise, and each must trust in some measure to the other's ability. I was the hidden and industrious spider who had woven the thread so slender and yet so strong upon which we all would hang. Bram was the experienced climber who would lead us, as fate allowed, or sacrifice himself should he as leader lose his purchase. Godfrey was the desperate but courageous amateur who had forged the trail alone and now would guide others in his successful footsteps.

The rope pulled as Bram let himself over the sill to the wall and the first foothold Godfrey had mentioned. It felt like a tug on my heartstrings. Then Godfrey was up on the sill and pulling me up beside him.

"For France and St. Denys!" he said with a swashbuckling grin.

"For England and St. George!" I retorted, too annoyed to gasp when he lowered himself out of sight. For France and St. Denys indeed! I pushed his leather gloves more tightly over my knuckles and turned to lower myself over the sill and down along the wall. It seemed a length of twenty feet before my toes touched the ledge he had mentioned.

But it was there, and quite wide enough for my footprint. I edged along, keeping my eyes on Godfrey's dark form ahead of me, barely seeing Bram's hulk in the darkness beyond.

I couldn't help thinking of three blind mice.

The wind was not strong, but it was sharp, and my eyes soon watered, an unexpected handicap.

Still, Godfrey called out the hallmarks of the route: the decorative stone that protruded, the fissure that bridged to the next ledge. We made our slow, painstaking crablike way across and down the face of the ancient stones.

The inching movement became so routine I felt like lava flowing. My feet followed Godfrey's every instruction, and I heard him guiding Bram ahead of him as well.

Tears were streaming down my face, but it mattered more what I felt than what I saw, and my hands and feet scraped along the stone as if attached to it.

Then, just as I believed I had attained a stability and a rhythm, a sudden jerk on the rope at my waist pulled me away from the wall, feet and hands, like an invisible current of wind.

I swung out as if snatched by a demon.

Then hands grasped my waist and I was lifted. I sat on a stone sill in an open window and the solidity beneath me felt like sand, and I grew so hideously dizzy that I had to cling to Godfrey while he pulled my limp form fully inside the window.

I leaned against a stone wall so like the one I had clung to for so long outside, my knees weak and my arms trembling.

Godfrey untied me like a nanny tending a babe from the nursery.

He and Bram were busy at the window frame and when I finally collected myself to ask what they were about, they explained that they had swung the rope away to dangle from our deserted chamber.

"If our absence is discovered, they'll think we climbed straight down to escape outside the castle."

"Could we have done that?"

Bram shook his head. "The rope's too short. Jumping loose would have killed us. Let them think our bodies are rotting on the rocks below," he added with the gusto of a true teller of gruesome tales. "That gives us time to explore the lower regions that Godfrey thinks might lead to an exit."

I did not mention that I had experienced my fill of lower regions in Paris.

My full sleeves had been judged the handiest carrier of candles, so I struggled to extract three of my supply from Medved's deserted candelabra from the narrow cuffs at my wrists.

Godfrey lit each one with a lucifer, and we moved through the massive chamber led by our personal fireflies of light. Our every step, no matter how soft, ground slightly on the stone floors unrelieved by carpets. Our progress sounded like the slither of some large snake.

We passed through two huge doors, both ajar so we didn't have to worry about creaking hinges, and into the dark tunnel of a hall.

All we could hear was the scrape of our footwear and the rustle of our clothing . . . and perhaps our own breathing. I had never before felt like such a scuttling, hidden insect and grew to appreciate their courage in venturing into vast buildings to find a crumb of sustenance.

"Stairs," Godfrey whispered, turning to us.

We each huddled against the nearest wall and cast our candlelight down as best we could.

Our gloved fingertips clinging to the surface that grew disturbingly slick the further we progressed, we inched downward.

Every moment I expected to take that final step that resulted in the jolt of level floor again, but down and down we went, and there was no level ground.

The silence had grown so intense that it became a kind of sound, a hollow, rushing emptiness like the passage of an invisible wind. Or . . . invisible spirits.

I thanked the season for being spring, rather than All Hallows Eve, then recalled something about another pagan festival day, Midsummer's Eve. Could that be near? All I could think of was May poles. And rats and mice. And ghosts. So in my mind rats and mice and ghosts danced around a grisly maypole crowned by an impaled severed head. I shut my eyes in the dark to banish the image.

When I opened them, I could just glimpse my fellow explorers' dark backs silhouetted by the candles they carried.

And I realized that the rush of blood and breath in my own body, that had seemed to be an internal wind I heard whipping around me, had been joined by the faint suspicion of another sound, a distant, actual sound, also of rhythmic nature.

Was it the sea? But none was near. An inland lake? The wind from outside rushing through a0tunnel, an escape tunnel?

My companions had become aware of it, too. I saw Godfrey's pale face as it turned over his shoulder, the candle casting grotesque light on the familiar features.

"Wait here, Nell. Bram and I will investigate below. One will come back and wave a candle if it's safe for you to proceed."

Irene would never have stood for being left behind like a piece of awkward luggage, midway down a staircase in the dark.

I dare not raise my voice in objection and betray our presence, and as I hesitated the men proceeded without me, making any attempt to follow in their withdrawing footsteps more dangerous by the instant, for both the light and sound of their motion had vanished as if swallowed by the gaping dark jaws of leviathan.

I huddled bitterly against the wall, clutching my candle and its feeble flame. Even as I debated that I still might stumble after them, I knew the opportunity had been lost to my hesitation. I was far too obedient to male instruction, I reflected. My parson father was the kindest man on earth, but he was a churchman and expected to be heeded. Unlike Irene and Pink, who found joyful opportunity in defying the strictures of men of power and influence, I went like a Shropshire sheep to holding pen! I had even ceded my sole weapon, the hat pin, to Godfrey and was now armed with only candle stumps that it would take minutes to release from their makeshift carrier in my sleeves.

What a ninny! So much for my brave climb down the castle wall. I was helplessly pinned against a safe interior wall now, unable to move or risk them returning and not finding me. Yet I could not say when they would return, or if. So I must stand here and know nothing, do nothing. Except worry. And wait. And not know what's really happening.

Irene, I knew, could worry. I knew that even at this moment she worried about me and Godfrey, but I had never known her to wait.

I was just about resolved to move ahead on my own when a moth of light flickered far below. I sighed my relief at having thus achieved that happy state for the meek of heart of doing exactly what I wanted to do while appearing to respect the wishes of others.

Keeping a hand to the wall on my right and my candle uplifted like Florence Nightingale's famous lamp in my left, I made my way down into the pitch dark as fast as I could.

And I was so relieved to see Godfrey and Bram—actually, Godfrey or Bram, since only one candle beckoned—returning safely from a first foray into the lower depths.

I came abreast of the candle almost ready to laugh with joy.

A bare hand seized my wrist to steady me, and the candles we each held almost collided like goblet rims in a toast.

The conjoined light revealed a horribly familiar face, the dark hair a disheveled frame to an even more disordered expression of frantic fear, the pale blue eyes staring into mine with confused recognition.

"The Master," James Kelly demanded, shaking my wrist. "Where is He? Tell me!"

I shrank against the wall, whose safety I had resented but moments before.

He looked around in the dark as if seeing other eyes that I could not.

"They did not want me here. They wanted me locked up in Paris, but I escaped them all and when I found the Master, they fled. Away from me. They left me to the dogs and wolves."

That I could well believe. Even in the flickering candlelight I could see that his clothing was as disordered as his hair and expression. He looked as if he had been clambering through wildwood for the past two weeks.

And perhaps he had been.

"The Master is the Only One," he murmured, his frantic tone becoming pleading, almost weeping. "He understands. He has walked the same way of the Cross. We know the suffering, the pain, the same happy flaw that all men do, that all women caused since Eve."

His diseased eyes fixed on me again. I remembered how he had taken a pocket knife and drilled into his wife's ear, for no reason, so that she died horribly a day later in hospital. He had been in the cavern under the Paris exposition grounds where the woman had been horribly mutilated by a madman. Had that been the Master? But Red Tomahawk's battle-axe had been flung into that devil's back even as he flaunted his gory trophy.

James Kelly held only a candle now, and the madness in his eyes, but he had seen me among the motley rescue party in the cavern and gone straight for me, as he had in his rooms when he was trapped there by Irene and Pink and I. And Sherlock Holmes.

Perhaps I reminded him of someone: his innocent and dead wife, or the poor girl whose breast had been sacrificed to some satanic ritual, or our mother Eve. . . .

"Where is He?" he pled, as if he did not recognize me.

Of course he didn't! My hair was wound in braids around my head like a peasant's. From the waist up I was dressed like a Gypsy, and we knew that the cult members had either employed or traveled with the Gypsies. The sight of my borrowed trousers might have maddened him more, but they were black and lost in the darkness. I looked, I realized, like any one of the Gypsy girls who worked around their camp outside or the castle inside.

"Is He not here to change wine into holy water and holy water into blood? He must be here! I have followed. *This is my body, in which pleasure resides. This is my blood, in which pain resides. Whoever shall drink my blood and share my sin shall obtain life everlasting.*"

He was reciting a chillingly garbled blend of Scriptures and Satanism.

I tried to twist my wrist free, but his grip tightened. He pressed me against the wall.

"You're coming to the ceremony, of course. To dance, and drink the Master's blood and feel the flames of the Spirit descend like a cloak and then comes the madness and then we renounce it all, some forever."

He clearly meant death. I recalled my unexpectedly effective kick with Medved the previous night and prepared to repeat it.

That is when he laid the knife blade against my throat.

This knife was longer than a clasp knife that could be folded into a pocket, long enough that blade and handle spanned my entire neck.

Fear was like a noose that would strangle me before he could cut me. I was entirely alone with a raving mad Jack the Ripper. No hat pin remained to strike out with, no companions bearing candles stirred anywhere in the vast empty dark to come to my rescue.

"Don't you want to wait for the ceremony?" I asked, trying to speak without moving my throat against the sharp steel brink it was poised upon like a diver on a cliff.

"Sometimes before, but usually after the ceremony," he said dreamily, the eerily vacant blue eyes becoming even vaguer. "I go and do likewise, as the Master commands. By myself. As I did with my wife. It was her fault, you know. She was on me for the drink, but the drink is the Life. The holy water is the Blood."

I didn't know how to answer such gibberish, but I didn't have to.

Out of the dark came a figure almost as dark. It caught James Kelly by the collar and pulled him away so swiftly and violently as if to fling him down into Hell itself. Instead the avenging angel smashed him into the wall beside me, and bent to strip him of something, probably the knife. Kelly's candle had gone out like a shuttered lantern.

In the flicker of my own candle, which I still held for some strange reason, I recognized the keeper of my silver smelling salts and Godfrey's note.

"You!" I burst out in accusation.

"Quickly!" returned a thrillingly, thoroughly English voice. "Step aside while I deal with this villain."

My free wrist was seized as I was pushed into the deeper dark so speedily that my tiny candle flame finally gave up the ghost and expired.

Footsteps pounded the hollow earth and stone as two men contended in the utter dark, one with the frenzied strength of the mad. I heard the huffing of wild boars. I heard boot-soles scrabbling like hooves as their owners fought for balance and dominance. It was easy to imagine two supernatural forces in contention.

I edged along the cold stone wall, for that fierce contention could propel them into me and I would be gravely hurt by that mortal struggle. And I needed to be ready to escape should the wrong man triumph. I had not been in the fearful presence of men meeting like wild stags since Colonel Moran had waylaid Quentin and me on the Hammersmith Bridge. In each case a defender sought my safety, but first he must fight for his survival in a mindless, fierce battle that made me momentarily irrelevant to either party.

I could not even witness this titanic struggle, but simply heard the rough violence of it. I should not know who had won until . . . until it was too late perhaps.

A guttural, anguished cry was followed by the thumping of a body to hard ground.

The winner panted hard in the dark silence. I could tell no man by his breathing and held my own breath.

In a moment a groping hand brushed my arm in the dark.

At that touch, I was possessed by a wild surmise. How could I have not seen! The swarthy skin, the bizarre, flowing, Gypsy garb . . . hadn't Quentin Stanhope been similarly disguised and dressed as an Arab when he had fallen unconscious at my feet in Paris more than a year ago? He was a spy . . . and more, he could go to ground in the treacherous East like a native born. Of course, the moment I had gone missing Irene would have called upon his aid. *Quentin* had been the Gypsy who had contrived to deliver food to my door. I should have known from the first, by that quite inappropriate wink from the supposed Gypsy.

How obtuse I had been! And now I knew that it was his hand that reached for me in the dark. My heart galloped as if my Gypsy boots were running off with me. I leaned against the wall, breathless, as I felt his form draw close to me.

"It *is* you!" I managed to whisper.

"Quite." A lucifer flared, and my fallen candle warmed to life and light again.

I gazed up at the dashing figure, his eyes cast down at the candle's stuttering flame.

When he had surprised me in soldier's guise on the train from Prague I had swooned, but he had caught me. I did feel oddly lightheaded now and wondered what form his greeting would take once the necessities were addressed.

"Are you all right," he was saying, "my—"

"Quentin," I breathed.

He froze for an unguarded instant as he saw my face in the candlelight.

"Good God, no! So you are indeed all right, Miss Huxleigh?"

The sentence was long enough, and the voice now strong enough that I realized my dreadful mistake in an instant.

"I am reasonably . . . well," I said stiffly.

"Good. I could use something to bind him with. You don't have anything—? No. I will have to improvise."

Sherlock Holmes in Gypsy guise lowered the candle to reveal the unconscious form of James Kelly as he bent over it.

I was so humiliated by my error that I determined to provide what he wanted.

"As a matter of fact, Mr. Holmes," I said, "I do have a bit of sturdy lacing if you will wait a moment."

I unthreaded the cord of my Gypsy corselet, which fell to the ground unnoticed and unmourned.

"Excellent," he said, testing the line's resilience. "Long enough, and strong enough, to keep Mr. Kelly out of mischief for a few hours."

He had absolutely no curiosity about where on my person I had found or stored such an item.

I watched him securely bind Kelly's arms behind him, then use the man's own belt to confine his ankles.

"How did you manage to overpower him in the dark?" I wondered.

"The dark had nothing to do with it. My advantage was Baritsu, an Oriental martial art that involves many quick and deceptive movements. Perhaps your Mr. Stanhope may know something of it."

"Perhaps. Have you any notion where he might be?"

Sherlock Holmes paused after finishing binding Kelly, then glanced up with a private smile. "In Prague, I imagine, with your friend Mrs. Norton and her shadow Miss Pink. My brother Mycroft has arranged to delay their intrusive rescue attempts."

I gasped. "Quentin is with Irene and Pink?"

"He joined them in Paris, why? You shouldn't be surprised."

I wasn't surprised, I was something entirely different. Quentin was with Irene. I expected no less. Quentin was with Pink. Quentin was with Pink while I was confined to castle and corselet and braids and lamb stew night and noon with Godfrey in Transylvania.

It was only after a few more agonized moments of supposition that I realized that Sherlock Holmes had admitted to interfering with my dearest friends' movements.

I drew myself up, sans the support of my fallen corselet. "On the one hand, Mr. Holmes, I find it presumptuous and utterly despicable that you would connive against my friends. On the other, I am glad that they have been prevented from risking themselves on our behalf."

"Where is Norton, by the way?"

"I don't know. He and Bram Stoker went ahead to explore. One or both was to return to the foot of the stairs with a candle when there was something to report."

"So you didn't go waltzing down into Kelly's clutches out of ignorance."

"I never go waltzing anywhere out of ignorance, Mr. Holmes, which you would know did you know me better. Kelly carried a candle, and it was too dark to see who he wasn't until I was too close to retreat."

"Quite," he agreed.

"And I would like my smelling salts back."

"What?"

"The sterling silver smelling salts vial that I gave the Gypsy violinist."

"Ah." He pulled something from the pocket of his ridiculous full trousers (that had seemed dashing when I assumed that Quentin wore them) and held it out. "You devised a clever if desperate plan. I imagine the barrister managed the Latin."

"My father was a parson in the Church of England," I rejoined as stiffly as ever.

"Of course. No Latin. My chemical, medical, and legal experiments have acquainted me with the language, dead as it may be. Cleverly done."

"We realized it wouldn't work when Bram Stoker told us later that the man Tatyana had introduced to us as the 'Count' was actually the village priest."

"Before we find your missing explorers, tell me who this Bram Stoker is."

"You don't know?"

"Should I? Please do me the favor, unlike Watson, of not assuming that common knowledge is *my* knowledge. I am an unabashed specialist and in a very narrow constellation of disciplines, including the telltale shapes of human hands and ears, tattoos and tobaccos, manuscripts and typescripts and other arcane matters. You may often need to explain what you consider obvious to me."

"I believe that situation works both ways."

He digested that. "True. So who is Bram Stoker? I don't have my Baker Street commonplace book to consult."

"I should think you could read the Gypsy tea leaves," I commented, but he refused to rise to the bait, and I realized I was being childish at a time when none of us could afford it.

"Bram Stoker," I went on, "is theatrical manager for Henry Irving of London, the world's greatest contemporary actor."

"I may have heard of him. Actors are not among my specialities."

"That is odd, since you often behave like one yourself. At any rate, Bram is well-known about London. We made his acquaintance years ago. In fact, I poured at one of his wife's teas, but of course it was in the pursuit of an early private inquiry of Irene's involving—" I stopped abruptly, aware that I was about to reveal her pursuit of Queen Marie Antoinette's Zone of Diamonds to the last person on earth who should know about it.

"More of Mr. Stoker and less of your friend's escapades, although I am sure that they make for sparkling conversation." Even by candlelight I could detect a very minor twinkle in his eye that made me wonder if he suspected more about diamonds than either Irene or I dreamed. I plunged ahead.

"As a theater manager Bram is man-about-town, a raconteur, a lecturer, and a world traveler. In fact, his idea of a holiday is a solitary tramp through the wild places of the world, even though he has a wife and child in London. He also writes a bit, but they are sensational stories."

"How did he happen to join the hunting party?"

"He was in Paris?"

"During the killings?"

"Yes, in fact . . . it's hardly relevant, because we all know who Jack the Ripper is, but Irene had pointed out once that Bram had also been in London during the Irving production of *Macbeth* all last year, and that if speculators were proposing respectable figures for the Ripper, who better than a theatrical manager who leaves work late each night and whose whereabouts are unaccounted for? That only goes to show how insane Ripper fever had become; even the royal family was tainted with suspicion."

Sherlock Holmes had dropped the lounging Gypsy stance he still affected like a second skin and suddenly stood straight at his six feet of height or more. He towered over me like a schoolmaster.

"Irrelevant? The very opposite may be true, Miss Huxleigh. The matter of the Ripper is not settled."

"But James Kelly . . ." I pointed to the bound figure still unconscious on the cellar floor.

". . . is a murderer, a madman, and is certainly connected to many of these woman-slayings, but he is not Jack the Ripper. Madam Irene's suspicions of Bram Stoker are not as unlikely as you think. I have studied the volume of case histories she unearthed in the Left Bank bookstalls of Paris and it is most scientific."

My mouth agape, I said nothing. Had I inched along a wall over a chasm tied to Jack the Ripper?

"As instructive as this *Psychopathia Sexualis* of Krafft-Ebing's is, however, and valid, it has little bearing on the true motivations of the one who slaughtered prostitutes in London, Prague, and Paris."

"You are deliberately trying to give me a headache, Mr. Holmes, and I will not listen further. Next you will be saying that Godfrey or Quentin could be the Ripper!"

"Indeed, a case can be made for almost any man, more's the pity. Quite a comment on the relations between the sexes, isn't it?

Which is no doubt why you and I so wisely refrain from such nonsense."

Well!

"I really require nothing further of you, other than a reunion with the missing Messieurs Norton and Stoker, and that you all stay out of my way when the time comes. I am up against the most vicious gang of my career and well out of my bailiwick. If only Watson and his trusty revolver were here!"

I could have responded in kind, "If only Irene and her trusty revolver were here," but that was the last thing on earth that I truly wanted.

45.

Trapped Like Rats

~∙∙~

A lovely weapon indeed. The trick is that you must use an air pump to prime it. After that you have twenty shots before it fizzles. For those twenty shots you have one of the most murderous weapons on the planet.

—QUENTIN STANHOPE ON THE AIR RIFLE

It was with great pleasure that I assisted Sherlock Holmes in depositing James Kelly for safekeeping in one of the large wooden boxes that littered the vast empty cellars beneath the castle.

I did not assist much, merely helped lift the man's bound legs into the box before Mr. Holmes replaced the cover.

The arrangement was satisfyingly like storing the man in a coffin as I had been when transported from Paris to this mountain keep in Transylvania. I was even pleased with my decision to appropriate Godfrey's trousers, for I never could have bent and heaved with propriety in ladies' garb.

The detective said nothing of my outré garb, nor my aid.

"That will keep the rest of the villains from stumbling over Kelly for some time," he concluded, "although I believe that they would be as unhappy to see him as you were."

"Really? Why? Is he not part of their cult?"

"Not a welcome one. Now. I suggest we retreat to the foot of the stairs and wait for the candlebearer you expected, rather than the one you were unfortunate enough to greet."

With my candle fresh-lit we retraced our steps back to that unhappy site.

By now there was a faint hum of activity throughout the cellar, as if a huge, invisible hive of bees had taken up residence. I cannot explain it, a sound both natural and unnatural and rather elemental, like the wind of the sea rushing through many small empty caverns.

This part of the castle remained, however, eerily deserted and I actually felt a pang for mad James Kelly awakening bound in the utter dark of that vampire box.

The snakelike shuffle of shoes in the dark brought Sherlock Holmes to attention at the wall he leaned upon. I had sat on a step near the bottom and leaped to my feet.

The candle flicker that approached bobbled like a miner's lamp.

Behind it came not one of my companions, but both!

"Nell," Godfrey whispered, his hand moving inside his coat jacket for what I well knew was a foot-long steel hatpin. "You have reunited with your Gypsy admirer."

"He is no admirer," I whispered vehemently, "and no Gypsy either. This is Sherlock Holmes."

"The devil you say!"

I refrained from agreeing that Sherlock Holmes was the devil indeed.

"Mr. Norton, I presume, and Mr. Bram Stoker," the devil himself said blandly. "Miss Huxleigh has had a bit of a fright and needs to be escorted to more civilized spheres upstairs."

"Nell?" Godfrey asked.

"James Kelly, the Ripper suspect, lies bound in a packing box only yards away."

"The fiend who had a knife to your throat in Paris?"

Of course Sherlock Holmes had to put himself in a good light. "He had a knife to her throat only minutes ago here, but I happened upon them in the nick of time."

"Good God, Miss Huxleigh," said Bram Stoker, for once more distressed by the nearness of ordinary mayhem rather than that shrouded in supernatural trappings.

"I'm quite all right," I tried to explain, not seeing why we should all be shuffled aside.

"We can't go farther down," Godfrey advised. "I was right about there being an exit from the cellar into the mountain, but what serves as an exit also serves as an entrance. A mob of people have been flooding into the great open room below."

"What sort of people?" Mr. Holmes demanded.

Bram Stoker answered. "People from the area. Peasants, humble folk. I must say that what first drew my attention to the castle when I visited the neighborhood were murmurs among the villagers. Their young people were coming to staff the castle in great numbers. Although they had glimpsed Madame Tatyana in her carriage and knew she was in residence, she and her associates were often gone for long periods, and still the castle swallowed village lads and lassies like the whale consumed Jonah. When the older folk came to inquire, they always found a surly encampment of Gypsies in the main courtyard preventing entrance. Only the testimony of the village priest to the great renovations the castle was undergoing quieted the villagers' unease."

Mr. Holmes snorted in an ungentlemanly fashion at the mention of this local priest. Dressed as he was, the reaction was in character at least. "When I have time I will be most interested in discovering how and when Father Lupescu came to lead this isolated little flock."

"You believe he is a fraud, a false priest?" I asked.

The face he turned to me was serious beneath its Gypsy insouciance. "No, I believe that he is something much worse." He appeared to think for a moment. (In fact, Mr. Sherlock Holmes made a great show of any act of ratiocination he troubled to undertake.

I believe this theatrical mannerism accounted for much of the awe in which his intellect was held.)

"I am here alone," he went on, "and we hardly number enough to deal with the mob assembling below and what it will all too soon become. I have resources, but they are remote, for now. I suggest we consider this a rescue mission first and a hunting party second. We must steal out of the castle from above."

"What of the Gypsies?" Bram Stoker asked. "Their numbers have grown into a small army, and it will be as hard to pass through going out of the castle as trying to come into it. And need I mention the number of enormous, fierce hounds that travel with them and treat all non-Romany like fresh bones to worry?"

"Sesostros the Mute will help gain passage," Mr. Holmes said, bowing with true Gypsy pride. "It would be best if Miss Huxleigh would feign some injury and the men assist her. But we will worry about the method when we have achieved the opportunity."

Sounds from below welled up for a moment, like the distant roar of a beast.

"They were assembling the wood for an enormous fire," Mr. Stoker said, looking backwards with a curious look of longing and fear.

"No time to be lost," Mr. Holmes declared, his very urgency of tone herding us up the stairs ahead of him before any of us could think to object. "Quickly! We must run for our lives until we reach the castle's inhabited sections, and then we must be as subtle as serpents."

I had seen enough of the violent doings under the Paris Exposition to sprint up the steps in my uninhibiting trousers, my cupped hand sheltering the candle flame.

When we reached a level passage, Godfrey leaped into the lead, for he had more thoroughly explored these regions than anyone present, even the vaunted Sherlock Holmes, who kept close behind him.

This level was also mostly empty except for broken shards of ancient furniture and the ubiquitous storage boxes. I wondered if anyone would find James Kelly. Then Godfrey and Mr. Holmes ran up another set of stairs, and Mr. Stoker cupped my elbow in his huge hand and pushed me after them until I was panting hard enough to endanger my precious candle flame.

The next level was close enough to the occupied portions of the castle that some dim beams of light penetrated its darkness, likely from unshuttered windows on the next level.

"Less haste and more quiet," Mr. Holmes advised in a whisper.

The two men bracketed me like an honor guard as the Gypsy detective struck out a few paces ahead of us, our advance guard.

If only Quentin had been here! He would have been much more useful. Once we reached the level upon which the library was located, Mr. Holmes slowed his pace to a stroll.

From above came the occasional thump or bang of persons moving about. We were now trapped between two busily occupied parts of the castle, both offering exits of one sort or another.

"It's a pity we loosened the rope from the library window," I whispered to Godfrey.

"What rope?" asked Mr. Holmes, who seemed to possess the keen ears of a Shropshire rabbit.

"Nell fashioned an escape rope from the bed linens in our chamber, which we used to climb from our window down to the library chamber, there."

Sesostros frowned darkly at my braided hair. "I had no idea that Miss Huxleigh's plaiting talents could be applied to more useful tasks. What do you mean that you loosened it?"

"We made our escape on an angle from the higher window to the lower ones," Godfrey explained. "Rather than betray our escape route should our absence be discovered, we let the rope dangle straight down. We can only reach it from Nell's chamber, and then it will only lead us back inside the castle, as it's too short to reach anywhere near the ground."

"I see," said Mr. Holmes, looking as if he wished he didn't. "I suppose it might do as a desperate measure, but our best choice is to try to walk out unchallenged. If we are spotted or stopped, let me deal with it, or Sesostros the Mute, rather."

With our duplicitous guide in the lead, we spiraled up a narrow staircase that led us to a place of noise and strong smells, the castle kitchens.

These rooms were fortunately deserted. Godfrey paused to snatch up a crumpled white linen towel, smash a tomato against it, and wrap my forearm with it.

In an instant I became the walking wounded, and it made sense that Godfrey and Bram supported me on either side.

Godfrey also seized a pair of chopping knives for himself and Bram to conceal inside their jacket pockets.

Mr. Holmes observed our acting and armament rituals without comment, but I suspect he found them nothing more than amusing.

He led us into the maze of hallways that connected the castle's main rooms on this level. Again, we heard noise and tumult from a distance, this time coming from outside the castle. We crossed the flagstones to the great entrance.

I glimpsed a twilight scene lit by torches, somehow dismayed that dusk had fallen. It did not seem possible.

In that half-dark, I saw figures limned against the glow of a bonfire, Gypsies and others. Perhaps a half dozen of their covered wagons were drawn up before the castle, and horses and dogs were silhouetted against both fire and the fading sunset.

From the costume of some of the women I glimpsed—white aprons and caps—I gathered that at least a portion of those present were villagers, for I never saw a Gypsy woman wearing white of any kind.

A tall figure crossed the open space by the castle entrance . . . the priest who was a Count who was a fraud!

I did not look forward to our motley party confronting him, no matter what mime the Gypsy mute who led us performed. Mr. Holmes was astute in thinking that people would shun a figure with such an obvious handicap . . . those who can hear, see, and speak shy from confronting those who cannot, although a touch of leprosy would have done our group more good if we wished to escape unchallenged.

Indeed, with half our number able to pass as Gypsies (although what anyone would make of me in Godfrey's shortened trousers I have no idea), it was just possible that we might stroll among and through them to freedom.

This vista was so welcome that we all stopped to draw a mutually liberated breath. And in that communal silence, harsh against the sounds of the gathering outside, we heard one sharp, snapping sound, like a stick shattering in a fire.

Alas, all of us were worldly enough (myself unwillingly so) to recognize at once that we had heard a firearm being cocked . . . behind us.

We turned, I and my three doughty companions, to face Colonel Sebastian Moran holding a most peculiar weapon upon us . . . a walking stick!

46.

A Midsummer Nightmare

 The brass handle of the long wooden cane caressed Colonel
Sebastian Moran's clean-shaven cheek. Since his stance was
that of a man holding a rifle to his shoulder, none of us
were inclined to challenge his presumed command of the
situation.

"An air rifle, lady and gentlemen and Gypsy traitor," he announced. "It can shatter stone at three hundred yards and what it
can do to bone at thirty feet none of you would like to see, nor live
to see again were you its target."

We said nothing.

"You are wanted in the dining chamber." He gestured abruptly
with the barrel of his . . . cane.

I really could not contemplate any more bizarre events of the
day, so joined my fellows in shuffling gingerly across the vast hall
and through the open coffered doors into the room that had become
so familiar to us all, Sesostros included.

No food and music occupied the room this night, only our

sinister hostess clothed in a voluminous red-black velvet dressing gown, her hair loosened like tongues of amber-orange fire over her shoulders.

She was writing in a small book covered in yellow moiré, but shut it when we entered the room.

"Do you know what day—I should say, night—this is?" she asked.

"We have lost track of time, for some reason," Godfrey answered.

She looked up at him and smiled almost gently. Almost.

"Always the barrister, Mr. Norton. Precision is your God. I do not know what my God is. Chaos, perhaps? Miss Huxleigh, how you surprise me, for an Englishwoman. Trousers, you minx! And a Gypsy swain in tow. I saw you two speak with hands across the room, a courtship in pantomime. Or was it conspiracy? I cannot decide whether I most wish to see you play the coquette or the two-faced fool. Either role is against your religion, isn't it, so both would be equally satisfying to me."

Tatyana next let her odd red-brown gaze, the color of dried blood, fall on Bram Stoker. "Well acted, my not-so-naive friend! I am almost inclined to let you play my Medved, since the original is unavailable for the time being, but I fear you lack his depth of character."

This was so outrageously insulting that I drew in an indignant breath on Mr. Stoker's behalf.

"Yes, Miss Huxleigh?" She taunted me with a supercilious lift of the eyebrows. "You are about to be brave and draw attention to yourself when any woman of sense would shrink into invisibility behind the men. Do you aspire to usurp the place of your bolder, brighter, more beautiful friend? Perhaps in Mr. Norton's affections? Perhaps in another's?"

Well, I would have run out of gasps had I expressed my full indignation at each of these ludicrous and irrational charges.

Instead I said, "I was about to say that the only time I was inclined to shrink from anything was when your pet Medved assaulted me in my room but since I was able to repulse him—a quite fitting verb, I might add, for such an uncouth person—no shrinking was required."

"Ah, yes, but were you able to repulse him when you lay drugged in your humble wooden crate? Although you mostly resembled a corpse during that time, I doubt that would have stopped Medved."

She had publicly laid bare my worst nightmare, and I had no response. Bram Stoker did.

"A most interesting choice of words, Madam. Am I to believe that you credit these local legends of the living dead, of those who seek corpses for sustenance? I fear Miss Huxleigh is far too lively to be a survivor of such a creature, and if she were, I would advise you not to sleep too soundly at night, for she would be far more dangerous than the usual Englishwoman."

"Ah, a man after my own interests. Are you anyone of note in your world? Forgive me, but I have never heard of you."

"Alas, no. I am as I appear to be . . . an enthusiastic traveler and a collector of arcane legends. I shall without a doubt add you to my roster, as a lamia perhaps?"

"I think you are much more interesting than a tiresome barrister. I would prefer to be a succubus, however."

For some reason, Bram Stoker blushed like the burning bush of the Bible.

Tatyana leaned back and pushed the yellow book away like a full plate she had partaken of too much already.

"I don't know what to do with you, my guests." Her eyes fell at last on the rakish figure I knew to be Sherlock Holmes, although he was behaving now like a rather bright bird, glancing from face to face, apparently attempting to understand without benefit of hearing.

"Gypsies," she said considering, "are so predictably loyal when paid enough. That you were not disturbs me."

Sherlock Holmes squinted at her speaking lips, then shrugged and smiled and glanced at me.

"What did you bribe him with?" Tatyana asked me without taking her eyes from the supposed Sesostros.

"Kindness?" I suggested. "A person who does not speak is much overlooked."

"Kindness! Just the sort of pablum I would expect from your lips. You really are too good to be true. It will be a pleasure to introduce you to the rites below."

"I have seen them already," I answered.

"But not as a participant."

I was quite surprised when I felt every man in the room, excepting Colonel Moran, tense like a cocked air rifle.

Although being a victim of the cult's bloody rites had long been my greatest fear since being captured, when the actual threat was made, I was surprised to find myself more angry than frightened.

Unlike our hostess, I knew that Sherlock Holmes carried a pistol and that Godfrey and Bram sported knives and one heretofore proven-effective hatpin. I myself kept custody of Kelly's knife. It is true that we were a piteous number compared to the hordes assembling inside and outside of the castle, but I could not help remembering another ritual scene where Buffalo Bill and his valiant companion Red Tomahawk literally leaped into the fray while the pistol-armed Rothschild agents held back in horror. Irene's was the only pistol to speak on that occasion, I recalled, so it struck me that a few valiant souls were far more defense than an army of the easily discouraged. For what was discouragement but a lack of courage?

If Tatyana could not discourage us, she could not defeat us.

I wonder if that ever had occurred to her.

It had certainly never occurred to her that we might be armed with more than audacity.

"Call the escorts to take our guests to the ceremonies below," she ordered Colonel Moran.

He hesitated. "I don't care to see Europeans—"

"Like myself, you have no true homeland, Colonel, no continent to call your own. We are our own island nation now and rule it. Call the celebrants of the season."

He left the room, and we four held our ground in silence. Tatyana's complacency, or perhaps her contempt, kept her from even suspecting that any of us might have managed to arm ourselves, much less all four.

"The study of mankind is man," Tatyana said, eyeing us. " 'What fools these mortals be.' "

With a chill I recognized Puck's final lines from Shakespeare's *A Midsummer Night's Dream*, whose cast included a fairy queen named Titania! This Titania had fallen in love with a lowly tailor who magically had been given the head of a donkey. It was all a trick that her lord Oberon—was that Colonel Moran?—had used to teach his contrary queen a lesson. Was Godfrey to play the ignominious part of the tailor Bottom, then? And Puck, the mischievous sprite, was that possibly . . . Sherlock Holmes? And who was I? Confused Helena, perhaps. And Irene? Hippolyta, Queen of the Amazons. And was Pink . . . Hermia, the object of both Demetrius's and Lysander's love? Were they Quentin and Bram Stoker, then? Or, more loathsomely, James Kelly and Medved?

"My God," Bram Stoker murmured beside me, openly despairing for the first time that night. "Curse me for a theatrical dunce who has lost track of time! It is indeed Midsummer's Night. Today is June twenty-first. The summer solstice. An ancient pagan feast day."

Only I heard his self-accusing muttering, but it was dire enough to divert me from my mad recasting of Shakespeare's play. Even I knew that ancient pagan feasts were a likely time for devilish rituals.

"And you," said Tatyana after a silence, gazing at Sherlock Holmes in his Gypsy guise. "Are you merely mute, or more clever than I think? Or simply stupid?"

I give credit to Mr. Holmes for nodding and grinning amiably through her roll call of questions, all the while making gestures that could be Gypsy signs or a mute's attempt at sketching out an answer.

"It's a pity that you could not stay where you were put," she said to the rest of us, her hand lifting from beside her heavy velvet gown to reveal the elaborately chased revolver she held, far larger and more ornate than Irene's trusty model of many years. "Too many unwanted guests are descending on the castle, and we shall have to leave sooner than expected. So shall you all, although not by the route you expected."

She stood, placed the gun upon the table before her, and pulled a heavy black wool cloak from the chair behind her onto her shoulders.

"I suppose, though, that you deserve the privilege of seeing Jack the Ripper at last, especially Miss Huxleigh, who has been flirting with the fiend for some time."

My mind reeled insanely through the possibilities. What Tatyana enjoyed calling "flirting" meant only that I had brushed shoulders with the actual killer and had never known it. Was it Kelly, secretly bound and hidden in the caverns below? Colonel Moran even? A man who had hunted heavy game was being outpaced by a world which was rapidly depleting the supply of such beasts. Had he descended to the mad stalking and butchery of helpless women? Was that why he was such a docile servant to Tatyana, rather than a colleague?

Or . . . was the Ripper the least likely suspect? Bram Stoker, also a secret tool of this terrible woman because of the knowledge of his secrets she held. Or even . . . I had cherished this suspicion, rather illogically, but perhaps my instincts were better than I knew . . . had Sherlock Holmes jumped the tracks of the straight and narrow, his raging cocaine habit and lonely ways finally driving him to madly seek and kill the women whose intellects and bodies he spurned equally? Baron Richard von Krafft-Ebing had made the matter plain, from what Irene and Pink said of his disgusting work, *Psychopathia Sexualis*: ordinary men often hid extraordinary obsessions and appetites that they could not control.

There was no doubt that devils walked among us and perhaps more closely in my own footsteps than I knew.

My last glance was at Godfrey. His expression was calm. There was no way anyone sane could suspect Godfrey of Ripper tendencies. I had one true ally, as I have always had, and we would stand shoulder to shoulder no matter what shocks and threats this night brought. As he had said to me earlier, so I swore silently back to him, "either both, or none," but I added another phrase of my own, "*or if only one, then you.*" At least Irene was not here to risk herself, and I was free to risk myself.

When Tatyana pulled the monk's hood over her hair, I felt a chill of apprehension that such a warm garment was never meant to impart. There had been three identically cloaked figures watching from the sidelines during the Paris atrocities: Tatyana, Colonel Moran . . . and who else? The third of that sinister party couldn't have been James Kelly, for he had spied me from the mob of insane worshipers and rushed forward. *So who had it been?* Did we have another mortal enemy among this lot whose identity we did not know?

Or . . . cruelest of ironies, had it been Bram Stoker and had his innocent arrival here been only a ruse to lull us into revealing our escape plans? Such a notion was fiendish, but it was possible, especially if Mr. Stoker were Jack the Ripper.

Steps ground the stones behind us. Colonel Moran returned attired in a cloak like Tatyana's, still flourishing the lethal cane. That made two of the three watchers of that night present. With him came a dozen men as well as three women clad in white robes of rough cloth, with no hoods. They had the look of peasants rather than Gypsies and in age went from youth to middle age. The women wore garlands of flowers around their heads, reminding me of Ophelias fit for drowning. All of them, men and women, had fixed eyes with a glazed expression, as if they had been drugged as I had been, only not so effectively. From outside I could hear the violins and cries of men and dogs: a Gypsy campfire guarding the gate.

This flock was to be our shepherds. I glanced at Godfrey and Mr. Holmes, but sensed no desperate attempt at escape brewing. Bram Stoker acted as confused as I, not quite believing that we were to retrace our steps into the bowels of the castle.

As it was, our ears told us that we were pincered between two assembling mobs of people who had no reason to help us and may have had many private needs to prey on us, those below and those outside.

Tatyana let her firearm vanish into the folds of her black cloak and came toward us. I saw the bright yellow blot of her abandoned book lying on the dark table like a square of sunshine cast through a window, save there was only dark pressing at the library's many tall apertures. The smoke from the Gypsy fire outside slithered into the room, woody and choking. I wished I knew more of Midsummer's Eve. It sounded a benign event, but so did All Saint's Eve, and look what had been made of it!

Silent, like lambs, we allowed ourselves to be herded below again.

The white-robed ones had gathered torches from the hall and held them high, thus surrounding us with a crown of fire. We glided together down the halls and passages and a series of steps.

I was struck suddenly by the scrape of our shoes on the stone . . . only ours, our party and Tatyana and the Colonel. The robed ones' feet were silent. Barefoot.

That one odd fact unnerved me more than anything. We were on the level above the noises that had first driven us back upstairs when suddenly Mr. Sherlock Holmes whimpered like an animal and went sprinting off into the dark, charging through the robed figures like a dark-coated wolf scattering sheep.

"Tiger!" Tatyana ordered. "Fetch back that mute fool!"

As the Colonel thundered off in pursuit, I glimpsed his face in the torchlight. It held an expression of unholy satisfaction. If Mr. Holmes had been a wolf among sheep, this man was a charging rhinoceros among wolves.

I felt a qualm for our escaped member, no matter how cowardly his action. Perhaps he fooled himself that he could bring reinforcements if he escaped, yet he struck me as too enamored of his own powers to turn craven and run. Tatyana lifted and aimed her pistol. At me.

"Gentlemen. If either of you does likewise, I shall shoot Miss Huxleigh in the head."

Bram and Godfrey said nothing, but I could feel their sturdy forms pressing against mine like shields. Such a gesture was well intentioned, but it forced my arms against my sides so that I would be much impeded should I wish to extract and use James Kelly's long-bladed knife.

I began to sense the roots of Irene's annoyance with social chivalry.

And I knew right where I would go with said knife if all was lost: the little robber girl would head straight for the Ice Queen so that Kay was free to rejoin his searching Gerda.

I do believe that I could now do, in the right cause, what I had never imagined I could, but what Jack the Ripper had accomplished night after night in Whitechapel and beyond.

We heard thumps and scuffling down the darkened corridor. In a moment the Colonel's black-draped form propelled a cringing, gibbering man back into our midst, making the sad, seal-like sounds of the mute. If ever I had cherished a wish to see Sherlock Holmes humbled, playing this pathetic role was not the form I had desired.

I assumed that he was exaggerating his submission to disarm his opponents, who still took him for a callow Gypsy not worth regarding as an opponent merely because he lacked the use of a sense most of us take for granted.

Still, I could not be sure about him, even that he was not one of them. Only Godfrey and I were who we thought we were. He seemed to harbor a similar thought, for he glanced down at me just then and nodded slightly.

By now the smoke from below was drifting upward, as were sounds of rioting and revelry. Odd how similar they are, cries of joy and cries of rage. Mobs are mobs whether threatening or celebrating. Or doing both at once.

Now I knew how condemned prisoners felt being marched down the prison corridors to the execution yard where their deaths would inflame the onlookers.

The end of our journey was only another flight of stairs away. Godfrey and Bram had peered down this last tunnel of darkness, but I had not.

I set my jaw and kept an eye on the steps so ill-lit by the torches, now being rubbed by the slither of many bare feet as well as our booted ones. Of we three, Irene and Pink and me, only my path had always been set on this path. I would walk down it and meet my fate.

47.

Nameless Practices

~∾Jᴄᴄ∾~

Case 17. Lustmurder
The murderer, known as Jack the Ripper, has never been found. It is probable that he first cut the throats of his victims, then ripped open the abdomen and groped among the intestines. In some instances he cut off the genitals and carried them away; in others he only tore them to pieces and left them behind.

—RICHARD VON KRAFFT-EBING, *PSYCHOPATHIA SEXUALIS*

Halfway down the last set of steps our "honor guard" of white-robed figures pressed close until we found ourselves moving down a narrow passage that forced us to go in single file.

It was strange, that insistent, mute shepherding, when from just below came the clamor of excited voices in tongues impossible to translate or even identify.

We were herded onto a sort of balcony, almost like a minstrel's gallery in a medieval hall. Our niche jutted out like the prow of a ship. Through its trio of Gothic windows bereft of glass we could see the cavern floor below. Because the cellar, or chapel, however vast, was upheld by low arches and thick pillars, its height even in the loftiest center was less than twenty feet. Our niche, clearly installed for the purpose of overlooking the area below, was only eight feet above the stony cavern floor. Nor was it designed for more than three or four watchers, so our party of four prisoners and two guards pushed against the bay of windows that formed both watching and listening post.

The cloaked figures of Tatyana and Colonel Moran pushed through the crude single door to our perch, sealing us in.

For the moment that fact did not disturb us. We were all held spellbound by the gathering below, by the multitude wearing white robes with rainbow-colored girdles, men and women, the women marked only by their long streaming hair and the wreaths of flowers in it.

While such a gathering in a woodland could be mistaken for a village maypole assembly or even, to the imaginative, a fairy circle, here in this dark, stone-formed cavern of a chapel their presence seemed more sinister.

I was startled to hear strains of music. . . . Not Gypsy violins, as I had thought, but something mellower. I searched the scene of milling human tumult and finally found the music's source: a man working an accordion like a servant pumping a bellows.

I cannot think of a less sinister musical instrument than the good-natured, sweet-toned accordion. It is impossible to make one sound melancholy, in my opinion. Yet, deep within this mountain where solid stone stopped any sound and threw back faint echoes of itself, I found the accordion music resembling the slow, mournful cadence of a great church organ, perhaps one playing at a funeral.

This solemn note was only slightly heard under the clamor of the agitated voices.

I mainly heard the rough laughter of men as they gathered to smack the heads of their sealed pottery jugs against large logs that two or three men would hold upright. It sounded like a convocation of carpenters, but I saw the wax that closed the bottles flaking off, and as soon as the seal was gone, the great logs would be hauled to the cavern's center where wood was forming into the great wheel of a bonfire-to-be.

I spied a black robe moving among the white: the third figure from the sidelines at the cavern under the Paris exposition!

Was this Jack the Ripper, if James Kelly was not?

I watched closely as it bent and bowed to present the jugs for opening and then turned to pass them among the flock with a measured deliberation that reminded me of a priest administering communion. He was tallish, and his deep hood often hid his features, but he did not seem loath to let the people recognize him. Many did, nodding with respect as he passed among them. Respect!

I watched with disrespect, glimpsing a sharp aquiline nose, a gaunt cheek, the brush of heavy eyebrows shadowing sunken eye sockets, thin but weather-roughened red lips, and quite white, strong teeth. Except for the teeth it was the face of age, and every feature was vaguely familiar to me, but not as a whole.

At last the figure finished distributing the jars of liquor and paused to throw back his head and take a long swallow himself.

The hood ebbed halfway down his skull. I saw the thick white hair that thinned toward his face, the pallor of age intensified by the black clothing. It was Count Lupescu! In village circles the man known as the local priest.

This made a certain demented sense, if one could imagine a regularly ordained minister participating in such a pagan travesty of Christian observance. This man, whatever his true name and role, had a head like a great bird of prey, taut and alert, as I had seen in engravings of Spanish Inquisition churchmen, or paintings of religious fanatics like the friar Savonarola. All Roman Catholics, I might add, since Church of England clergy do not tend to torture and burn in the performance of their duties. (The long-ago witchcraft trials do cause me a moment's hesitation, but that was a worldwide phenomenon with which England was unfortunately tainted before good sense took the high ground again.)

Apparently these peasant flocks are very easily led astray, though who can blame them when even their clergy succumbs to Satan?

Even the garlanded women who had at first looked so charming and pure of heart were now gulping from the pottery jugs that passed to every hand.

"I expected Gypsies," I whispered to Godfrey, "and more of those maddening violins."

He nodded. "I as well. Apparently the Gypsies are useful for transportation but not much else."

"Do you recognize any of those tongues?"

"They sound familiar for the region: German, Bohemian, Transylvanian. Dozens of dialects run amok in this remote portion of the world, Nell, where almost every village is its own little country."

As the pottery jars passed from hand to hand and mouth to mouth, so did lighted candles. A widening circle of the white-robed people began to dance and sing, but the others sat around them in circles, some on logs not yet assigned to the central pile. I began to suspect what was in the heavy boxes that had been carried here over the past weeks. I had imagined unconscious bodies like my own, but instead the freight was far less sinister: man-size logs for the fire.

In one sense, the sight of this festival singing and dancing could have been charming, even inspiring. But the jars of liquor that made the rounds both among the spectators and the dancers added a note of frenzy that increased both sound and motion.

I couldn't help making a disgusted face as I recalled those fiery contents splashing into my own mouth and nostrils.

Bram Stoker murmured as much to himself as to us, "It is a Midsummer Eve festival but why indoors like this? The solstice ritual celebrates nature. Why is this one held so far away from light and air?"

"Because," Tatyana's voice came from behind us, transformed by a kind of triumphal joy, "you are privileged to observe one of the world's most hidden spiritual traditions, quite literally an 'underground' sect that is extending its reach, centered as it is now around the leadership of a truly extraordinary figure of supernatural power."

"You do not strike me as one much interested in spiritual attainments," I answered.

"Always so correct, Miss Huxleigh, if not always right. I am ever intrigued by the delusions that drive mankind. Religion is the most powerful, I believe, and its power can be measured by how closely it treads toward evil, rather than what is generally assumed to be good."

"As I thought: devil worshipers."

"You thought wrong for once. Or is it only once? Perhaps after tonight you will reconsider the accuracy of your rectitude, Miss Huxleigh. No, these people are the *Khlysty*. You will notice the similarity to the word *khristy*, or Christs. This sect is Christian."

"No Christian I know imbibes raw liquors during services."

"No? What of the sacramental wine?"

"Wine is not strong spirits."

"No, but it is considered the literal blood of your Lord."

"Only by the Church of Rome."

"The libation here takes its name from the word for water in my language, *voda*. What is more worthy for religious use than the water of life?"

"The same phrase is 'whiskey' in my language," Bram Stoker put in. "Which is Irish, of course, though none but the old speak it these days."

"Is it really?" Tatyana sounded enchanted. "The convolutions of English, or Irish, always amaze me. My *voda* was also made from rye grain, as your whiskey is. It was used as a disinfectant at first but even then the people used it for religious purposes. I am speaking of six hundred years ago. A ceremonial cup that held a gallon of it would be passed around, not these paltry clay bottles, and anyone who abstained was considered impious beyond saving," she added with a malicious glance at me.

"So drunkenness is the state religion in Russia," I said.

Colonel Moran laughed sharply at my comment, but before I could bask in support from an unlikely quarter, Tatyana moved far too close for my comfort.

"Right again, Miss Huxleigh." Her basilisk eyes stared into mine and through me. "For nearly four hundred years Imperial banquets have begun with bread and *voda*. Bread and water. Bread and what we and the world now call vodka. But most of it is *samogon*, a brew made by the people for their own use. Thus vodka is the drink of both czars and peasants."

"It should be the drink of sewers," I said. "It tastes abominable."

"And when did *you* taste vodka?" she asked, bemused.

"When your servant Medved poured some down my throat, but I was able to spit most of it out."

"Interesting." She cocked her head like a bird who was hearing a worm say something astounding. "He was drunk of course. He almost always is; that's why I find him so amusing."

"In civilized lands, we do not laugh at the inebriated." This was not quite true. I understood that the music halls laughed a good deal at the drunkard's expense, but I had never attended a music hall so could afford to take a superior position.

Tatyana laughed at me. "Russia is not a civilized land. Thank God, I suppose? The peasants have nothing much to laugh at, save the inebriated. And the Irish"—here she glanced at Bram Stoker—"know much of both peasantry and inebriation, yes?"

"The report of our national inebriation is much exaggerated, Madam," Mr. Stoker said with great dignity. I had indeed never heard that he was anything but a sober man. "I will cede the honors to the Russians, on your testimony."

"I will take those honors." She leaned out the archway of one window and called out a throat-sticking arrangement of guttural sounds.

In a moment a man in a wide-sleeved robe had tossed a pale jar up to our outpost. The Colonel rapidly stepped forward to catch it, but our Gypsy companion forestalled him, holding the prize high above his head for a moment as if he refused to surrender it.

Sherlock Holmes had been so dormant since his foiled escape attempt that I was as surprised as anyone by his snake-fast strike in snaring the bottle.

He gave his mute's grin and shook the bottle by his supposedly useless ear, then shrugged to indicate that he couldn't hear the contents shift. With a bow, he ceded the bottle to Colonel Moran, but I suspected a point had been made.

"I could use a drink," Colonel Moran muttered, tapping the jar's narrow end against the stone whilst turning it expertly.

Wax dropped away like falling leaves, a process the Gypsy Holmes and I watched with equal fascination. Only now were we seeing the source of the wax traces we had tracked from Paris to this forsaken spot in Transylvania, where we were indeed forsaken ourselves and probably observing our last sights on this earth, unfortunately the height of human perversion.

Yet I was grateful that I would go to my death with at least that niggling mystery of the wax solved.

The Colonel pulled a small collapsible steel cup from his pocket and filled it with the clear liquid that poured from the jug.

"Tatyana?"

She nodded and sipped. He sipped in turn, then glanced at the rest of us. "Shall I offer tastes all 'round?" he asked her. "I know you are fond of educating the ignorant."

"Indeed, at least to those willing to use a common cup, which I suspect will not include Miss Huxleigh."

"I am a battlefield veteran," the Colonel said harshly. "We know that raw liquor is a great purifier, for throats and wounds. Nothing safer to drink in any clime."

"Agreed," said Mr. Stoker. "I'll try the whiskey of another land."

The Colonel filled the cup again and handed it to the huge Irishman, who tipped it back in one swallow.

He laughed. "Raw liquor indeed, Colonel. Not so smooth as my favorite rye whiskey, but clean and sharp."

"Mr. Norton?" the Colonel asked next.

"Why not?" Godfrey took the refilled cup, eyed the company, and tossed it back in two considered gulps. "Reminds me of the Blue Ruin, the gin of the common folk in London," he explained to Tatyana. "We don't have true peasants, for Englishmen have had a place in law since the Magna Carta, but we do have many poor souls who need to forget hard toil."

"The Gypsy must know this drink," Tatyana said.

He nodded eagerly, then pantomimed tossing back a cup. The Colonel murmured *memento mori*, a Latin phrase that made Godfrey's mouth tighten, then refilled the cup.

Unlike the others, Mr. Holmes sipped the brew, grinning at each of us between sips, like the simpleton he was playing.

I couldn't help wondering how much he liked the bottle, this man who regularly took, according to his physician friend, "a seven-percent solution" of cocaine. From the careful, birdlike way he imbibed the vodka, I concluded that liquor was not one of his vices.

I did have the oddest impression that he was *analyzing* the brew, using himself as a human chemical process. It made me wonder if he was acquainted with vodka and its variations already. And to wonder how, and why, and when.

While we had been indulging daintily in ancient Russian drinking material, the people below had been gulping the stuff down. No longer were they dancing a recognizable round. They reeled and screeched, sang and fell, laughed and cried, men and women together. And then they began to grope each other.

I watched with the unmitigated disgust of the truly sober.

Into the cacophony of accordion and song and hands slapping knees came a sudden sharp report, like a rifle.

I glanced at the Colonel, but his sinister cane was not in evidence. Another report echoed even as I stared at him.

Looking below, I saw a nest of dark serpents undulating among the dancers, lashing them to faster gyrations.

"*Khlyst* also means 'whip' in my language," Tatyana said, gazing raptly below.

I watched in horror as the white gowns, some girdled in crimson ribbons, ran red about the shoulders, back, and arms. I remembered the drops of spilled "wine" we had spied upon the rocky cellar and catacomb floors of Paris.

Most of all I recalled the sentence writ in blood, in French, on the cellar wall ... *The Juwes are the men That Will not be Blamed for nothing* ... only Irene had pointed out that form of the word Juwes in that construction was the feminine one. And Sherlock Holmes had concluded that the blood came from a man who had been whipped along the length of the graffito, using his own blood to inscribe the letters.

Although I had not drunk from the common cup the water of Russian life, my senses reeled. Everything I was witnessing I had seen the aftermath of, not once, but again and again.

The candle stubs, tossed aside as they were being so now, while the great central bonfire was lit to take their place. The flakes of wax and droplets of blood sharing common ground on the cavern floor.

I saw shredded robes slipping off shoulders slick with sweat and blood as men and women came together in an orgy that history had likely not seen since the days of the Romans.

Godfrey caught my head in one hand and turned my face into the darkness of his shoulder.

Despite the shelter, my mind combined images from the past few weeks ... the twisted remnants of the Paris courtesans on the Prince of Wales's amorous device in the French brothel ... the illustrations and descriptions of the gutted women of Whitechapel that Irene and I and Pink had put together from newspaper reports ... the naked dead bodies displayed daily at the Paris Morgue ... and the one real dead body I had seen placed into a waxwork vignette at the Musée Grévin in Paris ... the dead flower seller in Neunkirchen. ... the tale of the brutalized Madonna and hideously murdered child in Prague ... the severed breasts left on Mary Jane Kelly's table in the spare Whitechapel room that held what was left of her literally flayed and eviscerated body, a breast excised before a mob like this and my very eyes under the Paris Exposition grounds. ...

The dark of Godfrey's shoulder, however welcome, was no escape.

I lifted my head even as his fingers tightened onto my upper arm like a claw.

Some of the men lifted a huge, crude cross of logs bound into a figure "X" against the cavern's back wall.

The black-robed figure had come to stand between it and the snapping, crackling, roaring fire.

He held a pale jar in one hand and thrust his head back to drink . . . and drink . . . and drink until he had emptied the entire jar and cast it down before him to shatter.

. . . pottery shards and pieces of wax on a cellar floor.

He began to speak in no language I knew, but his voice was strong and flowing, like lava, and the people before him swayed left and right even as they continued to twine each other (in unspeakable acts that I luckily knew so little of) like a nest of snakes.

They answered him in many tongues and some of them were not of this earth. And still they writhed as one, sacrilegious mass.

I knew that I witnessed utter abandonment, sin on an unthinkable scale, but I could not see the specifics of the acts, as if some benign force had blinded my eyes to exactly what I saw, though my mind and heart were not so sheltered.

This was horror. This was the world I believed in, inverted. If it was not Satanism, it was a close neighbor to Hell.

And yet I must know. I had walked too far into the dark to shut my eyes at its triumph over the light.

The man in the black cloak threw back the hood as he drank the second jar of vodka, the water of life, and apparently death as well.

I saw revealed this time not the hawkish features of the old priest, but the stolid young features of Medved, his pale eyes blazing in his peasant face like holes into Hell.

I stared at the jar at his lips, unable to accept that merely twenty-four hours before he was urging this same raw spirit upon me.

He smashed the empty bottle to bits at his feet, then bent to pluck a burning brand from the fire. He turned and scratched a large symbol into the cavern wall, the burnt stick marking the stone like charcoal.

It was a Chi-Rho!

As he turned back to the fire, a girl clutched the tatters of her white robe around her and rushed up to him with a pottery jar, kneeling to offer him another full measure.

He took the jar and drank from it even as he drew up the girl, tore what was left of her robe from her, and bore her down to the ground beneath him.

I saw what could have been myself.

Other girls rushed toward him, covered him like leeches, until they formed a knot of slippery bloody skin and bones and tangled robes.

The accordion wheezed as if trying to push air back into Hell, people screamed and swooned and entwined with each other and began shaking and spitting out alien words as if giving voice to all the imps of eternity. It was agony and ecstasy. I knew I was hearing what had first been heard on earth when the Disciples had shut themselves away after Jesus's death . . . speaking in tongues. For the Disciples the gift had come from the Holy Spirit.

I could see no Holy Spirit in this mountain cavern. I could only see and hear the Evil One in human guise, which, come to think of it, was the only way he ever displayed himself.

I was shaking with disgust and fear, and Godfrey's heart was an avalanche beneath my ear. Bram Stoker was struck to stone, confronting a horror story beyond his ability to write it. Sherlock Holmes also stood transfixed, unable to take his eyes from the scene below, which I suspected appalled him almost as much as it appalled me.

I looked at Tatyana. Her expression was rapt, like a saint being assumed into heaven. She wished to be down there. She wished to be a maiden in a wreath writhing on the floor with a half dozen men. She wished to be Medved, inciting and leading and drinking and taking. She wished to be a mad dog.

Colonel Moran, I saw, was of two minds: the natural thirst for violence of the hunter slaked, the civilized club man both accepting the alien, even savoring it, yet instinctively, fascinatingly repulsed by it.

I felt a throb of sympathy for him. I admitted in myself a fascination with the inhuman. Yet no ghost in any story, however carefully wrought, could compete with the reality of the *Khlysty*. I understood that all this evil was done in the supposed name of God, and that this was not an utterly uncommon condition in the world every day, though never so extreme.

And I remembered the recent incident in my bedchamber, and the mesmerizing approach of Medved, who had played the Devil, the demon, more than once in the past few weeks. For the first time, I saw myself as Eve in Eden, under the fruited tree, noticing the serpent.

48.

Unholy Spirit

※

*Tyger! Tyger! burning bright
In the forests of the night,
What immortal hand or eye
Could frame thy fearful symmetry?*
—WILLIAM BLAKE, 1794, *SONGS OF EXPERIENCE*

 If Tatyana had wished to terrify and dispirit us, she had
been wildly successful. We would all meet whatever death
she chose, rather than face the rituals of that faceless mob.

In horror we watched a man brought forth, willingly,
and laid out on an "X" of crossed logs, his wrists and ankles
tied to the extremes of each board.

It was a moment's work to tear the whip-shredded robes from
his body.

I had seen once (and never looked again, as I was sure this was
not recommended viewing for a parson's spinster daughter) Mi-
chelangelo's evocation of a naked man as upon an invisible wheel,
with his limbs stretched out so that a perfect circle could be scribed
around him. I was sure the Renaissance artist had intended this to
be a tribute to the Deity's inimitable plan for all of life and humanity, the eye that is upon the sparrow and yet makes of man a
geometry pleasing to all nature and science.

This man laid before our horrified eyes was such a figure. While Medved held up his sinewy naked arms, his robe having ebbed to his hips, a knot of grasping young women clasped his legs as if they supported a heroic public statue. His manhood (for my father had kept a secret book of Greek and Roman statuary that I, in a childhood sin, had found and perused) enormously visible, Medved's followers took knives to the very same area on his supine worshiper.

I would have swooned, having good reason to do so, except that I was past swooning. Even Godfrey's hand over my eyes could not dampen my imagination.

Thanks to Godfrey's brotherly interference, I missed the most astounding event of the evening: not sexual misconduct, not orgiastic excess, not false religious ritual, but a figure darting from the shadows beyond the fire to the very feet of Medved himself, screeching, begging, pleading, all in English!

I heard the words and jerked my head free of Godfrey's control just in time to see James Kelly, slavering on his knees before the brute Medved.

"Master," he was shouting. "I have been faithful to thee. I have followed thee despite all barriers. Sin is salvation. Let me sin. Let me take this man's place. I have earned the sacrifice. Master, the blood is the Life, let me shed it for you and Drink your Blood in the Cup."

All eyes in the cavern had sobered to attend to Kelly's demented plea, though few could understand its words.

"Quick," came Sherlock Holmes's voice over my shoulder, harsh as a diving kestrel's cry. "Hold Tatyana while I bind Moran."

After an instant's shocked paralysis, Bram and Godfrey leaped upon the woman like dogs upon a hind to pull the black cloak down over her arms to bind her.

Sherlock Holmes had wrested away Colonel Moran's cloak and struck him a blow with the butt of a pistol. I watched as he used Kelly's trouser belt to lash the man's hands behind his back.

My own corselet lacing soon slashed into the air like a whip and then was servicing Madam Tatyana in similar fashion while she struggled like a wildcat with Godfrey and Bram.

"Kelly?" I asked no one in particular and everyone, wondering how the items used to bind him earlier had reappeared here.

"I freed him during my short sabbatical from your company," Mr. Holmes said, eyeing the chaos below, "expecting just such a distraction. Look. There's an exit from the cavern beyond the bonfire. We must be quick about leaving while Kelly distracts the crowd. Gentlemen, don the robes. Miss Huxleigh and myself are already in Gypsy guise. Jump down and be ready to catch the lady. I will follow. Draw any weapon you possess. This mob is mad with frenzy and hot for blood, their own first, but ours will do."

Barely had he finished speaking than Bram and Godfrey were bounding through the window frames, landing hard on their feet eight feet below.

I paused to stare into the bound Tatyana's eyes, which burned with some overpowering emotion . . . failure, blood-lust, or hoped-for revenge? I wondered if she knew the identity of who had foiled her.

I had no longer to dally. Sherlock Holmes lifted me over the sill like a sack of potatoes and cast me into the waiting arms of Godfrey and Bram Stoker, who absorbed my weight together as if I had been a thistledown, so that not a foot touched the floor.

He leaped down immediately after and pushed us in the direction he wished us to run. We went where herded, as had been our wont of late. Here on the cavern floor I smelled the raw power of vodka mixed with the ugly perfume of sweat and blood and other unmentionable excesses.

The glazed eyes of the celebrants barely noted our passing as if we were sparks from the fire rushing by. Their condition lent us an instant's invisibility. We darted through and beyond them and circled the fringes of the group, hunting Mr. Holmes's vaunted exit.

He was in the lead, with Godfrey and Bram on either side of me, practically carrying me along.

We felt the fire at our backs and saw a blot of darkness that expanded as we neared it. This could only be our exit.

As we raced for its welcome darkness, light bloomed and then swelled at its center. Torches flared into a mass like a sun as a new mob of people rushed to fill our only escape route with their thronging presence.

Like flood water in a mine shaft, they swept us apart and pinned us against the wall with an irresistible force.

I could see no one, hear nothing over the roar of the oncoming crowd.

But the mob had seen us. Perhaps two dozen unintelligible, ravening men pressed me and my companions against the wall into a prison cell constructed of human bodies.

49.

Journey's End

❧❧❧

My mother said that I never should
Play with the gypsies in the wood
—ANONYMOUS

The heat and the pressure were unbearable. My pulses raced. I felt once again confined in a box. I wrenched my head from side to side, the only portion I could move, hoping to spy my friends.

Angry shouts in a foreign tongue assailed my ears. I sensed a flutter of violence to my right and managed to see Bram or Godfrey being stripped of his borrowed cloak.

And still the fissure between the walls spewed an onslaught of new forces into the cellar.

If only we had made our race to freedom ten or fifteen minutes earlier. . . . As the men milled around us, I realized that they didn't wear the white robes of celebrants, but the full, colorful clothing of Gypsies. There was even a woman or two among them. I glimpsed long unbound hair under scarlet-and-gold scarves, but only briefly, as both they and I were below the common height and condemned to see only half of what occurred.

Bram roared like an angry bear behind me. I felt his cloak whip my shoulder as it was torn away and then I heard a shriek that almost sounded joyous.

One of the Gypsy women came tearing through the circle of men, knocking into their arms and shoulders left and right with some object in her hand.

She pushed past me, and as I turned to follow her impetuous progress, I saw Godfrey pressed against the wall only a yard's width behind me. If we survived this, I would have to speak with him about his lamentable and very unbarristerlike tendency to attract strange and fanatical women. . . .

Then I heard a voice shout "Godfrey!" It was the only voice in the world anyone could have heard in that chaos: one trained to shake the back walls of an opera house.

"Irene!" I cried, my own voice lost in the whirlwind, as a second Gypsy woman came in her wake, flailing right and left with a cane.

I had no trouble glimpsing Godfrey now, for Irene had cast herself upon him in an embrace so encompassing and with a kiss so ferocious that I looked away blushing.

My shoulders were suddenly taken in someone's hands and shaken.

"Nell! Can this be you?"

I stared into the astonished blue-gray eyes of Elizabeth Jane, also known as Pink, equally astounded that she was so uncertain of my identity and then very pleased indeed.

I had not long to bask, for Irene had somehow managed to relinquish Godfrey and leaped upon me like an unmannerly dog. "Nell? Are you sure, Pink? *Nell?*" She petted my braids and my full sleeves and regarded me with the greatest amazement and delight, glancing over her shoulder to Godfrey every other instant as if she dared not let either of us out of her sight.

"And Bram!" she exclaimed, for he had managed to fight his way to join us. Her entering our prison circle had made it into a charmed one. The Gypsy men gave way like courtiers, suddenly less keepers and more guards.

Another man crashed through the ring of Gypsies, as brown of face as they and also wearing a strange medley of clothing from here and there, which I could hardly criticize given my equally unconventional attire.

"They are safe?" he demanded of Irene, blinking to take in Godfrey and Bram, who looked quite ordinary divested of their sinister robes.

He looked right over my braided head.

"Yes, both. All!" Irene caroled, her voice carrying over the screams and chaos all around us.

"But, Nell. Where is Nell?" Quentin shouted.

I could not speak. I could certainly not make myself heard as they did.

Irene shook me slightly, as if pinching a dream to make sure that it is real. "Here she is." She whirled to claim Godfrey again, leaving me to face Quentin alone.

Can one be alone in a milling mob of madmen and six tribes of assembling Gypsies? Can two be alone in such a circumstance?

Quentin looked so different, but then he always did. I imagine I did too, and I never did. He stared at me, at my eyes, my face, my hair, my clothes, as if he did not know me and he feared he might never know me again. I saw not joy on his face but worry relieved and new worry as quickly born. Where Irene and Pink had pulled me into their commanding orbits as if we had been separated for a mere three weeks, which we indeed had been, Quentin regarded me across a chasm as wide as three years, or thirty. True, we had not seen each other in months. The cavern had become as quiet as a compartment on a train, though I could hear the dull roar of the entire world through which our isolated (and imaginary) railway car rolled.

His lips mouthed my name, but I could not hear the word.

I heard another voice, high-pitched with command and even a bit peevish. "Yes, 'journeys end in lovers' meetings,' but we've work to do in this *abattoir* of the Carpathians. I assume these are your trained Gypsies, Madam Norton. I need to direct them."

She took in the man's disguise in an instant, then without hesitation she pulled a large playing card from the gathered fullness of her borrowed Gypsy sleeve and presented it to Sherlock Holmes.

"The Tarot," he observed with a sigh. "And blood on the swords? Is that not a bit melodramatic even for a prima donna?"

"It always works in the operettas," she answered with an ecstatic grin, linking her arm through Godfrey's.

"I am translator," Quentin said, not yet taking his eyes off of me. "I will go with you."

They were gone and we five were left alone against a dirty dark stone wall, watching from the sidelines. I realized that it had become quiet in our corner for some time.

Irene, her arm still linked with Godfrey, linked her free arm with mine. She was smiling though her eyes were bright with tears. Bram Stoker grinned and pulled my free arm through his and patted my hand before he reached out to link arms with Pink. We stood, absolutely content in our own company bought at such cost, and watched.

Before us, the Gypsy troops, and that's what they indeed were, rounded up the poor deluded souls who had already punished themselves for their sins.

Mr. Holmes and Quentin were leading a party of ten to storm the monsters' gallery above the cavern floor and collect the bound prisoners.

Behind the mighty bonfire, which the Gypsies were beating with unburnt logs, scattering the great burning pieces of wood, sending up showers of sparks, pushing it all apart to burn down in small brush fires here and there, another knot of Gypsies were struggling.

From my vantage point they appeared to be squabbling among themselves, as if they were gathered around a game of dice and disagreed. I was reminded of the Roman soldiers gambling for the cloak of Christ after the Crucifixion.

I couldn't imagine what made me think of that, except that the great crossed logs against the far wall recalled the X-shaped crosses on which some of the Disciples were crucified, and the Chi-Rho of course.

And then a struggling, half-naked figure reared up against that awful black X-shape, throwing off the Gypsies as if they were children.

His naked upper torso was streaked with sweat and charcoal and drops of other people's blood. I was certain I was looking on the anti-Christ, and it was Tatyana's Medved, the leader of this demented ceremony.

Again the Gypsies rushed to hold him down. Again he exploded upright among them, not a tall man, but a powerful man, a man of almost superhuman strength. His nudity, his dreadful condition, were so evocative of the suffering of Christ that I stood transfixed by him despite myself, as I had been frozen by his burning ice-blue eyes in my room not long before. What if we were wrong? What if there was some divinity in all this? Good Christians should suffer meekly . . . was this not what this congregation was doing, walking in the tortured footsteps of Our Lord? I had heard of flagellants in the early church, in the Roman Church, of hideously tortured saints, even among the missionaries to the American Indians. Was what happened here any worse than what the Church would have us read about and revere in the martyrs? Did we not see the truth here?

I confess to confusion as I watched more pagan Gypsies converge on the lone struggling figure and finally bear it to the ground to be bound.

All the celebrants of the cellar chapel were subdued now and being herded to the castle's upper areas. I saw Mr. Holmes and Quentin moving among the Gypsy guards.

We five were too exhausted to do anything but watch numbly and savor our reunion.

Then as the sounds of riot gave way to the weeping and sighing and moaning of prisoners, Irene began to sing. It was nothing operatic, but it was, to my everlasting surprise, a hymn.

"Amazing Grace."

What was most amazing was how the rock chamber amplified and magnified her voice, as pure as a mountain stream as the simple

English words echoed off of hard stone and fell on our ears like warm rain.

Even Medved, upright and still struggling in his bonds, paused and lifted his shaggy head like a dog scenting something rare and held still.

Sherlock Holmes stopped halfway up the stairs, Colonel Moran and Tatyana at pistol point ahead of him.

At the first note, Tatyana's head of ungoverned hair snapped up and back, as if she had been shot. I could not see her face and didn't want to. I didn't even look at Irene, but merely swayed slowly left and right with my comrades as the music bade us. I wanted only to hear those healing syllables and notes, to let anguish and worry and fear of the past and the future rinse away like the road dust from a long and very arduous journey.

"Journeys end in lovers' meetings." It had sounded like a jibe from the lips of Sherlock Holmes, but I wondered if a trace of envy flavored it. It was from Shakespeare. I would have to look up the play when we were back in Paris and I had time.

Meanwhile, Irene sang like a benediction.

"Thro' many dangers, toil, and snares, I have already come.

" 'Tis grace has kept me safe thus far, And grace will lead me home."

The words and verses were short and simple. The song soon over. The memory of its absolute purity would never die.

When the last echo of the last note had died, we looked at each other, all petty rivalries or cross-purposes evaporated, all at peace, together.

This moment could not last, but it could be savored.

50.

Found and Lost

※

I once was lost, but now am found,
Was blind, but now I see
—JOHN NEWTON, *AMAZING GRACE*, CIRCA 1760–1770

We returned to our rooms, Godfrey and I, to gather what belongings we had before we left the castle forever.

Rather, Godfrey retired to his room with Irene, and I retired to mine alone.

As I lit the candelabra feeling an odd blend of practicality and horror, I heard the mysterious murmurs of a married couple beyond the connecting door. And the mysterious silences.

I felt a warm flood of security, like a child who knows her parents are in the house. I also felt the cold, hot, empty loneliness of a child who knows she must grow up someday, and then who will take care of her? *No one.*

This last rush of feeling was ridiculous. I would return to Neuilly with Irene and Godfrey. All would be as before.

No! I was not as before.

I had little to gather in this room. Godfrey's nightshirt to return, two books Godfrey had fetched me from his explorations. That was all. Everything I had brought with me was destroyed. Except the chatelaine in my pocket.

At the window, my rope of bed linens lay coiled like a great albino snake. Its head reared as if to strike . . . the end that Godfrey had looped and knotted around the window's central post.

I went to look out on the night, a full moon that shed light and shadow on the mountains and the meadows, gilding everything, making what was harsh and inhospitable lovely.

Bats reeled against the moon's fat face, looking like moths drawn to an irresistible flame.

The night was still . . . until something scratched at my door.

Rats and cats? I had never seen much of these supposed denizens. Perhaps only in human form.

I went to my door, afraid to approach it.

Another scratch.

"Yes?"

"Nell?"

"Quentin?"

"May I come in?"

"Yes, but . . . I am so used to the door being locked from the outside."

"Nothing simpler," he replied, and I heard the latch lifted.

"I'm sorry," he said on entering. "There was so much to manage."

"You are Irene's first lieutenant," I said, proud of both of them. "I have never seen her so willing to relinquish the leading role. Did you hear her sing?"

"Who did not? It was . . . amazing. I've always known she had been a singer. I didn't know that she was a Singer, like a Siren. From now on, when I think of the life I might have had, and regret it, I'll think of the life she had, and lost, and my regret will look very puny."

"Would you really prefer to be still living on Russell Square in London?"

"Would you really prefer to be living in Shropshire?"

"Sometimes."

"Honest Nell. You make hypocrites of us all."

"No! I've no desire to make anyone feel unhappy, ever."

"Sometimes it can't be helped. Sometimes it's even good for us."

I shrugged.

He glanced at the window. "So this is the famous rope."

"You've heard of it?"

"And you climbed down the castle wall with Godfrey and Bram Stoker."

"Between them. They would have caught me if I slipped."

"But your rope would have caught *them* if they slipped."

He stepped away in the moonlight, as if to look at me anew. This made me very nervous and a trifle irritated. It was as if he felt he had underestimated me, and if he had, then he didn't know me at all. And if he didn't, then my heart should break. And yet . . . I had been kept in a vampire box for a week and hung by a rope over a chasm since last we had met, and I do not think any part of me would break as easily anymore. And for that I felt very sorry.

"What is this?" he asked.

"What?"

He was smiling. . . . I saw his white teeth in the moonlight, like pearls. "This . . . arrangement."

His fingers touched the braids coiled around my head.

"That is how I got the idea for the rope. My hair was . . . impossible after a week being shipped across Europe in a box—"

"Nell," he murmured.

But I had not finished explaining myself.

"Godfrey was able to convince the Gypsies to get me the makings of a bath. The Gypsies! Can you imagine! Godfrey is a barrister St. Peter at the Gate would have to reckon with. At any rate, I was clean but lacked the simplest wherewithal of good grooming, so I braided my hair and in so doing thought of the rope when Godfrey proposed climbing down the castle walls by himself, which was of course unthinkable."

"Unthinkable," he repeated. His fingers still played in my plaited hair.

"I planned to undo the braids tonight, but the compression has quite destroyed my hair."

"Let me," he said.

"Destroy my hair?"

"Undo your braids."

Well, I didn't think he should. Really. An unrelated male. An unrelated male of a higher position in society. It was almost like undoing corset strings, wasn't it? Although I wore no corset, not even a corselet since Mr. Holmes had required the lacing to bind Tatyana, though I certainly could not tell *Quentin* that! Even though he had once most efficiently de-corseted me when I had swooned with shock from his appearance in disguise in a place and at a time I had never expected him to be.

Such as here. And now.

In the moonlight. By the window of a castle.

I had perhaps divided my hair into a dozen or so braids, and I could feel his fingers working at the first.

There was something comforting and parental about that steady tug, a service I had performed many times for my charges during the two short years I was a governess. For my dear charges. Where were they now, my temporary little ones? His niece Allegra we could certainly find at a moment's notice, but the others. . . .

His fingers tugged at another braid.

"What are we to do now?" I asked.

"Here? Now?"

"With all those people." I started up. "What has become of James Kelly? I don't remember seeing him once Tatyana and Colonel Moran were subdued."

"James Kelly?"

"Jack the Ripper. Only—Sherlock Holmes implied that he wasn't. Where is he?"

"Holmes or Kelly?"

"Kelly! I certainly don't care where Sherlock Holmes is."

"I'm glad to hear it."

"Ouch! That pulled."

"Sorry. If you would calm down and stop agitating yourself. . . . We're holding a meeting later downstairs to decide all these issues. But not for a while yet."

I leaned back against the wall and let Quentin continue my unraveling.

Questions pushed to the fore of my mind like nettles, but I bit my tongue and held them back. He was right. This was the first time in three weeks that I need not worry about something.

Except him.

He turned me to face away from him and began unbraiding the back of my hair.

"I wonder that you can do that in the dark," I said finally.

"A spy learns to do almost everything in the dark. It's a soothing facility."

"I braided my rope at night, mostly by feel. I had the fire-glow though."

"You cheated," he said, jerking playfully on one of my braids. I had never had anyone to tease me before.

This was the last one. I felt it unravel strand by strand, and it seemed every fiber of necessity of the past weeks, which was what I had lived on, had fallen away into loose, rolling waves as well.

Quentin turned me around to face him and combed his fingers through my hair as if admiring his own handiwork.

I couldn't breathe, but that didn't seem to be an unwelcome state.

His fingers slipped up into my hair at the back of my head and then he was pulling my face to his or pushing his face to mine.

I felt as if I had been dropped from a rope to hang swinging over a precipice, a feeling both frightening and exhilarating and thus utterly confusing.

He kissed me, as he had kissed me once before long ago, in front of a window, a light, slight kiss like a moth fanning its wings.

This was different and before I could even say how it was different Medved reared up before me like a devil summoned from Hell, his fingers clawing into my hair and pushing my face toward the hard, fiery lip of a pottery jar of vodka . . . and then James Kelly was lurching toward me against the marvelous painting of a spinning seascape, prodding at my bodice, as Medved had, leaving me locked in a dark space, sent spinning and bruising through time in a vampire box . . . the secret trapdoor in a stage floor which the monster will jump out of when the cue is given . . . the coffin, the prison, and you are left filthy and battered and alone and not knowing . . . not knowing even where you have been or what has been done to you in London, in Paris, in Prague, in Transylvania!

I felt a stunning terrifying plunge, Quentin's hands slipping over my shoulders, my bare shoulders as the Gypsy blouse fled like a ghost, and . . . I began shaking, as if I would shake myself out of my box, out of time. . . .

And I knew it was the worst thing to do, and I couldn't stop it to save my soul.

"My God, Nell, I'm sorry!"

Quentin had backed away, his hands raised as if swearing an oath.

And what could I say, how could I say, that I had discovered that good and evil were so close that I could for the moment stand neither one nor the other?

"I'm sorry." He reached again for me, then forced himself back. "I can't know—"

I could say nothing. I shook so hard I could not speak, could not explain, could not retract, could do nothing, a prisoner in an invisible box no one could see, that only I could feel.

"I can't stay without wanting to comfort you," he said, "and I can see that is the worst thing I can do."

He left then, and I sank down by my coils of rope and wept into their coarse and somehow comforting braids until they were soaked with my salt and regret.

⚜   ⚜   ⚜

A soft knock on the connecting door to Godfrey's room a half hour later roused me from my puddle of self-pity. Irene, of course, warned by Quentin. I both resented and secretly appreciated that inevitability.

When I opened the door, Irene peered in like a supplicant.

"We are having a war council in the library in half an hour. I thought you might not want to miss it."

"War council?"

"To decide what to do with our captives, and other matters. You'll attend?"

I nodded.

She stepped over the threshold, her arms full of clothing. "I thought you might prefer to wear ordinary garb. We brought only one carpetbag each on our journey, but this was most useful."

She laid my surprise dress on the bed. I was indeed surprised to see it, and dismayed.

"Who will be at the council?" I asked.

"Godfrey and myself, Bram Stoker, Pink. . . ."

"Why is she still with us?" I asked with uncustomary irritation. "She has no real part in this affair."

"Perhaps 'Pink' does not." Irene paused, looking rueful. "But she is also Nellie Bly, a daredevil reporter for a New York City newspaper. She was following the Ripper's trail from London to Paris before we happened upon her."

"Pink? *Elizabeth?* Is named Nellie! Nellie—?"

"Bly. The pseudonym comes from an American song."

"She isn't a fallen woman, then?"

"Not at all. So we can hardly exclude her from our conference."

"And who else cannot be excluded?"

Irene hesitated again, then came out with it. "Sherlock Holmes."

I made a face but held my tongue.

"Yourself, of course," she rushed on before pausing again, then plunging. "And . . . Quentin."

As I had feared. I fingered the gown's satin shirtwaist. Quentin had seen me wear it. I had seen Quentin while wearing it. But Irene was right; there was little to choose from, and I was anxious to shed Godfrey's trousers and my long-worn Gypsy blouse, as useful as the full sleeves had been for concealment and carrying.

"And these." Irene laid a full set of ladies' lingerie on top of the gown: corset, chemise, pantaloons, petticoat. For a moment these articles looked as foreign as a sari, though a good deal more complicated.

"I will help you dress," Irene decreed.

And so she did, fussing with the intricacies of the surprise dress while I donned the underthings and stockings and garters. My black walking boots had survived my kidnaping, but I decided to keep the Gypsy boots instead. Only the toes would peep out from under my hem, and they were a deep eggplant color that almost looked black.

"You will need this to fit into the surprise dress." Irene brought over the cotton and whalebone corset, its loosened strings dangling like skinny pink serpents.

I let her help pull the thing over my head and shoulders and then ply the laces. She tsked as she noticed the bruises still visible on my arms and shoulders, but tightening laces was hard work, and she did not waste her breath on words.

I donned the surprise dress, but fastened the black revers over the pink shirtwaist and had her lower the panels on the skirt that revealed the pink underskirt.

"But you look so pretty in pink!" she objected.

"This is a war council, you said. I do not wish to appear frivolous."

"I don't think you ever could." She sighed. "Now, as for what I can do with your hair, bereft of curling irons, rats, and combs . . . and with the braiding that has made it so thick!"

She sat me down before the dim mirror and began twisting my hair into a chignon, pulling pins from her own hair to anchor mine into a semblance of a hairstyle.

I saw myself swiftly reassembled as quite nearly my old self, yet all these artifacts of my old life hardly seemed to matter now.

Irene hummed as she subdued my hair into something resembling a coiffure. Lullabies.

"Would you like to talk?" she asked at last.

"No."

Her hands hesitated on my hair. "Where would you like to go from here?"

"Home."

She was utterly still again for a moment. "And . . . where is that?"

"Why, that bucolic backwater of a village, Neuilly."

"We could . . . there's no reason now—my presumed death is either known to be erroneous or I am sufficiently forgotten—that we couldn't remove to London. England."

"I may not know where we are now, but I know quite well where London is. Are you mad, Irene? That man Sherlock Holmes lives there and your interests would be forever tangling with his, I don't doubt. No. I wish to go home to Neuilly and supervise our impossible maid Sophie and that annoying parrot Casanova, and Lucifer, the devil of a black cat, and Sarah's poor little serpents." I could not bring myself to mention Messalina, Quentin's endearing little mongoose whose care I had assumed.

"If that's really where you want to go. You have never liked Paris."

"Oh, it is not so bad when murderers are not running amok in it. In fact, I would like to return to *l'Exposition universelle* and see the Wild West Show and ride the elevator on the Eiffel Tower, and I especially would like to visit the nautical panorama when it is open for viewing."

That last request was tantamount to a rider thrown by a thoroughbred deciding to get back on the mount. I watched in the mirror while Irene's careful expression finally relaxed into relief and even a modicum of joy.

"We shall!" she said. "We shall do all that and more as soon as we return."

She was not, or perhaps I was not, a person given to physical expressions of emotion, but her hands left my hair to squeeze my shoulders encouragingly.

I winced.

"Oh, you are hurt! That awful journey has battered you most dreadfully, my poor Nell!"

"It will heal," I said stoically.

"Of course it will."

"Except—"

She grew quiet again.

"I don't know what happened to me during the week I was transported here. Godfrey says I was kept drugged by chloroform. I was shipped like an animal, Irene, with no food and a little water slopped on me from time to time, unable to attend to my most basic needs. I arrived here thirsty and starving and filthy."

"I know, I know," she cried kneeling beside me so our faces were paired in the mirror. She spoke to my reflection. "Haven't I imagined every possibility a hundred times. It was barbaric."

"The only consolation is that I was too disgusting to be violated. Except that Tatyana's beast would probably violate a corpse, and James Kelly, too."

"Nell." She started to put her hands on my shoulders again, but lifted them away as if remembering to avoid a hot skillet. "Nell, if you had been ravaged, you would have felt great pain for some time. There would have been blood. Was there?"

I let out a long breath. "No. I ached and was bruised all over, but not that."

"Then you needn't worry about what you don't remember happening. Ever." She eyed me cautiously in the mirror, sideways. "And . . . once in Paris, what about the Rue de la Paix?"

"What about it?"

"Could we not find time for a small expedition to *Maison Worth*, do you think? As long as we are out and about anyway? Shall we go there, too?"

I understood that it was the will to make the journey, not the destination, the pretext.

"We shall!" I answered.

She lightly pressed her cheek against mine in the mirror. "We shall do astounding things."

51.

The Disposition

~∞∞~

In person 'Nellie Bly' is slender, quick in her
movements, a brunette with a bright, coquettish face.
Animated in conversation and quick in repartée, she is
quite a favorite among the gentlemen.
—*THE SOCIAL MIRROR*, 1885

We gathered at the library table that evening for what
amounted to a picnic. Godfrey and Irene had brought bread
and stew and cold cuts of meat and cheese from the castle
kitchen. Sherlock Holmes, still wearing the robustly youthful Gypsy guise that seemed so at odds with his fussy metropolitan self, complimented the absent Tatyana's wine collection
while importing two bottles of dusty but apparently impeccable vintage. I suspected that a postprandial pipe was inevitable, and that I
should not have the courage to object, since the man had saved all
our lives, at least partially.

Pink wore a new garment to me: a checked coatdress of most
modest and practical design; in fact, very like the one I'd had to
destroy after my dreadful journey.

It gave me a turn, as if seeing her in my stead, and I can't say I much liked the reminder of that gown and those circumstances.

I pulled the tiny silver notebook and pencil from my chatelaine and laid them on the table.

"Nell, no!" Irene exclaimed, pausing in constructing a roast beef and bleu cheese sandwich. "Don't tell me that you've managed to take notes of your ordeal?"

"I had to write very small, with many abbreviations, and will no doubt need a magnifying glass to decipher it all, but, yes, I did."

The dwarf who had served Tatyana made himself busy picking up napkins that had slipped to the floor and offered to pour the wine, but Mr. Holmes commandeered that role.

He was also apparently in charge of the disposition of our prisoners, for he sat down, demolished a chicken sandwich, then dusted his hands of such details of eating on his dinner napkin and began.

"The poor misled fools who provided the congregation here are best left to what they can make of their lives. It is to be hoped that lacking a leader and the resources for such private meetings they will regain their senses."

"Surely some more restorative action could be taken, Mr. Holmes." Bram Stoker began doubtfully.

"Perhaps, but who would take it? Would Mrs. Norton's Krafft-Ebing care to come here to the village and study mass hysteria? I doubt it."

"He is not *my* Krafft-Ebing, Mr. Holmes," Irene objected mildly.

The uncloaked Gypsy waved an elegantly dismissive hand quite incongruous with the role. "He will forever be so in my estimation, Madam. I am not sure what I owe you for introducing me to such a depraved work, but I am sure to find it useful in my future endeavors.

"The priest Lupescu will certainly be subjected to village justice, and perhaps the discipline of his fellow churchmen, although I doubt the full extent of the crimes here will travel much beyond the village.

"No. Our real problem is that the nearest telegraph office is in Oradea, some two days' travel distant."

"That is indeed a problem, Mr. Holmes," Pink said. "I am in desperate need of a telegraph office."

"That is something else that requires discussion, Miss Pink," he said. "Later."

His use of the diminutive shocked me. I sensed a grudging respect for her that I found quite unearned. Often she acted as imbecilic as her name, in my opinion, but perhaps that was youth and being American.

Mr. Holmes went on. "Our immediate and most pressing problem . . . ah, Stanhope. Have a seat. You may be just the answer to our discussion."

It was hardly a "discussion," but I didn't dare object or look up as I heard Quentin pull out one of the heavy chairs and sensed him settling at the only vacant spot, between Bram Stoker and "Miss Pink."

"You are just the man to ride to Oradea and set matters in motion," Mr. Holmes said. "We need a small military detail from Bohemia to convey our prisoners to Prague. The various foreign offices concerned will no doubt decide on some way to handle this difficult affair."

"What is 'this difficult affair?' " I asked without looking up from my notes.

"The difficulty is how these disparate individuals so deeply involved in so many heinous crimes in so many countries are to be dealt with. I refer to Madam Tatyana, of unknown surname. To Colonel Sebastian Moran, a retired British Army officer and renowned heavy-game hunter and London club man, but the second most dangerous man in London, for all that, and the most dangerous man in Europe, with the exception of Tatyana's trained bear. And to this . . . Medved, who is, of course, responsible for the Whitechapel murders attributed to Jack the Ripper and the similar murders in Paris and Prague."

"That . . . animal! I do not believe it."

"You honor him, Miss Huxleigh, by your terminology. Yes, he is undoubtedly the Ripper. I suspect that he does not even remember the crimes, however; we ourselves witnessed his immense capacity for drink. I am convinced that after serving as . . . ringleader at these secret rituals that play such sadistic variations on the carnal and the religious that even Baron von Krafft-Ebing would be confounded by them, and him, this Medved stumbled into the streets in a drunken state and continued to offer up sacrifices to the knife, only these were not willing participants."

"I cannot believe it! No women would let such a drunken, filthy creature near them."

"That is indeed a mystery to me as well, but if you had spent as much time as I have on Whitechapel street corners you would see that a great many poor women already suffer such unappetizing specimens. And remember that the women, too, are usually drunk."

"Even so," I said with a shudder, then felt Quentin's gaze upon me and spoke no more.

"And then there is Kelly," Mr. Holmes went on, "who has already been judged mad and escaped detention once. Each of these persons must be dealt with as best befits their crimes and individual backgrounds. And absolutely none of it must be made public."

Shocked silence reigned at the table as Mr. Holmes sipped his wine and nodded satisfaction.

"Now, see here, Mr. Holmes," came Pink's clear and rising inflections. " 'None of it must be made public.' That's my job, to make things public, and I did not expose myself to so much misery and danger to return home and let Bessie Bramble lord it over me with her latest sensational story."

"If you would persist in your notion to publicize these lamentable events, involving as they do interests of the ruling families of England and Bohemia, not to mention the French and Russian governments and Germany as well, you would discover that America is not so isolated from Europe as you think. It would mean your position, and still you would be silenced, or worse, ridiculed as a lying fraud."

"America doesn't let the Old World dictate to her."

"In the larger sense, no. But there are delicate issues always between countries, and your government would find it much to its best interests to be discreet rather than add to the reputation of Nellie Bly."

"Irene?" she appealed.

"I have not made up my mind," Irene answered, "but I don't know how you could possibly describe the actions of such a distorted cult in the public print. When you write of fallen women, the world in general has a notion of what their state is, and why. This cult is, quite simply, beyond belief, and you might consider your future reputation very seriously before you commit to unmasking what the world really doesn't want to hear about."

"Like modern slavery," Quentin added in rather melancholy tones. "England and America point to exact dates when they eliminated such evils. It still exists on as large a scale as before in other parts of the world. There are some things that no civilized nation wants to know, or its people to know."

"But this is a story of a lifetime! Not only Jack the Ripper, the most notorious fiend on the planet, but a whole set of people doing even more fiendish things. I cannot let it go unnoted."

Holmes sighed deeply over his fisted hands. "I would hate, Miss Bly, to have to go searching for you, or your remains, because our international friends had decided you were a person as dangerous to their political stability as Tatyana and Medved."

"They would go that far?" Pink glanced at Quentin, which allowed me to take the slightest peek.

He looked quite all right, but he kept his eyes on the tabletop.

"Holmes is right. This has become a political matter, and with the Russian involvement Tatyana's presence implies, it is too volatile to entrust to the public. Better that Jack the Ripper go unidentified through eternity than that such a scandal shake so many governments. There is the matter of emigration and the volatile state of native populations over that issue. This cult that drew so many of so many nations into its bloody toils would cause riots in the streets, not to mention stir up the always simmering anti-Semitism. The anarchists and socialists would leap upon the issue. There could be chaos."

Pink sat back, pouting and not bothering to hide it. "It is the story of the century."

"Perhaps," Godfrey said, "but this century will end in eleven years. Perhaps you can find a more uplifting subject that looks forward rather than back, not this last spasm of a remnant of ancient barbarism."

Bram Stoker nodded his agreement. "I love to study all the arcane practices of the past, but I write fiction. I don't believe my own stories, Miss Pink, and I doubt anyone will believe the truth from you on this matter. As well announce to the world that you have discovered an ancient nest of surviving vampires!"

That made a smile quirk her lips, and then she looked up, her eyes narrowed. "You are right, Mr. Norton, perhaps there is another story for me. I need a spectacular 'stunt,' that's for sure. My sister journalists never rest. In fact, I have just had a terrific idea, but I may need your help, my dear Quentin."

She glanced sideways at him, a dimple tucked into the corner of her smile.

"If it does not involve deranged religious cultists, I am your man, my dear Pink."

"Done!" she said, glancing around the table. "And if I need a favor from any of you, I expect to get it for being an unnatural reporter and keeping my lips sealed. That is a most uncomfortable state for me."

I, meanwhile, was writing down the exchange in script so tiny a mouse could hardly read it: *I may need your help, my dear Quentin. I am your man, my dear Pink.* My pencil point broke off. I stared at the much too large blot of a gigantic period.

I could feel my cheeks flaming. While I was bouncing around railyards in a box, *they* had been traveling together.

I heard a chair's legs scrape back from the table, but did not look up at the sound.

"If I am your only Mercury," Quentin said, "I will commandeer a horse with wings. And I'll contact the Rothschilds in Paris as well as the Foreign Office in London, to make sure the local satraps know that the mightiest of Europe and England support our needs."

"My name," said Sherlock Holmes, "will be your password with all parties but the Rothschilds and the King of Bohemia. There you may use Mrs. Norton's."

"Good. The sooner I'm gone the faster you will have help in keeping this monstrous crew confined. Be wary, and good-bye."

I managed to breathe deep and look up. Quentin was nodding farewell to everyone around the table. Our glances crossed and held for a brief moment.

"Godspeed," I mouthed, but no sound came out, and I fear he turned away before he could even see my lips move.

I sensed a motion at my right. Godfrey was looking at me with the same steadfast expression as when he had vowed that either he and I would escape the peril together or neither would. He put his hand out, as he had then, and I put my hand in his.

I do not know what he had been told, or how much he knew of what had passed between Quentin and myself, but I knew that Godfrey at least would never desert me.

52.

The Inquisition

⌇

Sin, if sin lurks in you... sin, then you will repent and drive evil from you. So long as you bear sin secretly within you... you will remain a hypocrite and hateful to the Lord. The filth must be expelled.

—MEDVED ADDRESSING HIS CONGREGATION

 "It is time," Sherlock Holmes said after Quentin had left, "to talk of many things with our captives. I suggest a minimum of inquisitors. Myself and perhaps Mrs. Norton."

I bridled at that "perhaps," although I did not much like the idea of Irene facing Tatyana again, an enemy as hateful and capable of untold violence as any human I had heard of, alive or dead. She was indeed a Messalina for our modern times.

Godfrey stirred beside me, expressing the same reluctance.

"Why not me?" Pink demanded. "I promise not to print a word of it."

"It should be Nell," Irene said, surprising everyone, including me. "She has suffered most at their hands, and, besides, she can take notes. For our private use only, of course."

"There is no point in us interviewing Medved," Holmes said,

"although the foreign office has people who can speak his language. I wish to interrogate Moran myself, with an armed Mr. Stoker and Mr. Norton for company. He is a fierce old warrior and would attack a pride of lions if necessary. I don't wish to betray my identity to the fellow, so will masquerade as Mr. Stanhope masquerading as a Gypsy."

"Colonel Moran has seen Quentin on more than one occasion," I pointed out. "He fought him to the death. Do you really think you can mislead such a canny opponent into believing you are Quentin?"

"I know Quentin Stanhope stands as inimitable in your eyes, Miss Huxleigh, but the foreign office employs dozens of spies who don native dress and operate under cover in foreign climes. I need not be the particular man, simply one of his ilk. And I need not explain myself to Colonel Sebastian Moran."

"But ladies first," he said, turning to Irene. "Are you ready to confront your worst enemy?"

"Nell?" she asked me in turn.

I nodded and stood. Across the table, Pink also stood and held something out to me.

I gazed on it without comprehension.

"My notebook. It is much larger than yours, and I suspect there is no need to conceal the notetaking from Tatyana."

"No," Mr. Holmes agreed. "It may unnerve her, but I doubt the Black Hole of Calcutta would unnerve that woman. Speaking of which, I wish we had such a secure cell to keep her in."

"Do report back," Bram Stoker called after us as we left the room.

Poor man. It must have killed him to have the last threads of this gruesome story unwound out of his presence.

We climbed the endless stairs and entered a wing of the castle I had never seen, though it was much like the one that Godfrey and I had called home for two weeks.

We needed candlesticks to navigate halls furnished with moth-eaten carpets and furniture whose aged joints were so dry they had begun to collapse at the legs and arms, rather like arthritic old people.

Pairs of grim men in peasant dress stood guard on either side of a series of barred doors.

"We learned from your adventures, Miss Huxleigh," Mr. Holmes informed me, "and chose rooms where time had not knocked out all the window glass."

I felt a flutter of appreciation most alien to me. Imagine! My exploits were daring enough to serve as a warning when incarcerating others. It was not an achievement to benefit all mankind, but it was certainly rewarding to hear Mr. Sherlock Holmes admit that something I had done had caused him to use more caution.

At the door he paused. "I did not ask you, Mrs. Norton, if you wished to be present at this interview. I merely assumed it."

"You assumed quite rightly, Mr. Holmes. I had warned this woman before against meddling with me and mine, and you saw how little she regarded that warning in the exquisite trinket with which she anonymously gifted me at the Bohemian National Theater."

"Indeed," he said with a bow that was pure London, "as vicious an assassin's trick as it has ever been my privilege to disarm. We will use no names within. I wish to hide my identity from this woman so long as allowable, to eternity if possible."

"Why?" Irene asked.

"She is one of those very few persons who seem born solely to cause misery in the world. Only death will quiet her mischief. If she lives and goes free to do harm again, I wish to have the advantage in pursuing her, that is all."

"You are saying that me and mine are in permanent danger from this creature?"

"Of course you are, as I am from a certain obscure mathematician who happens to be the mastermind behind all the organized evil done in London. I warned you time and again against meddling in criminal matters. This is the price you pay, as do all who know you."

Irene nodded, not so much in agreement as to hasten the culmination of our quest.

"There are certain facts and theories that I wish to test with Madam Tatyana," Mr. Holmes said. "You will let me satisfy myself on these scores, as well as learn something of the scheme she had set in motion, before you address your personal concerns."

"Of course," Irene agreed. "I was far too engaged in working to find my nearest and dearest to investigate anything else and, in fact, relied upon you to attend to that matter."

"Did you? I live only to serve," he responded with another ironic bow and nodded to a guard, who lifted the huge bar so we all might pass into the room.

It was like entering the lion's cage at the zoological gardens.

One first needed to know where the beast lay before taking in the scenery.

The chamber was large enough and filled with enough of the same fustian furnishings of my own room that at first glance it was hard to pierce the shadows and spy a person in residence.

For a moment there was the sinking feeling of certain escape. Yet the window glass winked back at me whole and enormously old and thick.

We three remained by the door, and I for one had mixed feelings when I heard the heavy latch fall into place again behind us. Was Tatyana locked in, or were we locked in *with* her?

I examined the bed's heavy hangings and the lumps under the coverlet, knowing my own device of hiding the rope there.

Mr. Holmes was taking a methodical inventory of the room from right to left.

Irene looked thoughtful for a moment, and then looked up.

I followed her gaze, and gasped.

The creature was crouched under the high ceiling like a spider in a corner! I cannot say what a turn it gave me to see a human being in such a position. It was an unearthly sight, and the evil expression on her face did nothing to allay my fear.

"We shall have to alert the guards to her climbing feats," Mr.

Holmes said under his breath. "She went from chair to paneling to candle sconce to ornamental plaster work. Madam," he said in a ringing tone, "will you come down to talk?"

"For a mute fool you certainly have acquired a voice, and a London accent," she answered.

"Many mute fools are more than they seem. Will you come down?" He stepped forward as though to assist her.

In that moment she leaped, or fell.

I gasped again, much distressed by my weakness.

It was an amazing descent, as though managed by someone half monkey, half cat. She swung for a split second from the candle sconce, fell twisting to land briefly on the back of a tall chair and then tumbled to the floor, rising instantly to her feet.

"Brava," said Irene, clapping softly. "The Russian Ballet teaches its company to defy gravity, among other things."

Tatyana then took a deep swanlike bow, her forehead nearly touching the tattered carpet before she stood again at her full regal height.

"How did you corrupt my Gypsies?" she asked, addressing no one of us.

"As you did," Irene answered. "With golden coins, only more of them."

"Ah, your personal fortune has been depleted, how sad."

I watched Irene hold her tongue from answering, but knew what that answer was as if I had heard it pronounced aloud: Irene's personal fortune was not invested in coins. It would not do to confirm that Tatyana's weapons of choice were so effective, however.

"And how is the admirable Godfrey?" Tatyana inquired.

Sherlock Holmes intervened, whether to stop her taunts of Irene and myself or simply because he was impatient to address the specifics of the crime, I cannot say. Given his cold-blooded nature, I would choose a thirst for affirmation of his deductions.

"I wish to confirm certain opinions about this cult and your role in it, and this Medved individual's as well."

"Do you always get what you wish, Englishman in Gypsy guise? Is it you, Cobra?"

He was silent.

"I have not seen you in your own semblance for some years. Is that why you retain that absurd persona? Your light eyes give you away."

"They also gave away Medved."

"Yes, aren't they most extraordinary? That a peasant should be gifted with such heavenly eyes . . . perhaps that is why he decided he had a religious vocation. I think he has misjudged his gifts, but who am I to dissuade an unlettered genius from following his natural bent?"

"So you followed him, Madam, even as you led him first to London and then to Prague and Paris. Why there?"

"Because that is where his flock was flocking." She laughed with pleasure at the very idea, and turned to Irene. "Have I not read of your figure of freedom in New York harbor, the Statue of Liberty sent by the French, those masters of liberty, fraternity, and equality, but the slaves of political havoc? What does that make America?"

"'A teeming shore,' says the poem." I quoted the striking patriotic phrase Pink had declaimed about the statue.

Irene smiled serenely. "A refuge for the 'wretched refuse' of Europe's shore." To hear her intone "wretched refuse" was to hear the term stripped of all opprobrium and elevated to an honored title. "The point is that one nation's exiles are another nation's gift. Nations, like every other human institution, always exile the different, the original, the independent."

"And so with my adorable Medved."

I nearly gagged at her adjective.

"Poor peasant lad. At an early age he showed signs of unusual talents, stopping the blood of hemorrhaging animals, for instance. He had a peculiar rapport with horses, could calm them by speaking to them. He had an uncanny instinct for detecting thieves and more than once pointed out the culprit to the entire village."

"This was in Siberia, Madam?" Sherlock Holmes inquired.

"I thought your knowledge was all of hot climes like Afghanistan and India. What do you know of Siberia?"

"I know that is where the peasants brew vodka in pottery jars and seal them with wax, requiring them to be struck against a tree or cavern wall to be opened, just like the bottles found at the site of cult rituals in Paris and Prague. And London."

I saw Irene's face tense. This was the first she or I had heard that these same vile ceremonies had been held in London, too. I saw her eyes fly to Sherlock Holmes. She was itching to know what he had learned in Whitechapel.

"How," he was asking Tatyana, "did you manage to supply Medved and his followers with Siberian-brewed vodka in the major cities of western Europe and the capital of the British Isles?"

"It was cumbersome and it was expensive, but nothing was too good to inspire my Medved."

"He is your protegé then?" Irene asked.

"*Agh!* You understand nothing! A protegé would follow in my footsteps. Medved as a dancer in the Russian ballet . . . how amusing. 'Medved' means 'bear,' you know, in Russian. It is my pet name for him. He will be known better by his real name, Grigorii Efimovich."

"Gregory, son of Efim." Irene said promptly.

"Ah, you know the Russian usage. Is he not fascinating? Not yet twenty-five and look at all he has accomplished? He has sent several great capitol cities to their knees."

I soberly contemplated that he was barely older than Pink.

"Or perhaps he is only twenty," she went on with a shrug. "They hardly know the year of their own birth, these incredibly hardy peasants. The year of the ice storm. Whatever sticks in human memory. I mentioned his talents, healing and also a certain clairvoyance. He recognizes character at first sight. Some call it second sight. But he is young and has other talents as interesting. By the age of fifteen, he drinks like a sperm whale. He fights like a wolf. He mates like a mink. Perhaps I should say sable."

"If he is such a beast," Irene said calmly, as though beastliness were a fine civilized subject for discussion, "and a foreign beast at that, who barely speaks a word of English, or French, or Bohemian, how was he able to approach the prostitutes of each city? As some have pointed out, he is drunken, dirty, crude. Even streetwalkers would be cautious of such a figure."

Tatyana laughed. And laughed. And laughed. It was a high-pitched, hooting cackle one would expect from a witch, not a fairly young woman, but it seemed oddly natural coming from her. She threw back her supernaturally long throat (reminding me of a serpent) and indulged in laughter the way I guessed some would indulge in liquor.

"Oh, my poor, foolish, ordinary, blind women! You and your prim little secretary there! He has this last and most wondrous gift, my Medved. He is irresistible to women."

"Not I," I said. "I repulsed him."

"Perhaps you did," she said with a denigrating look I much resented, as if she eyed me up and down and inside and out and found me wanting. Me, a decent woman!

"But I tell you," she said, stalking toward me with one foot crossed in front of the other, reminding me of the few times I had seen Sarah Bernhardt on the stage playing some *femme fatale* or other. "I tell you, *Miss* Huxleigh, that Medved, drunk as any lord in England and only half as drunk as a Siberian peasant in top form, can approach a queen or a Gypsy fortune-teller or a prostitute or a girl-child of twelve, and they will fall to him, succumb to him, like overripe fruit to a windstorm."

She was face-to-face with me before anyone could stop her. I held my ground. "Name one," I said.

"One what?"

"One queen he has seduced."

"Not yet. But there will be!"

"If he lives that long," Sherlock Holmes put in. "Step back, Madam, or I shall be forced to make you."

She spun to face him.

"You think you can, Cobra? Or are you someone else? I am not as gifted as Medved at sensing character. I cannot quite tell. I bow to your command."

And she fluttered back as lightly as a firefly, like a ballerina *en pointe*, a mocking, infinitely graceful figure of the gaslit stage.

"I should tell you," Mr. Holmes continued, "that I have had some little time to investigate these brutal rituals of yours and Medved's. Like everything evil under the sun, they are not without precedent. Nothing criminal ever is, in my experience.

"From the first I detected a similarity to the rites of the flagellants, a religious sect that crops up in many lands and that is as old as Greece. There is a thread in mankind that cannot unweave pain from pleasure, or that seeks to punish pleasure with pain. To this we owe many historic atrocities. I had never heard of the Siberian variety until your protegé's activities drew my attention in Paris. You were discreet in London, even having Colonel Moran find and procure the ritual sites. In Paris Medved went mad. I have a theory—"

"A theory! In the face of primitive nature? That is why the weaklings of the West will never resist the power of the East. If you have researched my darling boy's homeland, you must know that it has spawned dozens of brutal halfling children from the forcible rape of paganism by Christianity, sects, if you will, that the Orthodox church persecutes. His people retreated to caves and cellars and underground chapels in the icy climate, to fires and communal celebration . . . and then communal copulation and from there it was but a half-step to communal blood sacrifice. Today, in this day and age, it is still happening, this impulse that will not be quenched, that civilized men cannot explain and proper women cannot resist. It is the spirit of primitive man that will not be denied. Torture. Whipping. Slavery. Rape. Castration. Killing. It is in the blood and the blood demands to shed and be shed. The blood is the life."

Mr. Holmes cut through her gruesome rhetoric to pluck out the fact that answered his question. "So Paris, with its subterranean catacombs and cellars and sewers, was the very evocation of Siberia.

What of the religious elements, the graffiti invoking the Jews?"

"The Jews! That was my idea. They are leaving Russia like rats and no more welcome anywhere else. How easy to point the finger at them. And the Christian signs and symbols? They *are* Christian, these magnificent Siberian savages. Devoutly so, though twisted like ancient olive trees into such a divine and original obscenity of the Christian doctrine.

"Do you know, did you learn in your 'investigations' that a Siberian peasant, hearing of an official census, took it as the arrival of the anti-Christ. He buried mother, wife, and children alive, inspiring his village to beseech his services for their own families, killing twenty before he succumbed to suicide.

"Some men did likewise to their own families, counting on their leader to slit their throats as the *coup de grace*. Wherever there are sheep to be led, leaders will rise up to slaughter them. Religion is the distraction of the people from their poverty. Some peculiarities of faith in Siberia are less violent but no less odd. Some sects worship the sky through a hole in the roof, others a tree or a river, but most often there is a strain of such astounding excess, a combination of the licentious and the puritanical. The *Khlysty* date back at least two centuries and engendered, though that may be the wrong word in this case, the *skopstys*, who believed that the Disciples were castrated and that the Holy Spirit comes by fire, not the water of Baptism. That explains some of the self-torture and mutilation their rituals involve."

"They are not devil worshipers?" I couldn't help asking.

"Not at all. Like so many Christians, they claim their rituals offer the one and only true path. They seek spiritual purity. However, such acts of devotion as their religion demands requires the celebrants to be dulled by drink to their own pain. So they commit drunkenness in the search for holiness. They also manage, by a convoluted form of thinking that would do a politician proud, to conclude that the path to abstinence is overindulgence. To be pure one must first be impure. Especially their leaders are allowed every imaginable excess.

"My dear Medved calls it using sin to drive out sin."

Irene stared at her. "You have no religion but yourself. You thrive on chaos. International. Political. Religious. Personal. Why?"

"The blood is the life," she answered coldly. "People who make history are not afraid to shed it."

"She is right in this much," Sherlock Holmes commented when we stood outside the chamber that held Tatyana and far down the hall from the guards. "It would be better if the authorities executed her and this young Russian at once."

"Without trial?" Irene did not so much ask, as express disgust.

"I suppose that my observation is a heresy the *Khlystys* with their illogical goal of finding purity by committing sin would endorse: sometimes justice is best served by circumventing justice. But never fear, this region boasts enough obscure but impregnable fortresses to contain and hide Napoleon and his legions for decades. These two misbegotten souls will disappear into the bowels of such a place, never to be heard from again."

"And you are convinced that Medved—Grigorii—is Jack the Ripper?"

"He is by far the most likely candidate. I found sites in Whitechapel where cult members had met, littered with the same wax from the vodka bottles and cork from ordinary wine bottles, which the non-Russian of the cultists drank instead. Your companions have witnessed his incredible capacity for drink. In such a state, a man like him could do anything."

"I now believe," I put in, "that the crazed figure who came rushing toward me in the Paris panorama building just before I succumbed to the chloroform was not Kelly, but Medved. He was . . . pawing at the buttons on my bodice," I admitted with both shame and disgust.

"That is indeed a damning link," Irene said. "What of James Kelly?" she asked Mr. Holmes.

"It's possible he committed a murder or two along the way in imitation of his Master, but not in London. His swift departure after Mary Jane Kelly's slaughter was no doubt a vain attempt to catch up with the absconding Tatyana and Medved. Even she must have realized after that atrocity that things had gone too far. Certainly they could not count on the cover provided by the tangled byways of Whitechapel any longer."

"It does make sense," I said, speaking mostly to Irene. "When you consider the Chi-Rhos scratched into the meeting sites and the fact that all the murders we know of form a Chi-Rho upon the map of each particular city."

"Chi-Rho?" Mr. Holmes echoed me, sounding alarmed. "What nonsense is this?"

"Mere speculation," Irene answered quite disingenuously. "The Chi-Rho is the Greek symbol for Christ: an 'X' intersected by a figure that resembles the English letter 'P.' We noticed a certain pattern to the killings that duplicated the extreme points of the Chi-Rho on the maps of Whitechapel, Paris, and Prague."

"I must have copies of those maps . . . and Madam Tatyana's yellow book that she was writing in when we confronted her."

"Oh, that. I gave it to Quentin, since he will be reaching civilization before us."

"Gave it to Stanhope! I must read it."

"It is written in Russian."

"I will have it translated."

"I was planning on doing that. It does, after all, document matters that intimately affect me and mine."

"We will certainly get no more out of Madam Tatyana than she chooses to tell us, and Medved is too uneducated to provide any enlightenment except on the nature of his delusions. I must see that diary."

"Perhaps I can provide you with a copy of the translation."

A Gypsy scowl is fearsome to see when it is powered by an

irritated Englishman. "You had better do so. And I will not leave without copies of the maps Miss Huxleigh mentioned. This theory of yours sounds far-fetched, but I am willing to review it and give my opinion of its relevance."

Irene laughed. "A fair exchange. Your professional opinion of a series of maps that are moot now, as they too must be buried to history forever, and a translation of Sable's record of Grigorii's religious mania. I suspect the maps will be much easier reading than the contents of that yellow book." Irene glanced at me. "And the mouse-size scribblings in Nell's miniature chatelaine notebook. You shall have to copy it all out in normal size."

"I will," I said, rather glumly.

Not only was Quentin galloping away from me, but I did not know when, or if, I would ever see him again, or dare to.

Meanwhile, from the discussion here, it was all too obvious that we three would meet again in not too long a time to exchange artifacts and opinions on a case of such excess and cruelty that I could wish to fall asleep and awake having forgotten every speck of it.

It was indeed a cruel world when Quentin was a mystery I might never see again or solve, and Mr. Sherlock Holmes had become a reluctant associate we would have occasion to see again all too soon.

And then I recalled the most vivid memory among all the mayhem I had so reluctantly witnessed, events that had changed me forever.

It was Irene's marvelous voice lifted a capella in that murderous cavern singing the simple old hymn of conversion written by a former slave trader, "Amazing Grace."

I could only hope that some amazing grace would shed its light on me as time led us all far from our descent into the hell to be found in twisted hearts and minds.

Afterword

❧

*In this drink-sodden, low-class intrigue there were reefs
that Rasputin did not see.... For Europe, Rasputin was
an anecdote, not a fact. For us, however, he was not only
a fact. He was an epoch.*
—ALEXANDER YABLONSKY IN ONE OF RASPUTIN'S 1916

OBITUARIES

At last my painstaking piecework is done, and I can quote freely from Tatyana's yellow casebook without fear of betraying the astounding truth, for now it lies open to be read, and perhaps debated, by the entire world.

The identity of Medved, the Russian word for "bear" often used as an affectionate term, a shuddersome notion in this instance, must be plain to even the most casual student of history.

He is none other than the young Rasputin: Grigorii Efimovich Rasputin. This is the so-called "mad monk" whose influence on the last Czar and Empress of Russia, Nicholas and Alexandra, played a major part in their downfall and deaths.

In twenty-some years from the events of this narrative, Rasputin's remarkable and sinister charisma will make him a confidant of the imperial couple because of his apparent ability to arrest the hemophilia that afflicts the young royal heir. He will be the most notorious and powerful man in Russia and a key figure in the violent end of Czarist Russia and the Russian Revolution, that culminating and last great act of a dramatic series that began with the American and French revolutions in the late eighteenth century. That revolution will begin almost eighty years of Soviet socialist rule and the Cold War of the twentieth century.

The Rasputin of his glory days in St. Petersburg will be an older and more notorious man but no wiser in some matters. His prodigious appetite for liquor and women will remain. He will be able to walk up to aristocratic ladies in broad daylight and public company and begin undressing them. He will persuade women to sleep with him to test his chastity and theirs with predictable results: failure. The enormous size of his manhood will become a matter of such public knowledge that when challenged while drunk and disorderly on the streets, he will unbutton his fly and identify himself by his member. He will consort with gypsies and lose himself in their music, dancing to unconsciousness. His powers as well will deepen with the years, both the strange potency of his personality and his peasant constitutional stamina that made it almost impossible for his assassins to kill him even by a combination of poison, shooting, stabbing, and drowning in December of 1916.

Regard the oxymoron: Holy Devil. To anyone who knows Rasputin's unique history that epithet will apply only to him. In his own lifetime an enemy had already titled a book about him just that. He was not a monk, but he followed Christian religious practice and also drew on the more primitive powers of the shaman, for the people of his remote Siberian homeland are not so different from the native American Indians who occupied the frigid lands across the Bering Strait where Russia and Alaska almost touch fingers through the chain of icy islands that both separate and connect them. The Christianity that mixed uneasily with the harsh Siberian society in which captured thieves were beaten to the point of death provoked many strange growths.

No doubt Tatyana detected Rasputin's political usefulness and encouraged his excesses, perhaps to give her power over him in later years. Also, it is obvious, she envied his capacity for evil in the name of good. From reading the record of her association with the young Rasputin, like Krafft-Ebing she hoped to learn something of mankind from the acts of its most aberrant members. Unlike Krafft-Ebing, she was not a scientist and a scholar, but a master manipulator and a voyeur.

She herself is worthy of intense psychological study, but the age of Freud had not yet taken hold and what was done with her was what had been done with a "Lady Dracula" from a house related to Vlad Tepes line. Elizabeth Bathory in the sixteenth century, one of history's most prolific sadistic serial killers, numbering perhaps six hundred-some victims in her search for young girls' blood to keep her young, was locked away from the world forever, until she died.

Some attribute Bram Stoker's inspiration for Count Dracula, the quintessential vampire in Stoker's appropriately immortal novel, *Dracula*, which he began writing in the year following these events and published in 1897, to the incarnadine careers of Vlad and Elizabeth. The evidence, however, points to only a glancing acquaintance with their existence. It is far more likely that the trials he and his associates experienced during the period related here influenced his imagination and the novel that would debut eight years later. Some have found similarities between *Dracula* and *Macbeth*: the bloody content and brooding land and castle of both works, sleepwalking scenes, and such parallels as *Macbeth*'s three witches with Count Dracula's three brides.

Some also compare Stoker's novel to another published in 1894, George du Maurier's *Trilby*, which introduced the Jewish mesmerist, Svengali, who hypnotized the eponymous tone-deaf heroine into vocal feats. In *Trilby* as in *Dracula*, several Englishmen (and one American) all in love with the same woman (Trilby or Lucy) fight to save her from a predatory foreign male.

In fiction, Dracula is far the more sinister figure than Svengali, but in real life, Gregorii Efimovich Rasputin is the king of predatory foreign males in both the intimate and public arenas. He obviously did not stay incarcerated, though when he may have escaped back to Siberia to resume his grotesque spiritual and political journey to international notoriety is impossible to know.

Did Tatyana escape with him? Is she known to history after that at all, or by another name? That is a mystery that even Sherlock Holmes may not have been able to solve.

One thing is certain: Colonel Sebastian Moran was at large and armed again with an air rifle in 1894 when he attempted to as-sas0sinate Sherlock Holmes.

Fiona Witherspoon, Ph.D., A.I.A.*
November 5, 2001

*Advocates of Irene Adler

Castle Rouge

Reader's Guide

"Perhaps it has taken until the end of this century for an author like Douglas to be able to imagine a female protagonist who could be called 'the' woman by Sherlock Holmes."

—GROUNDS FOR MURDER, 1991

Reader's Guide

To encourage the reading and discussion of Carole Nelson Douglas's acclaimed novels examining the Victorian world from the viewpoint of one of the most mysterious women in literature, the following descriptions and discussion topics are offered. The author interview, biography, and bibliography will aid discussion as well.

Set in 1880–1890 London, Paris, Prague, and Monaco, the Irene Adler novels reinvent the only woman to have outwitted Sherlock Holmes as the complex and compelling protagonist of her own stories. Douglas's portrayal of "this remarkable heroine and her keen perspective on the male society in which she must make her independent way," noted the *New York Times*, recasts her "not as a loose-living adventuress but a woman ahead of her time." In Douglas's hands, the fascinating but sketchy American prima donna from "A Scandal in Bohemia" becomes an aspiring opera singer moonlighting as a private inquiry agent. When events force her from the stage into the art of detection, Adler's exploits rival those of Sherlock Holmes himself as she crosses paths and swords with the day's leading creative and political figures while sleuthing among the Bad and the Beautiful of Belle Epoque Europe.

Critics praise the novels' rich period detail, numerous historical characters, original perspective, wit, and "welcome window on things Victorian."

"The private and public escapades of Irene Adler Norton [are] as erratic and unexpected and brilliant as the character herself," noted *Mystery Scene* of *Another Scandal in Bohemia* (formerly *Irene's Last Waltz*), "a long and complex *jeu d'esprit*, simultaneously modeling itself on and critiquing Doylesque novels of ratiocination coupled with emotional distancing. Here is Sherlock Holmes in skirts, but as a detective with an artistic temperament and the passion to match, with the intellect to penetrate to the heart of a crime and the heart to show compassion for the intellect behind it."

About This Book

Castle Rouge, the sixth Irene Adler novel, opens in the Paris of June 1889 with Irene Adler facing two demoralizing disappearances: her husband, English barrister Godfrey Norton, has vanished into the uncharted wilds of Transylvania while on secret business in Bohemia for the Rothschild banking family. And Irene's longtime companion, Nell Huxleigh, appears to have fallen into the hands of either Jack the Ripper or a sinister cult acting with him in Paris six months after the vile Whitechapel murders. Even Sherlock Holmes, who had crossed paths with Irene and her cohorts in attempting to track the Ripper's Paris resurrection, has abruptly returned to London to reinvestigate the Whitechapel murders from a new perspective. So the usually indomitable Irene, sadly shaken, must draw on her circle of acquaintances to rescue her loved ones. Despite the proffered financial assistance of Baron de Rothschild and Bertie, Prince of Wales, Irene finds less aristocratic (if not less notorious) but more practical aid from Buffalo Bill and an Indian scout in his Wild West Show playing in Paris. Irene dragoons another American in Paris, Nellie Bly, the daredevil American girl reporter who has been passing as a courtesan named Pink while tracking the Ripper from London to Paris, into her rescue party. And then there's the famed theatrical manager, Bram Stoker, who's made a habit of hiking wild and lonely places.

How can this new and uneasy detecting alliance, its members all harboring hidden agendas of their own, retrieve Godfrey and Nell from the abyss into which they seem to have fallen? The trail will take the trackers back to Bohemia and the secrets of many-spired Prague, then eastward on to a darker land with an even darker history: the Transylvania of the legendary fifteenth-century warlord whose murderous deeds make even the abominations of Jack the Ripper pale in comparison, Vlad the Impaler.

For Discussion

⤫⤬⤫

1. Advancing historical suspects for Jack the Ripper, from British Royals to other notorious killers of the era, has become a popular fictional and nonfictional game over past decades. Rasputin's youth is shrouded in mystery, and he fits the classic serial killer profile: a boy already prone to binge drinking and blackouts becoming a man whose intense notions of religion deeply conflict with his need for sex. Why did the author develop this particular suspect given the particular direction in which she takes Irene Adler and her cohorts, far afield from the foggy London town and the Holmes Canon? How does Rasputin's candidacy alter the perception of the historical Ripper and his motivations? Although the authorities then often cited "religious mania" as a likely motive for the Ripper, why has it so seldom been used in later fiction and nonfiction explorations of the case? How does the role of religious mania in the life of James Kelly, the Englishman, both differ from and resemble the pagan/Christian sects that erupted in Rasputin's peasant Siberian culture for two centuries? Do elements of modern religious upbringing echo these eternal notions that sex is bad and that women who have

sex deserve punishment? Why must some men despise what they desire? And what has it to do with self-hatred?

2. Nell plays an entirely different part in this novel. *The Drood Review of Mystery* observed of *Chapel Noir*: "This dark tour de force proves by its verbal play and literary allusiveness that Douglas wants neither Irene nor herself underestimated in fiction. More important, she wants women fully informed about and capable of action on the mean streets of their world." Nell begins *Castle Rouge* as a helpless abductee, but proves to be more adaptable and resilient than her protective friends might suspect. Does she gain strength by being separated from her "leading lady," Irene? Her relationship to all the male characters in the series is changing in these Ripper-related novels. How and why, and is it for the better, or worse? Or both?

3. The immediate British public's reaction to the murders and mutilations in Whitechapel was: "No Englishman could have done it." What does this say about the attitudes of nineteenth-century colonial nations then busily engaged in making inroads into "dark continents" and unsettled places? Are the savageries of the Siberian wastes any less comprehensible than the atrocities of the American Indian wars? Are the Russian peasants, persecuted Jews, and itinerant Gypsies any less subject to control and eradication than the Native Americans? What would the young Rasputin have made of himself in the American West?

4. The mysterious author of the Yellow Book entries in *Chapel Noir* is revealed in this novel. Is this also another person displaced from a native culture, like the wandering Red Tomahawk and Rasputin . . . and Quentin Stanhope and Nell Huxleigh, and Irene Adler herself? If you have read *Another Scandal in Bohemia*, the previous novel to *Chapel Noir* by seven years, what foreshadowing of this person and locales and themes and events appear in the earlier novel? Has Irene Adler helped bring these disastrous eventualities upon herself? Through what weaknesses, or what strengths?

5. Bram Stoker's *Dracula* is central to this Jack the Ripper duology,

yet Dracula himself never appears in it. Although Conan Doyle flirted with the occult in his Sherlock Holmes stories, he always came down on the side of the rational explanation. Does *Castle Rouge* "flirt" with this alternate dimension of unreality, and why? What is Douglas saying about the man who imagined Dracula and his motivations? Are the fictional Dracula, the historical Vlad the Impaler, and Jack the Ripper brothers under the skin?

6. Douglas has said she likes to work on the "large canvas" of series fiction. What kind of character development does that approach permit? Do you like it? Has television recommitted viewers/readers to the kind of multivolume storytelling common in the nineteenth century, or is the attention span of the twentieth century too short? Is long-term, committed reading becoming a lost art?

❧FOR DISCUSSION OF THE IRENE ADLER SERIES❧

1. Douglas mentions other authors, many of them women, who have reinvented major female characters or minor characters from classic literary or genre novels to reevaluate culture then and now. Can you think of such works in the field of fantasy or historical novels? General literature? What about the recent copyright contest over *The Wind Done Gone*, Alice Randall's reimagining of *Gone With the Wind* events and characters from the African-American slaves' viewpoints? Could the novel's important social points have been made as effectively without referencing the classic work generally familiar to most people? What other works have attained the mythic status that might make possible such socially conscious reinventions? What works would you revisit or rewrite?

2. Religion and morality are underlying issues in the novels, including the time's anti-Semitism. This is an element absent from the Holmes stories. How is this issue brought out and how do Nell's strictly conventional views affect those around her? Why does she take on a moral watchdog role yet remain both disap-

proving and fascinated by Irene's pragmatic philosophy? Why is Irene (and also most readers) so fond of her despite her limited opinions?

3. Douglas chose to blend humor with adventurous plots. Do comic characters and situations satirize the times, or soften them? Is humor a more effective form of social criticism than rhetoric? What other writers and novelists use this technique, besides George Bernard Shaw and Mark Twain?

4. The novels also present a continuing tension between New World and Old World, America and England and the Continent, artist-tradesman and aristocrat, and as well as woman and man. Which characters reflect which camps? How does the tension show itself?

5. *Chapel Noir* and *Castle Rouge* make several references to *Dracula* through the presence of Bram Stoker some six years before the novel actually was published. Stoker is also a continuing character in other Adler novels. Various literary figures appear in the Adler novels, including Oscar Wilde, and most of these historical characters knew each other. Why was this period so rich in writers who founded much modern genre fiction, like Doyle and Stoker? The late nineteenth century produced not only *Dracula* and Doyle's Holmes stories and the surviving dinosaurs of *The Lost World*, but *Trilby* and Svengali, *The Phantom of the Opera*, *The Prisoner of Zenda*, *Dr. Jekyll and Mr. Hyde*, among the earliest and most lasting works of science fiction, political intrigue, mystery, and horror. How does Douglas pay homage to this tradition in the plots, characters, and details of the Adler novels?

An Interview with Carole Nelson Douglas

❧

Q: *You were the first woman to write about the Sherlock Holmes world from the viewpoint of one of Arthur Conan Doyle's women characters, and only the second woman to write a Holmes-related novel at all. Why?*

A: Most of my fiction ideas stem from my role as social observer in my first career, journalism. One day I looked at the mystery field and realized that all post-Doyle Sherlockian novels were written by men. I had loved the stories as a child and thought it was high time for a woman to examine the subject from a female point of view.

Q: *So there was "the woman," Irene Adler, the only woman to outwit Holmes, waiting for you.*

A: She seems the most obvious candidate, but I bypassed her for that very reason to look at other women in what is called the Holmes Canon. Eventually I came back to "A Scandal in Bohemia." Rereading it, I realized that male writers had all taken Irene Adler at face value as the King of Bohemia's jilted mistress, but the story doesn't support that. As the only woman in the Canon who stirred a hint of romantic interest in the aloof Holmes, Irene Adler had to be more than this beautiful but amoral "Victorian vamp." Once I saw that I could validly interpret her as a gifted and serious performing artist, I had my protagonist.

Q: *It was that simple?*

A: It was that complex. I felt that any deeper psychological exploration of this character still had to adhere to Doyle's story, both literally and in regard to the author's own feeling toward the character. That's how I ended up having to explain that operatic impossibility, a contralto prima donna. It's been great fun justifying Doyle's error by finding operatic roles Irene could conceivably sing. My Irene Adler is as intelligent, self-sufficient, and serious about her professional and personal integrity as Sherlock Holmes, and far too independent to be anyone's mistress but her own. She also moonlights as an inquiry agent while building her performing career. In many ways they are flip sides of the same coin: her profession, music, is his hobby. His profession, detection, is her secondary career. Her adventures intertwine with Holmes's, but she is definitely her own woman in these novels.

Q: *How did Doyle feel toward the character of Irene Adler?*

A: I believe that Holmes and Watson expressed two sides of Dr. Doyle: Watson; the medical and scientific man, also the staunch upholder of British convention; Holmes, the creative and bohemian writer, fascinated by the criminal and the bizarre. Doyle wrote classic stories of horror and science fiction as well as hefty historical novels set in the age of chivalry. His mixed feelings of attraction to and fear of a liberated, artistic woman like Irene Adler led him to "kill" her as soon as he created her. Watson states she is dead at the beginning of the story that introduces her. Irene was literally too hot for Doyle as well as Holmes to handle. She also debuted (and exited) in the first Holmes-Watson story Doyle ever wrote. Perhaps Doyle wanted to establish an unattainable woman to excuse Holmes remaining a bachelor and aloof from matters of the heart. What he did was to create a fascinatingly unrealized character for generations of readers.

Q: *Do your protagonists represent a split personality as well?*

A: Yes, one even more sociologically interesting than the Holmes-Watson split because it embodies the evolving roles of women in the late nineteenth century. As a larger-than-life heroine, Irene is "up to anything." Her biographer, Penelope "Nell" Huxleigh, however, is the very model of traditional Victorian womanhood. Together they provide a seriocomic point-counterpoint on women's restricted roles then and now. Narrator Nell is the character who "grows" most during the series as the unconventional Irene forces her to see herself and her times in a broader perspective. This is something women writers have been doing the past two decades: revisiting classic literary terrains and bringing the sketchy women characters into full-bodied prominence.

Q: *What of "the husband," Godfrey Norton?*

A: In my novels, Irene's husband, Godfrey Norton, is more than the "tall, dark, and dashing barrister" Doyle gave her. I made him the son of a woman wronged by England's then female-punitive divorce law, so he is a "supporting" character in every sense of the word. These novels are that rare bird in literature: female "buddy" books. Godfrey fulfills the useful, decorative, and faithful role so often played by women and wives in fiction and real life. Sherlockians anxious to unite Adler and Holmes have tried to oust Godfrey. William S. Baring-Gould even depicted him as a wife-beater in order to promote a later assignation with Holmes that produced Nero Wolfe! That is such an unbelievable violation of a strong female character's psychology. That scenario would make Irene Adler a two-time loser in her choice of men and a masochist to boot. My protagonist is a world away from that notion and a wonderful vehicle for subtle but sharp feminist comment.

Q: *Did you give her any attributes not found in the Doyle story?*

A: I gave her one of Holmes's bad habits. She smokes "little cigars." Smoking was an act of rebellion for women then. And because Doyle shows her sometimes donning male dress to go unhampered into public places, I gave her "a wicked little revolver" to carry. When Doyle put her in male disguise at the end of his story, I doubt he was thinking of the modern psychosexual ramifications of cross-dressing.

Q: *Essentially, you have changed Irene Adler from an ornamental woman to a working woman.*

A: My Irene is more a rival than a romantic interest for Holmes, yes. She is not a logical detective in the same mold as he, but is as gifted in her intuitive way. Nor is her opera-singing a convenient profession for a beauty of the day, but a passionate vocation that was taken from her by the King of Bohemia's autocratic attitude toward women, forcing her to occupy herself with detection. Although Doyle's Irene is beautiful, well dressed, and clever, my Irene demands that she be taken seriously despite these feminine attributes. Now we call it "Grrrrl power."

I like to write "against" conventions that are no longer true, or were never true. This is the thread that runs through all my fiction: my dissatisfaction with the portrayal of women in literary and popular fiction—then and even now. This begins with *Amberleigh*—my postfeminist mainstream version of the Gothic-revival popular novels of the 1960s and 1970s—and continues with Irene Adler today. I'm interested in women as survivors. Men also interest me of necessity, men strong enough to escape cultural blinders to become equal partners to strong women.

Q: *How do you research these books?*

A: From a lifetime of reading English literature and a theatrical background that educated me on the clothing, culture, customs, and speech of various historical periods. I was reading Oscar Wilde plays when I was eight years old. My mother's book club meant that I cut my teeth on Eliot, Balzac, Kipling, Poe, poetry, Greek mythology, Hawthorne, the Brontes, Dumas, and Dickens.

In doing research, I have a fortunate facility of using every nugget I find, or of finding that every little fascinating nugget works itself into the story. Perhaps that's because good journalists must be ingenious in using every fact available to make a story as complete and accurate as possible under deadline conditions. Often the smallest mustard seed of research swells into an entire tree of plot. The corpse on the dining-room table of Bram Stoker, author of *Dracula*, was too macabre to resist and spurred the entire plot of the second Adler novel, *The Adventuress* (formerly *Good Morning, Irene*). Stoker rescued a drowning man from the Thames and carried him home for revival efforts, but it was too late.

Besides using my own extensive library on this period, I've borrowed from my local library all sorts of arcane books they don't even know they have because no one ever checks them out. The Internet aids greatly with the specific fact. I've also visited London and Paris to research the books, a great hardship, but worth it. I also must visit Las Vegas periodically for my contemporary-set *Midnight Louie* mystery series. No sacrifice is too great.

Q: *You've written fantasy and science-fiction novels, why did you turn to mystery?*

A: All novels are fantasy and all novels are mystery in the largest sense. Although mystery was often an element in my early novels, when I evolved the Irene Adler idea, I considered it simply a novel. *Good Night, Mr. Holmes* was almost on the shelves before I realized it would be "categorized" as a mystery. So Irene is utterly a product of my mind and times, not of the marketplace, though I always believed that the concept was timely and necessary.

Selected Bibliography

Belford, Barbara. *Bram Stoker.* New York, NY: Alfred A. Knopf, 1996.

Brook-Shepherd, Gordon. *Uncle of Europe: The Social and Diplomatic Life of Edward VII.* New York, NY: Harcourt, Brace, Jovanovich, 1975.

Bunson, Matthew E. *Encyclopedia Sherlockiana.* New York, NY: Mac-Millan, 1994.

Coleman, Elizabeth Ann. *The Opulent Era.* New York, NY: The Brooklyn Museum, 1989.

Crow, Duncan. *The Victorian Woman.* London UK: Cox & Wyman Ltd, 1971.

De Jonge, Alex. *The Life and Times of Gregorii Rasputin.* New York, NY: Carroll & Graf, 1989.

Demetz, Peter. *Prague in Black and Gold.* New York, NY: Hill and Wang, 1997.

Doyle, Arthur Conan. The Complete Works of Sherlock Holmes. Various editions.

Du Maurier, George. *Trilby.* New York, NY: Oxford University Press, 1999.

Hibbert, Christopher. *The Royal Victorians.* New York, NY: Lippincott, 1976.

Jakubowski, Maxim and Nathan Braund. *The Mammoth Book of Jack the Ripper.* New York, NY: Carroll & Graf, 1999.

Krafft-Ebing, Richard von. *Psychopathia Sexualis.* London UK: Velvet Publications, 1997.

Kroeger, Brooke. *Nellie Bly: Daredevil, Reporter, Feminist.* New York, NY: Times Books, 1994.

Lehrer, Milton G. *Transylvania: History and Reality.* Silver Spring, MD: Bartleby Press. 1986.

Lottman, Herbert R. *The French Rothschilds.* New York, NY: Crown, 1995.

Moynahan, Brian. *Rasputin: The Saint Who Sinned.* New York, NY: Random House, 1997.

Oakley, Jane. *Rasputin: Rascal Master.* New York, NY: St. Martin's Press, 1989.

Pearson, John. *Edward the Rake.* New York, NY: Harcourt, Brace, Jovanovich, 1975.

Rasputin, Maria and Patte Barham. *Rasputin: The Man Behind the Myth.* Englewood Cliffs, NJ: Prentice-Hall, 1977.

Stoker, Bram. *Dracula.* Various editions.

Tully, James. *Prisoner 1167: The Madman Who Was Jack the Ripper.* New York, NY: Carroll & Graf, 1997.

Wetmore, Helen Cody. *Last of the Great Scouts.* Harrisburg, PA: The National Historical Society, 1899/1994.

Wittlich, Petr. *Prague: Fin de Siècle.* Cologne, Germany: Benedikt Taschen Verlag, 1999.

About the Author

~ひひ~

"Highly eclectic writer and literary adventuress Douglas is as concerned about genre equality as she is about gender equity," writes Jo Ellyn Clarey in *The Drood Review of Mystery.*

Carole Nelson Douglas is a journalist-turned-novelist whose writing in both fields has received dozens of awards. A literary chameleon, she has always explored the roles of women in society, first in daily newspaper reporting, then in numerous novels ranging from fantasy and science fiction to mainstream fiction.

She currently writes two mystery series. The Victorian Irene Adler series examines the role of women in the late nineteenth century through the eyes of the only woman to outwit Sherlock Holmes, an American diva/detective. The contemporary-yet-Runyonesque Midnight Louie series contrasts the realistic crime-solving activities and personal issues of four main human characters with the interjected first-person feline viewpoint of a black alley cat PI, who satirizes the role of the rogue male in crime and popular fiction. ("Although Douglas has a wicked sense of humor," Clarey writes, "her energetic sense of justice is well-balanced and her fictional mockery is never nasty.")

Douglas, born in Everett, Washington, grew up in St. Paul, Minnesota, and emigrated with her husband to Fort Worth, Texas, trading Snowbelt for Sunbelt and journalism for fiction. At the College of St. Catherine in St. Paul she earned degrees in English literature and speech and theater, with a minor in philosophy, and was a finalist in *Vogue* magazine's *Prix de Paris* writing competition (won earlier by Jacqueline Bouvier Kennedy Onassis).

Chapel Noir resumed the enormously well-received Irene Adler series after a seven-year hiatus and with its sequel, *Castle Rouge*, comprises the Jack the Ripper duology within the overall series. The first Adler novel, *Good Night, Mr. Holmes*, won American Mystery and *Romantic Times* magazine awards and was a *New York Times* Notable Book of the Year. The reissued edition of *Irene's Last Waltz* will be released as *Another Scandal in Bohemia* in January, 2003.

E-mail: ireneadler@catwriter.com

Web site: www.catwriter.com